# PARADISE
# SKY

## JOE R. LANSDALE

MULHOLLAND
BOOKS

HODDER

First published in Great Britain in 2015 by Mulholland
An imprint of Hodder & Stoughton
An Hachette UK company

First published in paperback in 2016

1

A CIP catalogue record for this title is available from the British Library

Paperback ISBN 978 1 444 78717 7
eBook ISBN 978 1 444 78719 1

Printed and bound by CPI Group (UK) Ltd, Croydon, CR0 4YY

Hodder & Stoughton policy is to use papers that are natural,
renewable and recyclable products and made from wood grown in
sustainable forests. The logging and manufacturing processes are expected
to conform to the environmental regulations of the country of origin.

Hodder & Stoughton Ltd
Carmelite House
50 Victoria Embankment
London EC4Y 0DZ

www.hodder.co.uk

*Dedicated to the Gillette Brothers:*
*Pipp Gillette and the late Guy Gillette, who keep and have kept*
*Texas history and Texas music rich and alive*

By trying we can easily learn to endure adversity.
Another man's, I mean.

—*Following the Equator,* Mark Twain

I can't stand a damn liar and have no respect for
one. But an artful exaggerator always gets my full
attention and my undying respect.

—Nat Love

# PARADISE SKY

# 1

Now, in the living of my life, I've killed deadly men and dangerous animals and made love to four Chinese women, all of them on the same night and in the same wagon bed, and one of them with a wooden leg, which made things a mite difficult from time to time. I even ate some of a dead fellow once when I was crossing the plains, though I want to rush right in here and make it clear I didn't know him all that well, and we damn sure wasn't kinfolks, and it all come about by a misunderstanding.

Another thing I did was won me a shooting contest up Deadwood way against some pretty damn fine shooters, all of them white boys, and me as shiny black as obsidian rock. There was some dime novels written about me as well, though there are some that argue with that and say I've merely latched onto the name Deadwood Dick, the Dark Rider of the Plains, as a way of giving myself a higher standing in life, and that those stories wasn't based on me at all. That isn't true, though the stories those writers wrote about me in those books was mostly damn lies, and I plan to set that record straight from one end to the other, and in due time. But I'm not starting where the story starts. I'm jumping ahead and wetting down the fire before it's been lit.

I think this is where it begins. I heard if you went out west and joined up with the colored soldiers they'd pay you in real Yankee dollars, thirteen of them a month, feed and clothe you, and give you a horse to ride. This was in the back of my mind when my adventure started. It was something that had been lying there like a hound in the sun that didn't want to get up. But on this day I'm talking about, suddenly some fire got in that dog's bones. It was due to what I heard a man once call the vagaries of life that it come to sound like a right smart idea and a good career choice. You see, I got invited to a lynching.

It wasn't that I had been asked to hold the rope or sing a little spiritual. I was the guest of honor on this one. They was planning to stretch my neck like a goozle-wrung chicken at Sunday dinner.

At the time of these goings-on, I wasn't but twenty years old. Thing I'd done was nothing on purpose. I had gone to town for Pa, to get some flour and such, and it was about a five-mile walk. I wasn't looking forward to carrying a tow sack of flour and corn and other goods back that five miles, but that was how things was. We only had one horse, and Pa was using it to plow the cornfield. That meant I had to walk.

The trip there was all right, as the sack was empty and without real weight, and the day was nice, the sun heating things up, birds singing in the trees, happy as if they had good sense. I whistled most of the way there. It was a good thing wasn't anyone with me, because I'm not much of a whistler. But there I was, on a nice morning, feeling pretty good about things, even if I was going to have to deal with white peo-ple—Civil War veterans, mostly. Folks who wanted to talk about the war all the time and to anyone come along. Wanted to tell how if good ole Robert E. Lee had just done a little of this instead of a little of that, we niggers would still know our place down on the farm, and when we didn't know it, whippings was needed now and then just to keep us straight cause our minds was like a child's mind. According to them, if left to ourselves, we would have been wandering around aimless, not knowing how to feed and clothe ourselves and humping the livestock.

On this day I wasn't thinking much on that kind of thing, though. I was just enjoying myself, walking along, going to Wilkes Mercantile and General Store and Emporium to buy some things with what little money

Pa had on hand from selling taters and maters last year. He had clung to that money tight as a crow to something shiny, but finally some of the staples had run low, and I was going to have to buy enough of those to last us until he brought in the next crop, all of it growed on land we owned free and clear, which for colored was as rare as a ride down Main Street in a buggy with fringe on top and white people standing on either side of the street waving and cheering.

It was a white woman that led to the trouble. I was traveling along, my empty sack hung over my shoulder, thinking how I hated to have to go to the back of the Wilkes store and stand there with my sack in hand till Old Man Wilkes or his son, Royce, decided they would ask what it was I wanted, then try and sell me the worst of the meal and flour for more than it was worth. I was supposed to sort of shuck and yuk with them until I got as good a deal as I could get without appearing uppity or pushy. It was a thing that wore a man out, young or old. But it was part of survival training.

I never got to the store. I decided on a shortcut, took a back alley, and come to a split between the handful of buildings that made up the town and walked past a backyard where a white woman was hanging out wash. That house five years ago had set on the edge of town, but now the town had grown out that way, and the house was tucked in among a livery and a barbershop. It wasn't much of a house, by the way. What real property there had once been was sold off after the war, and to hear the owner of that place, Mr. Sam Ruggert, talk, you would have thought before the war it had been vast farmland and bountiful orchards, but it hadn't. It had been covered in brush and thistle, and if Ruggert had spent less time in the barn with a jug of moonshine he might could have grown something besides all them thistles and weeds. His take, however, was different. He decided loss of the war had thrown him and his family into decline—and to hear him tell it, which he did on a regular basis at the store toward which I was walking, ever' hole in his long johns had to do with Yankees and niggers. According to Ruggert's way of thinking, I was a member of both groups: one by birth and the other by wishful thinking. He also had a reputation as a strange and angry man, right deadly if crossed. His hovel was always patched over with animal skins he was curing against the outside wall, and the roof sagged on one side and had a tarp stretched over it where some shingles should have been laid.

As I come along with my empty sack, I turned my head to see this young red-haired woman of generous but well-contained construction at the wash, hanging clothes on the line, clamping it there with clothespins. I knew this woman by sight, if no other way. She was Ruggert's third wife, one having died from working herself to death, a second having run off, and this one being the daughter of the woman who had run off. She was an attractive young lady from behind, but from the fore, with the way her face was narrow and her nose was long, she gave the appearance of the business end of a hatchet.

That wasn't the end I was watching, however, and I will admit to a bit of true curiosity as to how that backside of hers was far more attractive than the front, but I wasn't about no mischief of any kind. I just turned my head and seen she was reaching into her basket, pressing some serious butt up against her thin gingham dress.

It was in that brief and fateful moment that her husband, the aforementioned Sam Ruggert, come out of the back door and seen me looking. My having sight of what anyone that might have walked by could have seen just crawled up his ass like a wounded animal and died, and he couldn't stand the stink.

There he stood, eyeing me hard with his piggy eyes, wearing only a pair of pants and his boots, his big white belly hanging over his belt like a bag of potatoes, his mouth twisting around in his beard like a couple of red worms trying to get out of a tangle of grass.

Next thing I know the fly was in the buttermilk. He's bellowing at me, accusing me of being bold with a white woman, like maybe I had broke into their yard and jammed my arm up her ass. But I hadn't done nothing except what was natural, which was to admire a nice butt when it was available to me.

By this time his wife had turned around and seen me, ruining any joy

I might have had in her backside with the sight of her face. She started calling me this and that, and you can bet the word *nigger* come up two or three times. *Coon* was tossed in there for good measure, and the kindest thing I was called by the both of them was a goddamn darky. Of course they made mention of my ears, which stood out like the open front and back doors on a shack.

So there they was, yelling at me and carrying on, and Ruggert started looking around, hoping for an ax or a hoe, maybe even a rock to throw. None of that was on hand, so he rushed into the house. I knew he'd be coming out with a gun. Most likely a big one.

If he didn't shoot me dead, I could already in my mind's eye see a bunch of white folks loping up with a rope and a snarl on their lips, ready to string me to a tree or a porch overhang without so much as a questioning or a trial. I had seen it happen once. An old man, who the white folks called Uncle Bob, said something that went sour with some white person, and it was a thing so minor no one remembers what it was anymore. In the next instant Uncle Bob was dangling by a rope from a tree and had been set on fire by lighting his pants legs with a kitchen match. That was done after a nice churchgoing lady had opened his fly, sawed off his manhood with a pocketknife, and tossed it to a dog.

I was ten years old when I seen it happen. My mama was alive then and home, as it was after the war and her having been sold off became unlawful, and she had made her way back to us. By then Pa was free himself. I had only been a little slave boy for a few years and was fortunate enough not to remember it too good. We had been owned by a pretty nice fellow, if you want to consider it that way. I mean, he didn't beat us or anything, but we was certainly his property. Had we run off we would have been hunted down with dogs and men with rifles. And he had sold Mama, hadn't he? So to say he wasn't bad as some is a relief, but not a smooth satisfaction.

Mama got to come home, and things was better, but it didn't last. Didn't seem it was no time at all until she got the sickness and died. But this time concerning Uncle Bob was before her dying. Me and Mama had come to town to buy something or another with our small bit of trade goods, and next thing we knew here come old Uncle Bob running like a dog that had stole a ham.

A mob was right behind him, and then they was on him. It was like watching a mass of big ole horseflies settling down on a dog turd. Mama tried to put her hand over my eyes so I wouldn't see it happen, but a white man seen us standing there, said to Ma, "Get your fingers off his face. You people take a good look and know your place around here." It happened so fast and so furious that by the time you could have picked your nose only slightly, and without much in the way of a comfortable reward, it was over. Uncle Bob was cut and hanged, and a dead bird found beside the road was stuck in his mouth. I don't think there was any reason to that, other than it was something mean.

That day got branded firm in my mind, and that's why I run away from that place after seeing Mrs. Ruggert's ass. I ended up at the livery and stole a horse right in front of the colored livery boy, who said, "Oh, shit, you gonna be in some hot water now."

In a moment I had gone from being in trouble over a misunderstanding to being in trouble over an actual theft.

I didn't have time to saddle the horse, and I didn't pick too wise. That mare was old and near lame. Therefore I don't know I can say I rode out of town so much as my horse limped away with me on its back.

It wasn't clear to me what I should do, so I decided to ride out to our place to see Pa and explain to him what had happened. When I was about a half mile out, for some reason I abandoned the horse, thinking I might be forgiven for taking it. This was, of course, unclear thinking, as I was going to be killed for something that was a matter of accident and of no consequence. Had that horse gone back to the livery, and had it had the ability to talk, and had it explained the situation, given them a solid and true bill of events, about how I was in a frightened whirl and had only borrowed her, it wouldn't have mattered. Had the horse spoke up in my defense, she would have been hanged first and then me alongside her, the both of us with dead birds in our mouths.

I ran like a deer the rest of the way to our place and hadn't no more got there when I realized pretty soon there would be a rabble on my tail. By this time the story of what I had done would have been built on so a foot would become a yard. It would be determined that I had not only molested that hatchet-faced wife of Ruggert's and stole a horse but also assaulted every woman in town in some fashion or another, and of course that would be an insult to white manhood, which was a thing that couldn't be tolerated.

It also occurred to me that I might be bringing the whole bad business down on Pa. But by the time I had thought this through, I was at our place and had caught Pa out in the field plowing.

He stopped to listen to my story, and I explained the whole bad business to him. Unhitching the old horse from the plow, we both rode it back to the house. When we got there, he tied the horse up, and we went inside. He peeled back some floorboards. Underneath them was a tow sack, and inside it, wrapped in oil paper, was a pistol. It was a .44, Pa explained, and it was converted from cap and ball to a cartridge shooter. When he gave it to me, I damn near went through the floor it was so heavy.

"You had better run," he said. "I ain't gonna say I seen you. You ought not take the plow horse, cause it would be dead in an afternoon if you had to really ride it, and they'd know for a fact you come here and took it, which would put them directly on your path. You'd make out best if you run across the field and down into the draw, where them trees along it can hide you. Do that and keep moving down it until you get to the pine break. Go into them pines, head west, and keep traveling on in that direction. And son, it might be best you never come back, cause if you do, they'll be waiting. A white man has a long memory for unimportant things involving colored folks. And that Ruggert fella, he's one of the worst."

I nodded at him, feeling so weak I could hardly stand, not quite wrapping my thoughts around the fact I was leaving forever.

"You take that gun. It's loaded, and try not to use it, but they come down on you, you take it in both hands and aim at the biggest part of them you can see, and if they are going to swarm you, you ought to save a bullet for yourself, put it to your head, and let go, cause things is going to get a lot worse if you're alive when they lay hands on you."

Considering I was already scared, that bit of advice really lit a shuck under me. Next thing I knew Pa was taking out his old cheap pocket watch and giving me that, as if telling time under the circumstances was important, and then he hugged me. I shoved that watch deep in my pocket, dropped the Colt into a feed sack, and within minutes I was running out of the house, across the field toward that deep draw that was at the back of our place.

As I ran I heard Pa yell at me, "Run, Willie, run."

I made right smart of my run, and it wasn't long before I come to that draw, which was bordered by trees. I slipped down the side of it, stumbling, near losing that big cannon of a gun as I went. I got my feet under me, then took to running through the shallow water that crawled along the draw like a thin, wet snake. I figured if I was in the water I might put off any dogs they brought, and my tracks could get lost if there were enough rocks at the bottom of the stream. That plan went to hell quick when I realized I was just bogging in mud and leaving a path that a blind man with no more than a walking stick to feel around with could have followed. It also come to me that a dog didn't need to smell my feet, just me. Anyway, I continued on, and it didn't seem any time at all that I come to the spot I was hunting for: the big gathering of pines.

Scrambling up the side of the draw, I made it into the trees, and at the same time I heard horses splashing through the water. They had come on me quicker than I could have imagined. I paused a moment for a peek, and coming over the lip of the draw I saw a horse, and on it was Ruggert, shirted now and wearing an old black flat hat. There was a holstered revolver on his hip.

Ruggert had no more made the top of the draw than another man on horseback followed up. I didn't wait to see how many there was, cause I knew for certain there was more of them than me.

They broke apart, fanning out through the pines, and I started hoofing it. I decided it might be smart to go wide and backtrack on them and get behind them and into the creek. They didn't have dogs with them, but they had reckoned correctly that I would head to Pa's place, and it occurred to me then that was why they was on me so fast, having found my footprints out in the plowed field and then followed them down into the draw.

I went wide and cut back through the pines, back to the water, but well up ahead of where I had been. When I got to the draw it wasn't just a little run of water no more. It was wide in the spot I come to, and was in fact no longer a draw at all but a marsh. There was reeds and old dried wood and some trees growing up in it. I couldn't figure no other thing to do than to wade in and try and heel it to dry land, which was a considerable distance away.

Me and my feed sack full of pistol got into the water, and it wasn't deep, but it was mucky. I headed to where the trees was thickest in the beyond, and hadn't gone no distance at all when I heard a horse splashing along in the water. I turned to see that it wasn't none other than Ruggert riding down on me, though his horse was having considerable problems in the mud.

He yelled out to the others he had me cornered, and that's when the water got deep and I was suddenly up to my neck, still clinging to my bag of pistol but knowing I had most likely wetted it up to the point of not firing.

It was then that I took a step and found the water got really deep. I was under it before I could say, "Oh, shit."

I don't know how far I went down, but it seemed some distance. All I know for sure was it was wet and I come up out of it snorting. At that same time a shot was fired, and I felt the side of my head, high up over my ear, burn like a lightning strike, and then everything was black.

I couldn't have been out long, cause when I come to Ruggert and his horse was right over me. Still in his saddle, Ruggert swung out and down, trying to grab me by the collar, pull me up, trap me against the side of his horse, and ride me out of the water, where he could lay solid hands on me.

I was pretty light and thin compared to him. He was strong and was trying to back his horse out of the water, dragging me with it. It was then that I swung out with the bag of pistol, which I had clung to even during my time of unconsciousness. I swung it high, and damned if I didn't catch Ruggert a good lick—nailed him about the same place he grazed me with his shot.

He let out a sound like a cow that was dropping her calf, and next thing he was in the water, facedown and cold out. I ain't sure why I done it, but I rolled him over so he wouldn't drown. I looked down into his face, which seemed to be older than I knew he was, and took a quick study of it. There was creases on his forehead, along with a red knot swelling up where I had whacked him. His whiskers was wet and clearly shot through with gray. It was then, too, that I realized that though he was stout, he wasn't no big man, really, but was short and muscled with a big belly. I don't know why I noticed all this, but I did, and then I let him go a'floating and got to hustling out of there, thinking any minute the rest of them fellas would come up on me. An alligator couldn't have hastened through that marsh any faster than I did, though I was concerned I might come upon a real one in my progress, it being bottomland and close to where the Sabine run its course.

I didn't have no idea how far I went or how long it was before they found Ruggert, who at that point in time I thought was dead. I just kept going.

The swamp got thicker with trees, and the land got firmer, and after a long time I was on solid ground, moving along nicely through a stand of hardwoods and scattered pines. The day began to creep away, and I stopped a few times to rest, listening for horses, but didn't hear nothing. Being in such thick woods, I couldn't really see the sun and tell which way it was sinking, so I was firmly confused on directions.

When the trees broke there was a clearing. I looked out and seen I had made a loop all the way back to our property, only now where our house used to be standing, there was a pile of blackened ash and charred wood.

My first impulse was to charge out of there over to the house and see if I could find Pa, but I didn't. It was a tough decision, but I had been dragging and staggering through the swamp and the woods all day, and the sun was setting like a busted apple off to my right, finally showing me which way was west. I sat down among the trees and put the bag of Colt in my lap and waited until it was solid dark.

There was just a piece of moon that night, but it was good enough I could make my way across the field and over to our burned house. I looked around as best I could in the moonlight, fearing I'd find Pa's body, and that's exactly what I did. He was blacker than his natural black and was smoking like a heap of burning tobacco, his ribs and skull revealed, the fire having charred the flesh off of them.

They had throwed our hog up in there with him, probably shot it or beaned it in the head. It had burned up too, except I could see its legs poking up, its hog hooves puffing off strips of smoke like rips of cotton. The air smelled like frying pork, or at least I liked to think it was pork, cause it made my stomach hungry and sick at the same time.

I felt so weak I almost couldn't walk. It was too hot to go right in there and drag Pa out, and by that point it didn't matter. He wasn't going to cure up and be well between now and things cooling off. He was dead as dead could be, and they had either killed him there or done it and put him and the hog in the cabin and set fire to it just because they could. I wasn't sure what their problem with the hog was. Probably just wanted to kill something else, and without me being around the porker had taken my place.

I decided I couldn't leave Pa there until he'd cooled down, so I went out to the barn, which they hadn't burned, got a rope, and lassoed Pa's body and dragged it out of the ruins of our shack. I hauled him to a place beneath an old oak, got a shovel out of the barn, and buried him, his body still smoking. I didn't make a cross or heap up stones, cause I didn't want to let on where he was buried, in case the vengeful bastards might take it out on his remains. I scraped the ground good and dragged some leaves over it with the shovel, so unless someone was looking for the grave it wouldn't be easy to find.

Finishing up, I was considering if I could get away with sleeping in the barn when I seen outlined in the moonlight four men on horseback coming out of the pines along the draw at the back of the property. They was heading in the direction of the cabin.

Carrying the shovel and my bag with the pistol in it, the rope coiled and looped over my shoulder, I eased into the woods, hunkered down, and watched. I seen right off from the way he sat in the saddle that one of them was Ruggert. He wasn't dead. It was then that I wished the pistol hadn't gotten wet, because I didn't want to chance shooting it and it misfiring. I pulled it out of the bag anyway, poured water out of the barrel, checked the chambers, and discovered three loads. I couldn't have put up much of a fight with that if it was working, especially if I was saving one of the shells for myself. Still, I clung to it in case I had to give it a try.

So there I sat, back in the shadow of the woods, squatted down on my haunches, watching that string of horses ride toward the shack, starting to be able to hear them talking. The night air carried every sound as clean and sharp as if they was standing right beside me. I listened to them until they rode up to the burned-down house. They looked around for a while but never bothered to get off horseback.

"Looks like he's all burned up, Sam," said one of the men mounted next to Ruggert. "I don't even see no bones." He was a man I had seen around town but didn't know well, other than he was kind of a drunk and his name was Hubert something or another. The others I didn't know at all.

"It's that damn uppity coon I want," Ruggert said. "Want to cut him and rope him and burn him and whatever I can think of."

That uppity shine would be me, of course.

"We ought to burn down the goddamn barn while we're here," Ruggert said. "I think they got chickens we can kill."

"Ah, the hell with it," said the man mounted next to him. "Let's head on back in. I've had enough. We got us one tonight, and I'm satisfied enough."

"Wasn't your wife's butt he was looking at," Ruggert said.

"Hell, I think your wife's butt is about all she's got going for her," said another of the men. "I've taken a look now and then."

"But it was a darky took the look," Ruggert said. "I can understand a white man, but a darky? That's wrong, and you know it."

"We've done what we can, and I'm through with it," Hubert said. "I ain't gonna spend the rest of my night chasing some nigger through the swamp."

"I wasn't planning on starting out until tomorrow again," said Ruggert.

"You'll start without me," said a man.

"I got to get home to dinner," said another.

"I ain't never gonna give up till I get him," Ruggert said. "I have to get me a tracker to run him down, that's what I'll do."

That's when I heard a sound behind me, like something creeping up. I turned with the big pistol, hoping it would fire, and seen our old plow horse, who we called Jesse. He was wandering out of the woods, walking right at me. I stood up behind the tree, and the horse come over and looked down at me, probably wanting the grain it hadn't had. It made a nickering sound.

I heard Ruggert say, "There's that old nigger's horse." A shot was fired, and Jesse reared up slightly and turned and bolted away in pain.

Another shot was fired off into the pines where Jesse had departed, then there was silence. I laid down on the ground behind the tree and wormed my head around the side of it and took a gander. They was riding off then, having burned down our house, killed my pa and a hog, threatened the chickens, and shot at Jesse. Not to mention they had tried to kill me. They had had a busy day.

It was my thoughts to follow them into town and kill the four man jack of them. But even in the state I was in, I knew that wasn't a good plan. There I was, a kid compared to them, and them with guns that was fully loaded, and there I was with an old pistol that might work and might not, and if it did, I had three shots and there was four of them.

Much as it galled me to do it, I lay there and let them ride out of sight. When I was sure they was good and gone, I put the pistol in the bag and went into the woods searching for Jesse. I found him easy enough. He wasn't much of a runner, old as he was. I petted him up, saw that the bullet had grazed him under the belly. Ruggert seemed to have a knack for coming close but not quite getting there.

I walked out of the pines, and, as I expected, Jesse followed me to the barn. Opening the double doors, I let him in and fed him grain, went out to the well pump and got a bucket of water, and sloshed it into his trough. I looked around for something for me to eat, but there wasn't nothing. We had a few chickens in coops behind the barn, so I went out there and let the chickens out, since there wouldn't be no one to feed them anymore. I gathered about a half dozen eggs that hadn't been collected that day, put them in a feed bucket, and went back inside the barn. I took all the eggs out of the bucket and laid them out on a pile of hay.

There was some matches in the barn, and I used hay for a fire starter, brought in some sticks from outside, and made me a little blaze. I sat the bucket on some logs I dragged in. I cracked all those eggs and fried them in the bottom of the bucket. They stuck a little, but I scooped them out with my hands when the bucket and the eggs was cool enough for me to stand it. I licked the eggs off my fingers.

When I finished eating, I decided to lay down for a couple hours' sleep. When I woke up I was crying. I was crying for Mama being dead, Pa murdered. I was mad I had been chased and near killed for looking at a white woman's butt. On top of that I was angry about them taking a shot at poor old Jesse, who was about as dangerous to them as a wind-blown leaf.

Getting off the horse blanket I had laid out, I got the saddle and the bridle and such that was needed and dressed Jesse up. I led him outside. It was a still night, and the air was sharp. The moon was laying gold light over everything, smooth as butter being spread with a knife. It was odd the world could look so pretty and the air taste so clean and my pa was lying buried under a tree.

I walked Jesse out to the oak, where I said my good-byes to Pa. Mama was buried in a colored cemetery. I thought about visiting her grave but come to the thought that she and Pa was dead and that didn't matter none. Mama told me once she wanted a better life for me and thought being free would give me a shot. She said, "You get the chance, you got to take it."

I also remembered her lying sick, dying, touching her hand to my cheek, saying, "Willie, you're our hope. You got to go on and make something of yourself. You got greatness in you."

Well, I didn't know if that was true, but I know Mama believed it, and I wanted to. It was better to follow the dream she wished for me than to try and visit her grave. One had a future, the other just might not.

I started thinking on those stories I had heard about the colored army and made up my mind their outposts would be my destination, which was no short hop and a jump but way out in West Texas. I led Jesse to the draw, then guided him down into it. Once we was there I mounted, and Jesse splashed through the water, on to where that marshland was. We eventually come out on the draw and took the road alongside the marsh for a stretch. We passed where me and Ruggert had our tangle. Even with Jesse plodding like he was dragging a plow, we made a good many miles. The marsh was covered with a mist thick enough it looked like a cloud had fallen out of the sky. We rode through that cloud, the dampness of the mist clamping to us like a wet cloth.

Eventually the sun burned off the mist, and we left the road and wandered between the trees. The ground was mighty clean under them trees until we got close to the river, and then the brambles started to grow.

I had bagged some grain for Jesse, and when it was good and light I stopped and let him eat some of it right out of the bag. Not so much that when he took a drink of water he'd founder. What drinking water we had was what I had put in an old whiskey jug in the barn and tied over the saddle with a cord. And there was the Sabine River, which we was about to cross. That was all-right water for a horse, but I drank from it once when I was out fishing and got the runs so bad I thought I'd be in the outhouse the rest of my life.

The Sabine wasn't wide, but it was deep there, and Jesse had to swim it. The water was sluggish, but a couple of turtles was showing out and making good time. I watched their snaky heads as they drifted down the river and under the shadows of the overhanging trees along the bank. A fat perch swam by, and he was colorful enough and the light was bright enough so I could see him good, and just the sight of him made me hungry again.

There was a few times when I thought Jesse might tucker out, but he stayed with it, and we got to the other side. I slid down off Jesse, grabbed a handful of the rich, stinking mud from the riverbank, and slapped it on my head wound, which had opened up and was bleeding heavily. I packed some of the muck on Jesse's bullet graze, and then I walked him until I thought he had blown well enough for me to ride. We continued then, steady as the ticking of a clock, heading out west.

# 2

My journey out west didn't get much farther than the middle of East Texas on that day, and by that time I was so hungry I could almost see buttered cornbread crawling on the ground. I fed Jesse again and chewed some of his dried corn myself. It wasn't even close to satisfying. I couldn't figure what Jesse saw in it. It wasn't a thought with a lot of sense behind it, but by that time I didn't have a lot of sense. I was still sticking to the places where I was less likely to be seen, but I was so tuckered out from the events of the day before, and from sleeping only a short time, I knew only that I was following the sun. Right then, had Ruggert come up on me I would have been done for. I was covered in ticks and chiggers and itched all over, including my privates, and I knew if I stopped I might not get going again.

That's when the woods began to thin, and I come to a place that had been cleared, though there were still stumps scattered throughout the clearing. I could see some vegetables growing beyond that on some well-plowed land, maybe twenty acres or so. On the other side of the field was a comfy-looking house and a barn and some wood fencing, a feedlot and such. It all looked well cared for, which was a thing I could appreciate. I figured I could also appreciate eating something from the garden.

It had turned off hot by this time. I tied Jesse to a tree, took the gun out of the bag, laid the bag on the ground with the gun on top of it, and crawled out to the garden. I plucked about half a dozen maters off the vines—big, fat ones—then edged my way to the corn and took down about a dozen stalks, some of them bearing several ears of corn. I felt bad for doing it, plundering a person's crops, but I was at the point where I had to eat or pass out.

Creeping back to where Jesse was tied, I gave him the cornstalks I had pulled and ate the fresh corn. I would have adored to plunge them big, juicy ears into some boiling water with some salt. I ate the maters, or at least four of them. By that time I was full. I gave all that was left to Jesse.

We waited there during the hot of the day. I slept on the pine needles, hoping Jesse wouldn't step on me. I slept with my hand on the old pistol.

It was cool dark when I woke up. Jesse was standing with his head held low. I got my bag and put my gun in it, led Jesse along the edge of the crops until we got to the end, and began to mosey toward the barn and corral.

The moon was thinner this night, but still good enough to walk by. I could even see an old bull snake slithering over the ground pretty as you please. I felt low enough right then to crawl with him.

I got to the corral. There was some horses there. The barn was open to it, and the horses could go in and out as they pleased.

I took off Jesse's saddle and bridle and let him loose in the corral. I took Pa's watch out of the bag and laid it on a fence post. Right then that watch felt heavy as an anvil to me. That watch and Jesse was all I had left of him. Still, he wouldn't have wanted me to take a horse without payment, even if Jesse and that watch wasn't worth any one of those fine cayuses in the corral.

I petted Jesse, being sick about leaving him, but figuring whoever owned this nice place would take better care of him than I could. I wanted to leave a note about his plowing virtues and how his nature was and all, but I didn't have a pencil or paper.

I picked up Jesse's bridle and reins, dodged through the fence, and started easing up on the horses. I had the pistol in the bag and had tied it on my belt. The horse I chose was a big black one. I tried to calm it, but it kept moving away from me, and it was starting to snort.

I was cooing to it like a dove and was within a foot of laying hands on it when it raised up quick and kicked out with its front legs, knocked me winding. I wasn't hurt, but it was a close call. I was trying to get up when a big man wearing a droopy hat come out of the shadows, leaned over me, showed me a big hole in the end of a pistol. Even in the moonlight, I could tell he was wearing patched Confederate pants tucked into his tall boots.

"You might want to be still," he said, "so I don't have to shoot you."

He lifted from his bent-over position, and the way the moonlight laid on him I could see his face clear enough under the brim of his hat. It was a rough old face, sharp and ragged, like farm equipment. Part of that raggedness was the tangled whiskers he wore.

"I wasn't gonna steal nothing," I said.

"No?" he said. "You could have fooled me."

"I was leaving a horse and a watch in trade," I said.

"You was, was you?" He looked about, settled on Jesse. "That bag of bones there was any older it could be the Trojan horse."

I didn't know what the Trojan horse was, but I figured it was old.

"I left a watch, too," I said.

"You did, did you?"

"I did," I said, and wanted to get up bad, because I had fallen in a big pile of horse shit. Not only was it wet and coming through my shirt, it also smelled something vicious.

"How's that watch tick?" he asked.

I made a ticking noise with my mouth.

"No, not that," he said. "Does it work good?"

"Works fine, though the glass is a mite scratched from coins and such in Pa's pocket."

"But you can still see the hands well enough?"

"If your eyes are good."

"Thing is, though, I already got a pocket watch." After a few moments of studying on me, he said, "I ought to jerk a knot in your dick, son, out here messing in my horse pen."

"I'm kind of desperate," I said.

"Are you, now?" he said.

We settled in this position for a while, as if we was posing for a painting, then this fella looks at the sky, says, "You needed to come from the other side, by the barn, climb over the corral, chase the horse into the barn, where you couldn't be seen. A horse, if he's in the barn, isn't so excited about being bothered or about someone trying to separate him from the others. Less likely to make noise."

"I didn't know that," I said. I thought it best to be polite and let him keep the lead.

"Well, it's a minor horse-stealing detail, but I figured if horse thieving was to be your career, you might want a few pointers."

"Have you been at that kind of work?" I asked.

"I have, but it was in the war, so we considered it all right to steal a horse."

"I'm in kind of a war, so I reckon I was seeing it the same way."

"Were you, now?"

I was propped on my elbows, trying to get a read on the fellow, wondering if I could leap up and dart through the corral slats and make a run for it. But something about the way he held that pistol like it was one of his fingers led me to staying still.

"Tell you what," he said, after what seemed time enough for daylight to be on the rise. "Why don't you tell me why you was stealing my horse."

"You want to hear all that?" I said.

"Asked, didn't I?"

I considered some lies but decided I wasn't up to it. I told it like it happened, making sure to mention the first horse I had stolen I had let go and that it was probably already back at the livery doing whatever it was horses liked to do there in the middle of the night.

"That is quite a story," he said when I finished.

"It's the truth."

"Is it, now?"

"True as I can tell it," I said, which after I said it pained me a little, because it sounded like I had told a lie and dressed it up as the truth.

"You swear it's true?"

"I swear by it."

"Did you get along with your mama?" he asked.

"Right well. Got along good with my pa, too. And I like grits and ain't got no hatred for turnip greens if they're seasoned right."

"That pa of yours got burned up?" he said. "That's the one you liked?"

"He's the only one I had."

"I had two daddies," he said. "One that made me, and the one that raised me. I didn't get along all that well with either one of them. Well, I don't know how I'd have gotten along with the one that made me, on account of I never got the chance to find out. Him running off the way he did put a crimp in our relationship."

"I can see that," I said.

"You get those ears from your ma or your pa?"

"My pa," I said.

"That's a relief. If it was your ma, she was going to spend a lot of time wearing a head scarf. A man can deal with ears like that. All right. Get up."

He gun-pointed me up to the house, took me around to the back of it, and had me take off my horse-shit-covered shirt and pants and toss away my shoes. He marched me inside the house naked. I was starting to fear the plans this fellow had might be worse than Ruggert's.

Turned out he had some of his old clothes for me. I put them on like he asked. I had to cuff up the bottoms of the pants slightly; the shirt hung loose on me. I was a young man, but six-two tall, so you can figure the size of my captor. I reckoned him having two inches on me in height and about ten inches across. His shoulders was wide enough he had to turn a little sideways when we come through the door, and his chest looked like a barrel had been stuffed under his shirt. He had a bit of a paunch, but you couldn't really call him a fat man.

The house itself was good-sized. You could have put our old house into it three, maybe four times, and had a room for Jesse and at least a half dozen chickens and a visiting mule. There was other rooms off the one I was standing in. There was some rugs on the wall, which seemed like an odd place for rugs. There was a bit of a smoky smell in the room, and that was because the stove was leaking wood smoke, the damper not working just right. There was also in the air the smell of something good cooking. It made my stomach knot up like a hangman's rope.

I wasn't sure what was going on, but I noticed he put the pistol into its holster and hung his hat on a peg by the door. I took a good look at him now. My guess was when he was young he might have been handsome, but that face he was wearing now looked as if it had been whipped raw, left out in the rain, and sun-dried.

"You ate lately?" he asked.

"No, sir," I said.

"Let's fix that first. Got nothing but cornbread, but I got some good molasses to dip it in."

I studied on him to figure if he was serious. He seemed to be. I said, "That would be just fine, if you can spare the grub."

"It's you and me or the ants get it."

Now, he had lied to me a bit. There was certainly some cornbread and molasses, but it was fresh baked, and he had a big pot of pinto beans to go with it, seasoned with onion, bacon, salt, and a right smart bit of hot garden peppers.

He had me sit down and served me like he was working for me. It made me nervous. I hadn't never had no white person do anything like that for me. He heaped beans on my plate, brought out a big jar of molasses with a ladle in it, then he brought me a cup and poured some coffee.

He fixed his own plate then, sat down at the other end, and eyeballed me. I said, "Thank you, sir, for not shooting me and for feeding me."

"Well, I can still shoot you after you eat."

That stopped a spoonful of beans midway to my mouth.

"Nah," he said, showing me he had a nice set of teeth. "I'm just joshing with you. So you got old Sam Ruggert after you?" He of course knew about this, as I had laid it all out to him honestly while lying in horse shit in the corral.

"Yes, sir," I said, and by this time I was a little bold, knifing up some butter and putting it on my cornbread, heaping spoonfuls of sugar into my coffee, touching it off with milk from a pitcher. "You know him, sir?"

"Me and him went to the war together. I used to be a preacher in the church we attended."

"Preacher?" I said.

"Before the war. It was an easy living. They paid you for it, and you could empty the collection plates every Sunday. It's a delightful racket. It don't seem right to me now that I've quit being religious. I have come to think that if your job is to spread the message and get paid for it, then you don't believe it. And I got tired of having to figure out how to explain the Bible saying one thing in one place and another in another place. Mostly you just preached around it—picked out the things that sounded good and ignored the rest. Finally I decided I'd be a Christian without all that Christ nonsense."

"Oh," I said.

"I just try and do right because it's right, and I don't need no other reason. Goodness for goodness' sake. Which is not to say that if you mess with me I won't shoot your goddamn balls off."

It wasn't a smart question to ask, but I was itching to ask nonetheless. "Before the war, did you have slaves?"

"Four, and they were hard workers. Then one day, while I was still a preacher, I came across the stories about slaves in Egypt again, and about how they were freed by Moses and ran off, and he parted the waters, and all manner of shit that's just too hard to believe. But it got me thinking. Here I am talking about them poor Hebrew slaves, and tearing up as I preached on it like I was there with them, and I got me four slaves at home. There was what I like to call a goddamn conflict. How's them beans?"

"Fine, sir."

"Good. You see, I had me one older slave that was always telling me how close we was, how he was glad I fed and housed him and such, and when the War between the States come, I sold them other three and kept him. I left him to take care of the property while I was away fighting, thinking we'd have those Yankees whipped in six months. Well, we didn't. When I finally come limping back here, the whole place was run-down, and Chase, which is what I called the old colored man, had run off and made his way up north, taking some of my goods with him. I thought right then he didn't love me nearly so much as he said, and I thought, too: why should he? My wife, who was alive for another year before the pox got her, said she couldn't believe he'd do that after all we'd done for him. He even took a big shit in the middle of the floor. Right there."

He pointed out the scene of the crime, which wasn't too far from the table.

"Slipped in here and done that before he left so my wife would find it."

I studied where he was pointing.

"Don't worry," he said. "That's been years ago, and it's been cleaned up some time now."

"Yes, sir," I said.

"It doesn't sound like much, but that thing right there, him doing that, running off, got me thinking maybe a colored slave wasn't so different from a Hebrew slave, and I give in to another way of thinking. After I did I could never preach again. I was ruined for it. I had always used the sermon about Ham, who saw his father, Noah, naked and how Noah cursed Ham's son for it. Cursed him because his father had seen his balls. Not Ham himself, but his son — Canaan — and all his descendants. Made them black, is how I was taught, and doomed to slavery for that ball watching. It made sense to me then, cause I hadn't never thought on it.

After the war I did consider it. I didn't go around trying to spy me some men's balls, but I've seen a few, which is a thing that will happen if you're in the army or in a Yankee prison camp, like I was. Seeing them balls and them seeing mine didn't make me want to curse no one with slavery for generations. It was bullshit, and I seen that clear as a sunny day."

"You actually seen my balls," I said, referring to my changing clothes in front of him.

He recollected a little, then laughed. "I guess I have, though I didn't lay considerable observation on them."

"I could lay a curse on you," I said, "and from now on all white men will be slaves."

He really laughed then, so hard in fact I thought he was going to fall off his chair and roll on the floor. It wasn't that funny, but I guess it was causing him to let something stove up inside of him out. Laughing was good for that.

When he got his mind and mouth in line again, he said, "You know, Noah must have had one ugly set to have been offended so bad to have them spied on. I mean, that's something, isn't it? You've peeped on my nut sack, so a whole generation and their generations gets cursed."

"Yes, sir," I said. "Them must have been the ugliest nuts ever hung between a pair of legs."

He grinned, and then his mind settled into something darker. The grin washed off his face like a stick-drawn line in the dirt washed away by fast water. "You know, my son went off in that war, too. Got killed the first day he was in a battle. He's buried some sad place up in Virginia. He fought far away from me. Over in another part of the war — another theater, you might call it. Sometime after it happened, after I was out of the prison camp and home, a fellow that had been with him looked me up and gave me Tad's pocket watch. He said it had stopped the moment he was shot and therefore was some kind of recognition from God of his death. Well, I had already come to that realization about Ham and Noah and Canaan, and had come to certain conclusions about slavery, but this clinched it. I'm thinking, my boy gets shot, and his watch stops, and that's a sign from God? He couldn't make that bullet miss or bring my boy home to me or bring him back from the dead, but he'd go to the trouble to stop a watch? How can they be sure his watch stopped at the exact moment of death in all the confusion of battle? Maybe it just stopped because he fell on it or some such. Before that moment, little signs like that meant something to me. A cloud shaped like an angel's wings. A hawk flying overhead with a snake in its mouth.

"What happened to me when that fellow gave me that watch and went on his way was I gave the whole thing furious thought. God's bucket from then on didn't tote water. That bucket had a hole in it. I come to think on that watch some more, and it come to me that God wasn't all loving. He was like a big watchmaker, and we were the innards of his watch, and this here earth we stand on is the watch's slippery surface. Once God got the watch made, set it ticking, he sat back and said, 'Well, good luck to you son of a bitches, cause I'm done.' "

I studied on his reasoning a bit, and damn if it didn't make some sense to me, which scared me a little. If the big man was right, we was all on our own out here.

He looked at me just then, as if watching a bug crawl across my face, said, "Pie?"

"Excuse me, sir?"

"Want a piece of pie? I got an apple pie in the warmer, and it looked to me it might have turned out all right, though it's slightly sunk in the middle."

It did turn out all right, and we ate it up, the whole damn pie. Drank about a pot of coffee, then he took me out back and we walked to a field that lay beyond what I had seen before. It was cleared, except for a few stumps and a giant oak out there in the middle of it, and there were chairs under it. We sat in them. Above us was this big gap in the limbs, like a window between tree and sky. You could look up and see the stars real good. That's what we did, him explaining to me that there was things called constellations, and positioned as we were in our chairs, we was looking right at one. He told me what it was, but the name of it has faded from my mind now. I didn't really care about any of that right then, so maybe it never really stuck to me. I was full of food and felt worn to a nubbin, in spite of all that coffee. Somewhere along the way, between him chattering about this set of stars and another, my head tossed back and I closed my eyes and slipped off to sleep like I was gently sliding down a muddy slope into a field of soft, dry grass and darkness.

# 3

When I woke up the next morning I was covered in dew, or at least my face was, but I had a thick blanket tossed over me, and I was beginning to get a little warm. Cracking an eye open, I found I was still under that oak out in the middle of the field.

Getting up, I stretched and seen there had been a note laid out on the ground, held down with a couple of rocks. It was dew-damp but not ruined. There was an arrow drawn on it, and that pointed toward the house. I reckoned on it for a while, trying to decide should I go back up to the house, or should I light out west. Thing made me decide was thinking on that excellent meal I'd had the night before, and there being most likely some kind of breakfast back at the house. Maybe I could pay for it by working it off. I knew there was some all-right white people, but last night I had come to consider there might even be some good ones. Then again, it could be like putting cheese in a rat trap, and that dinner last night was the cheese, and I'd get down to the house, and there Ruggert would be, waiting with a tall horse and a short rope.

Giving it a final turnabout in my head, I started down to the house. When I come up to the corral, the big fellow was out there feeding the horses, pouring grain from a sack into the trough.

"There you are," he said. "I had a mind to think you run off."

"Considered it," I said.

"Tell you what," he said. "Here's how we'll do it. Go in the house, have you some biscuits—they're in the warmer—and pour you a cup of coffee. Have two cups if you like. You're going to get sweaty when you come back, cause I'm going to put you to work, but if you need to take a bath—and from the way the wind is blowing your stink on me, I suspect you do—then there's some hot water on the stove to put in the tub. It's enough for a good splash bath, not much more. It will make you better to stand out here in the field with. Do that, then come out to the far field and we'll pick some tomatoes. I done got the bags and such, so all you got to do is show. Is that fair enough to you, son?"

"Yes, sir."

I went in the house, had two biscuits slathered in butter, drank two cups of coffee that I put milk and sugar in, poured water in the number 10 washtub that had been set out near the stove, and worked on my filthy body with some lye soap. I picked ticks and chiggers till I thought I got them all, then dressed and did a turn at the outhouse out back. Having had a refreshing morning constitutional, I strolled to where my host was working.

He gave me a bag, said, "From what you told me, you're a farmer. You know how to gather ripe tomatoes without pulling down the vines and bruising the fruit, don't you?"

I afforded that I did and went to picking. He had one row, and I had the other. We worked right along even with one another, getting hotter and sweatier as the day rolled on.

He said from his row, "You know, the tomato really is a fruit, not a vegetable."

"It ain't."

"It belongs to the nightshade family, and there are nightshade plants that will poison you right down to the toes, but not the tomato."

"The mater has a family?"

"Not with a mommy and daddy and three kids and a horse. No. Everything, plant or animal, bug and such, is said by science to be part of a specific kingdom, class, family, subfamily, genus, species, and so on. I don't know all the names without having my books in front of me, but that's how it is."

"No shit?" I said.

"You don't know what I'm talking about, do you, son?"

"Reckon I don't."

"Then don't be so goddamn agreeable. Let me explain it to you."

Then he did. For most of the day I learned this about maters, that about corn, something about taters, and much about beans, which was called legumes; and there was a name for peas other than peas, though for the life of me I don't remember it now. Maybe it had the same name. I don't recall. Radishes had cousins. Sweet taters was distant cousins of the maters, which didn't seem right, and he threw in that they didn't belong to the nightshade family like the mater. He said this like I might be relieved to find out they wasn't. He knew everything there was to know about plants. I myself had plenty of experience plucking, picking, pulling, and digging all that stuff, and I knew how to eat them, but it was beyond me there was more to it than that, or that I was eating plants with family names, which somehow made me feel like a cannibal.

When he had worn down on that topic, I made the mistake of asking him about how he grew such big plants and juicy maters. I remarked on the dark soil, which wasn't common around East Texas, it being mostly red or sandy white. Well, now, that was like opening a door with a thundering herd of horses behind it, and here they come. It was all about how he turned the vines back into the soil and let them rot instead of pulling them up and tossing them out like lots of farmers do. That was what Pa had done—tossed them out. This fellow said you folded them back in with the plow along with the right amount of dried and cured chicken and horse and hog manure, and wood ashes if your soil was too acid, which it mostly was in East Texas.

I already knew about manure and wood ashes, which me and Pa had used, but by the end of the day I knew all about, or had at least heard about, how all the different kinds of dried shit could be mixed with all manner of wasted food, dead plants, and then heated up naturally as it broke down. He kept saying, "You have to layer it." All of this made me sleepy on my feet, but to my good I endured it.

Later he sent me up to hitch the horses to a wagon and haul it out to where we had bagged our maters. That trip to the barn and back was nice; the silence was a relief. I, however, was not one who learned from experience. When I got back to him, I asked, "How come you ain't got no mules, since you got all these horses? It looks like you could afford one."

"They are good workers, smart and the illegitimate children of the donkey and the horse. But I figure with me on the place, one ass is enough."

Gradually I was learning not to say anything that might start a discussion, cause he seemed to know a little about everything. Or, to be more exact, he seemed to know a lot about very little. I also had to take his word on matters. For all I knew, he didn't know raccoon shit from coffee beans. Come to think of it, how the hell was a mater a fruit? I was beginning to have suspicions on the sweet tater. Maybe it was in the nightshade family, too.

We got all those maters hauled in, and it was only midday by then. He was a serious worker.

He said, "I tell you what. I got some chores need done, and if you'd like to do them while I go into town and sell these tomatoes, when I get back I'll fix us up a good supper of fried chicken. I'll rewarm the beans, and we'll keep some tomatoes to go with it—some of the green ones I can batter and fry up. I might even bake us some sweet potatoes to split and butter. Hell, I'll buy some brown sugar. You like brown sugar on your sweet potatoes?"

For him this seemed a question right up there with the greatest concerns a person might have. I agreed I liked brown sugar on sweet taters and that I could do those chores. It was work akin to what I had been doing all my life, and by the time he was heading into town, I was on my way to toss corn to the chickens, slop the hogs, and so on.

As I went about the chores, I begun to think maybe this fellow was touched, or had caught a musket ball or a chunk of cannon shrapnel in the head and his brain had been knocked loose; maybe even some of it had been blown right out of his skull.

Then something else hit me, and when it did I felt weak in the knees. It wasn't a new thought, as you've probably already guessed, but it kept coming back, and each time it showed up it seemed as fresh as dew on a rose. I was worried again my farmer might be bringing Ruggert back with him. Could be he had just been making like he was nice so as to get a day's work out of me, then he would turn me over to an old war buddy for castrating and hanging, and then it would be them slicing maters and pouring brown sugar on baked sweet taters, not me. He might joke with Ruggert about how he fooled me about the nightshade family.

I didn't start thinking seriously on this possibility until late in the day, and about the time I had come to believe that was his purpose and was planning a swift decampment, here he come, clattering down the road in his wagon.

No one was on that road but my man himself, his wagon, and his team.

He was good as his word. After I helped unhitch the horses and we groomed them and put them away, he went out back and picked two fat hens and wrung their necks, doing them both by using his left and right hand at the same time. When he had their necks wrung out good, he popped them, causing their heads to come plumb off in his hands. The chickens hit the ground, spurting blood, running around like they had some place to go. I will tell you true, I have seen that done many times, and have done it myself, but I never did get used to it. It made me want to jump and holler.

Finally the chickens fell over. We took them, sat on overturned tubs, and went to plucking feathers. He had us toss the feathers in another tub, said they'd be mixed into his compost pile, as he called it, that being the layered business he had told me about.

It took some time, but we got them plucked, then he took a knife and cut them open, took out the sweetbreads, put them in a pan, then cut the chickens up quick and smooth, tossed their parts in the pan, too.

Wasn't long after that that the chickens was washed, flour-rolled, salted and peppered, and set to frying. When it was done, we took a gizzard apiece to start with, then came the livers and hearts, then a leg apiece, and so on right down to the necks. I even chewed open a bone and sucked on it.

"I seen Sam Ruggert today," he said when we come to the part where we was wiping our greasy fingers on nice white napkins.

"Say you did?" I tried to make the question casual, but for an instant I thought my fried chicken might come up, leave the house on its own, collect its head and feathers, and go back to the coop.

"Yeah. He was still all het up about the darky that come on to his wife and tried to take her womanhood, like he and everyone that ever knew her hadn't already done that. Hell, I fucked her once. He said he fought you off and you stole a horse and run away. When your old pa tried to stop you from a life of crime, you killed him and burned him up and his house. He didn't mention the hog."

"Ain't none of it like that."

"Oh, no one in town really thinks it's like that," he said. "Not really. They like to put the justify on it. They all know that old slattern of a wife wasn't attacked by nobody, and the horse you took come back home. Ain't no one really thought you killed your pa, though that's what they're putting on the wanted poster."

"Wanted poster?"

"Yeah. They wrote out your general description, making heavy note of them ears, and wrote on it what they say you done. They're offering one hundred dollars for you."

"Who's they?"

"Seems some of the townfolk got together and chipped in for a reward. It don't say on the poster that half of that goes to the sheriff, but it probably does. That's solid money, son."

"I better run then," I said.

"I wouldn't do that. Not just yet. They wouldn't expect to find you at my place. If we play our cards right, no one will know you're here. Give it some time, then you can be on your way. Again, you may not be safe here, but you're safer than being on the road. I don't get much in the way of visitors too often, as I'm not well liked."

This confused me. He seemed as affable a man as I ever met. So affable that at first I hadn't trusted him.

"I got different views on things than they do, and that upsets them enough to think I'm strange, and maybe crazy, and probably dangerous. I am dangerous, you know."

That last part, about being dangerous, I thought might be his way of joking.

"You think Ruggert will give up looking for me in a piece?" I said. "Actually, it's me ought to be looking for him after what he done to my pa."

"I'd get that vengeance out of your head. There might come a time, but this wouldn't be it. Let me tell you about Sam Ruggert. Told you me and him served together, but I didn't tell you how it was with the pair of us. He was a fellow that latched onto folks. I don't mean me. I sensed all the time I knew him that he had an outlook that could be discomforting, so I kept my distance. Thing is, Sam don't like to hear no."

"Who does?" I said.

"He don't like it a lot. He's one of them that if he wants something, like a woman, and she don't want him, he takes it in his head that they got them a connection anyway, even if one never existed. He takes to following her around. When she puts him off, that just makes it stronger for him. Before the war there was a very nice woman that lived in town, and Sam took to her. She didn't to him. He wouldn't leave her alone, and things got pretty bad. One day he came to her house and broke in. Turned out, though, there was three men walking in the street in front of the house, and they seen him run in. They dragged him out and whipped his ass. It took all three. Sam is rough as a cob.

"The woman was foolish-kind, though, said it was all a misunderstanding, and it was written off, as lots of his acts were written off in these parts. It was determined to just be his way, so to speak. Well, his way was ugly. About a month later that woman disappeared. No one could lay it on Sam, but there were those among us who thought he had done away with her.

"Few years went by, and there was more incidents like that, though maybe not as open. But it got so anyone Sam fixated on ended up dead or missing, and that included wives. No one could nail Sam to the wall on it. It wasn't just women, though. There was the first owner of the livery where Sam tried to get a job but was turned down. He kept coming back, wouldn't take no for an answer. That seems like a good work ethic at first, but in time you need to know the difference between if you're going to get a job or if you aren't. He didn't know that difference. Eventually he seemed to take the hint. But near a year later that liveryman was found beaten to death, lying up in a ditch at the back of town. I figured Sam for it, and some others did, too, but nothing could be proved. It's not like with colored folks, where you don't have to prove it. With a white fellow you do. You see, he nursed that grudge for a year, and it wasn't nothing other than that man not having a job for him. By this time Sam had got his growth, and it was a solid growth. He wasn't one to be contradicted, and people around town grew to fear him."

"You, too?"

"I'm not always smart enough to be scared when I should. Besides, Sam knew if he bothered me the undertaker would be wiping his ass. What you see sitting before you is a contented farmer with a chicken dinner in his stomach, but what I am is a man not to be trifled with. Follow me?"

"Yes, sir," I said, though I wasn't sure I did.

"We went to war later, being from the same part of the country. We ended up together. Not like my boy, who ended up as part of the Virginia bunch of soldiers that got pounded at Gettysburg, which is where his watch got stopped. But me and Sam went together. I was lucky he never fastened himself to me in any way, and he seemed fearful of me.

Which was a good way for him to be. During the war, though, he gained him some skills, which was mostly always falling to the back of the line during a big battle or faking a wound or some such. He did get fastened on this one young man, though, and wanted to be friends with him in the worst way. I think it was because that young fellow came from a good family, and Sam imagined himself being elevated to a higher position by association. Least I think that was what was on his mind. That boy may have been young, but he was a wise one. He kept Sam at arm's length.

"That didn't set right with Sam. Pretty soon he was following that boy around in camp, hanging with him in battle, even if the boy made it to the front lines, which he always seemed to do. As I was saying, before he got interested in that kid, Sam had nothing to do with the front lines. Yet it wasn't any good. Sam couldn't make the connection he wanted, whatever it was, and that boy told him off right in front of a bunch of us. About how he wanted Sam to get off his ass, cause he didn't need no set of tail feathers or some such. He dressed Sam down mighty strong. That was his undoing.

"One night we camped, and the next morning they found that kid facedown in the latrine we had dug. Back of his head was split wide open, like with a camp ax. No one seen it happen or knew who done it. There was an attempt to investigate, but it was wartime, and we were on the move by midmorning. On we went, and on we fought, then it was the end of the war, and we all went home.

"So Sam, he's put a brand on you in his mind, same as them others, and my thinking is he won't let go. He'll keep on coming or send someone to keep coming after you if he can't."

"No one is that loco," I said.

"He is."

"Then I ought to go back and kill him. Put an end to it."

"You haven't a chance. Ought to stay right here and work for me for room and board. I'll pick up a thing or two you need when I go to town. I'll teach you how to take care of yourself. Use a gun. Ride a horse like a real rider. We'll make it a better horse than the one you rode in on.

A better one than the one you was going to steal. Even then you should go on and forget Sam. In these parts even the people that hate him will hate you more because there's coffee in your color. Here's another thing, son. You don't need to go back for him, because he'll come for you. It might take some time, but he'll sniff you out eventually. When you least expect him, there he'll be. But for now, this place is as good a place as any, and you got me for backup. All that said, there'll come a time when you should move on. Let him look for you then. You got to lead a man like that out into deep water and drown him."

"I had a chance to actually do just that, and I didn't," I said.

He nodded, remembering my story.

"Well, son, what's it going to be? And if you're wondering why I would bother, it's because I need the help around here, and I haven't a good word for Ruggert."

I said I needed to think on it a spell, but it was a short spell. I answered within a few moments of putting my mind to it.

"All right," I said. "I'll settle on your idea until I have to fly away from it."

"Good, then," he said, and he looked really happy about it. "Now, I think it might be a good time for us to exchange names. I didn't do it right away in case you might need killing. I find it a lot easier to kill someone whose name I don't know. By now I think we can make that swap of information without fear of murder, dismemberment, the loss of an eye, or a stretch of hurt feelings."

"Willie Jackson," I said.

"Mine's Tate Loving," he said.

"Glad to meet you Mr. Loving."

This was the beginning of my association with Tate Loving.

# 4

**N**ow, at this point I'm going to jump ahead a bit, because after us giving each other our names it was the beginning of me planning to leave every day and then not doing it. I stayed there with Mr. Loving and worked out my room and board. He gave me a place in the barn, up in the loft, which had a door that opened out in the air so as to give a view of the house and the road that was up ahead of it. It was for forking hay down to the ground below, but it was a good vigil.

Some nights I would sit up there with that loft door open and find myself looking at those constellations Mr. Loving was always telling me about and the stories that went along with them. They nearly all seemed to end with someone getting killed or raped by a duck or a goose or a bull or some such and getting thrown up into the sky as a batch of stars by way of apology, though why that was supposed to be a satisfying reward I couldn't figure.

That loft was mighty cozy. Half of it was given over to stacks of hay, but the other half had a good bed in it with solid ticking. There was a table and chairs, a kerosene lamp, and some odds and ends that made it a nice little home for a runaway ass-looker, part-time horse thief, and sometime farmhand.

I was given a hive of clothes that had belonged to Mr. Loving's son, including lace-up work boots and riding boots with pointy toes made of fine, soft black leather. Them was for dressing up. If I had some place to go, you bet I would have worn them. As it was, I tried them on now and then with some of the finer clothes and walked around up there in the loft like I was about to strut off to a barn dance. It all fit like it had been made for me.

Thing that surprised me most was I was given plenty of time to myself at the end of workdays—or, rather, at the end of our dinners. We took plenty of time at those dinners, talking and such. Mr. Loving did most of the talking, but I was learning my way around a stack of words.

When I wasn't on my own time, me and Mr. Loving was working in the fields, bringing in this crop or that. While we worked he was telling me about something or another from one of his books. The books was stacked every which way in the house, and how he found what he was looking for I got no idea.

Some nights after we'd done our chores we'd sit in the main room and he'd read aloud for an hour or two from one of his books. In spite of myself I was learning a thing or two about all manner of subjects, some of which I thought might be helpful in life. Others I couldn't imagine being of use under any circumstance, but another thing I learned from Mr. Loving was that knowledge was a pleasure for its own sake and didn't need to have no day-to-day purpose.

I didn't forget about Ruggert, but in time I began to relax somewhat, because it was rare anyone ever come down that road to Mr. Loving's house. When they did, I was usually wearing my big hat and the clothes Mr. Loving had given me, so I wasn't someone to immediately be taken for myself. Mr. Loving told me it was like a story by a fellow named Poe who wrote about hiding a letter in plain sight so those that was looking for it would overlook it. But it's one thing to hide a letter and another to hide a large colored fellow with big ears.

One afternoon when the chores was light and I had plenty of rest time, Mr. Loving climbed up to the loft in the barn at just about the time I was thinking of playing with my pecker. Fortunately he caught me at rest, right before I came to that part. He snuck up on me like a ghost. He was standing on the ladder to the loft, and all I could see of him was his hat and his face peeking over the edge.

He said, "You got some time on your hands. I'd like you to meet me out at the sitting tree in about fifteen minutes."

Mr. Loving went away, and I got up and put on my boots and hat, climbed down the stairs, and drifted out to the sitting tree.

I got there before he did, sat in one of the chairs, and waited. It wasn't more than a minute when I seen him coming along from the house car-rying a big wooden bucket in either hand. When he got to me, he set the buckets on the ground. I seen one of them was filled with what I thought at first was a bunch of mud balls, though I couldn't figure on how or why that was. The other one had cardboard boxes of ammunition in it, and stacked on top of it was two pistols.

"You rub up against Ruggert, or them that might support him, it may be good if you could hit something with a pistol without having to throw it. I studied on that old revolver you had, and if the ammunition in it had been good, which it wasn't, and had the pistol been in good shape and well oiled and well cared for, which it wasn't, you'd have probably got so much kick from it that it would have come back on you and the barrel would have smacked you in the face hard enough to turn you into a white man. It's an old muzzleloader, cartridge-converted. Whoever done the job might have been a good farmer but was a lousy gunsmith."

"I don't rightly know how it got set up," I said, and that was true, though I suspected my pa might have been responsible.

"All right," Mr. Loving said. He plucked one of the mud balls from the bucket and flipped it to me. I caught it and realized it was a hardened ball of clay, not mud. I balanced it in my palm.

"I made these myself. You got to bake them in the oven like a chicken after you get them all rounded out. Takes a lot of mud and a lot of time, so kind of watch any you might miss, see where they fall. We'll try and collect what we can of them that don't bust."

"What about the ones you miss?"

"I don't miss. Well, now and again, if I'm drunk or sick or blind-folded."

He took the pistols out of the bucket, held one in either hand. "This here," he said, balancing one of the pistols in his left paw, "is a Colt Peacemaker, .45 caliber. Probably no one makes a better pistol, though Smith and Wesson has some fine ones. It's easy to use. Single action, which is a surer cock and better to aim with. Double action jumps around more, though with a single you got to take time to thumb the hammer back, but it makes for a more regular aim. This other one," he said, bouncing it in his right hand, "is rarer. Got issued to some of us in the Civil War. It's a LeMat revolver."

"Do I really need to know what kind of pistol it is?"

"It makes you less ignorant to actually know what you're talking about, so listen to me."

I shut up then. Mr. Loving said, "The Colt .45 uses .45-caliber ammunition. That's something even you can figure out, it being called a .45 and all."

"Yep," I said. "I got that part."

"It's a good gun, and this shorter barrel length is my choice, on account of it's less likely to get snagged. Holsters tend to grab at it like a hand when you try to draw it quick. Regular holsters, that is. I got some that are hardened considerable by use of salt water and proper drying around a wooden frame; they hold a gun much better, and they got a hammer loop on them to help hold the pistols in, so you see some business coming your way, you got to get that loop off the hammer. You don't like a holster, you can use a sash, but you got to file the sights off if you go that route. These pistols got their sights, so they wouldn't be of much use that way. Another thing to do is to line your coat or pants pockets with leather, lightly grease the inside so you can get a smooth draw.

"Now, this LeMat, this particular one, anyway, uses .44-caliber ammunition. The curious part about it is it's a nine-shooter. This big barrel underneath—a shotgun load goes there, sixteen-gauge. It's a little like holding a stick of dynamite and hoping all the juice comes out the end of the barrel. That actually makes it a ten-shooter."

"That sounds iffy," I said, staring at its blue steel and what looked like polished hickory grips.

"Naw, it isn't iffy. I'm just talking it up, but it sure will give you a kick if you aren't paying attention. The LeMat's not as accurate as the Colt, but it's got you three more shots and then one big shot. For self-defense, up close, which is pretty much how self-defense usually is, you can't beat that shotgun load. Hard to miss at ten feet or less. You got a little striker here on the hammer. Have it up, like this, it's going to hit them nine rounds. Push it down, and it'll hammer the shotgun load. I've adjusted it some, cause I've made this one over from pin-fire to center-fire so as to modernize it. You might call it the Loving version of the LeMat revolver."

He went on like that for a while, telling me about the pistols and the loads and how I needed to pay attention on account of ammunition was expensive and he didn't want it wasted on me just popping off shots.

Mr. Loving was a good teacher. By the end of the lesson I had almost hit one or two of the balls. He, on the other hand, wasn't kidding about his aim. After he got tired of instructing me, he took the Colt, said, "Toss 'em, Willie."

I went to doing that, and with that pistol held down beside his leg he'd wait till the ball I tossed got its full height and was just starting to drop, and quick as a tornado his hand would come up and he'd thumb that hammer and fire off a shot and knock that ball to shatters. He shot from the hip. He shot facing forward and standing sideways. About the only thing he didn't do was stand on his head. He shot that fine with his left hand or his right. Way that man could shoot either of them pistols was like poetry.

He'd say, "Thing to remember is it's good to be fast, but it's better to be accurate. You can fire six times and miss, and the other fellow can come slow as a turtle but be right on his shot, and you'll wind up with a hole in your chest big enough to shove an apple through. The chest is the best place to aim in a real situation because it's bigger and more likely for you to hit. Still, you ought to be able to shoot the hairy balls off an undersize squirrel if it comes to it. Hit the little stuff in practice, you're more likely to hit the big stuff in a real spot of trouble. Side vision is going to narrow some, get black on the edges, and you're only going to see what's right in front of you. Practice, some real experience, changes that. You don't get killed the first time or two, you'll get so you don't have tunnel vision like before. During a gunfight you'll be as alive as you ever were. Your hearing will most likely be extra sharp. Fact is your tongue will taste the air different. You'll taste your own fear, and them that's shooting at you, you'll taste theirs, too, a sour copper taste. If you blow a hole in someone solid, you'll smell shit and gut gas like it lived in your nose. You'll have the taste of it on your tongue. That's how alive your senses will be.

"Don't never draw a pistol on nobody that you don't plan to shoot. You draw it, and you shoot, you shoot to kill. A wounded fellow can kill you same as one that isn't wounded."

Over the next few months I was taught how to shoot a Sharps rifle and a brand-new Winchester he had bought last time he was in town. But the thing about that Winchester that he done was he put a loop cock on it, and on that loop he put a striker that could be flipped with a finger. The loop cock could be handled quickly, and that striker, if you pushed it down, would hit the trigger every time you closed the cocking loop. You could fire rapid-like. It was hard to hit anything that way, unless you was Mr. Loving, of course, but you sure could put a lot of lead in the air.

By the end of them months I was not only good at shooting but the love of them weapons had also gone away from me. At first I adored them, but Mr. Loving kept telling me how they was tools, and they wasn't in need of any more admiration than a hoe or a shovel. I took him at his word. If I didn't love them pistols, I did respect them, and I was mighty respectful of the LeMat revolver in particular. It was, as Mr. Loving said, less accurate than the Colt, but I took to it. Pretty soon what natural accuracy it lacked I made up for by learning to know it and my-self, and I liked them extra three shots. And then there was the shotgun load. He put a board up in the ground for that one, and I'd shoot at it at about a distance of ten feet and splinter it.

It was a good life. I liked the work. I liked Mr. Loving, and I liked my loft. I liked all that he had been teaching me. I could read and write a little, but he improved me. He had me reading all manner of books. I liked the ones about geography and history, and I liked stories, mostly adventure. But math, I never could make any sense of it, outside of basic arithmetic. I could add, subtract, do fractions, and divide, but I could never get a handle on what was called geometry or algebra. I knew what a triangle was, a rectangle, a circle, and a square, but beyond that I was bewildered.

I learned to ride a horse like a Comanche, which was another thing Mr. Loving could do. He said Texans in his day had learned it from watching the Indians. I could hang on the side of the horse, dangle under its neck and fire a pistol, cling to its belly, and swing back up with the pressure of my heels. I could grab its tail and run along behind it by mak-ing leaps like a rabbit. I also learned to grab the saddle, cling to it, and run that way for the long distance of Mr. Loving's property.

One thing I haven't mentioned is amid all these good times was the dark moments when Mr. Loving was like someone else. Not mean, mind you, but there was times when he wanted to be alone and sit up there under that tree in a chair and look out at the sun setting or the moon rising, and he could sit there for hours. I never went up there to sit with him unless I was invited. Somehow I knew he needed that time alone. My guess was he was thinking about his son and wife, but for all I knew he missed the easy money of preaching.

Within a day, sometimes within hours, he'd be his jovial self, dis-cussing Polaris, Ursa Major, and Ursa Minor, who were supposed to be bears, and there was the Big and Little Dipper and Cassiopeia, who was supposed to have been the queen of Ethiopia. My geography lessons let me know Ethiopia was where dark people like myself lived, though with their ears closer to their head, or so Mr. Loving said, but I think he was pulling my leg.

I think I could have gone on like that forever, but as I heard my pa say to a friend of his one day, "The good times, if you have any, eventually get shit in them."

# 5

I had grown yet another inch by the time things started to come to an end. I didn't know things was coming to an end, but one day me and Mr. Loving was walking back from the fields, both of us with a tow sack of taters, and I noticed Mr. Loving was lollygagging a bit, dragging behind, and I come up and tried to lift the sack of taters he was carrying. He wasn't having any of it. I think I hurt his pride.

Up at the house he had his dinner, which I fixed, having become more than a serviceable cook by learning from him. I got to say my pa was an all-right cook if it was something battered and fried and you was so hungry your belly thought your throat was cut. But Mr. Loving truly knew his way around a frying pan.

This time I'm talking about, Mr. Loving thanked me for dinner and took himself to bed. That was the first day I came to realize he was starting to get old. It got so I was doing more of the work, making him stay up to the house, pride or no pride. I'd come in at sundown and fix supper and read to him, which was a reverse of how we started. It was along there I realized I had been with Mr. Loving about four years and had pretty much lost my worry about being found.

Then one day I was slopping the hogs, and this fellow rode up. He tied up his horse and come walking past the house to where I was working. I recognized him right off. He was that town drunk I told you about earlier, one that rode that day with Ruggert. Hubert was his name, if you remember, and my first thought was I wanted to kill him. If I had decided on it, I'd have had to strangle him with my bare hands or beat him to death with one of Mr. Loving's piglets. Or the slop bucket. I had that in my hand, and that's what I decided on. He come strolling up to me with a grin on his face, said, "Hey, boy. Loving around?"

I knew right then he didn't know weasel shit from axle grease. It had been long enough for him to have forgot me, even if I hadn't forgot him. I guess, too, I had changed a mite, except for those ears of mine, but the hat I had kind of fell down on them in such a way they didn't quite look like swinging doors, and I had more hair. I had quit shaving it close to my head and was letting it grow out into a curly bonnet.

"He's up to the house," I said, keeping my voice as even as I could, which was like a man walking along the edge of a cliff trying not to look down.

"I want to talk to him about a matter of business," he said.

The only business I'd known Hubert to have was trying to get to the bottom of a bottle, but I did note he looked cleaner than I remembered. He had an air about him that was different. He carried himself like a wares salesman who had plans to con someone into buying a cheap set of pots for too much money.

"He's resting," I said.

"Well, you go get him, boy," he said.

I didn't like the way he said "boy." I didn't like that he helped kill my pa. I didn't like him. I went up to the house, trembling with anger, went in through the back door like I was supposed to do at a white man's house, though me and Mr. Loving didn't stand by that way of doing things. I should add, to keep it all on the up-and-up, I knocked first, then went inside.

It was East Texas warm, yet Mr. Loving was sitting by the cookstove, had a fire going in it, and had a quilt thrown over him. I felt like a ham on slow bake in there, but he seemed fine with it. I said, "There's a man to see you, and I know him."

"Oh," Mr. Loving said.

I told him quickly who he was.

"He used to be the town drunk," Mr. Loving said.

"Used to?" I said.

"He got the cure, took up with a widow that had money, and now he owns the Wilkes Mercantile and General Store and Emporium."

"Do tell," I said.

"Yeah, I've known about it for a while but didn't see no need to mention it to you. It has nothing to do with you being here. Knowing he's prospering is of no importance. I been waiting for him to fall off the wagon and lose it all, actually. We go back out there, you think you can control yourself?"

"I don't want to," I said. "But I will."

"All right, then. Help me up."

Before we went outside, Mr. Loving took the Colt pistol and stuck it in his back pocket, which was one of those lined with oiled leather. He slipped that blanket around him, sort of like a poncho, so that it covered his gun. He told me to get the bucket by the door we used for gathering eggs, put the LeMat in there, and throw a dinner napkin over it.

I did that, and we went outside, Mr. Loving not making it too good but holding his head up, trying to act like he was ready to punch a bull in the face.

Outside, Hubert was grinning like he'd just found a gold dollar in a pig track. He said, "You look all run-in there, Loving. And what the hell you got that blanket on for? It's hot as a whore's diddle out here."

"I got me a spat of something," Mr. Loving said. "I'm a bit under the weather with it."

Hubert eyed me again. I could see he was starting to feel like he recognized me but hadn't yet put a handle to me. I thought about going off to finish with the hogs but decided I'd stick. If Mr. Loving was nervous enough to put a gun in his back pocket and have me stuff one inside a bucket, I figured I should stay.

"What can I do for you?" Mr. Loving said.

"Well, sir. You and me done some business at the store, me buying vegetables from you and such. What I come to talk to you about is doing your hog killing for you. I started me a couple of services in town, and that's one of them."

"What's the other?" I asked.

I shouldn't have said nothing, and the way I said it was disrespectful. It wasn't the words, it was the attitude. Like maybe he had become a cocksucker for money and I knowed it and was going to offer him two bits for the service.

Hubert said, "You let that boy talk to me like that?"

"He's man-sized," Mr. Loving said. "He had a question, and he asked it. Fact is, I'm curious. What is the other job you got? Is one of them distilling?"

"I give up the bottle," he said. "And actually, it's another job. I've become a field driver."

Now, this ain't a term I hear much anymore, but it was a fellow that rounded up loose stock, even dogs and cats, and stored them in a corral or pound at the edge of town. You was missing an animal, went over there and found it, you got it back for a fee. There was always the problem that some of the critters ended up in the pound hadn't been loose to begin with and had been made loose, so to speak, due to that fee for their return. And if the stock wasn't claimed, it ended up in the field driver's smokehouse. Dogs and cats might not last longer than an evening due to the feed bills and the smaller fee. Field driving could be a sketchy business.

"Field driver isn't a job," Mr. Loving said, and I thought his tone was far more disrespectful than mine had been. "Anyone can round up a neighbor's lost stock, and a righteous person won't ask him for a dime to get it back."

"I'm not here to debate the merits of my professions," said Hubert. "I'm here to promote hog killing."

"I can kill a hog," Mr. Loving said.

"A dog can kill a hog," Hubert said, "but if you bring them in, I'll kill them, cut them, and smoke the meat, and you will be entitled to so many pounds of it. I will keep a bit of it for my troubles and for resale."

"So I bring the hog to you, you kill it, take part of the meat, and smoke it? What have you done that I can't do?"

"Why, I have saved you time, sir."

"How do I know I'm getting my meat back?"

"That isn't the issue," Hubert said.

"It is with me."

"We add up the pounds of your hogs, mark out what my portion is to be, and when you want that meat, you come in and shop for your other things, which you can put some meat toward, and if you want the meat, I'll give you what you have coming. I also got a couple niggers who can make head cheese and such, and you'll be entitled to some of that. It don't matter if it's your hog. What matters is you are entitled to a certain percentage of meat from a hog or to exchange it for goods."

"I raise good hogs," Mr. Loving said. "There's folks aplenty who don't. I don't want some wormy critter with more bones than meat or one that's nothing but fat. For that matter, I just don't want no one else's hog. You being the field driver, I might end up with a dog leg and a cat liver in place of the hog I brought to you. No, I'm going to decline with a degree of prejudice. I'll kill my own hogs, or this boy here will do it for me, but thanks for the offer."

"It would sure make your life easier," Hubert said, trying to maintain his politeness but giving me the still-curious eye. "I been going around to all the farms, and I will swear to you that over half of the folks have made the agreement."

"Slate me down for the half that hasn't," Mr. Loving said.

Hubert worked his top lip like he was trying to persuade a fly to get off of it, then said, "That's the way you want it, of course. Can't blame a fellow for asking."

Hubert had become quite the politician. If Mr. Loving had told him to eat shit, he'd have said he already had a mouthful.

Hubert mulled me over. "I seen you somewhere before?"

"You haven't," Mr. Loving said before I could answer. "He came from over in Jacksonville looking for a job, and I hired him. He isn't looking to work nowhere else."

"I wasn't looking to hire him on. It's like I said. I think I know him from somewhere. You know me, boy?"

"No, sir," I said.

At this point Mr. Loving started indicating in an almost polite manner that he was anxious for Hubert to get on his way so that he could go back to his fire and nurse his ailment. Hubert bid Mr. Loving good day and didn't bid me sour apples. He walked out to his horse, which he had tied out front to a hitching post. Me and Mr. Loving walked there with him, which was an old custom designed not so much out of politeness but out of a plan to make sure your visitor wasn't going to his horse to pull a gun.

Hubert got on his beast and sat there for a moment. It was then, me looking up at him and him down on me, that I saw a change in his face. He had remembered who I was. I blame my ears for it. They are memorable, and with me looking up, my hat and hair didn't hide my ears like before. I still had that bucket with the LeMat in it, and I wanted badly to pull it and blow his brains all over that horse, but I didn't. He didn't make any kind of move, either. If he had, before I could have got in that bucket or Hubert could have got his pistol free of that clinging leather holster he wore, Mr. Loving would have yanked that Colt and put a hole in him. He'd have been dead before he hit the ground.

"I think maybe you and me crossed some trouble once," Hubert said to me.

"I doubt that," I said.

"You remind me of a nigger that had a problem in town." I guess he thought rephrasing the remark would get the answer he wanted, but I was harder to corral than that.

"Wasn't me," I said.

"Wasn't him," Mr. Loving said. "It's time you rode on, Hubert. I'm worn out with looking at and listening to you. I got a farm to run."

Hubert boiled Mr. Loving's words around for a while.

"They got a word for a man like you, you know," Hubert said.

"And what would that be?" Mr. Loving said.

"Nigger lover," Hubert said.

"Now you've said it, and now you're through," Mr. Loving said. "Ride on."

Hubert wanted to say something more but proved himself smarter than I expected. He reined his horse away from us and started it at a trot down the road.

Mr. Loving turned to me, said, "He recognized you for sure."

"Yes, sir. He did."

"He'll be back, and with Ruggert and some others with sheets over their heads."

"I know," I said. "I'll save you some trouble and clear out."

"He'll go into town and let it be known you're here. They'll be on you like stink on shit, as that wanted poster on you is still out there, though it's dusty in the post office."

"I know," I said.

It all settled down on me like a hawk on a mouse. I realized that I had put Mr. Loving in a tight spot. I had no choice but to go on. I said as much.

Mr. Loving said, "Well, he's got a good trip into town, and that horse he was riding sure won't be confused for a runner. But you need to get your things together and ride out, not because I want you to go, but because you got to, for your own safety."

"Yes, sir," I said.

"We can stand together and fight them," he said, "and we'll mess them up a lot, but in the end they'll just keep coming after that reward money, which will probably go up another hundred by the time Hubert gets through telling how you're out here and all."

"Them Kluxers ain't going to like you none, either," I said.

"I'll be okay, but you won't."

By this time it had cooled just a little. The sun was dipping its head behind the trees, and the shadows was falling.

"You'll need to take more than one horse, and in fact you can take two, plus one to ride on. If you remember your math lessons, which have been a trial to you, that's three."

"Them's your horses, Mr. Loving. And they're good horses, and it'll cost you considerable to let me have them."

"I know that," he said. "You think I don't know that? You'll need those extra two to sell for seed money along the way. Keep the runner to ride. I'll go draw you up a bill of sale, which will make things easier for you. Meet me at the sitting tree in about twenty minutes, which I figure is all you'll need to throw your things together. Take just what you need, and gather up them horses. I know it'll be hard for you to leave that dresser and mirror, but you got to."

Mr. Loving went coughing into the house, the blanket hanging over his shoulders in a way that made him look like an old Indian squaw. I went out to the loft. I had come to this place with a pocket watch, an old horse—now dead, having not made the first winter—and here I was leaving with a horse to ride and two to sell. I guess it was a profit in a way, but it wasn't something I felt good about. I didn't want to leave Mr. Loving. I loved that man about as much as I had loved my ma and pa.

I packed my saddlebags. Lean as I tried to trim it, there was quite a bit of goods, including some food I had for late-night nibbling—bread and jerky and a few boiled eggs wrapped in a paper bag. I rolled up some clothes and other items in my bedroll. I put those nice boots Mr. Loving gave me, along with some nicer clothes and a coat, in another roll.

Following Mr. Loving's advice, I took the three best horses, saddling one, using another for a pack horse, and using still another as a change-out horse if I needed it.

I was just starting to head up to the sitting tree when I heard the shot. I closed the horses back up in the corral and ran up to the tree. Mr. Loving was there in his chair, his head tossed back, staring at the fresh stars. I could see his eyes was open. I could see starlight in them.

Nervous-like, I come up on him and seen his hand was hanging by his side, and in it was that little pistol, dangling there from one finger, him having put a load into his head right behind the ear. I looked him over, then I yelled at the sky, and then I screamed, and then I dropped to my knees and cried. I was so mad I hit him in the leg once.

The grief I felt isn't something I can describe with words. All I can say is that it was akin to how I had felt when Ma died and Pa was murdered, only maybe a little worse, because it seemed no matter where I was in life, someone I cared about was going to die on me.

It was then I saw there was a big envelope in his lap. It had my name on the front of it. I opened it up, and three letters spilled out. One said simply that he had taken his own life and that I was not to blame, and it had his signature on it. He left all his worldly goods to what he called a solicitor, which is nothing but a ten-dollar word for a goddamn lawyer.

Opening up the second, there was a bill of sale for the horses, and some other items was listed, them being pretty much the things I had packed on the horses and some things I had chosen not to bother with but would have taken with me had I had the room. He knew me well.

There was another letter, and that was the one to me. I read it in the moonlight. It said:

Willie,

If you asked me if I'd done this a couple of years ago, I would have said no; it is the coward's way out. But my trips to town have also included trips to the physician, and I have a cancer big as a dry horse turd inside of me, or so says my sawbones, and a litany of health problems that assure me of a soon acquaintance with the grave.

I did not want you to see me in that state of waste, and though I know there is discomfort to you in me taking this method to depart, please understand I did it because I can no longer protect you, and the pain was such I couldn't wait another minute. I thought I'd wait until you left, but I couldn't, and so I'm going to do it.

They will come, and you must go. They will blame you for my death, but I have left notes and my will with my solicitor, a Mr. G. O. Freemont, to be opened after my death. The letter stating my suicide will be announced about town, so it will be understood that I died by my own hand. I told him that any day I would take this way out, and that I was leaving my goods to a young man who worked for me, who may in fact have to take to the road.

I told him you had been accused of a crime but were innocent. I have known him for years, and he can be trusted. He is my cousin. I gave him all the information he needs. It assures this farm and all its assets will be sold and that the money will be banked in your real name. You had better take another handle for a time, and upon your return it would be best if you showed him this letter to confirm your claim, though other identification may be necessary.

Now, you look just fine, but I told him about your ears so you can be recognized whenever you show. Make sure it isn't anytime soon. Keep the ears covered on the trail, because you will be identified with them sure as shit. G.O. is a fairly young man, looks healthy, so I'm expecting him to be around when you set your sights back on this part of the world.

Look under my chair and see the bucket there. It has the Colt and the LeMat, which I have placed in a holster that won't grab at the gun when you pull it. Also in there is ammunition for all the weapons, including some shotgun loads. You will find the Winchester leaning against the tree. The Colt ammunition fits it. I have sighted it some since you last used it. Stay firm in life and know you're as good as anyone else, but don't take to anger too much, as it will be your undoing, especially if you got a gun on you. Wear a wide-brimmed hat in the sun, as I have taught you, because your ears, even with black skin, will take a sunburn.

I'm tired now, and I see you out at the corral, so I got to finish this up and shoot myself in the head. Make sure all the livestock is good and fed, and when word gets out I'm dead, my solicitor will come out and manage the sale of all items. Head out west, but go east first. Cross the draw and cut back to the west when you get past Pine Ridge.

Leave me here in the chair. They will do what they do with my corpse, which they can have, it being of little use to me or them at this point.

*You are as a son to me, Willie, and I give you my dearest and loving wishes as would a father. Ride like hell.*

*P.S. Be careful of women. They can cause you trouble.*

I folded up the letters with trembling hands and put them back in the envelope. Gathering up the guns, ammunition, and holster, I went down to the corral and loaded up the weapons on my riding horse. I put the loop-cock Winchester in the saddle sheath. I put some of the ammunition on the pack horse. I fastened on the holster with the LeMat in it. I fed all the stock quickly. They would be all right for a couple of days. Of course, there was nothing that said the wrong people wouldn't take them, but there was nothing I could do about it. I considered letting all the stock go free, but decided that wasn't a better idea than leaving them, but to this day I feel guilty about it.

The moon laid a bright path over the ground. It was good for me to see by, but it was good for anyone following as well. I set out east, like Mr. Loving had said. It wasn't long until I was on a path through the pines. It was the same way I had come to the farm some few years back. Soon I was in the swamp water, going toward Pine Ridge. If all things went well and I wasn't castrated and hanged by morning, I would be striking out hard for the far west.

# 6

During the night, as I was making my way through the pines and into the swamp water before cutting westward, I was worried as could be. Sometime near morning I realized I was being followed, and I come to the thought that Ruggert and his men was closing in on me. I had all them horses with me, and that slowed me a lot. I thought about letting them go save for the one I was riding, but thinking on how them beasts was gifts from Mr. Loving, and how much care me and him had put into them, I just couldn't. Instead I determined I might have to stop somewhere and just fight it out before I let them loose.

It turned out what I heard behind me was a wild hog tramping about, and I was glad then I had kept hold of the horses. I stopped during the day in a cluster of trees that didn't have but one way in, which was a little narrow trail. The trees was packed up tight together in a big mess on a hill, and vines and brambles and stickers had twisted in there among them, making them like a fence.

Tying off the horses, I went into the trees first on foot, seen that the center was clear of growth. It was blackened there where lightning had hit, burned trees flat so quick the fire hadn't spread. I got the horses and led them inside the clearing.

I took a chance, removed the saddle off my riding horse so as to give it some comfort, and took the pack goods off the other. It was risky. Should someone come up on me and I had to make a retreat or a fight of it, there wouldn't be time to put everything back the way it was supposed to be, and the only way out, other than trying to push through thick limbs and tight brambles, was the way I had come in. So I was hid pretty good, but I was also trapped if I was trailed there. It didn't matter none to me right then. I was tuckered out. I hobbled and fed the horses some grain and let them drink water I poured from my canteen into my hat. I had a simple meal myself, a strip of jerky and a chunk of salt bread.

Stretched out there on my blanket on the ground, my head on the saddle for a pillow, I was feeling about as low as a man could feel. Right then I could have walked under a fat snake's belly wearing a top hat and tall-heel boots. I tried to think of the good times me and Mr. Loving had, about the cooking and reading and all that, but it wasn't any use. I could at that point only remember him dead under the sitting tree with that little pistol dangling from his finger.

My plan was to sleep through the days and start out again when the nights came, provided the nights was bright enough to travel by. When I come awake it was firm dark. I could see the stars glimmering between the gaps in the treetops. I lay there and took them in for a while, still feeling lonesome and scared. I had me another piece of jerky and the last of the bread, grained the horses, watered them a little, and then set out.

I went along like that for three days. Traveling by night, sleeping by day, keeping to the wild country as much as possible. I guess it was on the fourth day I decided they wasn't right on my trail and had maybe never found it to begin with. It was then that I started to keep regular hours. Traveling by day, camping by night. Eventually I rode into a town that was pretty much the border between East Texas and the beginning of the Texas plains. At the livery I was able to sell one of the horses for a fair price.

The deal went easy because I had that bill of sale on me. Another town over and I was tired of dragging that pack horse along. I sold it and most of the goods I had that it was carrying. Again, I had signed the new bill of sale with my name, and it was at this point I knew I needed another moniker, as Mr. Loving had suggested in his letter. I decided I would take part of his name or something similar. Tate became Nate, and Nate become Nat, and Loving became Love, and I became Nat Love. That's the name I am still mostly known by and have kept ever since.

I crossed out of the trees and into the plains, and there wasn't much in the way of water or shade. I rode where I saw the brush grow, finding a creek or two that way, though the water in them was little more than a trickle. It was enough to water myself and my horse and fill my canteen. This became harder as I went, because the brush got more sparse and so did the water. I took up riding at night again and sleeping during the day, because it had grown very hot. Though the nights was pretty cool, with my coat on they was bearable, and there was no longer trees and tree shadows to make the going rough.

There was one night when I was riding and I looked up at the sky, trying to recognize some of them star heroes Mr. Loving told me about. All of a sudden that sky looked so large and wide I felt as unimportant as a speck of dust in a dry creek bed, then in the next moment a different feeling rushed over me. I saw it as freedom. I wasn't tied to nothing no more. My future right then felt as large and wide as that sky.

One early morning, as the dark was dying and the light was rising, I come to a town that was so damn small the coming and going sign was pretty much on the same post. It said RANSACK on it. As it looked and smelled like a heavy rain was coming, I stopped there and spent a night in a barn for a dollar, which seemed like robbery without having to put a gun in my face. What made it less worth a dollar was that it was infested with rats, and though there was a cat in there, it hid out from them. Those rats was near big enough to straddle a turkey flat-footed, so I could see the cat's point of view. They scampered about me all night, loud as if they was wearing boots.

Lightning flashed and could be seen clearly through the splits in the slats of the wall. That and the hammering of thunder, and the rain blowing in through those gaps, made for a bad night of sleep. When I awoke right before daybreak, somewhat damp and not much rested, I found I had rolled over on one of those rats and crushed its head like a walnut.

Morning light come, the rain had passed, and for two bits I was able to go to the back of the hotel and buy some oatmeal with sugar and butter and a dollop of not-too-spoiled milk in it, along with one short cup of coffee so weak you could see the bottom of the cup when it was filled to the brim. It tasted like coffee grounds had just been waved over the cup.

After I'd choked down the lumps of oats and swallowed that coffee, I rode out of there and passed by a freight wagon that had lost a wheel and turned sideways, dumping a load of buffalo bones someone had been collecting on the prairie. Around those parts buffalo bones was gathered and sold to be ground into fertilizer. I was studying on their whiteness, considering fixing the wagon and trying to haul them myself for a few dollars, but decided it wasn't a job for one horse. And sure as hell, someone might come back for them, and there I'd be, a thief.

I happened to look behind me and seen there was three men on horses on a rise looking down at me, but still a good distance away. I rode around on the other side of the buffalo-bone wagon and got off my horse.

I thought maybe one of the men was Ruggert, but I didn't know for sure due to the distance. I thought it looked like him, and the other white man looked like Hubert. The third man was colored, which didn't seem right, but I wasn't taking no chances. I pulled the Winchester off my horse and settled behind the wagon, peeking through gaps in the stack of bones.

They stayed where they was for a long time. I think they took it in their heads, whoever they were, that I had a good position, better than theirs, and if that was what they was thinking, I had to agree. I stayed where I was for a stretch, watching to see if they was trying to come around on me. The rise tapered at the ends, and to ride or walk around on either side of it, they'd have to reveal themselves against the skyline. From the cover of that wrecked wagon I could have shot them off their horses like they was bottles on a post.

I kept my vigil for what was near an hour by the sun, and then took my chances and rode on so as not to give them time to go wide and come up on my flanks or behind me. I rode glancing over my shoulder the rest of the day but didn't see them again. I began to think they wasn't who I thought and wasn't after me at all, and we had just happened to cross trails.

I was about a half day out of Ransack when I seen this colored fellow taking a dump near some mesquite bushes, wiping his ass on a handful of rough leaves. Had I been a desperado, I could have shot him out from over his pile and taken his horse, cause he was deeply involved in his undertaking—so much, in fact, that though I was still some distance away I could see his eyes was crossed with the strain.

Being glad I was downwind, and hating to interrupt a man at his business, I sat on my horse until he finished leaf-wiping, and then I called out. "Hello, the shitter."

He looked at me and grinned. "You ain't planning on shooting me, are you?"

"No. I thought about stealing your horse, though, but it's swayback and ugly in the face."

"You sound like you're picking a wife, not a horse," he said. "When I left the plantation I took that horse with me. Wasn't much then, less now."

He was still standing near the bushes and his pile. He'd fastened his pants, and I watched carefully as he picked up a Winchester that lay on the ground near him. He walked toward my horse. The Winchester was in his left hand, and his right hand was extended for a shake. He walked prim and tall, like maybe there was a rod up his ass. I politely refused to lean down from my horse and embrace his invitation for the reason his fingers looked brown to me, and to let my right hand be taken by a man with a rifle didn't seem wise.

He nodded at my refusal, taking it in stride. I surveyed him, saw he was a tall man and skinny, wearing a hat with a big feather in it. His face was smooth, and his nose looked to have white man in it. He had green eyes, too, and that didn't come from any African. Somewhere in his bloodline there had been a peckerwood in the woodpile.

He put his rifle away in its boot, mounted himself on his horse. He said, "I'm riding out to Fort McKavett to join up, if you care to ride along."

"I'm of the same mind," I said, and that's how we rode off together. By nightfall we had struck it up pretty good. We found a creek where he could wash his hands with lye soap from his saddlebag and make a handshake more inviting; and shake hands we did. He had some coffee and biscuit makings with only a minimum of weevils. He got out his cookware, made a fire of mesquite brush, and pretty soon we was resting against our saddles, the horses hobbled nearby, eating flat biscuits and drinking bad coffee. My new companion was one of the worst cooks I have ever known.

I thanked him for the meal, and since all I had to offer was some conversation, that's what we did. His name was Cullen, but he kept referring to himself as the Former House Nigger, as if it were a rank akin to general. He told me a long story about how he got the feather for his hat, but it mostly come down to he snuck up on a hawk sitting on a low limb and jerked it out of its tail.

He come out of that story and said, "When my young master went to war against the Yankees, I went with him. I fought with him and wore a butternut coat and pants. I shot at least a half dozen Yankees."

"You leaking brains out of your gourd?" I said. "Them rebels was holding us down."

"I was a house nigger," he said, as if he hadn't already told me that about a half dozen times. "I grew up with Master Gerald, the young master, and didn't mind going to war with him. Me and him were friends. There were lots of us like that."

"Y'all must have got dropped on your heads when you was young'uns," I said.

"That war wasn't just about us slaves, you know. It was about states' rights."

"And what was the main states' right?" I asked, and then answered for myself. "The right to own us like cattle. States' rights be damned. Set fire to states' rights."

"The young master and the old master were all right," he said.

"For masters," I said. "They owned you."

"Maybe I was born to be owned," he said.

"Born to be owned?"

"They were always quoting about it out of the Bible."

"That damn Ham fellow again," I said.

"Yeah, that's it; someone called Ham."

"It's a story has to do with Noah's balls," I said. "Noah's the fellow that had all those animals in his boat, and his balls and us being slaves is just as silly as it sounds."

"Oh, I know the story," he said, but he didn't make any more comment on it. Instead he looked into the fire awhile, as if he might see someone he knew there. "I loved Young Master like a brother. I was his special servant in the home. We did everything together. He got shot in the war, in the throat. It killed him deader than a tree stump. I sopped up his blood in a piece of his shirt I cut off, mailed it back home with a note on what happened. As a house nigger, I can read and write pretty well. After the battle, I had to bury Young Master not far from where he fell. Wasn't any other choice. I went home then, as there wasn't any call for me there, and I was needed by Old Master."

"You chose to go home?"

"I did. When the war was over and slaves were freed, I stayed where I was comfortable, which was on the plantation with Old Master and his wife. By then, though, it was all coming apart. Damn Yankees coming in and telling how things were to be done. All the other slaves didn't have any loyalty. Not a drop. They ran off. Including that high yellow bitch that was Old Master's mistress. He had treated her good, and his wife had to put up with it, so I'm not sure of her complaint. She had nice clothes and perfume and so on.

"Old Master and his wife died, him first, her right behind him. I buried them under an elm near the house. It was a good spot. Uphill and a good distance from the privy or any pooling water. That just left me and Old Master's dog.

"That dog was as old as death and then some. Couldn't eat good, fell down a lot, so I shot it. That hurt me almost as bad as the death of the family. That dog was eighteen years old if he was a day. Not long after that I took some goods from the house, took to the road, not having any more mind where I was going than a blind chicken. I came upon the news about the government signing up coloreds for the army. I'm not any good on my own. I need someone to tell me what to do, so I decided the army was for me."

Well, now, I decided the Former House Nigger had a shingle loose, but I didn't say nothing about it, least not right then. We was riding companions, and it was wise to stay peaceable.

About three days later we rode up on Fort McKavett, between the Colorado and the Pecos Rivers, near the head of the San Saba River. Grand as a kingdom, that fort, or so it seemed to me back then. It was situated on a wide mount of land and had a good view of everything below and around it.

Out front was colored fellows in army blue drilling on horseback, looking sharp in the sunlight, which there was plenty of, it being so bright you had to squint to stand it. It was hot where I come from, sticky, even, but you could find a tree to get under. Out here, all you could get under was your hat, or maybe some dark cloud sailing across the face of the sun, and that might last only as long as it takes a bird to fly over.

But there I was. Full of dreams and crotch itch from long riding. Me and my new friend, the Former House Nigger, sat on our horses checking that fort over, watching them horse soldiers drill. It was a prideful thing to see, for they did look sharp, but that was their looks, not their abilities. Them uniforms kind of lied to you. They couldn't ride a horse if they was tied to it. They fell off so regular you almost got to thinking that was their plan. Ride out, fall off, remount, do it all over again. Still,

it was colored troops, and I was glad to see them doing something besides following a plow or plodding along after white folks, ready to chop
their wood or wipe their children's asses.

We rode on down to join them.

In the commanding officer's quarters, me and the Former House Nigger
stood before a big desk with a white man sitting behind it, name of
Colonel Hatch. He had a caterpillar mustache and big sweat circles like
wet pie pans under his arms. His eyes was aimed on a fly sitting on a stack
of papers on his desk. That bug would lift its wings now and then as if to
fly, but it was just a posture. He stayed where he was. Every time those
wings lifted, Colonel Hatch would hold his breath, as if fearing it would
take to the air and buzz away. Way he was watching that damn fly you'd
have thought he was beading down on a charging Apache. Nearby a colored soldier, probably fifty years of age if he was a day, stood at ease, not
showing any expression. He might have been dozing with his eyes open,
he was so still.

Colonel Hatch said, "So you boys want to sign up for the colored
army? I figured that on account of you both being colored."

He was a sharp knife, this colonel.

"Yes, sir," I said. "I've come to sign up to be a horse rider in the Ninth
Calvary."

The colonel reluctantly took his eye off the fly. "We got plenty of riding niggers. What we need is walking niggers for the goddamn infantry."

I figured anything that had the tag "goddamn" in front of it wasn't for
me.

"I reckon ain't a man here can ride better than me," I said, "and that
would be even you, Colonel, and I'm sure you are one riding son of a
bitch, and I mean that in as fine and as respectful a way as I can muster
it."

Hatch raised an eyebrow. "That so?"

"Yes, sir," I said. "No brag, just fact. I can ride on a horse's back, under
his belly, make him lay down, and make him jump, and at the end of the

day, I take to liking him, I can diddle that horse in the ass enough to make that critter smile and brew my coffee and bring my slippers, provided I had any slippers or coffee. That last part about the diddling is just talking, but the first part is serious."

"The diddling part ain't fact," he said.

"No, sir, it ain't."

"But will the horse bring you your slippers and make your coffee, even without the diddling?"

"Absolutely," I said.

"Maybe you are a riding son of a bitch," Colonel Hatch said. "What about you?"

He was addressing the Former House Nigger, who said, "I haven't any intention of diddling horses, but I can cook and lay out silverware. Mostly as a house nigger I drove a buggy."

"A buggy, huh?" Colonel Hatch said, and at that moment he come down on that fly with his hand and got him, too. "Bastard," he said.

He peeled the fly off his palm and flicked him on the floor. The colored soldier, who I had thought might be standing asleep, showed me he was not. He come alert, bent down, picked up the fly with a pinch of gloved thumb and forefinger, took the smashed varmint to the open door, and flicked him into the great outdoors.

Hatch wiped his palm on his pants, eyeing me the same way he had that fly, said, "Let's go outside and see how much of you is fact and how much of you is fart mouth and horseshit."

They had a corral nearby, and the horses in it was rough-looking, like they was in line for the soap factory and anxious to get it over with. But there was a separate, smaller corral, and in it was a horse that nearly filled it up. He was a big black stallion, and he looked like he ate men and shitted out saddlebags made of their skin and bones. He put his eye right on me when I come out to the corral. When I walked around on the other side, he spun around to keep a gander on me. Oh, he knew what I was about, all right.

Hatch took hold of one corner of his mustache and played with it, then turned and looked at me. "You ride that horse well as you say you can, I'll take you both into the cavalry, and the Former House Nigger can be our cook."

"I said I could cook," the Former House Nigger said. "I didn't say I was any good at it. I can make a peach pie, though, and it ain't bad if you can imagine it with a crust. I mostly just make the pie slop. Crust defeats me."

"What we got now," Hatch said, "ain't even cooking of the lowest order. There's just a couple of fellas that boil water and put stuff in it, mostly turnips. It's just one step up from eating horse turds. So if you can do better than that, out here you're a goddamn chef."

By this time four colored soldiers had caught up the horse for me, one of them being the sleepy-eyed fellow that was the colonel's assistant. During the process, the would-be wranglers came close to losing an eye in the gathering, and all of them at one point or another got banged from side to side and rolled along the hot, dusty ground like doodlebugs. They finally looped the horse's nose with a rope, got him bridled and saddled, and led him into an empty corral. When they come off the field of battle, so to speak, two of them was limping. The sleepy fellow was holding his head and looking amazed that he was still alive. They had tied the horse to the railing of the corral, and he was kicking at the wind like maybe he could knock it down.

"Go ahead and get on," Colonel Hatch said. "Show us your Bellerophon to his Pegasus."

I figured Hatch didn't think I knowed who they was, but I had Mr. Loving to thank for the fact I did.

"I will show you my Bellerophon *and* my Perseus," I said, just to let him know I wasn't as ignorant as he figured I was, but he didn't give any show that he thought a thing of it. My remark was as wasted as a nod to a blind man.

"I figure I'll be on my way shortly," the Former House Nigger said, leaning close to me, "and without a cooking job."

"That ain't any show of confidence," I said.

"I am looking at a thing straight-on and seeing how it's bound to turn out," he said. "Have you got any last words?"

"Bury me under a tree, if you can find one," I said. "Better yet, bury me with this horse, and him with a stake through his heart."

Having bragged myself into a deep hole, I had no choice but to get on that beast.

# 7

wasn't stretching the blanket about how I was one fine horse rider. I had learned a lot from Mr. Loving on that matter. But I had never been given a mount like this one to ride. He was blacker than the bottom of a silver mine. Had muscles on top of muscles, had the air of the devil, and was scary just to look at.

I climbed onto the corral, and that monster turned his piggy eyes on me. I swear I seen sparks in them. As soon as I swung on him, he jerked his head, and them reins was snapped off the railing, and I went to grabbing at them. Now, I had been taught to ride Indian-style, using my knees to press in tight to the horse, but that was when a horse had been trained to know what you was doing. This one hadn't been trained for nothing. He was a natural-born killer. But I managed to stay on and was able to grab the reins. Still, I was tottering from side to side like a whiskey bottle that had been whacked. I maintained the center of the saddle, one hand on the reins, the other clutching the saddle horn. My knees was turned into him so hard my nuts was swelling up.

And fellows, did he buck.

He went up so high and for so long I think I seen some ducks flying northward, though none of them mistook my ride for a horsefly, I will guarantee you that. Down we'd go to the pits of hell, among pitchforks and devils, and up again to the land of harps. Then it got so I couldn't tell down from up. All I knew was my butt felt like I was bent over a stump and someone was beating me with a stick and my bones was jarred so bad I figured I'd be spitting teeth out of my asshole.

I come out of the saddle a few times, my butt going skyward, but each trip I was able to bring myself right back into the leather. Finally he took to another plan and come down on his side and rolled. This mashed my leg in the dirt, then my side and head. It was loose dirt that had been kicked up by a lot of horses, so it was soft, and when he rolled I rolled with him, losing my hat and keeping my head. Had that dirt not been spongy, my bones would have been mixed into it so close you couldn't have sorted it with a flour sifter.

After that roll he came up, snorted, and run me along the corral railing, trying to scrape my leg off. I managed to swing my leg over the saddle horn and stay in the saddle. When that didn't work, he run to the middle of the corral and made one more great leap skyward, this one so high I thought I wasn't never going to come down and might bump my head on the moon. But come down I did and when I did I wished I hadn't, cause it pained my rear something fierce; a bolt of lightning rode up my backbone and into my head and made my sizable ears wiggle like hummingbird wings.

When we landed he kind of stumbled a bit, gave a couple of sad bucks, and then started to trot around the corral, snorting as he went. I leaned close to his ear and said, "You call that bucking?"

He seemed to take offense to that and run me straight into the corral. He hit the rails with his chest, dug his feet in so tight they was as rooted as oaks, and I went sailing off his back and over the upper railing and landed on top of some watching soldiers, scattering them like quail.

Colonel Hatch come over, looked down at me. "Well, you ain't smarter than the horse, but you can ride good enough. You and the Former House Nigger are in with the rest of the riding niggers. Get you a uniform and boots that mostly fit, and with those ears you got, I figure you can pretty much hold up any size hat. Get all that figured out and put on, and come the crack of light you start training to be a member of the United States Colored Cavalry."

"Yes, sir," I said.

"Ain't there some papers to fill out?" he said to that sleepy colored soldier.

"Yes, sir," said the soldier.

"Well, then, fill those out, too." He walked away, and the sleepy soldier and the Former House Nigger helped me to my feet.

Over the days we drilled with the rest of the cavalry recruits up and down that horse lot and finally outside and around the fort until we was looking pretty persnickety and thinking we was a lot sharper than we really was. I sure felt better about being part of the cavalry than being in the infantry, who always seemed to be tired and pissed on, sweating and fretting and looking as if they needed a place to lie down.

The horse they gave me to ride was that black ogre I had tried to break in and had done so enough to loosely call him a mount. He really wasn't as bad as I first thought: he was worse. You had to be at your best and alert every time you got on him, cause deep down in his bones he was always thinking about killing you. If you didn't watch it, he'd act casual, like he was looking at a cloud, a bird, or some such, then he would quickly turn his head and take a nip out of your leg. I still got scars on my knee.

Anyway, the months passed, we drilled, and my buddy the Former House Nigger became the second-best rider in the troop. Me being the first, of course. He also cooked, and wasn't nobody died during that time, though there was some sickness of the belly now and then. We mostly had grits and an occasional potato. Thank goodness there was weevils in the grits, or we wouldn't have had no meat at all.

I thought it was all good at the time. I was uniform proud, I'll tell you that. I sat on that black horse, which I had named Satan, like I was something special.

My pride got washed over by boredom in short time, though. We mostly did a little patrolling. Sometimes we'd go out for a few days, leaving some soldiers to guard the fort. What we did was ride around and see the countryside and collect our thirteen dollars a month, which was just so much paper, cause there wasn't any place to spend it. It was all pretty much of the same from day to day. I did get to know a few horny toads by name, and I could have sworn a couple of crickets I'd seen was familiar, too.

Colonel Hatch was our overseer, though most of the training and such was done by a white lieutenant and a colored sergeant everyone called Tornado, this being the fellow we had met that first day in Hatch's office, the one who seemed sleepy and had tossed the fly away. He had got this name from when he first came there and rode a horse for the first time and could only make it go in circles. Even though now he was a good rider, the handle had stuck. Still, I always thought of him as Sleepy or the Fly Catcher.

Colonel Hatch was an all-right fellow, by the way, and always treated us fair and square, if a little rough. He had faith in us and was a good soldier and polite in his own way. I had seen him leave the circle of the fire to walk off in the dark and fart. You can't say that about just anyone. Manners out on the frontier was rare.

The rest of the country, unlike Colonel Hatch, saw us as a little suspicious. I even read about it here and there in the newspapers that come our way, many of them being weeks and months old, a few of them smelling like long-dead fish. They said how we was an experiment. The government had its worries about us, too, and seemed to figure we was just a bunch of ignorant niggers who might at any moment have a watermelon relapse and take to getting drunk and shooting each other. They had already made up their mind who we was, and every day we had to prove we wasn't that and hadn't never been.

Our hopes of showing folks we was prime and ready didn't seem to have any chance of coming to be. We hadn't seen any action, unless you want to count the morning Rutherford got into it with Prickly Pear — I didn't name him; that come from his mother — and they fought over the last biscuit, which was due to the Former House Nigger actually cooking a good batch for a change. It was a hell of a fight. I have never seen fists thrown as fast or so much biting. Colonel Hatch, either to teach a lesson or out of hunger, come over and ate that biscuit while they was scuffling, so it was a wasted bout.

But then there came a morning when things changed. We was given an assignment. Our orders was to go out to a nice run of creek water branching off the Colorado River and stop there. Some trees grew near the creek, and there was frequent dead wood. We was to pick that up and cut down some of the scrubby trees for firewood, giving room for the other trees to grow. That way we'd have a regular woodlot.

It took us most of the day to get to it, the twelve or so of us assigned to the job. It was near nightfall when we showed up. The white lieutenant, Scufford, was leading us, and we had Tornado with us, too. He was Top Soldier among the colored troops, though he didn't always ride out with us, having duties to attend to for Colonel Hatch, like fly tossing and such.

Now, I don't know why I done it that day, as I'd mostly left my Winchester under my bunk along with my pistols for the time I was a soldier, but it occurred to me on that dark and early morning to take them along with me to supplement my army Springfield and pistol. You wasn't supposed to do that, but I done it anyway. I can't put any reason on my choosing to do it, but I did.

The horses, except for mine, was all tuckered out by the time we got to the creek. We strung the horses on a long rope like catfish, and cut down some greenery to let them eat, but not so much they'd get the serious squirts. The wind blowing through the leaves was pleasant, though the tops of the trees wasn't all that high above us. Fact was, after living in East Texas, I thought they seemed right scrawny. But they was trees, and you didn't see many out there, so I was glad to be among them. The night came down and the moon rose up and the wind was cool.

We built a good fire on account of we wasn't sneaking from no Indians, cause we didn't think there was any, least not within our range. The lieutenant wasn't worried anyway, as we had a good position along the creek and in the trees, and there was twelve of us, counting him, and we was well armed. He stationed some of the men as guards, and the rest of us sat around the fire until one of us was called to replace them. The fire was mostly old, dead mesquite, and it crackled as it burned and the smell from it was rich and smoky and made my nose itch.

The Former House Nigger did his best meal, grits and biscuits, and as we sat there eating, talk started up about this and another, horses and women, who among us had the biggest pecker, and then the Former House Nigger went into praising them that had owned him, talking about the men they was and how they had fought nobly for the Confederacy and so on. I don't know what brought him to that, but his carrying on about their nobility was to the rest of the troops like a mouthful of dirt.

Prickly Pear, who was low to the ground, wide in the shoulders, and dull in the face, and who usually had little more to say than "I'm hungry" or "I'm gonna go shit," said, "You is the biggest dummy ever walked, you house nigger, you. You is someone ain't learned no damn thing, cause you was up in that house sucking up to them white folks. You learned to read and such, and you think you is white, or you ought to be. But me, I was a field nigger, and I tell you the man owned us had five hundred slaves. He couldn't remember which nigger was which, was how it was. We was as similar to him as blackberries on a vine. He got mad at one of his slaves, he liked to tie them down, have a pot heated up with grease, which he made the slave's own family heat till it boiled. He had him a rack on which he put it, then he go on and tip it a little, letting spots of grease come down on that runaway's chest. He whipped his niggers, too. And hard."

Prickly Pear took off his shirt then, turned his back to the firelight. The scars was plentiful and looked like dark ropes across his back. He put his shirt back on, said, "He done it now and again to make sure niggers knowed who they belonged to. Once a couple slaves slipped off to another plantation and stole a ham and some wine, and he had no bother about that long as they didn't get caught and he got part of it. But they did get caught. They was ham bones and bottles in they hut, and they hadn't shared it none, and he called them out, and with the owner of that ham and wine standing right there with him, he took one of them bottles and beat them two men, giving that other man, the one got thieved, his chance to swing the bottle. He swung until it broke. Then master got him a bat he made for just that sort of thing, and went to work on them men, who was tied and on their knees and had no way to fight back—whupped on them until they was coming apart, they heads busted up like squash. Beat them until they was dead, making us all stand there and watch, mens, womens, and chillun screamin' and moanin' and carryin' on about what they was seeing. And when the master told them all to shut up, they did, cause they knew they didn't, that bloody bat would be on they heads next. That's my kind of learning with masters and white folk."

"Not everyone was like that," said the Former House Nigger.

"No, some was worse," said Prickly Pear, "and I guess some was better, but one don't weight out t'other. You owned, you owned, it don't matter if you being beat or you up in the master's house humping him in the ass and him reaching between his legs to fondle your nuts. You owned, and you doin' what he wants, cause you don't, he sell you off, trade you, kill you, cause you ain't as good as a dog, which he treats better, feeds good, lets lay up on the porch. Me, I be in the fields all the time, and when I was freed I left out of that Southern country so fast the hat on my head spun around. You can paint over it any way you likes, but it don't make them old times good.

"Tell you one thing, though. Heard the old master died, and I went back and found his grave one night. He had been buried for a time, but I dug him up and busted open his coffin, took the money off his eyes, dragged his rotting body out in a clearing, pieces falling off the bones, went all over his stinking self with a switch, like he felt it. I let him lay that night, and I settled down under a tree, watched the next morning till buzzards gathered on him, thick as seed ticks, and when they was eating good, I left out of there and I ain't never gone back and ain't got no mind to. I bet them ole buzzards choked to death on him."

"You didn't no more do that than fly away like a bird," Tornado said.

"All right, I didn't go back there, but that's what I want to do when I hear he good and dead. It heavy wishful thinking, I admit, but I run it through my head so many times, it almost the same as I went and did it."

After that, there was some throat clearing, and the white lieutenant looked as if he had suddenly come down with the miseries. The silence fell down heavy enough we could hear a night bird breathe. Even as tough as that old boy was, he must have thought it might be a good idea to calm things down, perhaps fearing, heavy as some of us was with our memories, we was about to revolt and beat him to death with a stick. The lieutenant cleared his throat, and to get us on his side went directly into a story about how he had fought for the Union, making sure to mention the bravery of colored troops, then he told a couple of jokes about army folk, and then two or three long, windy ones I didn't get. Then he commanded everyone to bed, except them he put on watch as replacements for those that had been standing and was now brought in to eat their supper.

He put me and the Former House Nigger on vigil, and then a couple hours later we was replaced and got to go to bed. It seemed as if I had just put my head down, and then the sun was up, and we was, too. The Former House Nigger prepared a breakfast of beans that contained what he said was black pepper nuggets but looked like rat turds to me. Taste was similar, too. I think it was his way of making us all feel better about the dining.

I ate it anyway, and was sopping up with a finger in the bean juice when I seen the lieutenant coming. We jumped to attention along with the other soldiers that was eating there by the creek.

The lieutenant said, "Boys, there's a patch of scrub oaks off the creek, scattered out there across the grass, and they aren't growing worth a damn. They're going to be your concern. I'm going to take some of the troops and see if we can pot us a deer or two to take back to camp. It would beat beans and grits and inconsistent biscuits—no offense, Private House Nigger."

"None taken, sir," said the Former House Nigger.

"Besides, I'm bored," said the lieutenant.

"I'm bored, too," I said.

"Looks like you're going to continue to be that way," he said, "unless cutting scrub oak livens you up. I want you fellows to cut that scrub down and saw it up and load it in the wagon to take back for firewood, so it doesn't look like we just come out here and rode around and spent the night at the creek, which is pretty much what we did."

"Yes, sir," I said.

"I thought we could use that oak to smoke the meat I plan to bring in."

"That's a good plan," I said. "That part I can help with. I can smoke meat." I didn't mention, of course, that I was a pretty good cook. That was the Former House Nigger's job, and it wasn't one I wanted.

"What if you don't get no meat?" Prickly Pear said.

"We can still burn the wood, but it won't be for smoking deer shanks. But hell. I saw those deer with my binoculars no less than five minutes ago. Big, fat deer, about a half dozen of them running along. They went over the hill. I'm going to take most of the troops in case I run into hostiles, and besides, I don't like to skin deer."

"I be the best deer skinner around, and I love to do it," Prickly Pear said.

"That's some disappointing shit for you," the lieutenant said. "I got Tornado with me, and I need you here, Prickly. Nat, I'm putting you in charge. You get bit by a snake and die, then the Former House Nigger takes over. I'm also going to put Rutherford, Bill, and Rice, couple others in your charge, and Prickly Pear. Prickly Pear, you take charge if everyone else is dead, got it?"

"Yes, sir," Prickly Pear said, and he looked right proud to hear this.

"What about Indians?" Rutherford said.

"You seen any Indians?" the lieutenant said.

"No, sir," said Rutherford.

"Then there are no Indians," the lieutenant said.

"You ever seen any?" Rutherford asked the lieutenant.

"Oh, hell, yeah. Been attacked by them, and I've attacked them. There's every kind of Indian you can imagine out here from time to time. Kiowa. Apache. Comanche, a stray Kickapoo, and some kind of Indian always looks like he's got dog shit smeared on his face or some such. And there isn't a thing they'd like better than to have your prickly black scalps on their belts, cause they find your hair funny. They think it's like the buffalo. They call you buffalo soldiers on account of it."

"I thought it was because we're brave like buffalo," I said.

"No, that isn't it," he said. "It's the hair."

"That's kind of disappointing," the Former House Nigger said.

"You haven't seen any action for any kind of Indian or anyone else to have an opinion of your bravery," the lieutenant said. "None of us have seen an Indian in ages, and we haven't seen sign of them, either. Not yesterday, not today. I'm starting to think they've all caught a boat to China, and I do suspicion them of Chinese heritage, but that's just my thinking. Someday I want to write a treatise on it. But as for thinking they're all gone, I've thought that before. Indians, especially the Apache and Comanche, they're hard to get a handle on. They'll get after something or someone like it matters more than anything in the world, then they'll wander off if a bird flies over and they make an omen of it. They find omens in squirrel shit, they take a mind to."

Leaving us with those mixed thoughts on Indians, buffalo, and squirrel shit, the lieutenant, Tornado, and the rest of the men rode off, leaving us standing in the shade and me as the leader over a small band of men. I had never given an order in my life, so I didn't know how to start.

First thing we did when the lieutenant and his men was out of sight was throw off our boots and get in the creek. I had been carrying my army Springfield around with me, and I laid it up on the bank with the cavalry pistol. My other guns, Winchester and such, was with my bedroll, which I had fastened up and put near the remuda, near my mount, Satan.

I finally decided to take off my clothes, get a bar of lye soap, and slip back down in the water and scrub myself with it until I didn't smell like my horse. After I was clean as an eastern society lady on her way to church, me and the others, all of us about as carefree as tramps, dressed, went up, and got the wagon hitched to the mules. I left Prickly Pear and another soldier to guard the goods and horses. I had everyone else get in the back of the wagon except for Rice, who I put on a horse to serve as a kind of range rider alongside of us. We traveled wide of the grove of trees, around to where there was just a trickle of creek water and nothing but hot sunlight overhead. We crossed there and made our way to where there was a scattering of miserable-looking oaks, spaced out a few feet apart, with drying leaves. We set to sawing them down with a cross-cut, and then two men using axes took to trimming the limbs. When we finished, we loaded the wagon with the wood.

As we was preparing to go back to camp, Rutherford said, "You know, I hear them Apache will cut off your eyelids and stake you out in the sun or split your pecker and put ants in it."

"I know there's things like that have been done, but I don't know we need to hear about them," Rice said.

Bill put a last chunk of oak in the back of the wagon and said, "Them Indians. Ain't no use hating them for being what they is. Like hating a bush cause it's got thorns on it. Hatin' a snake for biting you. They is what they is, same as us."

"And what are we?" the Former House Nigger said.

Before that question could be answered, Rice, who was in the wagon rearranging some wood, said, "I think we got a problem."

# 8

It was a white man without any drawers, just wearing a red-and-white-striped shirt and a red neckerchief, and he was running down a little rise of dried grass, going fast as a jackrabbit, and in a moment we seen what had given him his inspiration.

Behind him, whooping and having as good a time as kids at a birthday party, was Indians. Apache, to be right on the money, dressed in little to nothing but sunshine and headbands. Four of them was on horseback, six of them was on foot, and for a moment I thought that naked man, his johnson slapping about, was going to outrun them horses. Closer he got I saw that the stripes on his shirt was crawling and running together, and I realized it wasn't no shirt at all but that his chest was all cut up and his throat was cut bad, too, but still he was up and running.

Them Apaches was so interested in chasing him down they didn't even see us. He had either escaped them or they had let him go to have a game, cause I guess living out there with nothing but mesquite berries and some bushes you had to find your fun where you could get it.

The white man, though we was still a considerable distance away, had seen us by this time, and he started yelling at us and waving his hands as he run, flicking them left and right like birds taking flight.

"They're funning him," Rice said, figuring same as me.

It was then that I remembered we was soldiers. I climbed up in the wagon and pulled that government-issue Springfield out of it, got down, and took me a spot standing, prepared to fire at the Apache that was closing in on the white man.

Rice said, "Hell, you can't hit them from here, and neither can they bead in on you. We're out of range, and I heard Indians ain't good shots at all."

One of the running Apaches had spotted us, dropped to one knee, and pointed his rifle. When he did, Rice flung his arms wide, said, "Go on, shoot, you crooked-shooting heathen."

Rice was wrong about the distance and Apache marksmanship. That Indian had beaded him down good with what appeared to be a Henry rifle. Rice got it right on top of the nose and fell over with his arms spread and thumped against the ground on his back, dead.

The Former House Nigger said, "I reckon they been practicing."

It was in that moment that I learned a valuable lesson. Don't never wait on shooting at something if you're going to shoot. Had I not hesitated my shot would have most likely covered the distance and stopped that Indian from firing.

The Apaches that was on foot came down on that running white man then, and they was close enough now I knew I recognized that white fellow. He was none other than the one who had been the town drunk until he became a store owner and field wrangler. He was of course the same that had helped Ruggert kill my pa. It was Hubert. I couldn't decide if I should shoot him or the Apache, and cause I was stunned by these developments, I didn't shoot neither. The Apache took him to the ground, and we could see knives and rifle butts flying up in the air, coming down, and we could hear that poor bastard's head and bones cracking like someone was crushing walnuts in his fists. We opened up on them with our weapons, and it sounded like whips snapping. I fired, and it was a good distance of a shot, but I was square on aim. My Apache target was dead before he hit the ground.

One of the Apaches on horseback rode right at us. Someone in our group fired, and the horse took the shot. The Indian toppled to the ground, rolled, and came up on his feet, his horse having turned completely over on its back with its four legs in the air, like someone had upended a table.

All the other Indians had scampered back behind the rise, and the riding Indians had dismounted and pulled their horses down to the ground, out of sight. But that one Apache, he didn't go nowhere. You can say what you want about the Apache, but they are about the bravest thing that ever lived—outside of a drunk preacher who thinks God is on his side and when deep in his cups thinks he *is* God.

This brave come running right at us, all of us having gone to our knees and firing away at him fast as we could. I had excellent training with guns, but my long-gun shooting was a mite off with that Springfield, having done most of my education with a Winchester. I was used to firing rapidly and not reloading after each shot.

I figure that Apache notioned he had some big medicine, cause not a one of our shots hit him. He run right through that hail of bullets in haint-like fashion. As he got closer, I could see he had some kind of muddy paint on his chest and face, or maybe he was just filthy. He had a big grin, too, like he knew he was beyond the powers of our hot lead. He even paused—and I swear if I'm lying I'm dying—then he started to prance sideways, first to the left, then to the right. Our bullet-bees hummed around him, but none of them landed for the sting. With that big grin still on his face, he stepped in a hole and went down. Even from where we were, we could hear his ankle snap like a yanked suspender. Without meaning to, every one of us troopers went "Ooh." It was so nasty-sounding it made us hurt.

That fall must have caused that Apache's magic to fly right out of his ass, cause we all started firing at him again, and this time he collected all our bullets. He was deader than a government promise before the smoke cleared.

The Apache didn't move from their spot on the hill. I'm sure seeing their partner made into a cheese grater gave them pause, brave or not.

We popped off a few shots in their direction, killing one of the horses, whose head had managed to poke over the skyline. But to the best of my knowledge we didn't hit nary an Apache.

We hustled up on that wagon and clattered it across that little creek. I crouched in the back, looking for Apache. Sure enough, they had come back down the hill, none of them with horses, having hidden them somewhere. There was more of them than before; it was like they had split into other Indians.

Firing commenced from within the trees, and I knew Prickly Pear and the other soldier, who I think was called Dash—though the years have clouded my memory of him, as he was the silent type—heard the commotion and was shooting at the Indians, covering what we would later politely call a retreat.

We come around behind the trees, banged the wagon down a little rise, and fetched up in there among the growth near the creek. Prickly Pear and this other fellow was spread wide of each other on their bellies, aiming their rifles across the creek, firing, reloading, firing. The Apaches was ducking into dips and draws we didn't know was there until they disappeared into them like rabbits.

I had the horses unhitched quick-like from the wagon and placed with the remuda, which was between the trees. I made a firing line there at the creek. I put Bill to the rear with a tree at his back and one near his front for protection. I told him to watch for creepers and to yell out if he seen any. As it was, I was hoping we just had a front attack to worry about. The hill was long enough they could go wide on us, but even with them being Apache and the land being a confusion of drop-offs and gullies, I took it in my head that it would be hard for them to flank us. This from an old Apache fighter of about fifteen minutes.

I dug into my goods, got my Winchester, and strapped on that holster Mr. Loving had made with the LeMat in it. I stuck my Colt in another holster that slid toward my back, jammed the service pistol under the gun belt, then crouched over to the creek and dropped down on the ground flat as a leaf. There was a bush in front of me, and I hoped it might hide me. Someone among them Apache was a pretty good shot, having picked off Rice like that.

I watched as the Apache come along on their bellies, a head rising now and then to check things out, and then ducking out of sight. They somehow managed to cut the pecker off the dead Apache's horse without us being any wiser until they shoved it in Hubert's mouth, then propped him to a sitting position with a stick or something. This was meant to scare us, and it worked.

I was surprised Hubert had showed up, of course, but had suspected for a while that he and Ruggert and that big colored fellow I had seen was after me, but so much time had passed I thought they might have quit. Still, I figured they had come upon me by accident and might not even know they had found me. Maybe Ruggert and the colored man was lying dead and chopped up on the other side of the hill with a horse dick in their mouths. By the time it came to the Apache shoving one between your teeth, a stick of licorice, a cigar, or a horse dick was all pretty much the same to you.

I was trying to consider if it was possible for us to make a quick mount and ride off, but I concluded that would be a bad idea. It would put us in a busy way as they rushed down upon us, for surely they would. It seemed wiser to hold our ground, as we had trees for protection from the sun and we had plenty of water, something they might not have. The water might have led them to us in the first place.

It was then that Hubert reached up, partly pulled and partly spat that horse dick out of his mouth, and started moaning. He rolled off of what was propping him up, which turned out to be a hatchet, the blade of it stuck in his back. He went to crawling into some high grass and out of sight, but a couple of Apache came up on him then. They dragged him back and disappeared behind the grass, and we could hear screams.

It went on and on, and I began to feel sorry for Hubert. I tried to picture Pa burned up and lying next to the hog, but it wasn't enough. It was just awful hearing him caterwauling.

Prickly Pear called out, "I can't stand it no more. I'm gonna go get him."

"No, you're not," I said. "I'll do it."

"Why you?" said the Former House Nigger, bellying over close to me.

"Cause I'm in charge."

"I'm going with you," he said.

"Naw, you ain't," I said. "I get rubbed out, you're the one next in charge. Lieutenant said so. You don't want it to get down to Prickly Pear, do you?"

"Oh, hell, no," the Former House Nigger said.

That crying out hadn't ceased. It carried on and on. The sound of it was starting to make me sick to my stomach. It was like they was peeling his skin off an inch at a time, and for all I knew they was.

I turned to the Former House Nigger.

"When I get out there a ways, you and the others keep them busy as a hive of bees, but don't send a blue-whistler up my ass. I'm going to see I can get to him, pull him out of there, or if I have to, finish him off."

"Hell, we can't even see them," the Former House Nigger said.

"Then you got to shoot where you think they are, make them keep their heads down, or clip the top off one if it pokes up."

I laid the Winchester on the ground next to my Springfield, deciding it was too burdensome to crawl about with. I had the two pistols from Mr. Loving, which I was highly familiar with, so I laid the service pistol on the ground with the rifles. Pulling my big knife, I put it between my teeth.

I waited a moment to listen and hope Hubert had quit crying out, but he hadn't. He was still at it, louder than before. In that moment I couldn't think of him as no one other than a poor man in a horrible situation.

I slithered alongside the creek as the men put up a line of fire, and then slipped into the creek bed. I was able to stoop and stay hid because the bank was high on the Apache side. I hunched down and ran along that way until I made it to where there was a wide swath of grass and the creek bank broke open in a sandy V. The wind was moving the grass. I stuck my face in it and parted it just enough for a line of sight, hoping I wouldn't be seen and that the movement would be mistaken for the breeze at work.

There wasn't anything to see but more grass. I bellied up in it like a snake and began to slide along, going quiet as the guest of honor at a funeral. Finally I come upon a drop-off, a gulley, actually, and by moving the grass slightly with my fingers, I could look down the length of it and see two Apache down there with the body of Hubert. He was good and dead, his throat slit, and them two Apache was trading out with the moans and cries and such, doing all they could not to laugh about it. The sneaky bastards; if that didn't beat all. I was mighty impressed.

It was then one of them seen me.

They jumped up and come running at me, one with a knife, though he had a cap and ball pistol stuck in a sash around his waist. The other was toting the hatchet he'd pulled from Hubert's back.

I didn't have no other course than to pull the knife from my teeth and jump down in that gulley with them. I didn't want to shoot a pistol and make noise and bring the whole batch of them down on me. The one carrying the knife lunged at me with it, and though I was able to avoid his strike, his body hit me like a cannonball, and away we went a'rolling.

The other was almost on me with that hatchet. I caught sight of him out of the corner of my eye as I struggled with the other, but that buck had made a mistake by raising his head above the gulley line. One of the troopers got off a shot that knocked his noggin apart. His hatchet went flying, and he went tumbling.

Now it was just me and the one with the knife. I was trying to cut him, and he was trying to cut me. We was using our free hands to hold each other's knife hand at the wrist. I managed to squeeze his wrist enough he let go of his knife, but he jerked his hand loose and went for the gun in his sash, got it pulled, fired at me point-blank. I was moving, though, so the shot only singed my hair and made my ears ring like a church bell.

I got hold of his gun hand, partly covering the gun with my fingers, slipping one of them down on the hammer so he couldn't pull the trigger. This didn't work long. He yanked his hand free and stuck the gun in my face and squeezed the trigger again.

The pistol misfired. He was so startled by its failure he let go of my wrist with the knife in it, and that's what cooked his goose. I stabbed him in the chest, kicked him off of me, leaped on top of him before he could shoot again, and went to stabbing wildly. Finally I put the edge of the knife to his throat and pulled it across. He gave me a look of disappointment, like maybe he'd just discovered I had my finger up his ass. He gurgled blood out of his mouth and nose, kicked once like he was stepping down on a bug, and went still.

Wasn't nothing to be done for Hubert, so I put the knife away, pulled the Colt, and started crawling back to the creek the way I had come. The Apache saw me this time, as I had raised quite a ruckus in the gulley. Now I was making haste where before I had been trying to sneak. A bullet singed the butt of my trousers, but other than that I got back to the creek bed, and finally back to the soldiers, without any real wound.

When I was there, I said, "Who made that shot on the Apache?"

"That would be me," said the Former House Nigger.

"Listen here," I said. "I don't want you calling yourself the Former House Nigger anymore. I don't want no one calling you that no more. You're a buffalo soldier, and a good one. I tell you another thing while I'm telling how the hoss ate the apple: ain't none of us need to be called riding niggers, so we damn sure as hell don't need to be calling one another that. I say we don't. I won't, and I'll fight the man that can't resist it. Rest of you men hear that?"

They all heard me well enough, including Bill, up the hill between them trees.

"You getting paid for that preaching, nigger?" said Prickly Pear, and everyone laughed.

"This here is Cullen," I said. "He ain't nothing but Cullen, or Private Cullen, or whatever his last name is. That's what we call him. You hear that, Cullen? You're a soldier, a top soldier, at that. You saved my life."

"It was a good shot," Cullen said, so only I could hear it.

"Damn sure was," I said.

"What about the white man?" Cullen asked.

"Dead. Apaches was making the noises we heard."

"That ain't fair," Cullen said.

"It ain't a card game," I said.

"Thing worrying me," Cullen said, "is pretty soon we got to worry about when the sun goes down."

"That is a concern," I said.

I got my Winchester, stuck the service revolver in my belt, stretched out beside the Springfield, and took a breather, having concluded that I had the men positioned as best I could. We had a good view, and it would take some work for them Indians to come out of that grass and us not see them, but as Cullen had said, what about when the sun went down?

# 9

As the light faded, I began to fret. We had a lot of ammunition on hand, which was a good thing, but my feelings that I had the men well positioned dimmed with the sun. I rushed down our firing line and spaced the men along the creek in what I felt was better positions, having the last man on either end turn slightly to their side to protect from any kind of surrounding maneuver. I left Bill up there between them two trees, giving him strict instructions to watch carefully and not fall asleep, though I couldn't imagine anyone nodding off under the circumstances, which would be a bit like finding a bear's cave with a bear in it and being inclined to nap next to it.

Night crept up on us. It turned blue over the top of the hill, then the blue spread, went black. Shadows tumbled over us and wrapped themselves in the trees like torn canvas. A piece of the moon rode up. Its light hit the top of the hill, caused the tips of the grass to gleam like sword points and the little run of water in the creek to shine. Mosquitoes buzzed, and not too far from us we heard a big frog bleat.

I told Cullen I was going to check the line. I left my Winchester with the Springfield on the ground and hurried along, keeping low as I went.

I started with the rear, which wasn't no line at all but was Bill. I found him lying between the trees where he was supposed to be, but he was facedown, and the ground around him was wet. I turned him over and dug a match out of my soldier shirt, struck it on one of the trees. His throat was cut.

My skin goose-bumped, and the service revolver sort of leaped into my hand. I eased away from him and back down toward the creek, my ass crack clenched up like a fist. Starting at the far end of the line, I found that soldier whose name I could never remember and now didn't need to learn. There was an arrow through his head. It had gone in above his ear and come out the other side.

I scrambled down the line, such as it was, came to Prickly Pear, and said, "You alive?"

"Why, hell yeah, I'm alive," he said.

"There's two that ain't," I said.

"Oh, shit," Prickly Pear said, and he followed me as I went at a stoop down the row and found everyone else alive, right up to Cullen. When I told Cullen what had happened, he said, "Jesus."

"They're like ghosts," I said.

I turned to look at the horses. The remuda rope was still there, but two of the horses was gone. About then I heard Satan snort, saw him kick out, heard a slapping sound and a release of breath. I ran over there in a hurry. There was enough moonlight through the gaps in the trees I could see Satan had kicked an Apache in the head, one of his hooves cracking his cheek, causing the eye to roll out on its strings and hang there. I don't know if that Apache was dead or not, but I seen then there was another darting away. I raised my pistol and hit him square in the back, and he went down. I shot the one on the ground for good measure, twice, then hustled back to the others.

I had by now what you might call some serious misgivings about my leadership. I said, "What we got to do is get on our horses and try and ride for it. We ain't safe up in here. This just gives them a way to get to us and us not see them."

"You don't have to tell me twice," Prickly Pear said, and he and the others started running for the remuda. I picked up my Winchester as well as my Springfield and followed Cullen to the horses in haste.

I let everyone saddle up and mount, while I turned nervously this way and that with the loop-cock Winchester, the Springfield on the ground at my feet. When I was sure everyone was mounted, I got the bridle on Satan, loosed him from the remuda, and just as I got him saddled, he took that moment to rear up, jerk the reins from my hand, dart through the trees, and was gone.

"Now, ain't that something," I said.

Cullen said from horseback, "We'll ride double," and he held out his hand to pull me up.

The boys was all sitting their horses, ready to go, when there was a whoop, and an Apache leapfrogged over the back of one of the horses, taking a soldier off of it with him. They went rolling on the ground, the Apache pounding the trooper a couple of times with a hatchet, then darting into the woods swift as a rabbit.

The soldiers flurried like startled quail. Wasn't no military drill about it. It was every son of a bitch for himself. I swung on the back of Cullen's horse, hanging on to the Winchester but having forgotten the Springfield on the ground. We rode out of the wooded area and came out in the open. The partial moon was surprisingly bright.

I looked back, seen those soldiers was still up in the trees, having lost control of themselves and their horses. I saw the shadowy shapes of horses and men go down, and we could hear them screeching like children. There was gunfire, probably from both sides, and then it all went silent.

Did we wheel about and go to the rescue? Hell, no. There wasn't any rescue to be done. We had been outsmarted, outmanned, and outfought. If we didn't want to be down there among them, we had to ride faster than a blue norther blows. That's when a shot came our way, hit our horse. It fell down, sent Cullen plunging. I was able to come off the falling beast and land on my feet, still clutching my Winchester.

Then the horse got up, the wound not being a finisher. Cullen, like a grasshopper, leaped on its back and took the reins again. I grabbed the horse's tail and said, "Go," cause behind us those Apaches was coming, and though what they was yelling at us I couldn't understand, I doubted it was compliments on the cut of our uniforms.

I told you how Mr. Loving had taught me that horse-tail trick, but Cullen bolted off so fast I nearly got my arm jerked out of the socket. Still, I managed to hang on, and Cullen pulled back on the reins and let the horse lope, but nothing beyond what I could deal with.

The Apaches was mostly on foot, but there was a few with horses, and they had gathered them up. Some had our horses, leading to a high number of them becoming mounted, and pretty soon they was all coming after us. Since I had managed a little space from them with that horse-tail trick, I yelled for Cullen to stop. He reined that horse so sharp it near sat down on me. I swung up behind him, knowing if that horse had anything left we were going to have to use it. That tail trick wasn't going to work anymore, not with them on horseback.

The critter was favoring the wound in its right hip, but we couldn't let that stop us. We had to ride till there wasn't any riding to be done. It was starting to look like we had us a chance, and damn it, all of a sudden the horse crumpled and tossed us over his head. When we got to our feet the animal was panting loudly, down on its bent front legs, its neck bowed, mouth wide open, the moon in its eyes.

It was done for.

I swapped the Winchester to my left hand, pulled my service revolver, and shot the horse through the head. It dropped dead, but it was still stuck there on its bent front legs, its ass in the air. I put a boot to its side and knocked it over. We hustled in between its legs and peered over its body at them that was chasing us. And believe you me, they was coming right smart. There was more of them than I figured, as I hadn't exactly been able to take a head count before. They had been hidden out there in the grass, and then the trees, and now all of them was on horseback, bearing down on us like a dose of the flu.

I had hung on to my Winchester, but Cullen had lost his Springfield when the horse tumbled. It was on the side of the horse where the Apaches was. He pulled his revolver, and we both laid up behind the horse, making a fort of the poor thing. I was stretched over the dead critter's neck, and Cullen was hanging over its ass. I beaded down on an Apache and fired, then fired again. Two of them came off their horses and hit the dirt.

My eyes was on their horses, as I was hoping to nab at least one as it ran by so we could make a run for it, but it was like the beasts knew what I was hoping. They spread wide to either side and run, disappearing into the night like it had swallowed them. Truth was, it was unlikely we could have snatched one before them Apaches come down on us.

Cullen was firing his pistol, and though he didn't hit any Apaches, he killed a horse, and that threw one of the riders pretty hard. The Indian lay there on his back a moment, rolled over, and pushed up with his hands. He was stunned and hardly knew where he was. I took that moment to shoot him in the top of the head. It was so easy I almost felt bad about it. I had killed three of them now. It had put a stop to their headlong ride. They heeled up their horses, leaped off, and pulled them over on the ground by biting their ears and dropping their weight. You get your teeth in a horse's ear, you can pull it to the ground like it was light as a feather.

When they got their horses pulled down, they shot them to make their own forts. I had been told that an Apache wasn't like a Comanche, who would try and keep his horse no matter what. The Apache was a practical Indian. He'd run one until it couldn't run, and when it fell over, he'd stick it with something sharp so that it got to its feet, and he'd ride it till it fell over and couldn't get up no matter how much you poked it. After that, he'd cut its throat, drink its blood, build a fire and eat some of it, then he'd cut off its nuts and take those with him as something to nibble on.

They had a half circle of horses out there, and they decided they was going to camp out and wait on us. It was a pretty good plan, considering we didn't have nowhere to move that they couldn't see us. We was two on foot and they was still six or seven at least, and that was a considerable number against us under the circumstances; though there was no doubt my shooting was whittling them down a bit.

They was firing at us, and the bullets were plopping into our horse and throwing up blood and sweat, and that dead cayuse was fluttering farts out the back end and through them bullet holes.

After a bit they tired of shooting and took to saving their ammunition, which was what we was doing. I reckoned their plan was to rest in shifts, and when we was tuckered out and needing water, they'd put the sneak on us. I offered to shoot Cullen if it looked as if we was about to be overrun and tortured.

"I'd rather shoot you, then shoot myself," he said.

"Okay. You shoot me, then shoot yourself."

"What if I shoot you, then I make an escape?"

"I'd rather it not work that way."

"But it could."

"Here's the deal: you shoot me only if you have reckoned you're going to have to shoot yourself, otherwise we'll try for escape together. I don't want no idle shooting going on, especially since one of those shots will be for me."

"All right, then," he said.

That wasn't quite the end of it, though. We kept tossing this back and forth, wanting to make sure we was clear on these matters, and there wouldn't be any willy-nilly shooting going on. When we felt we had it straightened out, we shook hands on it.

It was a bright night and the land was flat and there wasn't a whole lot of creeping they could do without us noticing, but they could still outflank us because they outnumbered us. If they made a mad rush, they'd have us. Then again, they knew we'd get a few of them, too. I was hoping that wasn't an exchange they was high on making.

After a while we seen a fire flare up from behind that curving wall of horses, and then we could smell horse meat sizzling. They had chosen one and dug into its insides and made themselves a nice, late supper. We, on the other hand, had one horse, and eating our fort didn't seem like too good an idea. Still, I pulled my knife and cut the horse's throat, and we took turns putting our mouths over the cut and taking in some of the still-warm nourishment, though there wasn't any real flow to the blood anymore. It tasted better than I figured, but at that point in time I was so famished I would have eaten a buttered pile of buffalo chips and thought them tasty as apple pie.

When we had all we could suck out of the drying wound, we lay there peeking over our horse, listening to the Apaches laughing and cutting up. There's them that says they don't have no humor, but I tell you sure as hell they was tickled about something that night. I figured we was a part of it. Or maybe one of them had told a good joke. If things wasn't bad enough, after a while they began to sing in English, "Row, row, row your boat."

"Goddamn missionaries," I said.

"They've got some kind of liquor," Cullen said. "I know drunks when I hear them."

We had to listen to that go on for a couple of hours without them tiring of it. They was so good at it, in good voice and well in tune, and having such a big time over there I almost wanted to join them. Now they moved to further humiliation by having one of them stand up, bend over, and pull up the little flap he was wearing and show us his butt. There in the moonlight that redskin's meat was as white as an Irishman's ass. I was about to pot him when he turned around and showed us his dangling business, humped at the air like he was doing a squaw. That was enough. I had taken all I was going to take. I lifted up quick from behind the horse's neck and shot at him. I was aiming at his pecker, but think I got him in the belly. He let out a bark and fell back, and we didn't see him again. I bet right then they was wishing they had moved those horses back a few yards before killing them and using them for protection.

I dropped back down behind the horse.

"Bad enough they're going to kill us," Cullen said, "but they got to act nasty, too."

"I gave him a bellyache," I said.

We watched for a long while, but those Indians was as quiet as the dirt. After a short time, I'm ashamed to say I was so exhausted I nodded off. When I awoke it was daylight and my throat wasn't cut and I still had my hair.

I looked and saw Cullen was awake. He had gone out and got his Springfield and had it laid across the horse. I said, "Damn it, Cullen. I'm sorry. I fell out."

"I let you. They're gone."

I sat up and looked. There was the dead horses with buzzards lighting on them. A few of them birds was eyeballing our horse and us, but I didn't see any sign of the Apache.

"I been watching close," he said. "They're gone. They just picked up like a circus and left. Guess they figured they'd lost enough men over a couple of buffalo soldiers, or maybe it was like the lieutenant said: they saw a bird and figured it was a bad omen, and it told them to take theirselves home."

"What I figure is they got too drunk to think straight, woke up with hangovers, and went somewhere cool and shaded to sleep it off."

"Reckon so," Cullen said. Then: "You meant what you said about me being a top soldier and all?"

"Consider it came from someone left in charge that got everyone killed but you and me. I got the horses wiped out as well, and on top of that I left a lot of army equipment back there and fell asleep on guard duty hanging over a dead horse's neck. Only thing I didn't do was join them and lead them on a raid to burn down the fort. Taking all that into consideration, it might mean a little less."

"Lieutenant shouldn't have split us up in the first place. I am not Napoleon, but even I know that. It was his fault for leaving a private in charge. But I do appreciate what you said."

# 10

The day turned off blazing hot. We made our way back to the trees and the creek to look about. No Apaches was hiding in there, and the soldiers was all cut up and shot up, except for Prickly Pear. We found him standing against a tree, or so it seemed, but he was just propped there, having fallen back against it. He didn't even look to have been hurt. His eyes was open, and he had an expression like he was about to make some joke or other. I went over and touched him, thinking he might be alive and just stunned, but he wasn't. He fell over, and I saw a wound right behind his ear, a bullet hole, and from the looks of it, the shot had been fired close. It was my guess he did it to himself. I found his pistol on the ground nearby, so that made it even more likely. Why they hadn't cut him up like the rest I couldn't be sure. He didn't even smell ripe.

We looked about for any of our supplies that was left, but there wasn't none. The Apaches on their decamping from their horse fort had come back and taken everything but the wagon with the cut wood in it and Prickly Pear's clothes and gun. Cullen was convinced it was because he had backed up against that tree and put up a brave fight, and it was a sign of respect. But ain't no one can be sure.

We didn't even have a shovel to bury the men, and had no choice but to leave them where they fell for fear the hostiles might return. I think about that from time to time and wonder: should we have stacked them up and burned them? But in the end I guess there isn't any right answer. I hope when they was found, as they was bound to be by others from the fort, there was enough left of them to give them a burial.

Me and Cullen walked back out to the wall of horses the Apache had made, cut off a piece of horse meat, peeled the hide from it, and with some matches we had and some of the wood we had cut earlier, started a fire and cooked it. The meat was a little rank, but we cooked it black and ate it anyway.

We drank some water from the creek, started walking in the general direction of our soldier fort with nothing but our weapons and our good intent. Went on like that for several hours, that sun beating down and us without even a canteen of water to refresh ourselves.

"I hate being a soldier," Cullen said. "I don't like getting shot at or chased by Indians. And now we got to go back and tell them how things didn't go good. It'll all be put on you, how it all went bad. And my feet hurt. And we always got to get up early in the morning. And I don't want to cook."

I was considering on what Cullen was saying when we came upon a pair of binoculars on the ground. I picked those up, and not long after we saw a couple of shiny buttons off cavalry uniforms lying on the ground. Following that we came upon the deer-hunting party, or what was left of them.

Their bodies and those of their horses was dotted over the landscape. The soldiers was stripped and had been scalped and cut up and such; missing eyes, ball sacks, toes, and assorted things deemed necessary for the living. The lieutenant we found partly burned up. A fire of mesquite bush and items from saddlebags had been put on his belly and set ablaze. It had burned right down into his stomach and made a hole, sizzling his innards. His body was still smoking, and there was that horrible smell of burning human flesh in the air, something I recalled from when Ruggert and his friends had burned up my pa. The saddles, bridles, the whole shebang had been taken off the horses. Apaches like leather.

"I guess it worked out best we didn't go on the deer hunt," I said.

"Appears that way," Cullen said.

We looked around cautious-like, but it appeared we was on our own; no Apaches and no survivors. We went around and counted the dead and figured there was the right number there, though most of the troopers you couldn't tell from a slaughtered steer. Only the lieutenant and one or two others was recognizable, one of them being Tornado. They had chopped his head off, but I knew it was him from the way he was built. They hadn't taken his shirt and pants and boots, just his belt, and they had cut the buttons off his outfit. That's all they took from him. And his head, of course.

The flies was something awful, and like the others we didn't have no easy way to bury them. So there we stood, out in the hot sun amid those stinking bodies, and Cullen said, "Do you see a black horse? Or am I imagining it?"

"I see him," I said.

"Do you see some dancing soldiers?"

"Nope."

"Do you still see the horse?"

"I do," I said.

"Is it Satan?"

"Yes. In more ways than one."

"Good. Then I'm not imagining it."

"He looks strong and rested," I said. "Figure he found a water hole and some grass somewhere and maybe even a piece of horse ass. He has been taking it easy while we've been dealing with hellfire and damnation, the bastard."

"Don't talk mean," Cullen said. "He might hear you. Look happy to see him."

We started smiling, and I tried to whistle, but my mouth was dry as dirt.

Satan lifted his head and put a steely eye on us. I put my rifle and the binoculars down and started walking toward him, holding out my hand like I had a treat. I don't think he fell for that, but he dropped his head and let me walk up to him. He still had on the bridle, and the reins was hanging down, so I reached out slow and careful and took hold of them.

I swung onto his back with more than a little effort, and as I was about to settle into the stirrups good, he bucked. I went whirling through the air and hit the ground so hard my breath flew out of my mouth like bees from a hive. When my head quit swimming and I could take a breath, Satan was poking me with his nose, making a noise that came as close to a laugh as was possible; a horse laugh, I might add.

Wobbling to my feet, I got hold of his reins and led him over to Cullen, limping slightly.

"He loves a good joke," Cullen said. "But deep down, I think he likes you."

"It's pretty damn deep," I said.

We gathered our rifles and the binoculars, climbed on Satan's back, me at the reins, and started out in the direction of the fort, judging its location by the position of the sun. As we rode along, Cullen said, "You know, I right respect the buffalo soldiers, I surely do, and my short time there has been interesting, if not that rewarding. They are a fine bunch of individuals. Them that are still alive."

I studied on that comment, said, "You saying something between the lines, Cullen?"

"I'm saying everyone is dead, and why not us?"

"I thought we was doing all we could not to be dead," I said.

"And I'm suggesting we might keep that going for quite a while longer."

I love these here United States, primarily cause I don't know nothing else. That said, it turns out, even for thirteen dollars a month, I wasn't all that in love with the cavalry. I didn't like taking orders, for one, and I especially didn't like being nearly killed by Indians. And then there was eating Cullen's cooking.

"So if they're all dead," I said, "it stands to reason that we might be dead, too, just not found."

"What I was thinking," Cullen said.

We rode on a piece more, and then without thinking too hard on it, I started turning Satan away from the direction of the fort.

Satan had my canteen strapped on his saddle, and it was near full, and there was a couple bites of jerky in the saddlebags, so we ate that, and along with the fact we was riding, not walking, things was better than they had been shortly before. You could add to that our change of career plans, which was starting to appeal to me.

We had gone for most of a day when we seen something in the distance we couldn't make out. I lifted the binoculars and seen there was a red-shirted colored fellow lying out there with his leg under a dead horse. A big sombrero lay on the ground nearby.

I assumed he was dead like the horse, or right near it, cause buzzards were circling overhead. One of them had lit down near the horse and was staring in its direction as if waiting for a signal. A little black cloud of flies was buzzing about.

Riding over there, we discovered the colored fellow wasn't dead at all. Even with his leg trapped, he lifted up slightly on an elbow and pointed the business end of an old Sharps .50 at us.

"Hold up," I said. "I ain't got nothing against you."

"You're money on the hoof is all," he said, then sighed and gently laid the Sharps on the ground. "It ain't like I'm going to spend it, though."

We dropped off Satan, and I gave Cullen the reins to lead him. I pushed the Sharps aside with my foot. The man didn't try and stop me. I don't think he had the strength to lift that heavy old rifle again. He didn't have a handgun strapped to him.

I squatted by him. He had a face that looked as if it had been chopped out of dried wood. His eyes was so black they looked like blackberries. I said, "Just resting?"

He took a deep breath. "Me and my horse thought we'd stop in the middle of the prairie, under the sun, and take a nap. It seemed like a nice enough day for it. Feeling pleasant, I asked him if he would lay down on my leg."

"You had on that hat, you might could block out some of the sun."

"I can't get my leg out from under this dead bastard," he said, kicking the horse with his free leg. "Not even enough to reach my hat. I like that hat. I had to kill a Mexican for it."

Cullen picked up the hat and brought it to him, leading Satan as he came. The man was too weak to lift his hand and take it. I lifted his head, Cullen pushed the hat on him, and I settled his noggin back down on the ground. The back of the hat bent under him, the brim in front tilted so that it covered his face in shadow. I could see now that the horse had a couple of bullet holes in it. Sombrero Man had a hole himself, in his left side, between chest and belt. He was leaking out pretty fast.

"This ain't how I was expecting things to work out," he said.

"I reckon not," I said. "Having a horse fall on you and getting shot up don't seem like a good plan for nobody."

"Can't say as I can recommend it."

"You're the one hunting me, aren't you?"

"I recognize your ears. I was told you had a set."

"Why would you help those men? They despise colored folks."

"They hired me because I'm a tracker, part Seminole, out of Florida originally, late of Nacogdoches, Texas. That Ruggert fellow heard about me and my tracking, come and hired me. Money was good."

"Money's no kind of reason," I said.

"Thought I might grow up to do the ballet, but my legs looked bad in tights. So I do what I do. Only profession I got, tracking and killing people. Pays good, and I have a lot of time off."

"Time to relax and get hold of yourself is always good," Cullen said. "I didn't have much of that and always wanted more. I liked my work, and was good at it, but more time off would have been good."

"Yeah," I said. "That's a holdup on being a slave. Not enough time off."

"That's a good point you got there," Cullen said. "Very true."

"What I'd like to request is two things," Sombrero Man said. "Could you get this horse off my leg, for one?"

"I'll consider it," I said. "Tell me—has Ruggert given up by now?"

"He took it right bad you raped his wife."

"I didn't," I said.

"Other one told me you just looked at her ass. I can understand that. I've had a piece of ever' color ass I could find that would give out, and the thing is, an ass is an ass when you add it all up. But Ruggert, he didn't see it that way. He is an odd piece of work, and he ain't a forgetter."

"So I've figured," I said.

"We just stayed at it, and he kept paying me with money he got somewhere or another, so I stayed on. We come upon you first out by that abandoned buffalo wagon."

"I remember."

"Not much else to tell. We come to the conclusion you was in the army. Thought you'd leave the fort at some point, and we could cut you from the herd."

"That has been one long wait."

"I'll say. But he paid, and I stuck. We camped nearby on the sly. Used a spyglass to see where you were. Followed your troop out when you took to the woodlot, lagged behind on purpose. I don't know what he planned there, how he wanted to get you away from the others, but as I said, he was a determined cuss. I think he was considering on that when the Apache come upon us. I rode off when I saw it was hopeless. A couple of them redskins followed me on horseback. You walk out that way a piece, you'll see the blood from one of them. He was the one shot me and killed my horse, brought it down on my leg. I got him, though. Made that shot with this fine horse lying on my leg, me stretched out here in God's wide open. The one didn't have a hole in him threw his pal across the dead man's horse, mounted his own, and led the other after him. I wanted to shoot him, too, but the Sharps got heavy. I don't know what happened to Ruggert and the other fellow, Hubert, who I figured for a drunk. Didn't see him take a drink, but he rubbed his lips a lot and looked lonesome plenty. Usually got grumpy at suppertime. I'll tell you, though, he only called me nigger once. We had an understanding after that."

"Hubert is dead," I said. "Apache got him."

"Can't say I miss him."

"You never said the second thing," Cullen said.

I had forgotten there was a second thing.

"No, I didn't," Sombrero Man said. "Number two's this. Stay with me till I pass on. Take me some place where there's a real graveyard. I don't want to lay out here on the prairie. I want to be in God's soil, have some words said over me."

"I don't owe you a thing," I said.

"I ain't got no hard feelings. Why should you?"

"Because you were going to kill me," I said.

"I understand your point of view," he said. "It's a clear one."

I studied on the problem a moment. "I should leave you for the buzzards, but I'll do it. Ain't getting you no headstone, though."

"That's all right," he said. "No one would know who I was anyhow. For the record, my name is Cramp, or that's what I'm called. Man got my Seminole mama's belly full of me called me that. He run off early. I got a second name, but nobody used it much when I was little, and finally they didn't use it at all, and now I don't remember what it was. There ain't a single person I know of alive that's kin to me. But I was thinking God might forgive me some things if I was buried proper in his own ground."

"It's dirt," I said. "And that's all it is."

"I think I've spoken enough for this life," he said and started to breathe like a dog panting.

We dug around his leg with our hands. It was hard ground. Finally I got my knife out and broke the ground up good enough to slide his leg out from under the horse. The leg was a mess, bones sticking right through his pants, and he had bled out something awful. We dragged him around so he could rest his back against his horse. He closed his eyes, and after a bit he breathed less heavy, and finally he wasn't breathing at all.

# 11

We figured as payment for taking him to a graveyard, anything in his saddlebags was ours, which was good, because the meager bits of grub we had was ate up. There was dried jerky in his bags and some pickled eggs in a leather pouch. The eggs was out of the shell, and they had broken up. They not only tasted pickled, they tasted like sweaty leather. We ate them anyway.

There was some oats in a bag on the horse, and we gave that to Satan, and from the dead man's canteen we poured water in the sombrero and let Satan drink from that. When he finished drinking the water he ate part of the sombrero.

We also found a change of clothes in his possibles, and since the shirt fit me better than Cullen, I threw away my stinking army shirt and put it on, keeping my army coat and pants with the stripe. The extra pants didn't fit neither of us, so we tossed them.

There was also a book of poetry in one of the saddlebags. It was handwritten, and I figured between tracking and killing, Cramp had liked to rhyme a little. I ain't no great judge of poems, though Mr. Loving had me read a considerable number of them, but I can tell you these were so bad they hurt my feelings. I threw the book away and had an urge to bury it lest a coyote come across it, read a few lines, and get sick.

"There's a town I come through on the way here to joining up with the soldiers. Ransack," I said.

"I come to it myself," Cullen said.

"We might go there. They're bound to have a graveyard."

"We could just leave him here and wouldn't nobody ever know," Cullen said.

"I'd know."

"I think I could know and get over it," he said.

"Maybe I could in time," I said, "but a promise is a promise."

"How we going to do it? We just got the one horse."

Cramp had a lariat and a bedroll. I stretched the bedroll on the ground, then me and Cullen laid Cramp on it and wrapped him in it along with what was left of his sombrero, which we laid on his chest. I wound the lariat around his body and tied it so we could drag him behind us. We got his Sharps then, climbed on Satan, and started out.

That bedroll idea wasn't perfect, but it's what we had. Fact was, once we got loaded up and headed out, the bedroll began to come apart on the boot end, and after a few miles one of Cramp's boots slipped free of the blanket and thumped along the ground.

In time we come across enough small trees to cut a couple of limbs with my knife and make a travois—and this took some work, I assure you. The travois lifted the body off the ground more and kept what was left of the blanket from wearing. Parts of Cramp, including his face, was starting to peek out of it. He was also growing a mite ripe, and his face, which first swelled up, was now withering like an old potato.

We come to Ransack near nightfall.

Seeing it from a distance, Ransack looked like a series of large fireflies in the midst of shadow shapes, but it was kerosene lamps and fires, and the shapes was buildings.

As we rode in it was as silent as death, us having a very recent companion who belonged to that club, and then suddenly there was sound. At first it was like the hum of a fly, then we could hear clattering and a bit of music coming from one of the bars——a tuba, a piano, a banjo, and some kind of horn that might have been a trumpet or some idiot blowing through a pipe.

We went wide of that, as I was thinking if there was any colored folks around they'd be at the back of the town and wouldn't be welcome around white folks' saloons, stores, or women. When we come to the back-streets, it wasn't my people I seen but China folk. I had seen pictures of them in books Mr. Loving had, but here they was now, in the flesh.

There was four or five Chinamen and a China girl next to a big fire with a metal rack over it and a large, black pot of boiling laundry on it, the likes of which the China girl was stirring with a long, thin board. The firelight was so bright you could see the colors of the shirts in the churning laundry. The men was all about the same size and wore loose clothes. The girl was dressed the same and was almost as thin as the board she was holding. Her hair was long and black and bound behind her head, and the men had a single pigtail hanging off their partly shaved heads. Along with the pigtails they wore curious expressions, like maybe we was the first colored they'd seen, though it may have been on account of we was dragging a body you could smell from about three acres away and Cramp's boot was hanging out of the blanket along with an arm that had come loose and was dragging in the dirt.

A Chinaman we hadn't seen before, kind of fat with a greasy pigtail, come out from behind a big barrel that was blazing with enough fire to light up the ground around us. He waved his hands at us. I reined to a stop. He said. "Want girl?"

"Say what, now?" I said.

"Sell girl for cheap, you want."

The girls came out of the shadows and into the firelight. One was perched on a wooden peg leg and had a crutch to help her, and she was by far the comeliest of the three, though she could have used about ten gallons of water and a bar of lye soap to set her straight. There was two other China girls, and they wasn't of the appearance to hurt anyone's feelings, either, though they walked as if they had been horse-hobbled.

They wore enough powder and rouge and such to paint the whole Sioux Nation. A fourth showed up, and she was so ugly she could have chased a bobcat up a tree, but then again maybe I wasn't one to talk. She didn't have the same kind of stunted walk but moved same as anyone else. I was later to learn this was because them other gals had their feet bound since they was children to make them small and to make their movements littler and their opportunities for running away slimmer. The bobcat chaser had not had the same experience.

"Half woman, she cheaper," said the Chinaman. "Five penny."

I realized he meant the woman with the wooden leg.

"Actually, she's more than half a woman," I said. "Way more."

"Then cost more," he said, leaning toward Cramp, holding his nose as he did. "Friend on blanket, he have to clean first. Stink up girl."

"We got other plans for him," Cullen said.

"Yeah, he's past interest in such things," I said. "And we're going to pass on your offer. Though we could use some food."

"Got chop suey," he said. "Good. Ten cents."

"That's more than the woman," I said.

"Chop suey not have wooden leg."

"Thought we were burying Cramp," Cullen said.

"I haven't the strength," I said, and I meant it.

The Chinaman paused to study Cramp. "Man dead."

"Nothing slides by you, does it?" I said.

"Not going to get better," he said.

"Nope," I said. "He won't."

The Chinaman studied me for a moment. "Still want food?"

"Sure. But ten penny for two meals."

The Chinaman studied on my offer. "Okay. Put dead man away. Come eat."

I looked back at Cullen. He shrugged.

It may seem harsh, but we parked Cramp and his travois over by a sort of lean-to, because the only thing I could think on clearly was getting my stomach wrapped around some chow.

We tended to Satan. He was tired and hungry himself. I was able to buy some oats from the Chinaman at a dear price and will admit to taking some of the money from a bag worn around Cramp's waist. I had become his gravedigger and his banker.

When Satan was unsaddled, fed, and watered, I combed him down with equipment borrowed from the Chinaman, and then me and Cullen sat down on the ground to eat. We had to pay first, and we did, and the chop suey was only a little better than the horse meat we had eaten after the Apache fight. I came across a chicken foot in the bowl and what I thought might be a mashed calf's eyeball. I fished these out and ate the rest of it without too much study on it and even paid for seconds for both me and Cullen.

After we chowed down, we saddled Satan and hooked Cramp and the travois up. I turned to the gal that was perched on the wooden leg, said, "Where's the nearest graveyard?"

She stared at me.

"We need to bury him," I said, pointing at Cramp.

I waited to see if she spoke American, and she did, or at least understood it enough, because she pointed right down the street. All we had to do was go on forward until we got to it, it seemed. The Chinaman came over and cuffed the cripple alongside the head, knocking her down in the dirt. He said something fast to her in China talk. Then in English to us: "I do talking," he said.

"There's no call for that," Cullen said.

"My woman," he said. "I give talk. Not her. She for sale. She do as I say."

"Well, you lighten up there," I said. "That ain't called for. I was the one spoke to her."

To show us who was in charge, he went over to a hunk of wood with an ax in it, pulled the ax out, and came back. "I chop wooden leg off," he said.

"No, you won't," I said.

"I chop your leg off."

"You won't do that, neither."

"His leg," he said, motioning at Cullen.

Cullen said, "I need these legs."

I rested a hand on my Colt, measured my words so he could understand me. "You hurt her, I will shoot a hole in you. If you live, you will wake up with that ax lodged in your ass so deep it will take all of the town and a team of big mules to pull it out. You savvy?"

He backed up. I reached down, helped the girl to her feet, and gave her the crutch.

The Chinaman said, "She go to work."

Away went the China girl on her wooden leg and crutch, under the tenting and into the little hovel. I figured I had done what I could and might have made matters worse for her. The Chinaman smiled at us like it was all a big joke and went back to the chunk of wood and slammed the ax into it. I tried to borrow a shovel and a lantern, but our recent dealings had soured him on us. I ended up paying him two bits to rent both. With those and Cramp in tow, we led Satan up the street toward where the cripple had said the graveyard was.

A little breeze came down off the prairie, and it lifted Cramp's stink and blew it along the street and gave it some serious authority, and before long a promotion. As we come to the end of the street we seen there was a slight rise at the end of it, and on that rise there was a wood-slat fence, and inside the fence was some crosses and large, flat rocks that had been set on edge for headstones. There was a cluster of trees at the back of the graveyard, inside the fence, and I figured those had been planted there, as they looked to be struggling and not of the land's nature. Another long, hot summer and they wouldn't be no better than posts for clotheslines.

I looked back and seen the Chinaman going down the street into the town, chattering loud enough we could hear him all the way up the hill, though what he said didn't mean a thing to us, as none of it was American.

The front of the fence was open, there not being any gate, as few wanted in and none could come out. We pulled Cramp to the back of the graveyard, where the row of trees was, and picked a spot. Cullen held the lantern while I started digging. It seemed as if the more I dug the more Cramp smelled, and that helped me dig faster.

I had put on my old army jacket as we come into town, hoping that might elevate our status, though it hadn't, and now I paused and unbuttoned it and went back to my work. I had dug about two feet down and two feet wide when Cullen said, "We got some folks coming, and I don't think they're coming to pray over the body."

They was led by the Chinaman, who had a lantern in one hand and the ax in the other. The men with him was white folks, and they was coming at a good and determined clip. Including the Chinaman, I counted eight.

"I knew this was a bad idea," Cullen said.

I stuck the shovel in the ground, said, "Set the lantern over to the side. Not in front of us, and not behind us."

Cullen did just that. Now, Satan was nearby, and so was my loop-cock Winchester, but I didn't want to make a lunge for it and get the ball rolling when it might not be necessary. I had the Colt and the LeMat on me, both of them fully loaded. I was hoping if blood got stirred they would be enough to calm the situation.

When they was into the graveyard and about twenty feet from us, they stopped walking. The Chinaman took a step forward and waved the ax with one hand. "I tell them no Chinaman, no niggers here."

"You scoundrel," I said. "You rented me the shovel and the lantern. You're just mad because I didn't want you slapping that crippled girl around."

"Not bury nigger," he said.

One of the white men, a tall, bearded fellow with a hat so big you could have hidden a horse under it, and suspenders that pulled his pants near under his armpits, said, "This here is a white graveyard. Christian soil."

"What if he's a Christian?" I said.

"He's got to be a white Christian," one of the other men said. "You others got your own heavens, if you even go."

There was a grumbling agreement from the crowd on this matter, as they seemed to have given it some serious speculation at some point or another.

"All right," I said. "We'll take our dead man and go. No harm done."

"You got on a Yankee jacket," said the tall, bearded man.

"We just got mustered out of the soldiers," I said. "We ain't fought in no war except against Indians." It came to me right then that my idea about status had been a stupid one. A black man in uniform in Texas didn't have no status. Fact was, that jacket was like painting a bull's-eye on my back, a fact I should have considered but hadn't.

"I fought against them colors," the man said, nodding at my jacket.

"We ain't shot Southerner a one," I said.

"I say we lynch them, even the dead one." This from one of the other men, a fellow that looked as if he had gotten his jaw broken at some point and it had grown back crooked.

"If we carry him on, no harm done," I said. "But he's starting to stink, so we thought he might need some ground, and he asked for a Christian burial in a Christian graveyard, and here you have it."

I noticed one of the men in the back was edging to our right. He had a shotgun, which at that range was sure enough a deadly weapon. It could take both me and Cullen out, kill Satan, and kill Cramp all over again.

I don't know what come over me, but all of a sudden I was through talking. My hand went quick for Mr. Loving's Colt. I thumbed back the hammer and fired. I hit the fellow with the shotgun a smooth shot in the forehead, and whatever was between his ears that he had been thinking with was knocked out the back of his head.

Then they was all moving.

The Colt, which I had cross-pulled, was in my right hand, and now I cross-drew the LeMat with my left. I was firing them both, moving to the left, then to the right, ducking down, twisting, and firing, shooting as fast as I could, and somehow in the midst of my speed I can say I was taking my time, too. I was willing and accurate, and they was scared and wild.

Bullets cracked near me. I seen Cullen out of the corner of my eye, heard him say, "Ah, shit," and he toppled over. And damned if that Chinaman, who had stood right up front with that ax in one hand and the lantern in the other, didn't sort of come unstuck from the night. He dropped the lantern, cocked back that ax, and rushed me. I had mostly shot around him, the ones with guns being more my concern than him. I had fired quick, sometimes two shots to a man. I had emptied the Colt and the nine-shot LeMat. I had just enough time to flick the lever on the LeMat to the shotgun position, and as the Chinaman came up on me, I fired. It was a hell of a blast, and it tore a hole in his chest and put him on his knees. He chopped out at me. The ax went right between my legs but missed my vitals. He was held up by the ax for a moment, leaking his insides, until I kicked his hand loose. He came forward on his face then, his heels sort of snapping up in the air, throwing some graveyard · dirt with them.

I went over to Satan, who hadn't even so much as moved. Wasn't no figuring that horse. I reckon he was trying out all possibilities. I pulled the loop-cock Winchester off his saddle and went over and found Cullen lying on his back. I knelt down beside him and looked for a wound. A bullet had only grazed him across the head and had knocked him out. I said, "Hell, Cullen, you ain't hardly touched. You fought Apaches, and now you're lying on the ground taking a nap and I'm shooting it out."

I helped him up and got him steady on his feet.

It was then that them four China girls came up out of the dark, rattling along in a little wagon with loops of thin wood over the back of it and a striped tarp that was pulled down off of it and gathered at the rear of the wagon in a wad. The wagon was pulled by a couple of horses. It was the cripple driving the wagon. The others was in the back, and they had carpetbags with them that was near their size. It was like they had been ready and waiting for just such a moment. They said almost together, "We go with you."

"I don't think so," I said.

"We seen what you do," the cripple said. "Kill them all. You bad men, and we need bad men. We cook. Give free pussy."

"We can't take you with us."

"They kill us," said the cripple, who seemed to be the mouthpiece for the three of them, but I noted the ugly one seemed to be paying right smart attention, and this was a thing that would matter later. "His brothers, they take us and chop us up. Make chop suey."

"Oh, come on," I said.

"He done it before," said the crip. "You ate some white man tonight. No Chinese girl yet. But white man."

I sorted that one around in my bean, said, "You mean that wasn't a calf's eyeball?"

"No calf's eyeball."

"Hell," Cullen said. "It tasted all right, though. Salty, but all right."

The cripple kept talking. "Fat man sleeping. Chun kill him with ax. He do the same to you, he got chance."

"He won't," Cullen said, nodding at the Chinaman on the ground.

Down below in Ransack there was starting to be a stirring. White men and Chinamen was both moving in our direction. I said, "Cullen, you was a buggy driver. Can you drive a wagon?"

"I can," he said.

Cullen climbed up, edged the cripple aside on the driver's seat, and took the reins.

I looked out across the dark prairie, seen a storm was coming. Lightning was working its way across the sky in angry yellow slits, and thunder roared like big cannons. I could see the shadows of a fine and rare stand of trees down there, about a quarter mile away, most likely along a little creek.

"Take the wagon into them trees," I said, "and don't spare the horses. Get down in the creek bed if you can. You can hold out better there."

"What about you?" he said.

"You worry about you and them women," I said.

Cullen turned the team, started across the prairie, clattering away, urging the horses on. From where I stood it seemed to me that wagon and those horses was hardly touching ground. I could see those China girls bouncing around in the back like they was popping corn in a greasy skillet.

There was a half dozen mounted men riding my way, followed by a bunch of screaming lunatics on foot—whites, mostly, and some China-men, all of them on the run and sounding like someone had invited them to a free dinner of boiled eggs and hog leavings.

Still holding my Winchester, I leaped on Satan's back, hoping after the day Satan had been through he still had some serious horse left in him.

# 12

Satan was a black grass fire shoved by the wind, the fastest, smoothest-running critter I'd ever climbed on. He left those horses and riders that was after us like they was standing still. Compared to him, Pegasus was a nag. And for a change he wasn't trying to buck me off or bite me or kick me to death.

That quarter mile melted away. As I come up on the trees, I seen the wagon was pulled down into the creek mostly, but the tail end of it was still sticking up. I could hear Cullen yelling to the horses, "Go on" and such, and gradually the wagon bumped over the bank and out of sight and into the shallow creek, which wasn't really any more than a trickle of water.

I rode Satan down in there, flung myself off of him, led him into a run of trees alongside the bank below the firing line. I tied him off and took the saddlebags of ammunition and climbed up with the Winchester and found me a spot. That posse of men was coming and would soon be on us.

I beaded along the Winchester and shot the horse in the forefront of the line through the chest. It went down, and so did the rider. It was a bad thing for the horse but a good thing for us. The rider struck the ground so hard on his head I could hear his neck crack like someone had stepped on a clay pot. He got up, crawled in our direction for a short ways, determined that wasn't a good idea, and like a dog looking for a place to lie down, turned about on his hands and knees a couple times, then flattened out and didn't move. All the while he had done this with his head at an odd angle, like he was trying to look back and see if his asshole was properly centered. I think his neck finally come loose of something it needed, and it done him in.

The others had already turned their horses and rode back in the direction of town. They stopped about halfway there where they met up with all the men on foot that had been running behind them. They grouped up to consider their situation. I turned and seen Cullen had climbed up on the edge of the bank with the Springfield I could see the women in the wagon down below.

"I think you discouraged them, Nat," Cullen said.

"Yeah, but I don't know I've given them enough of it," I said. "I was them, I would try and flank us. Though they'd have to come down through the trees or along the creek if they did that, and that still ain't positions to their good."

"They could come up behind us," Cullen said.

"Two men, one on either side of the creek, could hold them off pretty damn good cause we got the cover and the better shooting position, and they ain't Apaches. We done dealt with some of the best sneakers there is, so these boys don't worry me the same."

"We got to come out of here eventually," Cullen said.

"That's true," I said. "And they got to decide how many men they want to lose before we do."

"They could rush us," Cullen said.

"They could, but I bet they won't. We got to wait until the right moment and roll out. I think we might do better to leave the wagon. Make some reins and bridles out of those lines, put the women on the wagon horses, get you on Satan with me, and creep out of here like a medicine show."

"I don't know," Cullen said.

"Damn it, Cullen. I'm trying to be on the ups about this. Quit putting a weight on my head."

"I don't know," he said again.

The rain was starting now, lightning was blasting away, the thunder was still rumbling. The rain was cold, and it rolled off my hat and run down the back of my shirt and made me tremble. I was thinking that with the clouds growing thick, maybe we could steal out under cover of darkness, but the constant lightning flashes made that tricky. I was turning all this around in my mind, trying to figure the odds, when I seen someone coming on horseback, all alone, sitting ramrod straight in the saddle. It was an old horse, and it walked with its head down. It rambled here and there and finally set a course toward us.

"What in the world is he thinking?" Cullen said. He propped the Springfield against the bank and took a bead.

"Wait a minute," I said.

On came the rider, stiff in the saddle, dark as night, hat pulled down over his eyes. His arms dangled at his sides. There was a flash of lightning, and in that quick glow I could see the reins was tied to the saddle horn and there was a big pole fastened to it, too; the rider was fixed firmly against that saddle horn and pole. I saw all this in that flash. Saw, too, that he was a colored man, and the wind carrying his stink, along with another flash of lightning, announced that it was Cramp.

The horse trotted right up to the bank. I stood in front of it so I wasn't being sighted by a rifle, took the reins, and guided the horse down into the shallow creek bed, Cramp wobbling in the saddle.

I tied the horse to the back of the wagon, nodded at the China girls in the rig, and hustled back to my spot and peeped over the bank. There was shapes of men and horses out in the distance, lights from the town flickering behind them.

"There's your friend," a voice called out from among them. "Bury him somewhere else. You done gonna fill up our cemetery with all them men you killed. We don't want no more trouble, now. We're giving you your chance. You go, we'll leave you alone."

I hadn't planned on going back for Cramp. I had done my best, and the whole promise had been a dumb one to begin with. This was as good a time as any to make our retreat. They had opened the door and wanted us to run through it. Course, I didn't believe that part about letting it be over and done with.

"Go on, then," I yelled loud as I could. "And we'll leave you be!"

"All right, then," said the voice. They turned their mounts and rode back into town, a clutter of riffraff walking after them, lightning flashing fast and furious, thunder echoing, rain coming down in cold, dark sheets.

What we did was we skedaddled.

Me and Cullen cut Cramp down and put him in the back of the wagon with the women. It wasn't a thing they liked, and they let us know in a burst of China talk, except for the ugly one, who said, "Why not leave him?"

"Say what, now?" Cullen said.

"Why not leave him here?" she said.

"We got that," I said. "But you speak English?"

"We all do," she said.

"You speak it so it makes sense."

"I have had more experience."

"So why didn't you say something before?" I asked.

"I was waiting to see how things were," she said. "I learned to speak English in missionary school and to be quiet in any language. Missionaries liked to take a stick to you if you talked in a way they didn't like. I think they just liked to paddle little girls."

"Well, here's how things are," I said. "I was going to leave old Cramp back there, but now that we got him, we're going to get out of here fast as we can, cause they are a pack of liars and will most likely be on us by daybreak."

And that's what we did. Cullen took the old, broken-down horse Cramp had been tied to, and Peg Leg, as I had come to know her, took

the wagon lines and drove it on down the creek until there was a break
in the trees and a gradual slope where she could drive it up and onto the
prairie. The rain was still coming down; it had knocked our hats near flat
on top and bent the brims down. The women didn't have hats, but they
had produced umbrellas I didn't know they had. One of the women sat
up by Peg Leg and held the umbrella over her head and her own while
Peg Leg drove the wagon. The others protected themselves, scrunching
under their umbrellas as best they could.

We rode across the prairie into wet darkness. A streak of lightning
ripped the sky so wide and white I went blind for a moment. The lightning struck the ground, and there was a flare of fire from some mesquite
bushes out there, then the fire and bushes smoked white from the rain.
It made me more than a little nervous to be out there in the naked world
with all that lightning and us its only targets.

Only good thing I can say about that night was the rain took some of
the stink off Cramp's body, which was starting to swell in places and fall
into itself in others.

Right before the night ended, the rain stopped and the sunlight edged
up like a busted apple. As the day seeped in I saw three men riding at us.
They was coming slow but steady. Cullen was riding beside me on that
skin-and-bones horse we had taken, and I said, "They have sent three riders."

"I can see that. Seems stupid of them, considering what you did to all
them men back there. I ain't never seen anything like that, Nat. I just
thought you was a badass in the Apache fight, but you done come into
your own."

"Think I just surprised them, but I bet these three ain't cowards like
them was, all except that Chinaman. He was a game rooster."

"Hired killers?"

"Most likely," I said.

"We going to stand and fight?"

While I was figuring on that, one of the men raised a white flag tied
to his rifle and rode a piece toward us. He was a fat man with a big head

and a little derby hat and a red kerchief around his neck. He was wearing a greasy buckskin shirt and black-and-yellow-checked pants.

He stopped when he was within earshot, said, "Can I have a palaver with you?"

I cupped my hands over my mouth and called out to him because I wanted them other two to hear me, see that I was making the rules here. "Drop that rifle and ride forward some more, and keep your hand away from your pistol."

He dropped the rifle and the flag on the ground and come on toward us. I told Cullen to stick and rode out to meet him. When we was about ten feet apart, I reined my horse in, said, "This will do."

"We been sent to hunt you down and kill you," he said.

"We'll see how that works out for you."

"We don't want to do that," he said.

"No?"

"No, cause we think it might not turn out as well as we'd like. We seen all them you killed by your lonesome, and we figure you to be a fair hand with a gun. What we was wondering is, could we just say we killed you and you not come back anymore?"

"I'll deny such a thing for the obvious reason. I'm alive."

"So we got to shoot it out?"

"Why don't you say you couldn't find us? That gets you off the hook."

"We was paid twenty dollars apiece to kill all of you," he said.

"That's a lot of work for twenty dollars apiece, considering you might not be going home again."

"But they did pay us twenty dollars," he said. "You know how it is, honest day for an honest dollar."

"And you know how it is with being dead," I said. "Ain't none of them dead folk make it home for supper."

He studied on that a moment and gently reached for his derby as if to take it off.

As his fingers touched the brim, I said, "If there is a gun in that derby, you'll be dead before you get it off your head."

"All right, then," he said, and left it on.

"My name is Nat Love," I said, "and it would do you best not to lie about killing us. The lie about not finding us I can live with. My pride doesn't care for the other."

I know how that sounds. Small of me, but I felt exactly that way.

"Ah, hell," he said. "We'll just say you all got away."

"Good. I see you or them other two again, I'll kill the lot of you."

"They're gonna think we was chickenshits," he said.

"You are, aren't you?"

That didn't set right with him, but he considered on things, probably recollected on the stories about how I had killed all them men with my revolvers, which as I have said was mostly because they didn't know what in hell they was doing. To be honest, I think some of them might have shot their own comrades trying to kill us, so it's possible I've given myself a shade more credit than I deserve.

He licked his lips, nodded. "Guess we're settled, then," he said, rode back to where he dropped his Winchester, got down out of the saddle, slowly picked it up, and remounted. I watched him carefully, having pulled my own rifle from its boot and laid it across my saddle. The man rode back to join the others. I rode back to the wagon, pulled up next to Cullen.

"You think he'll say we run off?" Cullen said, having heard our conversation.

"He'll say he killed us all, but I wasn't going to make it easy for him by agreeing. I have come to the end of catering to white folks."

"I don't really care so much one way or the other," Cullen said.

We watched them ride well out of sight, then we turned and headed on toward the northeast.

# 13

After a couple of days I come to think we wasn't being followed and they had gone back to Ransack to tell whatever lie soothed them. We was moving toward the Texas Panhandle, and there ain't no more desolate stretch of empty land than that. Coming from East Texas, I thought West Texas was bleak, but that northern part was sad on the eye and the mind; it wouldn't surprise me that anyone that lived out that way did so because their horse died there or their wagon broke down. I couldn't see no other reason for wanting to be there on purpose.

We got in a rhythm of traveling by night, sleeping in the day. Those China girls turned out to be right friendly, which was good, because the nights could be brisk. I found out the one with the wooden leg was called Wing Ding, Ling Ding, or some such, though as soon as I thought I was getting a handle on her name she'd laugh and correct me. In the bedroll she was prone to stretching a man's back to the breaking point and leaving splinters on one outside thigh; she really needed to sand that thing down. The ugly one turned out to be a real pistol. After a few nights of us taking turns and doing our pleasure with them all, we spaced ourselves better, due to weakness setting in.

We pulled the cover over the wagon during the day, when we was doing business in there, and the way we done it was me and the girls would stand outside of the wagon modest-like and talk about what we could understand from each other, and I do remember having quite a conversation once about beans. The ugly girl's name was Wow or some such. She was a good English speaker. She had read some books, some of the same ones Mr. Loving read. She knew, too, about a fellow whose name for a while I thought was Corn Foolish but finally came to realize was Confucius. He turned out to be some wise Chinaman and had a saying or two for just about every situation. Soon as you thought you was getting the hang of old Confucius, he'd turn on you and would mean something other than what it seemed like he was saying, or so Wow explained. I figured if a man had something to say, he ought to just go on and say it and not make it some kind of puzzle. I can honestly say I didn't care for him much, though the two of us never met, which can make a difference in your opinions.

Now, I suppose you're wondering about Cramp and where he was during all this time, and the situation is like this. About two days out no one could stay in that wagon but him. He was the sole owner of the wagon bed, and he commanded his area by stench. We finally pulled him out and dug a hole with some tools in the wagon and buried him. Turned out Wow knew a few Christian words, though she was what she called a Buddhist, and we buried him with those words and a rock on his well-covered hole and moved on. Had we done that early on, even without Wow's words, we would have been a sight better off.

That wagon was full of all manner of goods, the Chinaman having been a man of commerce. We got rid of our soldier trappings, as there was clothing in the wagon we could wear. We made our way toward the Dakota Territory, for no other reason than we had heard while at the fort that there was strikes of gold and silver there and that even a colored man could make a large stash. Frankly, it seemed as good a direction as any. In time the old horse they had sent out with Cramp on it began to wear down, and I felt bad about it, cause it was a sweet old horse and would nicker ever' time you got up close to it. It was friendly and would push its nose against you to be petted. But it got real weak, and I had to shoot it. We ate part of it. I had to not think on who I was eating to enjoy it. After that, Satan kept an eye on me, had a brisker step, and held his head high just to make sure there wasn't any confusion on his health.

One time, after we had traveled all night, we pulled the wagon to a stop just as the morning got bright and put the cover up. But as we was about to crawl in the wagon, Cullen said, "Look yonder."

Out there on the prairie we could see what looked like a dark sea rolling in with a loud rumble. After a bit of watching, we seen it was a sea of fur. Buffalo. They stretched far as the eye could see. They was right close to us, and we kept our spot, least we might somehow stir and stampede them. We watched them cross near us, and I didn't know it at the time, but what I was seeing was something that was soon to be no more. It wasn't but a few years beyond that when near every buffalo that had walked the earth was dead. Some of them buffalo was killed for food, some for hides, and finally just for sport, to be left rotting on the prairie. It was partly done out of greed, and partly for no other reason than to deny the Plains Indians breakfast and supper. It was the destruction of the Indians' on-the-hoof grocery store, and it done them in surer than smallpox-diseased blankets or repeating rifles.

We needed meat, and we watched for at least an hour as they passed, and then we shot a straggler on the end who looked as if he had already hurt a leg bad enough he would soon be for the wolves. Them buffalo, big and mighty as they are, was also dumb. They didn't seem to understand what the shot was about. If they missed the old boy on the end, there was no note of it we could see. Maybe at the end of the day one of them would turn and say, "Hey, boys, where's Bill?"

We skinned that buffalo out, made a cook fire using dried buffalo turds, which burned real good but smelled, as you might guess, like dried buffalo shit. We cooked some buffalo hump and stripped out some of the meat and salted it with the wagon supplies. Later on during the trip we ate it. The salt cured it enough it didn't rot, but I got to tell you, it was hardly worth the thirst it gave you; watering holes was far apart.

There was plenty of goods in that wagon, but one of the ones we had to scrounge for was water.

Still, all in all, that trip was one of the finest and most measured times of my life. With those China girls and us taking turns in the wagon, living off the land, laughing and hooting and such, Wow telling me about this and that she had read, it was one of the greatest pleasures of my life. The trip took us a long time, from the inside edge of West Texas, across the Panhandle, on through Indian Territory—without seeing any Indians—climbing up to South Dakota. Those days and nights seemed to float by like turtles in the river.

Before we actually seen the town we seen the hills, and they was thick and dark with trees. Along the hills a considerable fire had raged, gnawing up wood like a fiery beaver. I later learned that burned-up dead wood was how the town got its name.

We smelled the place before we come up on it. It was the stink of sewage tossed in the streets and that which had run down from outhouses built on higher land. As we come nearer you could add to that body odor and sweat and whiffs of cooking smells and a waft of burned wood breezing down gently from the trees on the rise above us. That burn smell, compared to the other, was a kind of refreshment.

There was a main road that was so muddy and deep with washouts it made the wagon jump as it come along. We had to pull ourselves to the side to keep from being crushed by an ox team that was rolling out of Deadwood, most likely on its way to gather fresh supplies of some ilk or another. The team was led on foot by a stout woman with a big old whip and a dress that hung over her boots, except for the toes. Her boots and dress was splattered in mud. It was quite a train of critters and wagons and such, and when it passed us we continued into town, though calling it a town seems overly polite, like calling a pimp a gentleman.

The buildings was thrown up willy-nilly along the sides of the street, as if some drunk had been given lumber, hammer, and nails and told to go at it. A few buildings had seen paint at one time or another; some rambled nearly into the street, as if they was trying to slink across it and into the hills and return to timber. Here and there were clusters of lumber due to some buildings having toppled like stacks of dominoes. A number of houses had low-slung wooden fences built around sad gardens where weeds grew and bugs lived, though I figured them bugs was embarrassed at their quarters.

There was placer mines right there in the big middle of things. As we come by, I seen a man at one spot, a woman at another, eyeing us as if they thought we might at any moment fly off the handle and steal whatever goods they had dug up. The woman, who was fifty if she was a day, wearing a big blue bonnet, stood with a Winchester in her left hand and a rock in the other. When I looked her way, she tossed the rock at us and winged Wow, who was at the wagon reins this day. After bouncing off Wow's arm, the rock landed on the seat. Wow scooped it up, swiveled from her position, and with a fine throw beaned the old woman hard enough in the head it knocked her down, slinging her bonnet to the wind. She was up in a flash, tossing more rocks at us, but by that time we was out of her aim and the strength of her arm. To our advantage, she was unwilling to move too far from her claim.

"This is a real nice town," Cullen said from the back of the wagon. "If it was to catch on fire."

We had the cover rolled back now, and Cullen and the three China girls was sitting back there like frogs on a log. Wow was clucking at the horses as they plodded through the mud. I rode Satan closer to the wagon. "Don't you know they're glad to see two coloreds and some China girls?" I said.

"I don't know that old woman is glad to see anybody," Cullen said.

We passed a building on a hill marked as a Congregational church. There was ragged, crooked stairs that climbed up to it. On a kind of porch, I could see what appeared to be a small buffalo, but as we passed I seen it was someone under a buffalo robe, having passed out there either from exhaustion or too much rotgut whiskey. We rolled past a place called the Gem Theater, which was two stories high and not a bad-looking building.

Now, for us colored and China folk, the only place we could go was somewhere on the edge of town, which is how it always was. It was a thing that caused a boiling anger in me and in some ways made me wish I had stayed with the army. We was about finding that place when a man with a tree limb under one arm for a crutch, the skin on his head peeled back from a probable attempt at scalping, limped out from between two buildings and nearly got hit by the horses hauling the wagon. Wow pulled them up, and the fellow put the spy on me so hard I could almost feel his eyes crawling under my skin. His jaw was broke on the left side, and the bone had heaped up there like a snake coiled under leaves. His skin was burned and puckered along the same side of his face, and the other side was a series of ridges made by scars, most likely carved there by a knife. There wasn't no way to know how he might have looked once, and I felt sorry for him. He not only had that face and a limp, his clothes looked to have been taken off a smaller man than himself. They was wore through with holes, and one of his boots had a flapping heel. He made it across the street with some effort and hobbled between the buildings and out of sight. Wow clucked to the horses and continued.

I seen a place called the Big Horn Store and ragged buildings that served this or that, mostly whiskey, and finally we come to a place that was somewhat cleaner and more organized. This was the Chinaman section of town. The air had a smoky aroma and a peculiar nose-twitching scent that I later learned was opium, and all this was hitting us as we parked in a yard where we was charged a bit of money for currying the horses and storing the wagon. It was a considerable bite in the loot me and Cullen had laid by, so it struck me we was going to have to find work, and pretty damn quick. I still had enough for a meal, and there was a chop suey place near us, but the idea of eating there made me nervous.

I said to Wow, "That China fellow that cooked a man in that stew we ate—that ain't regular with the China folk, is it?"

"He was a savage. Been around whites too long," she said.

"Haven't we all?" I said.

"Yeah, but he took it to heart," Wow said. "And he cooked the meat too long."

When we got ourselves over to the chop suey house, it took about five minutes before all the women, including Wow, discovered they could have jobs as whores out back of the place or as someone who served up the food. It seemed there had been an angry customer the night before, a white fellow, and he had got into the opium, mixed it with whiskey, and had gone wild with a bowie knife, killing off about a quarter of the whores. He was took out and hanged by a couple of white boys who had been waiting in line for their turn, but in the end it was a rough way for there to be a job opening.

But that was the case, and the girls took it. Wow was the only one said she was going to work at the chop suey house, not the bedding, at least for as long as she could afford it. As for Wing Ding, or whatever the peg-leg China girl's name was, she found in Deadwood she was worth more than back at Ransack. Here there was plenty of men that was missing limbs and eyes and such, and they liked the camaraderie of someone they felt was more an equal.

Anyway, we settled in there, and after a day or two of asking around, I got a job at one of the saloons, Mann's No. 10. Cullen got a job driving a honey wagon, which he'd pull up to houses and businesses, go in and empty the slop jars and such into it. It was nasty labor, but it paid all right, cause no one else wanted to do it, including me. Swamping at the saloon was bad enough, emptying spittoons and mopping out vomit and blood and whatever was wet on the floors, but driving a wagon full of shit wasn't something I wanted even part-time.

# 14

Me and Cullen took to living in the China quarters. We was accepted there well enough. There was a few other colored spotted here and there, some with placer-mine claims. Any of them that had a mine wasn't friendly, as they had this feeling anyone that spoke to them or associated with them might be claim jumpers. In truth, that was often the case.

We had a small room in the center of the China folk, and we locked and bolted it up like we had the crown jewels in there, but we didn't actually keep much stored for fear someone would decide they needed it. Locks are for honest people, when you get right down to it, and the thing about Deadwood was, it was a collection of some of the meanest, orneriest, and most thieving son of a bitches that ever stood on this earth. It wouldn't have surprised me to come in after a day of swamping to discover our entire shack had been stolen.

The room was tight but large enough for us to lay out bedrolls at night. We had two chairs, which we had to stack together and hang on nails on the wall when we wasn't using them. We had a board that swung down on chains for an eating and writing table, and we had a kerosene lamp hung on a nail.

The walls was double-planked and filled with all manner of junk to make them firm. I found one of the boards would peel back, and I pulled out and threw away the junk that was in there and took to wrapping my Winchester and a few odds and ends in a blanket and stuffing them behind the wall. Like most men in town, I toted my money and pistols with me—the LeMat and the Colt, anyway. The service revolver I kept back in that stash with my Winchester. When I put the board up and pushed the loose nail back in place, you couldn't tell it wasn't a proper part of the wall. Cullen also had a few goods he kept in there. It wasn't a cheerful place.

You woke and slept to the smell of food cooking. China folk was always cooking, feeding miners at all hours. It was nice to wake or bed down to those smells, though when you didn't have the coin to buy a bite to eat, it could also be depressing. Cullen and me had full run of the whores we had brought with us, as they considered it lifetime payment for what we had done to save them, but in time I drifted away from that, except for the now-and-again occasion. I didn't like them thinking they owed me nothing, especially their bodies, for what we'd done.

Cullen found he could live with that situation, and he not only partook of their joys but also soon came to have quite an affection for Wow in particular. I could see how that could come about, and had he not moved in on her, I might have. She was a little dumpling of a woman with a head that belonged on a broad-shouldered six-footer and a face made for going away, but inside that head was some real brains and personality. She had a smile that could make her seem right pretty as compared to others who was fair of features but dull of spirit, and vain to boot.

Wasn't long before they was a couple, and she didn't go back to whoring. She kept slinging that chop suey.

Time passed from summer into fall, and that's when I decided that I'd carry on as a swamper, but as a sideline, I was going to become a ratter. This, however, turned out to be a job with some competition.

Deadwood was prone to a horde of vermin, and sometimes at night, men, and women, too, would sit on their porches with a lantern lit and watch rats run along the edges of the street. This led to a number of low-caliber rifles being used to pop them, and in the act of that at least three people, two men and one woman, had died in the practice of rat tapping, as it was called by some. A few small dogs and cats had met their demise in much the same fashion.

Rat tapping and rat trapping also jobbed up a mess of young boys who was paid by the pound of dead rats brought to the general store in tow sacks. The bags was weighed up, same as gold nuggets, and the boys was paid off, sometimes in penny candy. This led to a clutch of the little heathens running around at night with two-by-fours whacking at rats and causing a general disturbance. But they was less of a worry than the rats themselves.

Them critters scuttled about in squeaking, sniffing, scratching, biting hordes. They came at night and hustled along with great excitement. They'd climb right up on you if you had a crumb on your shirt or a spill of beer on your pants. We even had them come directly into the saloon through the open doors, as if they was there to belly up at the bar and order a beer. They was bold, I tell you. The working girls in them places would scream, and so would some of the men, and then the revolvers was drawn, and rats was shot, or shot at; the quicker ones scampered to safety while the patrons ducked and hoped they didn't catch a round of hot lead.

Night I decided to be a ratter was the same night I was at the Gem Theater, my job having expanded from Mann's No. 10 during the days to the Gem at night. It was a busy place, what with troupes of Shakespearean actors, recitations of this and that, singing groups, jugglers, acrobats, and magicians. They all came through Deadwood, and the best of them usually ended up at the Gem Theater, which is not to say that some nights the entertainment there wasn't of a more unprofessional nature. It frequently was, and that's the case concerning the night I'm talking about.

I was emptying spittoons, and a fellow come down the aisle during an act, striding toward the stage, where a woman was howling like a wolf over a deer corpse, this being some of that less professional entertainment I mentioned. All of her bellowing was done to the numbing tinkle of bad piano; it couldn't have been no worse if the player was playing with his toes.

This man coming down the aisle had a pistol, and he started firing off shots at the piano player. I could understand this, as that was some racket that fellow was putting out, and combined with the woman's hollering, I could see how a fellow might fly off his bean. But unfortunately for the music world, it turned out the piano player was a better shot than the other. He pulled a little gun and popped a shot at him and laid him on the floor, leaking blood. We all gathered around the shot man, who said, "That singer is my wife. She run off with that goddamn piano player."

By then the piano man had come over and was standing with the rest of us over the dying man. His gun was taken from him by a big bruiser who served as a bouncer for the theater, and a heavy hand was laid on his shoulder.

The dying man said, "I am dying. There's a cloud settling over me. I chased them here, and I've been undone. But boys, you got to get a preacher and make this cad marry her, and now, over my dead body. You got to promise me that."

He talked just like that, I do not kid, and the men around him started nodding, and promises was made. When the old boy died, which was pretty quick after that, a preacher was brought in, and the howling woman was hustled over in her little feathered outfit, and her and that piano player was married right away, for what it was worth. When that was done, the dead man was laid out on a table, his hat was put on his chest, and a wad of dark cloth was stuck in his wound to stop the leaking. The bullet hadn't gone out the other side of him, so it wasn't as messy as you might think.

The preacher said some words over him, and his bravery was attested to, though the piano player made a few grumpy sounds during this. The preacher went on and on, extolling the virtues of this fellow who he had never met. You would have thought they'd grown up together and had spent many a night on the trail and had fought a grizzly bear to death in tandem, the two of them having only pocketknives and each other's asses to ride all the way down the mountainside. It was a preaching to beat all preachings. A few men was sniffling, and there was a couple who had gone beyond that and was right-out blubbering. I was a little sick to my stomach.

When this finally got over and we could put our hats back on, the dead man was given to what passed as the town undertaker, and the body, supported by four volunteers, was carted out.

I mention all this to give you the tone of the place and to get back to the bouncer, who was a husky white Southern boy; a redhead with a bad attitude. He come by me carrying that piano player's gun, shoved me with a shoulder, saying, "Out of the way, boy."

I had a spittoon in my hand, and I had on heavy gloves I was using to hold the lip of it, and I brought it around and clocked him. He was lucky I had already emptied it and was returning it or he would have been covered in tobacco spittings. He dropped so fast I figured him dead, as only the week before I seen a man throw a beer glass and kill a fellow. They was going to hang the glass tosser, but he said he had to pee, and they let him go out back. He was never seen again. Such was the vigilant law enforcement in Deadwood.

A crowd gathered around the bouncer—Red, as he was known—and I felt a little better when he rolled on his side and spat out blood. Soon a stout man come shoving through the crowd. I recognized him right off as Al Swearengen, the owner of the place and my employer.

"I seen what you done," he said, "and it was a good whack."

"Yes, sir," I said. "I put my full arm into it."

"Listen, put that down, come over to the office, and see me."

I put the spittoon down and followed him into a very nice office with ornate furniture and a painting of a naked woman on the wall doing something with a swan. He said, "Take a chair there."

I took a chair in front of his desk. I studied the girl and the swan. She had one leg halfway wrapped around it, and the swan was looking back at her. I couldn't figure if he was surprised by the leg wrap or if he was somehow in charge.

Swearengen gathered his hands together, made a steeple of his fingers. He was a man that would look oily fresh from the bath. His hair had enough grease on it a small moth had got hung up in it. I started to point it out, then decided not to. Swearengen pursed his lips as if in thought. I could tell right off he was the kind of man that would try and give you goat shit and tell you it was raisins.

"Now, listen here," he said. "Red, he's a pocketer."

"What?"

"He steals from me."

"Oh."

"I need a new bouncer, and a man your size might be just the ticket. Red, he's done here. I was trying to decide if I was going to fire him or have him whipped. I'll count that spittoon as a licking, and when he wakes up, I'll kick his ass free. So the job is yours."

"Well, sir, I don't know."

"Look at it this way," he said. "Red there could press charges."

"To who?" I said.

"To me," he said. "I'm the law in this saloon."

"I see," I said, and did see, and didn't like it.

"But you come to work for me as a bouncer instead of a swamper, and I will say he shouldered himself into you on purpose."

"He did," I said.

"I know. I would like to have you take the job. Lot of men here are scared of colored."

"Lot of men here hate colored," I said. "That ain't exactly the same thing."

"You got that working against you, I admit," he said. "But I pay well."

He told me what he paid. It was good, but I still had my doubts. I tried another tack.

"I was considering a ratting job," I said, and I took the tone that there just couldn't be any profession more glorious and profitable.

He didn't fall for it, though. I seen a smile work its way across his broad face, and his dark eyes lowered like he'd just realized he had my neck in a noose; no one in their right mind would see a ratting job as a high profession.

"You would in fact be dealing with rats here, but the two-legged kind."

I didn't say that I thought he himself might be a prime example. I just sat silent, which is sometimes the best thing to do, as Wow had said.

"Tell you what," Swearengen said, pursing his lips, looking at the ceiling like he had just called in a favor from the heavens. "I'll put five dollars a week on top of that offer I made you, like a cherry on a hot pie, on account of you got the colored factor—meaning, of course, you're putting your balls on the block a little more than someone else might be."

"You mean someone white," I said.

"There you have it."

I studied on that and thought maybe I might be able to still swamp during the day at Mann's No. 10 and possibly start a ratting career as well, at least part-time. With two jobs and a bag of weighed rats once or twice a week, I could put me together a nest egg that could allow me to move on from Deadwood in a little more style than I might otherwise.

"I'll take it," I said.

That's how I come to bounce at the Gem Theater and realize that Swearengen had maybe fooled me after all. It was good pay, but it was a dangerous job, right up there with kissing rattlesnakes and milking a she-bear's tits.

I started the next night.

Since winter had set in, I pretty much always carried my LeMat under my coat in its holster, but as bouncer I was allowed to do it open-like. I actually went to carrying both revolvers and tucking the third, the army service revolver, in a pocket inside my coat. I asked Wow to sew leather inside that pocket, and for a reasonable price she did, and then I oiled that leather so if I needed to pull my pistol, it was easy to yank loose. I was told I could carry a shotgun as well, but this seemed like a bad weapon for the work, being as how it could spread out and kill most anything on either side of the intended. I instead took to my loop-cock Winchester, which would be almost as bad if I was to go to firing it with the catch on the loop pushed down. But at least with it, I could take a singular and cautious shot if I chose, and if things called for it I could click the striker into place and open up a line of fire as fast as I could cock it.

As you might expect, the Gem stayed rowdy. Killings was too constant to have any real effect on the people who came there; it was just how things was. The piano player still played, though now he had a wife, and she had come to worry his ear something furious. She no longer sang, having decided marriage made her respectable, which as rumor had it meant she stayed home with a bottle. Her new husband was having to bring in extra income by working longer shifts, which was no treat to my ear as far as I was concerned. If anything, his playing had gotten worse, and had turned angry.

There was seldom a night at the Gem that I didn't have to ask someone to leave or end up buffaloing them with a blow upside the head with my Winchester barrel or one of my revolvers. It was a living.

But good as that money was, it cost to live in Deadwood, as all the prices was jacked up. Pretty soon I found that I was working nights at the Gem, emptying spittoons at Mann's No. 10, and on my day off, which was a Sunday, I was ratting a little, but I still wasn't putting that much away. Now and again Cullen, who had turned into an ace honey-wagon driver and such, would give me an assist with the rats. He, too, had taken on an "associative job," which meant instead of only driving a wagon that collected night soil, as he preferred to call it, he also had a job where he scraped horse and bull manure off the muddy streets with a large shovel and tossed it in a wagon. All this he took out to a spot where he was paid for it, the buyer having the intent to mix it with ground buffalo bones and turn it into fertilizer. This fertilizer business was owned by a near blind man and a woman who had gnawed her teeth down to the black gums. They smelled near as strong as their product and was constantly wearing it in its fresher state on their clothes and shoes.

* * *

One Sunday night after hitting drunks in the head, I went ratting. Cullen wasn't with me this night, having decided to stay in bed with Wow at the whorehouse, which was most certainly a better decision; fact was, he had moved in with her, leaving me the luxury of more room.

But the bull's-eye of the matter was, I was about my ratting. I had a heavy bat made of hickory for dispatching the little boogers and was aiming for a three-bag night. But two things happened, both of them life-changing events.

You see, the best rat time was just as the cold winter darkness was coming in over the hills, settling down on Deadwood like a black sack. Lights would get lit, and the street would have a glow, and you would see the rats in rapid march, moving down the byways in search of food and mischief. They was so thick in their packs and so determined to be about their business it was easy to put the crack on them, shove their bodies into a sack to be weighed the next morning at the general store.

I was leaning on the bat, watching them rats starting to stream out of the shacks and such. They was making a thick grouping toward the general store, which is where a large portion of the goods they liked best was kept—the same goods everyone else liked but preferred not to share with the rats. I was about to step out of the shadows, where I was hid between two buildings built so close together there was only enough room for me to stand sideways, and then I paused as I saw a peculiar sight.

It was a young woman, and in the moonlight I could tell she was dark-skinned, though I couldn't say right then and there she was colored or Mexican or some other blend of the races. She was tall for a woman, and lean. She had a great head of dark hair tied back and it fell behind her shoulders like night tumbling over a mountainside. And I tell you, for me, it was kind of a landslide, cause it was like that hair and that woman fell all over me, knocked me for a loop, and cracked my head. My God, she was something.

She was at the head of the line of rats, knowing, like me, where they was going, but she was a better thinker. She had a large bag held open by a wooden frame. It must have had a mouth on it three feet wide, and there was a stick going into it at the mouth. She was softly playing a little flute. It was like the rats was being called by it, cause they started to come faster and faster, filing into that bag like fish swimming into a tunnel.

When the mouth of the bag was so clogged with rats they was standing on top of one another, trying to force their way in, she all of a sudden held the flute to her side, and with the other hand snapped up the stick, which somehow pulled the bag together. The bag wiggled and squeaked.

I stood there flummoxed. She shoved that bag aside, and a mound of rats humped and squealed past and over her feet in a black boil of rodent meat and moved on. She didn't move a muscle, unlike the dance-hall girls, who when frightened by a rat or mouse could leap from the floor to the bar and even jump up and grab hold of the chandeliers and other light fixtures that hung in the various saloons about town.

Well, I seen then that there was three other of them bags next to her, and she shoved that stick into the mouth of one and put it in place quick as you could snap your fingers. And what happened but it began to fill up with rats, too. Pretty soon she had four heaving bags of rats.

My next thought was to wonder what she would do with them now, as them bags was big and heavy with them critters, but it was then that I seen an old white woman, pale as the moon, with a bonnet on her head, come along leading a mule that was dragging a sled over the mud. The young, darker woman and the white woman worked together to heap the rats onto the sled, then the older woman rolled the bags on their sides and went to work with a big stick, whacking them furiously, which calmed the rats pretty quick. Next they got on the sled themselves with their bags of rats, and the old woman took the lines and clucked her tongue at the mule, and away they trotted.

I let them go on a piece before I stepped out in the road and followed. I walked along by the buildings so I was in shadow and was surprised to see a match flare. My pistol found its way into my hand.

There in the light, as surprised to eyeball me as I was him, was that man I had seen our first day in Deadwood, the one with the scalped head, burned face, and the stick he used for support. The way he glared at me went into me like an arrow.

We stood there staring at one another so long you would have thought we was long-lost cousins giving each other the once-over, then he stepped back in the shadows, and the match went out. Reason he had fired it was to light a cigar he had tucked in his pie hole. It glowed with a round red light at the tip. He turned away from me, and I heard him clumping away down the alley on his crutch, which he had now in place of the stick.

I put my pistol away, gathered myself, and tried to catch up with the women and the rats. I followed them until they went up a skid of a road that came to a shack built on a hill. There wasn't no stairs to it, just that mud-slick path. They drove the mule up and onto a firmer lay of land in front of the shack. There was a big barrel out there, and pretty soon they was lifting the bags off together, toting them to the barrel, and one at a time lowering them in. They let the bags settle in the barrel a while, and when they pulled them out I seen water slosh over the sides. They was about the job of drowning what rats the old woman hadn't beat to death with a stick.

When they was on the third bag, which was fuller than the others and causing them to struggle a bit to lift it to the lip of the barrel, the younger woman looked down the hill and seen me. She studied me for a moment, half smiled, and waved me up.

I trudged up quickly. When I was within a yard of her, the young woman said, "You watching pretty close. You got a reason?"

I loved her voice. It was clear and as sweet-sounding as the flute she played.

"Curious," I said.

"Well," said the old woman. "I'll tell you this much. It's the flute."

"Like in that story," I said, it being another one of the many I had read when I was with Mr. Loving.

"Pied Piper," said the old white woman.

The girl giggled a little.

"You're pulling my leg," I said.

"All right, the truth," the old woman said. "It's a mixture we got that we rub inside the bags. It will pull a rat to it the way a hound will come to a pork chop. That's all you get, though. The mixture is ours, and it wouldn't be prudent to share it."

"I do like the flute, though," I said.

"We like to think it helps matters," said the old white woman. She gave me an examination up and down, said, "You going to watch, or you going to help? Or is all of chivalry dead?"

"I'll help," I said. I lifted the last bag into the barrel of water, and admit freely my skin crawled a little when them vermin squeaked their last right before going under.

"Now, you ain't going to get no money," said the old woman.

"That's all right," I said. "I'm just lending a hand."

I was looking over that young woman. She took my breath away. She was a fine mixture of races, with dusky skin and black hair that managed to be thick and smooth at the same time. She had fine, full lips and a slightly wide nose, and her eyes were like wet, shiny holes in the sky — at least that's how they looked with only the moonlight to shine them up. She wore a long dress that I figured was blue, though that was guesswork in the moon shadows, and the way she moved was light as an Apache, and it was then that I thought maybe she was part Indian as well, the way her forehead was, the way her eyes was spaced. She was everything that was fine and beautiful in anybody, far as I was concerned, and I won't lie or exaggerate one inch when I say the sight of her made me feel as if I might swoon. In that moment, like in all those romantic novels that Mr. Loving made fun of, for me it was love at first sight.

"You going to look at that girl or you going to finish with these rats?" said the old woman.

Finishing meant pulling that bag of dead vermin out of the barrel, stacking it back on the sled with the others.

"Come morning we'll weigh them up," said the girl. "I see you again, I'll buy you a stick of penny peppermint candy."

"My name is Nat Love. And I wouldn't mind a bite of peppermint."

"Well, my name is Win Finn," she said, "and this is Madame Finn."

"Formerly of the Finns of Georgia," said the old woman. "But after the war we wasn't much of anything besides broke and tuckered out."

"They burned the place down where we lived," said Win.

"You mean the Yankees?" I said.

"That would be them," Madame Finn said.

"I have taken the name of the Finn family," Win said. "But don't entertain the idea I took it as a slave girl takes a name."

"Course not. Lincoln freed the slaves," I said.

"There's no dearer person to me than Madame Finn," said Win. "And that includes the poor deceased and magnificent Mr. Lincoln."

This led to small talk about the rat-drowning barrel, and finally some other kinds of talk, where I gave them a bit of a rundown about myself, leaving out some of the less flattering points, like having to run off over seeing a white woman's butt. Also, I didn't mention I was a deserter, but I did say I had been in the army. It was really more than I should have said, I guess, but something about the two led me to talk. They talked, too. We got on the war for a while, and I said something or another about Lincoln, and that got the old lady stirred.

"And a good thing it was he freed the slaves," she said. "It was a bad thing all around, that business, and I always said so. Not like it mattered to anyone about my opinion, though. Not when there was cotton to be brought in and my family wanted to sit on the veranda and watch it picked. When the war was over, it was just me and this little girl, her mother having died and her father being my own husband."

"Oh," I said.

"Yeah," said Madame Finn. "Oh."

"My mother was a slave that was part Cherokee," said Win. "She was bought from Cherokee slavers."

"She was comely," said Madame Finn, "I will give her that, and I don't blame her for my husband's transgressions. She didn't have any choice in the matter. But look what it wrought—this lovely child. Like a daughter to me. Look here, Ears, tie those rats down, damn it. I don't want them toppling off the sled when we take them down in the morning. Make sure the knots are as secure as the Gordian Knot."

When I was finished tightening the bags down, Madame said, "You can go now."

"Okay," I said, but I didn't move and just kept looking at Win. I think Win was amused by me, mostly, and kept giving me a going-over in the manner of suddenly seeing a dog strike a match and light a cigar for itself.

"I said you can go now, Ears," Madame said.

"Yes, ma'am," I said, and I started down the hill, but paused and looked back up. I said, "Miss Win Finn, will I see you again?"

She smiled, and the moonlight lay on her teeth and made them shine. "Our paths could cross," she said.

Just those words, simple as they was, put a fire in my heart. I worked my way on back to the main street of Deadwood, feeling light and free as a storm-blown feather.

# 15

I had given up on ratting. That very night I had seen professional ratters, and compared to them I was a joke. Also, I didn't want to compete with Win, as she was suddenly the apple of my eye, and a shiny apple she was. I decided to take myself back to my so-humble abode, as Cullen called it, and pine over the beautiful Win Finn.

I was fetching myself in that direction, striding along near a rise of dirt and stairs and upper streets and buildings, when I heard a voice say, "I would suggest you men take your leave. It will be far better a choice than taking a bullet between the teeth."

It was a clear, firm, and fearless-sounding voice, and it was coming from a row of stairs that wound up from Main Street to Williams Street, which was little more than a terrace built into the hillside. There was one man at the bottom of the stairs, and he had moved his back to the stair railing.

It was light enough that night I could see he was a tall one, solid-built, narrow of hip, with hair that dangled down to his shoulders, and he had one of them drooping mustaches. The pearly handles of his pistols gleamed in the moonlight. The pistols was tucked down in the front pockets of his trousers, and the bottoms of his trousers was stuck down in tall boots with heels on them so high they made his already considerable height more than it was by some inches.

"There's more of us than there is of you," said one of the three in the street. They was all gangly and hungry-looking, like wolves that had cornered an old bull and meant to make a meal of him.

"Soon there will be less of you," said the long-haired man, who I thought sounded remarkably calm.

That's when I seen a fourth man coming down from the terrace above, creeping along the stairs, making his way behind the long haired bull.

"We just want your money," said one of the bony fellows, "though we'd oblige them pistols, too."

"These are Navy Colts, year fifty-one, cap and ball, and you will certainly be obliged to them within the moment."

It wasn't any of my business, and I could have gone on, but it was never in me to let someone be bullied, outnumbered, or hurrahed for no good reason than the bullies' own satisfaction or greed. I had seen that done enough to folks just because they was dark, like me, and had gotten to the point where I couldn't even stand for that to happen to a white man.

I stepped out of the shadows slowly, said, "There is a man behind you, sir. He's coming down the stairs on you."

The man on the stairs stopped creeping, looked madly disappointed. He said, "Damn. I was almost there."

"You was, wasn't you?" I said.

"Thank you, my friend," said Long Hair, and he shifted so that he was mostly still facing the men in the street, but had put his left shoulder to the one above. "I heard him squeaking along up there, but I appreciate it."

"I think you're still in a tight spot," I said, "so let me spare you the one on the stairs."

"You asking for dead," said the man on the stairs to me.

"We will see who's asking," I said.

Then the ball rolled. The man on the stairs pulled. He had decided his first target should be Long Hair, but I chose him. I jerked the LeMat, fired, and seen what looked like a black swarm of bees jump out of the back of his head, and then he come tumbling down the stairs as if it was some kind of circus act and fetched up about three steps above Long Hair.

All this was going on as Long Hair pulled his pistols, one with each hand, from his pockets. It was as fast as any pull I'd seen Mr. Loving make, and he, like Mr. Loving, didn't fire wildly. Took his time quickly is the best way I can explain it. Them revolvers of his snapped a shot apiece, almost at the same time, and two of them men went down while they was still trying to get their guns out of their holsters. The last one had his gun out, and he shot at Long Hair and missed, then turned to me to shoot, maybe thinking he'd nailed his first mark. I shot him before he could fire off another round. My shot hit him in the leg, and he dropped his gun and crumpled down and lay there, grabbed at his wound, rocked and moaned and started begging us to help him, like we had all been boon companions before.

"You'll have your bullet and enjoy it," said the long-haired man, strolling over to him.

I come over for a look. The man who had plummeted most of the way down the stairs was surely dead, and the two in the street Long Hair had shot had both took it through the heart and was pumped out of blood already. The man on the ground was still rolling around and moaning and making quite a spectacle. I was sort of embarrassed for him.

"Shut up some," said Long Hair to the man, putting a foot on the fellow's hat, it having dropped off during his writhing. "There's folks trying to sleep."

"Yes, sir," said the man on the ground, and he rolled about some more, but was mostly silent as he did it.

Long Hair picked up the wounded man's pistol and tossed it under the stairway. He caught up with him as he was trying to roll his way down Main Street. Long Hair bent over him and said, "You have been spared, and I reckon we could get the judge, or some kind of law, but why don't we let that bullet be your law? You get you some help if you can, but you will then be gone from this gulch, for if I see you again, on the street or in any establishment about town, I will kill you without remark. Is that fully understood? I would not want there to be any confusion."

"None, sir, none," said the man. "Oh, God, it hurts."

"I bet it does," Long Hair said. "And to tell the truth, looks to me my dusky friend clipped an artery in the leg there. Minor at first, but it's growing bad as you roll."

"Oh, oh," said the man, and then he stretched out and quit moving after saying "Mama." The ground around him turned dark.

"He has bled out," said Long Hair. "The devil is handing him a pitchfork and a slop bucket this very moment."

"I was a bit hasty with the shot," I said. "I was trying to shoot his kneecap off."

"Well, you have done him in, but he would surely have done you had the opportunity been reversed."

People had come out on the street, but when they seen us, two men holding guns and a bunch of dead men lying about, they went back into their shacks and hidey-holes, one of them pausing long enough to say, "Good evening," and seeming to mean it.

"Who are you, sir?" asked the long-haired man of me.

"Nat Love," I said, slipping the LeMat back into its place.

"Mr. Love, they call me Wild Bill. But my given name is James Butler Hickok. You may call me Wild Bill."

Well, now, I about messed myself, but I took his hand, and we shook. He threw an arm around me, said, "I have a bottle among my possibles, but it is hidden in a corner crack between buildings, as I have yet to figure out where my lodgings are. I have no place to offer you to drink except the great outdoors. But I will tell you square—and I would only say this to a man who had saved my life, and I beg you not to tell— truth is, I'm frightened to death of the goddamn rats, and they are everywhere."

"I know a place," I said.

We went on then, leaving them four dead there for the undertaker to pick up and tote off to the graveyard on the hill, or possibly to be dropped down some abandoned mine shaft, or into some varmint hole. I can't say I felt any real sympathy for them.

We got Wild Bill's possibles, which was a carpetbag and a rolled-up blanket with the butt of a rifle sticking out of one end. He had hidden them, as he said, between two buildings that was built so close together they was almost as one.

"I stashed my goods here and went strolling about, looking for a friend I know. I'm supposed to stay with him, but this place is like a rat maze. I was about to get my bag and find a tree to sleep under when those ruffians came along."

I led him to my room, which, as I said, had become all mine since Cullen had moved in with Wow. Wild Bill pulled his bottle from the carpetbag, took a swig, offered me a jolt, but I declined with good nature, saying I didn't have the stomach for it.

"Suit yourself, Nat," Wild Bill said and swigged some more, saying, "I am always prepared for snakebite this way. I figure one bites me, I already got the cure in me or enough liquor to kill the snake."

"You ain't got no place, Bill, you're welcome to fetch up here for a few days, seeing how we've rode the tiger together."

"I thank you for that," he said, "but a friend of mine, one dandified fine son of a bitch name of Charlie Utter, has laid me out a campsite. Only thing is I have no idea where, but I will catch up with him tomorrow. So I may take you up on that offer for one night. I came here planning to do some mining, but upon arrival have decided a pick handle doesn't fit my hands as well as a deck of cards or a pistol."

"Mining is nasty work," I said.

"Yes, and though there can be a reward of considerable size, it strikes me as easier to take your share at a card table after the miners have cashed their gold into chips. That way they do the work, and I spend the money."

"For me, no cards and no mining."

"What else is there in Deadwood, Nat?"

I told him about my jobs, and because I couldn't help myself, I told him about Win, how I had met her and how I was smitten with her, and that so far the only thing we had done together was drown rats.

"It's a start," Wild Bill said. "I suggest you lay about a plan to meet up with her and woo her, but leave the rats out of it. I also suggest you make a move to get out of the bouncing and the spit-emptying business. A woman needs something more respectable. Life is short. I myself was recently married to Agnes Lake, a retired circus performer."

"I've heard of her," I said.

"I was charmed by her, for she is quite flexible," Wild Bill said, "and she owns the circus, having inherited it from a former husband who was murdered in what I believe was a business dispute. I might add his will left her with a considerable bankroll as well as horses, tents, and elephants. But I find that even a good woman gets on my nerves after a time, even a flexible one, and I told her I was off to make my fortune. Part of my departure might be due to the fact that despite her profession she is quite the lady and wouldn't suck a dick if it were coated in peppermint oil. She was far more interesting as a performer and willing to show me her stretching abilities prior to marriage, but that marriage license put the respectable brand on her, and damn if she isn't trying to live up to it. Her retirement put a damper on my ardor. Did I mention she could put both legs behind her head?"

"You said she was flexible."

"Well, she is a lady and my wife, and I don't want any of that misunderstood," he said, "but outside of the flexibility and the money, she is one boring bitch. Shit, I am already drunk. It must be from not eating. You got anything to chew on, Nat?"

I had a strip of moldy jerky, enough for us both. I cut it in two with a pocketknife and gave him half.

"I will never forget this, Nat, though I ask you, unless we were seen and recognized by them that came out on the street, make no truck of what happened tonight. I have a reputation enough without suddenly finding out I have killed some backshooter's brother, nephew, or asshole buddy. Being a gunman at my age lacks the charm it did at twenty-five."

"I will keep it tight to myself," I said, and until this very moment I have. I figure by now it's a promise without purpose.

Wild Bill drank some more of his snakebite medicine, and when he spoke he became even more theatrical in tone. "You know, I am losing my sight. I shot on instinct alone tonight. I seem to have gotten a fever in my drawers—the French disease—from one of the night ladies, and it has gone to my eyes. I am especially troubled in the dark. Pretty much moon-blind. I waver some days on the value of feminine charms versus the value of my sight. I usually come down on the side of romance, but I can't help but have a doubt now and then."

"That eye problem wouldn't be a thing to be let known," I said. "Not with your reputation."

"You're right," he said. "I have in recent years become quite a talker. Perhaps even a blowhard, revealing far too much about this and that. But while I'm drunk and laying it out there, I want you to know that in spite of the pleasures of my wife's bed and her amazing flexibility, due to her decline in those activities I haven't always been true. In a night of need, and with too much liquor in me, I took an offered enjoyment that was less joyful than one might think and marred by a stink I still smell upon myself after many a bath. I tell you, once she took her pants off, it was like being trapped in a barn with a herd of shitting cows."

"I'm not sure I follow," I said.

"God help me, I fucked Calamity Jane. In the midst of it my stupor began to wear thin, and I saw her face really good, and for a brief moment thought I had been so drunk as to mount my own horse. But because I was quick to figure, even in my drunkenness, that I wouldn't be looking my horse in the face if I was about the business of breeding, I knew I could discard that possibility. Sometimes I wake up with that face burned behind my blinding eyes, and now she is following me about like a kitten. I haven't the iron about me to treat her rough. The word is getting out, though, and I'm ashamed of myself, not only for what remark of it might do to Agnes, my wife, but for what it might do to my reputation. It is bad enough my pecker had to suffer through it, but my reputation could also be abused. You know why I'm called Bill and not James, my true name?"

I didn't have a guess, and I told him such. I also had no idea who Calamity Jane was, and I had never known a man so worried about his reputation and yet so prone to soiling it.

"It is because of my upper lip. It hangs over my teeth a bit, and that is why I was called Bill, as in duck bill. I grew the mustache to hide it. I think it works well. What do you think?"

"I think it does," I said.

"This meat isn't very good," he said, referring to the jerky. "But the bugs seem fresh." He laughed then and went on like that for some while about this and that, some of it making sense, some not so much—and when the bottle was finished he pulled out another that was half filled with laudanum. He took a couple swigs of that, corked it back up, held the bottle up to the lantern light, said, "That's it," and collapsed. He was out for the night.

I blew out the light and tucked myself in, contemplating on the strangeness of the night, and then slept deep, without dreams, the best gunman ever known lying crumpled near me on the floor, a corked bottle of laudanum clutched in his fist.

Next morning when I awoke, Wild Bill and his carpetbag was gone, but he had left a nice hunting knife on Cullen's former bed, and there was a rough written note on a torn piece of sack paper.

It read:

*It's yours, and I owe you a big favor if you ever need it, Nat. I also believe I may have said some inappropriate things about some women I know, including my wife, and I would oblige you to indulge me and forget what I said. I think I exaggerated Calamity's aroma, and for that I apologize, though I would not want you to think she was all perfume. Also not saying about my upper lip would be good, too.*

*Wild Bill*

I kept that note for quite some time, though I never showed it around. Over the years, wettings and heat and crawling time took care of it, so now I have only the memory of it. I no longer have the knife. I'm not sure what happened to it.

I seen Wild Bill frequently after that, and he was always friendly and would have me at his table for a drink, even though a colored man was not usually invited by others. Sometimes his companions would stand up and leave us to it when I arrived, not wanting to share a drink with a nigger, though they wouldn't have said that in my presence or Wild Bill's. I had a reputation of my own by this time, it coming from how I handled myself at the Gem.

I appreciated Wild Bill's friendliness and never so much as said a thing about them men we killed, same for the note, until now. I also managed to help him dodge Calamity a few times, though I felt small over that, as she seemed a nice enough woman. I admired the way she could handle a cuss word, and her ability to string them together was unmatched by mule skinner, miner, and bullwhacker alike. When she come around, Wild Bill often found he had forgotten to do something or another, or needed the outhouse, whatever excuse he could muster. I was sometimes given the job of serving her whatever lie Bill had cooked up in that moment. I'd have to tell her his lie and have her look at me with her kind eyes and her hard face, made that way by time and men and alcohol. What good looks there might have been had fallen behind the crags of her bones, and lay there in hiding, unless you stared at her long and hard and she turned her head just right.

However, the main thing in my life back then was that I took to watching Win Finn like I was a viewer of rare birds. I would check on her during breaks or the few times when I was off work or at night, in hopes of seeing her and the old lady about the ratting business. I was fortunate to come across them at times, and made it a now-and-again job to help her drown the rats, though I never grew used to it. The ratting business all went to hell, however, when some half-breed figured out there was a major nest where the bulk of them was housed, and he burned it out with coal oil. This didn't entirely eliminate the rat population, but it put a dent in it, and what with them boys and their clubs and the men with their popping rifles and Win and Madame Finn with their traps and drowning, the rat infestation was knocked down to a gray dribble.

It was then that the two women became laundresses, and though I could hardly afford it, I took to having my shirts cleaned by them at a dear price. It was worth it, though, and one day as I brought in some shirts, Madame Finn said to me, "Son, let me have you aside here."

She took my shirts and put them on the board outside next to a big pot of boiling water set over a fireplace built of rocks. The shirts was boiled in there like pears for jam.

Me and Madame walked down the hill, and at the base of it, out in the street, she said, "You hear me on this. You must have the best of intentions with Win."

"I don't know it's a mutual feeling between me and her, but on my end my intentions are purely good," I said.

"To speak bluntly, Mr. Ears—"

"Nat."

"—a man finds he sometimes has needs, and so does a woman, and them things can lead to something don't neither of you need, something that can turn wrong on a cat's hair."

"I don't follow you." That was a lie, but it seemed the right thing to say.

"Yes, you do," she said. "You are thinking of linking up with my girl like the beasts of the fields."

"I ain't never thought of such a thing for a moment," I said. Which was, of course, a big goddamn lie. It's about all I thought about.

"I will tell you this," said Madame, and she put her face close to mine as she spoke. "You ask to see her, it will be with a chaperone, and I will be well armed with a pistol."

"You think she would see me under courting circumstances?" I asked. "You can carry two pistols if you like."

"I hoped she might choose more wisely than riffraff," she said, "though it's natural she would gravitate to a colored boy. You are not hard to look at, though you could easily hang laundry on those ears. I suggest you let your hair keep growing and get yourself a bigger hat."

"Thanks," I said.

By this point my hair had grown out considerable and was as bushy as mulberry bramble. I had also taken to wearing leather chaps I didn't need over blue-and-red-striped pants. Like Wild Bill, I had bought me some boots with high heels on them at a dear price, and they gave my already goodly height a greater measure. I thought I looked pretty good, though my hat didn't quite fit me anymore on account of the thickening hair. I tended to pull it down tight over my bushy head so that the hair fanned out like a parasol half open. During the day the hat would ride up on the hair and finally sit atop it like a bird on a rock.

"There is a dance being held this Saturday," Madame said, "and you may ask her to that if you must. No one cares what color you are at a barn dance, because it costs a dollar to get in. But you should do the asking with me nearby. I will not have done to her what was done to her mother."

"She's not a slave," I said.

"That is why it will not be done, Ears. Times are different."

That's how I come to walk back up that hill and go directly to Win and say as if it was my thought all along, "There is a dance this Saturday, and with you and your chaperone, Madame Finn, I would love to invite you to attend."

"I would be delighted to come," she said, and there wasn't a moment of hesitation. I hadn't actually expected a positive answer, and so quickly. I stood there stunned.

"You will come by to walk us to the dance, then?" Win said.

"I will. Whenever it is."

"The time can be found out," Win said.

Well, now, if I was floating the first time I met her, I was flying now. I went down the hill and hadn't gone far when Win caught up with me and took my elbow. She said, "I want you to know I asked Madame to ask you to ask me to the dance. I thought I should start out being honest."

"I'm glad to hear that," I said.

"I didn't know anyone else who is of the same color."

"I was the only pig left at the slaughterhouse?"

She laughed. "Well, you got a kind of ignorant country charm about you, but we should start soft, don't you think?"

"I suppose we should," I said.

"I look forward to it, then," she said.

# 16

It was a tent dance, and it was a big tent, striped red and yellow, having once belonged to a circus. It was lit up with all manner of lanterns and candles and things that led one to think a fire could get started real easy. The ground had been covered in sawdust and patches of hay around the sides. There was barrels to sit on and stools and assorted chairs and over-turned buckets. The tent had a musty smell to it, and I could almost imagine the animals that had paraded beneath it. In fact, on this night a whole different batch of animals paraded about. A band was brought in, one with horns and fiddles and banjos and the like, and there was food and drink and people was dressed up in their finest, which meant there was a lot of color and a rustling of women's dresses. Even the China folk was there, though except for Wow none of them came to dance. They came to see what this crazy business was about and mostly stood over to one side near the hanging tent wall.

It was a cool night, and the door flaps was wide open and spread back so you could have rode a circus elephant in there without having to duck your head, which was something I'm sure had been done in the past.

Wild Bill and his friend Charlie Utter showed up. I had been intro-duced to Charlie briefly one night at the Gem, where I was bouncing. He was a dandy, like Wild Bill, only a shorter version. Even Calamity Jane came, and she was all dressed up in women's clothes. It was the first time I had ever seen her that way. Her hair was fixed a little, and her face was washed. Normally she was dressed in buckskins, her face twisted up in a scowl, hair tucked inside a hat like a caged animal, a revolver stuck in her belt, and foul words flowing out of her mouth like loose sewage.

I had bought myself a new black hat, and it fit me better than the old one. I was tricked out in a fire-red double-breasted shirt with blue buttons, and I was wearing dark blue pants with a thin blue stripe in them. In the style of Hickok I had tucked the pants into my boots, which was shiny with polish. I had on a coat made of dark leather with fringes on it.

By the time I had checked my guns, the music had already started, and people was dancing. It was the dandiest sight you have ever seen. They was flashing elbows and lifting knees and a'gallivanting about the place, kicking up their heels like young horses. The faster the music got, the faster the dancing crowd got. And dang if Wild Bill wasn't out there dancing himself. He was at first with Charlie, and they was a reeling about like regular fools and starting to wave their arms in all manner of flapdoodle, and then women was dancing together, and then it all switched out, and men and women come together, and then the men. One man did a big jump and tried to land with his legs wide split, but ripped his pants and had to leave, clutching the back of them together with a thumb and forefinger. No one was kind about it. They laughed that poor fellow right out of the tent.

I seen Wow and Cullen, too. Wow was dressed in American clothes and was quite light on her feet, though Cullen danced like he had his shoestrings tied together. He had ended up with a green shirt and orange trousers and some two-tone shoes, brown and white with big red ties in them. It made him look a bit like a circus clown and in some ways reminded me of a painting in Mr. Loving's book of a court jester called Hop-Frog.

Everyone danced and changed partners, so that it finally come mostly to men and women together, though it didn't seem to be by design. Just whoever come up in the shuffle was grabbed. This man with that woman and this woman with that man and so on, and pretty soon it ended up that Wild Bill was dancing with Calamity Jane. If they wasn't having a good time it was the best performance I've ever seen. They had big smiles and was starting to hop like rabbits. They was obviously drunk as flies in persimmon wine.

The band started growing. New members with new instruments fell into place. There was a fellow picking up a beat with a pair of spoons and another scratching on a washboard with thimbles, and one guy had two pieces of cow ribs he was snapping together. The band was made up of white folks and black, and even a Chinaman who had a triangle and a stick he was whacking it with. Fortunately the horns, fiddles, banjos, and such covered up the clanging noise. A bit of the music would run off the rails now and again, but it always managed to come back.

I was ready to get out there. I turned to Win, who was lovely in a dress green as sin, with little green shoes and a green pin through her mound of hair. I said, "Would you oblige me a dance?"

"I would, sir," she said. "Let's get to it. And I hope you know how."

"I'll figure it out as we go."

Win looked at Madame, who nodded her consent, and away we went.

Now, I am going to brag on myself here and say I am a natural dancer. I caught that music and rode it like a bucking horse. The notes was butterflies, and I had the net. We started prancing a little here, a little there, picking up speed, like we was windup toys. Charlie Utter, drunk as a bull moose and dancing with himself, sashayed by us, totally out of step with the tune, and fell over a barrel and lay on the floor not moving.

We didn't pay him no mind. He was one of a handful of drunks and dizzy folks who had fallen out. Me and Win was on display for sure. We reeled and spun and bounced and even went vulgar with a hump or two in the air. I don't know what come over us there, but we did it, and when I looked at Madame she give me the eye, so we quit that foolishness.

Me and Win was the toast of the dance. We caught everyone's eye, or at least Win did, cause when she'd spin that green dress would fly out and about, and she was moving fast as a child's top. Around and around she spun, and me with her, us linking arms and kicking, moving sprightly about to such an extent everyone started trying to mimic us; and damned if the band didn't pick it up a step. It led to some of the kids doing cartwheels and handstands and the like. Everyone had caught the disease. It got even wilder as the drink got to flowing more loosely, and me and Win had to stop finally and take our rest and have some punch that wasn't spiked with liquor, and that amounted to one bowl that was served up by the Congregational church ladies. It was not a popular bowl. We found ourselves there primarily with the kids and a few women and henpecked husbands, sipping punch from cups and looking sour due to the drink being heavy on the lemon.

As you would expect, with there being drunks and women and music, some fights broke out, and some of the deacons from the Congregational church, following the laws of their creed, just beat the ever-living dog shit out of a couple of them and threw them out of the tent. When I went out once to find a place to relieve myself, I discovered them rowdies in a ditch behind the tent, and in fact found I was making water on one of them. I retreated quickly because the damp seemed to be bringing him around.

On my way back to the tent, I seen that Wild Bill had Calamity Jane bent over an outside water barrel, which he had dragged beneath a tree. Her dress was hiked up, and he was going at it like he was a hammer and she was a nail. It disgusted me, to tell you the truth, not because they was taking their pleasure, but cause they was so drunk I don't think they even knew they could be seen clear as a hot pie in an open window. I lost a smidgen of respect for Bill after that. Not because of Calamity, but because I seen him then as two-faced and a little too prone to drink. Being a legend was wearing, I reckoned.

Back under the tent, I found Win, and we went at it again, danced to near every song until my legs and feet began to hurt, those new high-heeled boots I had not really being made for that kind of springing about.

It finally come to me that I hadn't seen Madame in a while, and we went looking for her. We found her passed out on a smattering of hay by the side of the tent wall, a cup hanging on her finger, her tongue dangling out like a drying towel. What she had been drinking had not been provided by the Congregational church.

"She takes a nip now and then," Win said.

"One nip after the other, it appears."

"That describes it," she said.

It was about then I seen that poor man that had been on the stick and then a crutch—the one with his head peeled and his face scarred up from burning and maybe being rough-carved with a dull knife. He was over by one of the punch bowls. He had a dipping cup and was doing some serious dipping, throwing it down like he was trying to put a fire out in his belly. He didn't have the crutch no more, and in fact had a very fancy cane and expensive clothes and a bowler hat.

Win caught me looking at him, said, "He is mysterious. He never speaks unless he's got business, and lately his business has been good."

"Shoveling horse manure?"

"He quit that," she said. "Way I heard it, he earned enough to buy a claim, and two weeks out he hit it. It was hard work for him, too, having that limp, but it and shoveling what the horses left seems to have been good for him. He's gotten stronger than he used to be. Hired him three Chinamen and two white men to dig for him. Stands around and watches them, is what I hear."

I looked at him again. There was something oddly bothersome about him, and he had his eyes laid on me as steady as a man sighting down the barrel of a rifle. But then again, he was that way with everyone. I think had my scalp been peeled, my face worked over like that, and me given a limp, I'd have had a suspicious nature myself. I was glad for him, though. At least he had money, and if he was wise about it, wouldn't end up begging for coins with a tin cup, which was often the case for such that was in his kind of condition.

I collected my guns, and me and Win went out of the tent, took a walk back along Main Street. We went up to her shack because she wanted to get something there, and that turned out to be a picnic basket and her flute.

"Are we hunting rats?" I asked.

"Not hardly," she said. "I arranged us a picnic. I figured Madame would be on the ground after a snort or two. As for the flute, I just like it. I was taught by a white girl who didn't have anything in her life but to play it and the piano, sing, and dress up nice. She was all right. She was Madame's daughter. Her name was Jane, and she died of diphtheria."

"Madame's gonna be mad when she wakes up," I said.

"Oh, I've seen this before," Win said. "She couldn't be woke up if you poured a bucket of cold water on her and fired a cannon over her head. She has to come around on her own time, which will be sometime to-morrow morning, well after the birds first sing. Though I suppose we should gather her up before the night wears too thin. We got time for that, though. The dance is just getting wound up."

We went to the livery, where I kept my horse. There was a colored boy there, around twelve, and he was in charge of things. I gave him a few coins to saddle Satan. I usually came in about once a day to check on him, and when I had time I took him for a ride along Main Street, out and about a bit, without getting too much out in the wilds, where the Sioux and the Cheyenne roamed. Not to mention Blackfoot and Crow.

The boy's name was Easter, like the Resurrection, and he got Satan ready and hitched him up to a one-horse rig I rented. He had been teaching Satan to pull the rig for me and so far had not lost an eye in the process. Damn horse liked him from the beginning, which is more than I can say for how Satan had treated me.

Easter gave me an apple for Satan, and we took off into the night, under the moonlight, along Main Street and out of town, venturing a little far, but we both felt brave about it.

We took a side trail. It was rugged, but Satan managed it all right, and the buggy held together. We had the buggy top down, and we could see the sky and the source of all that moonlight, a moon so big it filled the eyes, though there was a few drifting clouds, soft ones, almost clear. They tumbled along the heavens like cotton-soft dreams.

I parked the buggy under a tall tree, got out our goods. I gave Satan his apple, proud of the fact he had learned to pull a wagon and a buggy good, and he didn't try to bite my hand off for a change.

We put out the food. The picnic was simple. It was good bread and sweet cheese, a jar of apple jam, a big bottle of sarsaparilla, glasses to pour it into, and there was a striped ground cloth and some metal plates and forks and spoons. Win had also brought a blanket for us if the air got too nippy. She cut us big slices of bread, slathered them with apple jam. It was delicious. This was my first taste of sarsaparilla, and from that point on it was my desired drink when I could get it. I can't say as I remember all we talked about, as most of it was kind of silly, as it often is when you're getting to know someone. But finally we talked about our lives and how it was we wanted more than a hoe and row to use it on. We had dreams, and we both agreed they was big as white people's. We also agreed that out here in the wilds we was more like everyone else than anywhere we had been before. Yet neither of us was all that set on Deadwood. That's how the talk ran.

Win said she planned to find some way to take care of Madame, as the old woman had taken care of her all this time, and now she was starting to get old and miss a step. I agreed she should do that. After a while Win brought out the flute and started playing. It was a strange and lonesome tune she played, full of all the sorrowful feeling you could have, and I certainly had me a list of sorrows. My ma and pa was in that song, their deaths, and me being chased by Ruggert, losing my friend Mr. Loving, and the deaths of them soldiers, which I still partly blamed on myself. The more she played, the sadder I got. Pretty soon there was tears in my eyes, but it wasn't a terrible way to feel. It was like that music, them notes she was playing, was getting down inside of me and taking hold of that sadness and pulling it out and tossing it away from me. At least for the time being. It was both a good feeling and a painful one, kind of like having a bad tooth pulled or a bullet dug out.

After a time she quit that tune, played a livelier one. I got up and danced a little to it. I did it in a funny way, and Win got tickled and couldn't play no more. I dropped down on the cloth then, and when I did she grabbed my head and pulled my face to hers and kissed me. It was for me the finest moment in my life. That kiss was like fire. It lit my lips. It lit my head. It lit my heart. It lit my soul. I was ablaze with passion.

That first loving kiss, the one that comes out of you from the source of your personal river, and the one that comes from her that is the same, there's never another moment like it; never another flame that burns so hot. It can never be that good again, ever. All manner of goodness can come after, but it's different. And that's a good thing, because if we burned that hot for too long, we'd be nothing but ash.

What followed some might think was better than that kiss, us taking off our clothes and all, bringing ourselves together with excitement on that picnic cloth, under that blanket with the weather turning cooler and cooler and there being the smell of pine and oncoming snow in the air, but it wasn't better than that kiss.

Don't misunderstand me. It was well worth doing, and if I was making me a list, it would be listed second in goodness and something that works better in repetition, but everything in my life from that point on lay under the mountain of that single kiss, and try as I might, I have never climbed that high again.

# 17

We gathered up Madame just as the dance was winding down and the drunks was piling up under the tent and around it. She couldn't walk, so we hefted her like a tow sack of potatoes out to the buggy. She wasn't a small woman, so it was something of a strain. We got her in it, and then I rode them home in the buggy. When Win and I had Madame in bed in the one room they shared, Win took the pistol out of Madame's purse, which had been strapped to her arm, and showed me the pistol wasn't loaded.

"You're the first man that she didn't carry bullets in the gun for," Win said. "Usually she expects to shoot them, and actually shot at one, but he was swift. With you she felt confident enough to just run a bluff."

"Well, how many men you seen?" I said.

"Let me say it this way. You seen more of me than any of them."

"I like that," I said, and I did, though I will be honest with you and say it wouldn't have made me no never mind. What had come before for either of us was way back then, far as I was concerned. What we had done and was doing was now.

This was the beginning of a routine, though we was a little less open about it due to Madame. Madame liked to get herself a bottle now and then, though Win made a point not to provide it or encourage it. But when she was in her cups, me and Win seen each other, either in my little room or up on that hill beneath the tree and the big wide sky. It was no trouble for the buggy, if there was enough moon and starlight or if the lanterns on the sides of the buggy would stay lit.

Under our tree it was shady in the day and dark at night, and there was a slope that went off one side of the hill that was covered in green grass when the spring come, the soil around there being tucked full of natural richness.

It was good times, but during them I thought all the while on what Wild Bill had told me. I needed to make some major money or have a real job if I planned to get married. The thought buried itself in my head like a chicken bone in a dog's throat. I couldn't cough that thought up no matter how hard I tried.

I thought about it more and more when I had to knock heads over at the Gem Theater and on long days when I was emptying stinky spittoons. I had to keep stashing enough money back for me and Win to light out from Deadwood, set our sights on something better. The better thing seemed to me Mr. Loving's money he had left me, provided it hadn't all been stolen from me. I tried to keep in mind that Mr. Loving had a lot of faith in his cousin, but when it come to taking advantage of the money or giving it to a colored man with big ears, I feared he might lose some of his loyalty. But if the money was there, it was a good nest egg, and I was thinking of having my own farm, which was something I knew how to do.

Plans was one thing, life was another.

As a rainy spring moved on and summer limped in, and the muddy streets dried and became spotted with holes deep enough to lose a leg in, I was feeling at the top of my game, having stuffed myself tight with plans and ambition.

One night, working at the Gem, a big man came in. And when I say big, I mean big. You will think I exaggerate when I say he was about seven feet tall. It is your privilege to doubt me. I didn't wrestle him to the ground and put a ruler to him, but I am a fair judge of height and weight from my time with livestock, and that was my figure. He was broad-shouldered, had a chest like a nail keg and legs like tree trunks. I reckoned him for three hundred pounds, thereabouts, and I might add we're talking lots of muscle and trim on the fat. His hat seemed to sit on top of his head and was in danger of falling off at any moment. His feet was so big his boots looked like rowboats to me.

What struck me as most interesting, though, was he came in with the fellow that had been scalped, cut, and burned. The busted fellow still had a limp, but as I said before he had abandoned the cane. There was also with him a little man with a sunken chin and a dimple in it like a bullet strike. This man was thin of shoulder and chest. His eyes were always darting about the room, which made me think of a weasel, which was the name he was known by. When he sauntered in he had on a set of guns and a belt full of cartridges.

Like a lot of cowboys and miners, there was them that didn't like to check their weapons, their manhood being tied so closely to them. This often meant I'd have to beat them about the head and ears with my own pistol, since as bouncer I was allowed to carry mine.

Weasel and Big Boy was among them that wanted to hang on to their goods. They grumbled when I asked for their weapons and promised them a claim check in my best handwriting. I pointed to a sign right by the door that said CHECK YOUR GODDAMN GUNS. AND WE MEAN IT.

"A man's guns ought to stay on him," Weasel said.

Like a lot of the others, I believed my manhood was tied to my weapons, too; it was easier to prove it with a pistol than it was with an idea, cause that took brain work and consideration and someone on the other end of it that was willing to listen. Problem with trying to be rational all the time is the other fellow ain't always concerned with how logical your argument is.

What I said next hit Weasel solid as a brick. "Your johnson stays on you, your guns go behind this counter."

Weasel leaned over the counter, got close to my face, letting me get the full measure of his breath, which was already wet with alcohol and onions and something that came from deep down inside of him like a mating skunk. His clothes smelled, too, mildewed and musky. Sweat was dripping down from under his hat and onto his forehead.

"I fought for the Confederacy, and now I got a nigger telling me I got to give up my guns?"

"I'm telling you to check them," I said. "I don't plan to auction them."

"You getting smart with me, boy?" said Weasel.

"I'm telling you the rules," I said.

Big Boy stepped up and loomed over me, even though I was standing behind that counter. He was so tall I felt like I was sitting down. The look on his face was frightening, not because he looked mad but because he didn't. There was some kind of mark in the center of his forehead made with what looked like fresh chicken shit.

"Fellows," said Burned Man, and his voice seemed to come from some dark mine shaft in which there had been a cave-in. "This man has rules to follow. Like all servants, he knows his job and his place, don't you, boy?"

Here I had been feeling sorry for this fellow, burned to a cracker, scalped, and pretty much shit on by life, and now he was making those kind of remarks with his tunnel voice. My job wasn't to avenge every sour remark that come up on me, because believe me, each night I got a washtub full of them, but any pity I might have felt for his burned-up self flew right out the window. Fact was, something about him made my neck knot up and my spine grow tight.

"It's my job," I said.

"Very well," said Burned Man, and he reached under his very shiny black suit coat into the inside pocket, came out with a lady's pistol, and laid it on the counter. This led to Big Man pulling his hog leg and smacking it on the counter alongside it, along with a bowie knife about the size of Saint George's sword, which he thrust into the wood point first, so that it stood up. Weasel just looked at me. He was breathing heavy, and his oily face shone in the lights. As his lips curled back, his twisted yellow teeth came out of his mouth like a groundhog checking for sun. For a moment I thought he was going to pull his pistols. I determined if he should make that motion, I would beat him to it. I laid a hand on the LeMat and watched him, tried to keep one eye on the other two, cause from time to time not all the weapons got corralled; now and again a few got through. I figured Big Man, however, could just fall on me and kill me.

"Now," Burned Man said, laying a hand on Weasel's shoulder. "It's for everyone, and we want to be cooperative." He was smiling wide enough I could see his gapped and snagged teeth, and he was speaking in that voice I told you about. I sensed deep down inside that tunnel there might actually be some honey, but it was spoiled honey.

Weasel slowly removed his gun belt and placed it on the counter. I gave them all a claim check with a number on it, tied off a tag to the weapons with the same number, and put them under the counter. All the time I'm doing this they gave me their full attention, and Big Man loomed over me like a cloud. Burned Man had a way of holding back, being behind them, letting them be the first line of defense. All that money he had come into had made him powerful.

They wandered off, Weasel the most unhappy of the three, and took a table where a card game was starting. Wild Bill appeared, laid an elbow on the counter, said, "I watched you deal with them fellows. Right nice job."

"Frankly, Bill, I was a little nervous."

"Ought to be," he said. He pulled his revolvers from his pants pockets, laid them on the counter. I knew he had a hideout gun, but thought it prudent not to ask about it. "I was near, though, and I would have come into the fray had the situation called for it."

"I know that," I said. "I seen you over to the side, and that gave me comfort."

I hadn't really seen him, but I thought it was a nice thing to say. I wanted him to know I trusted him, and in my mind the respect I had lost for him earlier had been regained.

"They were about the business of picking a fight, Nat. I should know; I've had many a one picked with me."

"Suppose you have," I said.

It had gotten noisy in the Gem. The cigar, pipe, and cigarette smoke had started to fill the air and drift across the room in little gray clouds. The piano player was really loud that night, and no more in tune or aware of what tune he was playing than he was any other time. There was a new girl singing, and she couldn't hit a note any better than the piano player's wife—not if she had had a boat paddle and the note was tied to a string just over her head. I put my hands behind the counter so Bill couldn't see them shake.

"Buy you a drink?" Bill said.

"Sarsaparilla," I said.

As I mentioned earlier, Wild Bill didn't much care who said what to whom as long as you didn't say it to him. He didn't mind sitting with a colored, and because of his reputation and ability with them pistols, everyone gave him a slide. It was better that way. There was people to cross, but Bill, pleasant as he could be, wasn't one of them.

"I get a reprieve in about half an hour," I said, pulling out my pocket watch and reading the face of it.

"That's when we'll do it, then," Bill said. "Well, going to get me a drink, find some cards, and if the night is right, line me up some feminine companionship, preferably before drunkenness has set in, so my choice will be better and cleaner and of a more satisfying nature when I awake in the morning."

For a married man with a disease, he was pretty cavalier about things. He wandered off into the crowd, them making way before him like he was Moses parting the sea. I went back to my work, and in about a half hour I turned over the gun gathering to another worker, a white fella with a drinking problem and a runny nose. I went out to find Bill.

Bill was holding down a table with three others, playing cards. Bill, as always, sat with his back against the wall. When I seen he was in a game, I started to walk away, but he called out, "Nat, come on over, friend."

I came and stood by him as he was tossing in his cards. He said, "I'm done with this round." He said to them others, "I would appreciate it if you would abandon this table so as to leave me and my friend to it for a private conversation."

Now, I can swear without exaggeration they was studying him and me, trying to put the whole thing together. It wasn't like the problem was they was all Southern boys, because they wasn't. There was plenty who fought for the North wouldn't give a colored man the time of day or piss on him if he was on fire. As I heard one Yankee say one time, "It was more about territory than niggers."

But this was Wild Bill, and after a moment of consideration they got up and scraped their chairs and went away. Bill watched them lest one should turn on him, cause the truth was, excluding Charlie Utter and a few others, Bill had few friends that was solid, and many of them that he had was really more like suckasses. Some might even be looking for a moment when his back was turned to pop him. Me he trusted cause I had thrown in my hand that night without knowing who he was or caring.

"You may be off duty, but pull your chair around here by me, the back of it against the wall," he said.

Like I said, he liked his back to the wall. I did that, and he said, "Nat, there's some that don't like you hereabout."

"I suspect they are legion," I said, "but it ain't for anything I done."

"You are a tribute to your race," Bill said, not realizing there was an insult in that. "But there are some that would shoot a dog that brought them a rabbit, and just because the dog was black. You following my drift, Nat?"

"No insult to you, but I have been in this position before and have been worse off in times past."

"Uh-huh," he said. "But I tell you now, that big man, he is one of the breed that killed Jesus, and he has your number."

It took me a moment, and then I got it. The big man was a Jew.

"Furthermore," Bill said. "The little fellow, he don't have nothing but dead in his eyes. He likes to kill."

"Some might say such of you," I said.

"Some might," Bill said, his teeth showing slightly beneath his mustache. "They would be wrong. I don't like to kill, but I'm willing to if the need arises. I prefer to go to bed at night without having killed a man, for it only furthers the desire of others to pull down on me so as to build a rep. But I can sleep with who I am. I have never killed a man that didn't need killing, except for an unfortunate accident with a deputy once. But I'll not discuss that. Weasel, though, he's one of a bad breed, Nat. He was not only a soldier, he used to be a buffalo hunter, and by all estimates a fair shot. He is said to have shot buffalo calves for fun and was known during the war as a man that liked to shoot the wounded; it didn't matter North or South. He was Northern, but it was for the blood, not for any kind of cause. That could just be a story, but I tend toward believing it because he has the look about him. I am a good evaluator of character, having used my good judgment to avoid being shot by many a scoundrel."

"How do you know all this about him?" I asked.

"I was in the war, Nat, and I knew of him through Custer. They were at Bull Run together. The little bastard was deadly, but mostly from behind a tree or from a ditch. He isn't exactly a coward, but he measures his odds out, I can promise that. No one ever saw him at the forefront of the battle if he could dodge it. He is a backshooter, if he gets a chance.

"The giant, his name is Finklestein, or so he claims. There are those that contest his story of being a Jew and say he is a German or some other foreigner, but it hardly matters, does it? They say he took his wife's last name. His family, as the story goes, were all killed when he lost his mind and took an ax to them. They say it was a fever and he didn't know what he was doing and he lives in constant sorrow. That's why they say he is here in the Territories, to avoid the law."

"Who is 'they'?"

"That is a good question, Nat. But I have heard the story from several. However, they always got it from another person. And it changes a little here and there. I'm telling you the version I prefer, the one Charlie Utter told me. Anyway, the big man went kind of mad and decided he was a Jew and that he had been turned into something called a golem, if I hear correctly. Fact is, he calls himself Golem, like that's his name."

"What's a golem?"

"It's a Jew thing. Some kind of monster they say will whip the ass of their enemies. He thinks he's that monster. That mark he's put on his forehead, says that stuffs him full of power, whatever that means. Charlie was a little unclear on the matter."

"Think there's anything to it?"

Wild Bill grinned at me. "I figure a .44 slug will straighten things out. As for the other, the walking Yule log, I think he pulls the strings on those two due to his having a reservoir of money. There is something wicked about him, of that you can be assured."

"You may be right, Bill," I said. "He makes my skin crawl, and I don't think it's just because of the way he looks. I like to think I've got a better heart than that."

"Let me get right on the matter. I have been told they have been following and asking about you. I have heard it this very night in Mann's Number Ten from a man said he overheard the greasy one say such when he was in his cups. According to what this fellow told me, and this fellow is something of a wind blower, Ole Yule Log has a thing for you, Nat, and that's why he has the crazy bastard and the grease bowl with him. He plans to plow your crop, come soon, and I don't mean he wants to mount your ass, least not in the carnal way."

I searched through the crowd and spotted the three at a round table not far from us. A fourth man had joined them. He was dirty and small with carrot-colored hair sticking out from under his hat. His nose had been broken and was bent; the tip of it pointed to his left ear. He was cross-eyed, too, but he had eye enough to do what them others was doing. They was all staring right at me.

"They have added another," I said.

"Jack McCall. He came out of his mama's wrong hole and she forgot to wipe. So there he is. But he is of no concern. I've played him in cards, and he's a coward. You can tell a lot of things about a man by the way he plays cards. I even felt sorry for him a few days back after I'd taken everything he owned in a friendly game of chance. I gave him a dollar and my best wishes to buy him some food and a rope to hang on to. He took it, but resented it. I stepped on his pride. I thought he didn't have any."

When Bill spoke of hanging on a rope, he was referring to what some called a trot line. When a man needed sleep but had little money, there was a building on the back side of Deadwood that tied ropes up, and you could hang between them as a way of sleeping standing up. That way the owner of the place could really pack them in. I figured I'd just as soon curl up on the ground and get nibbled by the rats.

It was in that moment my eyes settled firmly on Burned Man, took full notice of the way his eyes flashed across the room, hot as a prairie fire. It was like someone had slapped me in the back of the head. I knew what should have been obvious all along—scalped head, burned-up face, smoked-up voice or not.

He had survived them Apache and was still after me. It was Ruggert.

# 18

A rare bout of common sense and my love for Win saved Ruggert that night.

Believe me, I wanted to stand up right then, march over with my LeMat, the striker flicked to fire that sixteen-gauge shell, and blast his head off. But I didn't. I knew that I didn't have a chance of coming out alive, even if I was a bouncer in the Gem. I could get away with doing my bouncer work, but killing a white man for a past grievance I couldn't prove, even in the wilds of Deadwood, was going to be a hard pill for most of the cracker population to swallow. You could backshoot, card-cheat, and maybe even steal a horse and screw the preacher's wife and not be hung for it if the folks was in the right mood, but a colored man did any of those things, instant they caught you your boots would be off the ground and your neck would be stretched. I might have Wild Bill on my side, a few others, but even with that deadly man in my camp the numbers would be against me. It would be like trying to bail out the ocean with a teacup.

And I didn't want to lose my chance with Win. She was what I had been looking for all my life, and I didn't even know it until I come across her, seen her for the first time in the moonlight, playing music to rats.

We could have a life. I figured Pa would want that more than he would want me to shoot Ruggert.

I didn't even tell Wild Bill I knew who it was that wanted me dead and why. I let out my breath easy, made my excuses to Bill, and hit the street. I found myself walking very fast, becoming madder and madder, wanting to turn around and go back for Ruggert.

Finally I thought of how he looked and what had happened to him. I didn't know how he ended up in Deadwood, but it never occurred to me it had been on purpose. Probably figured me dead by Apache, and my guess is that was a disappointment for him, not having the chance to get his hands into the act. And then fate had brought us back together. He had somehow made his way to Deadwood, was little more than a beggar, and here I came riding in with Cullen and the China girls.

From the time he seen me that day, his fortunes had steady climbed up the ladder, and it may have been giving him too much credit to think he had improved them purely to hire the help he needed to take me down, but I wouldn't put it past him. It fit with what Mr. Loving said. He latched onto notions like a thirsty tick and wasn't happy until he had sucked all the blood out of them.

By the time I got to my room, I had begun to feel sorry for Ruggert again, the way he had been tortured by the Apache, and though it wasn't enough to soothe my burning hatred of him, as he had done just as bad to Pa, it was enough to throw a damp towel over my feelings, at least to some extent.

Pushed under my door was a flyer. Inside my room I lit a lamp and gave it a gander. At the top of it there was a couple sentences penciled in:

*This here sounds like your meat. It could mean big money.*

*Cullen*

The flyer had a drawing of a man with a rifle, and he had long hair and was dressed like Wild Bill. It was about a Deadwood shooting match, and the prize money was considerable. There was an entry fee and a sign-up deadline. I had two days to beat that.

I considered on it a bit.

I thought about that contest money, and then I began to think about Ruggert again. I decided he had paid enough for what he done. Maybe that was a greater punishment than death, and I should be content with it.

If I won that shooting contest I'd have plenty of money, and there could be more made with side bets. I could shorten my time in Deadwood considerably, making more money in one day than I might in months of working at the Gem, having to look over my shoulder all the time for Ruggert and his dingleberries. And if I won and left, and Ruggert followed, then a rifle shot on the wind needed no explanation to anyone.

The shooting event was set a week from that night. It didn't seem unrealistic to me to be able to avoid Ruggert for a week and take my chances at the shooting match, and it didn't seriously occur to me I might lose. I figured on winning that event, leaving Deadwood with a solid purse that would get me and Win and Madame clear across the country. I was so confident, had I been a smidgen more confident, I'd have had to hire someone to walk alongside me and help carry my confidence.

I pried open the wall space, checked in on my saved money, which I had stuffed in an old flour sack, pulled it out, and by lamplight counted what I had earned. There was nearly five hundred dollars in there. I added another twenty to it, keeping a few silver dollars in my pocket for needs. I was so excited about all that money, I counted it twice. I had earlier been overcome with the knowledge Ruggert was alive and still trying to kill me over seeing his wife's butt (and where was she now?), but right then I was shot through with excitement and a kind of joy. I packed the money back in its hiding place, got myself ready for bed, the revolvers lying on either side of me as always, leaned over, and blew out the light.

I was deep into a visit with Morpheus when I heard my door being beat on. I came awake immediately, the LeMat in my fist, the hammer cocked. I sat up, said, "Who's there?"

"It's me," Cullen said.

"Goddamn, Cullen," I said, sliding up to the door. It was so close in there I didn't even have to stand, just rolled off my pallet and knee-walked to it, spoke at him through the wood as I unlocked it by sliding back the bar. "You drunk? You don't live here anymore."

"No, I'm not drunk. Let me in."

He came in and sat in the spot where his bed used to be. I laid my pistol aside and lit the lamp. When I looked at him his mouth was hanging open and his lips was quivering. For a moment, I thought he had been shot or stabbed, but it was an injury of another kind.

"I am on fire with love," Cullen said.

"You been in them damn dime novels again, ain't you?"

"I want to marry Wow," he said.

"Well, my glorious congratulations to you," I said, and meant it.

"We decided on it tonight. Just got through doing what we always do at night, and she said, 'I think we ought to get married,' and I said, 'I think that's a good idea,' so we're going to."

"Usually you don't bed the woman until after you marry her," I said.

"And I suppose you have been chaste," Cullen said.

"I won't answer on the grounds that you know the truth," I said. "But I am glad for you. Very much so. Wow is a wonderful woman."

"She is," he said. "I know she ain't pretty, not like Win. Hell, not like a lot of women, including the China girl with the wooden leg. You know, I still don't know her name, can't get it right. Ring Ding. Ping Sing. Wing-a-ling. I don't know. I think she gives me another name every time I see her. Hell, like I was saying, Wow ain't a natural beauty, but she's grown pretty to me. There's the way she turns her head. She's got that sparkle in her eye, and the way her teeth are so straight and white when she smiles; she spends time on them, Nat, and has taught me a lot about what she calls personal hygiene."

"You're so in love you're making me a little sick to my stomach," I said, but I was grinning when I said it.

"She's got the best heart, but she's tough, too, if she needs to be. And she can talk about things I didn't know there was to talk about."

"She can do that," I said, thinking about her telling me about Corn Foolish, as I still liked to call him.

"Wow knows about ants and birds and diseases and doctoring. All kinds of shit I don't give a damn about, but she can make me think I want to know about it, at least while she's talking. She can sing like a goddamn bird, cook good, fix tasty things I would have never thought I'd eat. And she is really a treat in the night—but hell, you know that."

"Not the way you do, Cullen. I think she saved the real business for you. What me and her did was just dallying."

"You think so?" he said.

"I do. When is the event to take place?"

"We're going to do it as a Chinese wedding among them Chinamen and the China girls. That's what she wants, and I don't mind. I'll have some preacher say some Christian words over us to make it a well-tied knot from East to West."

"Again, Cullen," I said, "I am glad for you, but now that I know of the great joy that has come to you, go home. I'm frazzled out and need to sleep."

"Sorry, Nat."

"Not at all. You come anytime, just as long as it isn't at this time."

Cullen laughed. "I see you got the flyer."

He was looking at it lying on the floor by the bed. "I did. And I'm going to enter, and I'm going to win."

"Never doubted it," he said.

We shook hands. I gave him my best wishes again and let him out.

Fact was, I got him out of there quicker than I would have under normal circumstances, for I was busting to tell him about Ruggert. Yet it didn't seem right to spoil his big announcement with my news. Furthermore, Ruggert wasn't hunting Cullen, may not have known about him at all.

I lay there in the dark on my back staring at the ceiling I couldn't see. I had been in a deep sleep, but knew I wouldn't find that spot again, not tonight. I was too worked up over Ruggert and the shooting contest, and I was also happy for Cullen and Wow. It was an odd mix of feelings.

# 19

I kept a better watch on myself than I had before, was careful about corners and alleys and being out after dark except when I had to be for my jobs. I seen that fellow Bill said was called Golem from time to time. It wasn't like he was trying to conceal himself from me, which due to his size would have been like trying to hide a buffalo in a small barn with all the lanterns lit.

I tried to act like I didn't know he was there, or just pretended he meant nothing to me, would walk past him like I had never seen him before, but I kept an eye cocked and a loose hand near one of my revolvers.

More frequently I saw Weasel, who always seemed to be scuttling about, looking at me, showing me those nasty green teeth as if they was a prize of some kind. Ruggert I didn't see much—a glance of him now and then. I guess his newfound wealth allowed him to keep tabs on me while he rested up at one of the saloons with a glass of beer.

Once I knew Ruggert and Burned Man was one and the same, I asked about, discovered that his mine, though it had delivered big for a while, had played out like an aging whore. All that could be got from it was got, and now it was abandoned. What he had plied out of it let Ruggert go about town dressed in nice clothes with a built-up shoe (turned out the Apache had shaved off one of his heels and clipped a few toes), and he was eating at the finer places, such as they was. Places where colored wasn't supposed to go unless it was to sweep out or do what I did, bounce drunks and empty spit. I began to think Ruggert's punishment from the Apache wasn't enough after all. He was living pretty high on the hog. Still, I stuck to my plan.

All my good feelings was cut short the next day, when after signing up for the match, word come down that Custer and his command had been wiped out at the Little Bighorn. Tensions was high in Deadwood, and most likely everywhere else except back east, though they may themselves have felt a little queasy about matters. I wasn't fond of getting killed by Indians, but their side of things was clear. We was in their world, and we was shitting on it pretty big. Digging in their sacred lands, wiping out their food, and finding all manner of reasons to justify it.

This, however, didn't keep me close to camp, so to speak. Next day was my day off, and I joined up with Wild Bill that morning. We gave Ruggert's men the slip, rode our horses to the spot where me and Win did our romancing. I had told Wild Bill of my plan to enter the shooting contest, which he somehow already knew about, and finally revealed to him that I knew the burned fellow and that we had a past. I told him all of it. He was a good listener. I told it to him as we rode out of town, side by side.

When we got to the hill, we stood under the big tree and looked at the drop below. Grass and wildflowers flowed down the hill like a carpet had been rolled out. The air was crisp as a fresh-baked cracker.

"You know, a man could get used to living in a spot like this, having him a house and a wife," Wild Bill said.

"You have a wife, Bill," I said.

"I know. That's the one I meant."

"You thinking about hanging up your guns?"

"I'd like to," he said. "But it's harder than you might speculate. I have become the Prince of Pistoleers, which is a title sort of like Soon to Be a Fucking Leper. There ain't nowhere to go with it, Nat. I feel that Old

Man Time is soon to drop on me like a brick on a bug, as you don't get better at being the Prince of Pistoleers. You get older at it."

"Go back east, Bill. Peg your guns. There you'd be a hero and wouldn't nobody be expecting a shoot-out."

"Who would I be there? Just some old blowhard with a lot of windies to tell, no way to make a living unless I went into show business. I tried that with Buffalo Bill. I felt like a damn fool. Other than that there's the plow, and I have no hankering for it. Out here I'm still a man to be reckoned with. There have even been suggestions they make Deadwood a real town with a real town marshal, and I have been recommended by some for the job. I don't want it. I've done it, and it's just more gun work. I am good at the work but tired of it. I keep trying to figure on a way out of this cage I've built for myself, but haven't come upon a solid idea. Sometimes I think the best thing would be a quick exit on hell's shingle."

"Don't talk like that, Bill."

"Right enough. Let's don't talk about it at all. I am in a morose mood for no good reason I can figure. That's not true. I know why I'm that way."

"Custer?"

"Yep. I knew him. Always was an impulsive ass. Got through the war when he should have been killed ten times over. I think he got to thinking he was invincible. That his luck couldn't run out. I used to feel that way. Age has a way of pissing on those kinds of thoughts, though. Hell with it. Let's get you ready."

What he meant was we had come to practice shooting for the match. Wild Bill himself wasn't going to enter. He told me, "I have nothing to gain but a possible loss of reputation. If I have a bad night, that's all that will be remembered, and my stock will plunge like beaver hats against silk in popularity. Fewer will be scared of me. More will be willing to try me."

That made sense to me.

While we was pulling out our paper and clay targets from the saddlebags, laying out our ammunition on a blanket, Bill said, "I have spoken to Jack McCall."

"One was with that bunch at the Gem?" I realized I hadn't seen him about town with the others.

"The very same broken-nose, wandering-eye son of a bitch. He has given me some information, but its usage might be more important if we consider the source. He is telling me what we already know. This fellow you call Ruggert and I call Yule Log wants you dead. And now that you've told me the story I know why, though it makes about as much sense as spit-polishing a pickle. He has plenty of help beyond them we've seen. You degraded many a white man in your job as bouncer. Sometimes in front of white women."

"Only them that acted like fools got a whacking," I said. "In front of women or in front of the stove."

"Be that the case or not, the attitude is the same. There was, by the way, talk of banning your dusky breed from competing in the shooting match, as they felt that was putting colored on equal footing with whites. I had a lively debate with the organizers of the match myself."

"And how did that come out?" I asked.

"They came around to my point of view."

"Thanks, Bill."

"No need to speak of it. I know your prowess from a night not long ago. Those were some fine shots in the dark. But to not drift too far from my original point, you haven't got many turned out in your favor. Jack McCall, that squirrelly son of a bitch, claims to be a defector. Says he's telling me the insides of it, but I figure he is merely trying to keep my eye off things by leading me to look in the wrong directions. I think it's his mission to keep watch on me and report to them. I can't see him with the guts to attempt to dispatch me, but he might have plans to keep me busy or lead me into a trap with the others. Were he to pull his shitty little revolver on me, I could sing a song and take a piss before I needed to pull my weapon. Then I'd have time to shoot him twice."

"Don't underestimate a sneak," I said. "I done that with Ruggert, and he just keeps on coming. A man warned me about him, but I thought I had outrun him by time and distance. He got burned on and cut on by Apache, left out on the plains to die, but sure as the sun comes up and the moon goes down, here he is, and wealthy now. I knowed him when he didn't have a pot to piss in or a window to throw it out of, and now he has——"

"Minions," Bill said. "Still, I am a good judge of character and gunmen. And Jack McCall is no gunman. It's the others you——or I——have to be concerned with."

Bill had brought a few bottles with him, and they had corks in them, and he put them out at a goodly distance, say, thirty feet, then went on to shoot the center of those corks, driving them and the lead into the bottles. I tried it using the Colt Mr. Loving had given me and did the same, though I have to say with a bit more concentration between shots.

Bill was like Mr. Loving. He could be talking to you, scratching his ass, and shooting at the same time and not have any chance of missing. I have heard some say that the things Bill was able to do with his pistols was just big talk, but I'm here to tell you that ain't so. I might also add that Bill did all this with cap and ball weapons, which he preferred.

When those bottles was busted up, he had me toss some hard clay targets from the edge of the hill, sailing them way out and high over that falling carpet of flowers. He hit ten out of ten, then had me flip a dime in the air. It didn't go too high before the wind caught it, floated it out beyond the hill, but Bill shot it, sent it spinning into the distance.

"Damn, Bill," I said. "I thought your eyes was bad."

"Mostly they give me trouble at night. I can't figure on that, but it's a kind of moon-blindness that I have. The product of those whores I told you about. I can see shapes, but I can't get the distinctness of a thing. It's like there's sleep in my eyes or someone has rubbed oil over them."

"You shoot better on instinct than most men shoot by plan and practice."

"In my line of work, which is mostly gambling, being a good shot is only part of it. Weapons that are finely tuned and oiled and have proper ammunition are what make the difference in living another day. I also load my own ball and powder and therefore have control of its quality."

He spoke with a certain enthusiasm, but there was behind it a weariness, like he was struggling up one last hill and hoping to get to the top so he could lie down.

"Try the dime, Nat. It will catch on the wind, but if you shoot at the shine, you'll hit it."

Bill flipped the dime for me. I used the LeMat, flipping the swivel in such a way I fired off the shotgun round, blasting that dime most likely around the world.

That made Bill laugh like a braying donkey. "That was some trick, Nat. Let me see that thing."

I handed it to him to look over, and when he was done, he said, "I ain't never seen nothing like that, ain't even heard of such."

I told him about the gun, all that Mr. Loving had told me.

"That's interesting," Bill said, "but now let's see how you do without a trick."

I reverted to my Colt. I tried to remember all the tips Mr. Loving had given me, the main one being point that pistol like a finger. First time I pointed at that dime I might as well have left the pistol in my leather-lined pocket I missed so bad. I told Bill I had been trying to hit a cloud, which made him laugh. Second time I made the shot without too much thought and sent the dime spinning off my bullet. I think it was one of the more unique shots I had ever made.

That was it for wasting dimes. Bill said, "You don't need that kind of shooting to kill a man, but you do to win a contest. Fact is I can kill better than I can contest. That's as natural to me as the moving of my bowels. Targets, over a period of time—well, I start to get distracted by everyone else, start seeing the gals in the stands, get it in my mind I have to style for them, and so on. Shooting off the cuff, when needed, or out here shooting targets with a friend, not for a contest, I'm in my place. You, my companion, have the ability to do both and well. You are focused. That is a skill that is hard to teach. You have to come with it

in your bones. In a real gunfight the only way to survive is to not think
about winning, getting shot, or losing. You have to be in the instant.
Your only thought is your target. Pull it and point and gently squeeze
the trigger."

"Take your time slowly," I said.

"Exactly. And you are cool under fire, Nat. I have seen you in action.
That will win you more fights than a quick draw. I'm not telling you anything you don't already know and do."

I set some paper targets on sticks that raised them about three feet off
the ground; they had black bull's-eyes painted on them. At forty yards I
used my Winchester, pumping the shots with the special lever Mr. Loving had made. I hit six out of ten as fast as I could cock and fire, which
for fast shooting with a weapon like that is pretty good. Bill gave it a try
and couldn't hit a thing.

"I never was good with that sort of weapon," he said. "Too much haste
and uncertainty about it."

We packed our ears with cotton and burned through quite a few shells
and loads that day. It was some cost into my savings, as I was supplying
Bill with his fixings as well. I figured the trade-off was worth it, spending
time with one of the finest shootists that has ever walked the earth.

I practiced dry-firing my guns the rest of the week, except for going up
to our spot one afternoon with Win, day before the match. I had plenty
of live rounds with me. I wanted to fire a few shots to give me the feel of
live ammunition burning through the barrel, but not do it so much my
arms got tired of holding up my weapons. I didn't want to start tomorrow's shooting match with a liability of tired arms and a powder scorch
on my eyes.

I had taken the day off, becoming bolder about my job, knowing full
well I was leaving. There was also the fact that Swearengen was sponsor-
ing me for the match. I was representing the Gem. Swearengen, wanting
me to know how much he was on my side, said, "Look, you're going to
shoot in that match, I expect you to win. I don't think it matters if a

nigger or a white man wins, long as he represents himself and the Gem well."

This from a pimp.

I asked if he would like to front some money for ammunition or supply it directly, but here he drew the line. "No. I don't want to give you an unfair advantage against them that might have to purchase their own," he said.

He was quite the sport.

Win, who was sitting on a soft blue blanket watching me shoot, said, "You brought me up here to fire pistols?"

"Not entirely," I said, and I came over and sat beside her on the blanket.

"You're entering that shooting contest, aren't you?"

"I am." This was the first time I had admitted it to her.

"I figured as much. Why didn't you tell me?"

"Wanted it to be a surprise."

"Isn't much of one. It's been as obvious as those ears on your head."

"Not much gets by you."

"We been together a short time, but I know you, and I think you know me."

This was a lie. I never could completely figure Win out, and maybe that was the attraction, but I nodded because it seemed like the right and pleasant thing to do.

"You're making big plans, and I must believe they include me," she said.

"They do," I said. "And Madame."

I told her the whole thing, about Loving's place down in East Texas, the money I hoped to collect.

"A white man left you all that?"

"He was a white man, a good man, like a second father," I said, realizing I sounded like Bill; him talking about me being a credit to my race.

"I know precisely what you mean. Madame has been awfully good to me."

Our talk didn't go on too long before we were leaning in close, and my lips were touching hers. They trembled against mine like a struggling butterfly, and then they were soft and pressing.

She pulled me back on the blanket, said, "Show me how you can fire your own sweet pistol, but really take your time to aim and slowly pull the trigger."

"Yes, ma'am," I said.


Later that day I went over to Mann's No. 10, the saloon Bill liked to frequent and of course where I worked from time to time. It wasn't much of a place—a shack, really, with a few boards hammered together to make a bar. I went there to draw my last pay for emptying the spittoons and hoped to find Bill at a card table. When I got there, Bill wasn't in the room. There were three men at a table, and they eyed me the way you would a pile of buffalo chips on the floor. But no one said a thing to me, even though I came through the front door like a white man. They didn't mind seeing me empty spittoons, but they weren't crazy about me bellying up to the bar. I admit I was playing on Bill's friendship there, because they knew me and him was friendly, but I could live with that. It gave me a chance to rub my black ass in their face.

I was standing near a spittoon I had emptied many times, talking to the bartender, Snuffy. He was a tall fellow in a dirty white shirt and striped pants. His hair was oiled down and parted in the middle.

"Where am I gonna get another nigger on short notice?" Snuffy said.

"You might try an Indian or a cripple," I said. "Might even be a loose Mexican about, and I know there's some Chinamen."

"Ain't the same, as you was the best spittoon emptier I ever had," he said.

"Bullshit," I said. "A blind bear could empty a spittoon if it took a mind to it and was willing to wear an apron."

Snuffy studied on that a minute, perhaps trying to consider if a blind bear might be found around those parts—one that was willing to work, I mean.

"Ah, come on, Nat. You don't need to quit."

I had told him I was quitting but not that I was leaving Deadwood, and I kept it that way.

"Nope," I said. "I'm done."

Anyway, there I was taking the last of my back pay across the bar, and even ordering a sarsaparilla to irritate the men at the table, when Bill come strolling in. He was grinning when he saw me. He was dressed in blue pants and a leather jacket, had on a wide-brimmed, creamy white hat with a low crown. His revolvers was tucked in a wide red sash around his waist, near his hips, handles set forward so he could make with a cross-handed draw. Besides them two 1851 Navy pistols, he was carrying at the near center of his sash a Smith & Wesson Army .32 revolver with shiny bluing and rosewood grips. It wasn't a gun he carried often; guess you could say it was his dress gun. His hair was combed out smooth and long, and his mustache had been waxed lightly. On his left hip he had a large bowie knife in a sheath dangling from under his sash, fastened most likely to a belt. He was all dressed up and had no place to go.

"Nat," he said. "Let me stand you to a drink."

"Thanks, Bill. You know I'm only for sarsaparilla."

"That you are," he said. "It's a damn shameful girl's drink, but if you must have it, dear sweetie, I will order it, and if I pay for three in a row, you have to lift your skirt for me."

Bill, still grinning, leaned on the bar and propped his boot on the footrest beneath it. I could smell his breath, and it was stout as a mince pie; he had already been in the whiskey. He ordered us two swigs—me a refreshed sarsaparilla and him his usual poison, although from time to time he broke tradition and had a Champagne flip with fruit juice.

Snuffy, now that Bill had entered the room, was stepping lively, trying to look like he was the most pleasant, ass-kissing fellow on earth. He poured us a set. Me and Bill placed our backs against the bar, holding our drinks, looking over at the card table.

Bill was watching the game intently. He was a man who loved his gambling. He wasn't near as good as some folks claimed, but he could play cards well enough to keep himself in whiskey and bullets, a steak now and again. I recognized the men at the table, including the owner of the place, Mr. Mann.

"Any minute now my shadow, Broken Nose, will come through that door," Bill said. "He will most likely be snorting a little wind on account of when I first noticed he was trailing my scent I picked up my step. He will come in and act like he is my best friend that ever was."

At just that moment, Jack did come in, blowing a little. He blinked a few times, seen Bill and me leaning against the bar, and came over. He stood in front of us, his bad eye wandering about in his head as if on a secret mission. He had on a ragged coat, a moth-eaten hat, and his boot heels had laid over on the sides due to wear.

Jack said, "Wild Bill, how are you, sir?"

"I am tight with life," Bill said. "And how are you, Broken Nose?"

It seemed like an unnecessary insult, but Bill could be cruel.

"I am fine, sir."

"Can I stand you to a drink?" Bill said.

"Well, sir, you have been most kind, and I could use one."

There was something about Jack's words that didn't go with his tone or the look on his face. It was like he was trying to gleefully accept a turd and pretend it was a diamond.

"Pour this man a drink," Bill said. "Some of the cheap stuff."

"Yes, sir," said the bartender. He brought out a bottle of whiskey, so watered you could see through it. He poured Jack a drink in a fly-specked glass. Jack took it and downed it. He brought out money of his own, said, "Give me another, and stand Wild Bill here, and even the nigger. Make it the good stuff."

That went all over me, but Bill reached out and gently touched my arm. "Enjoy your drink, Nat."

Bill picked up his glass when it was filled, said, "To the Union, and to the freedom of slaves. And to the snake that bit you. And may even drunkards, beggars, and cripples be saved by the all-merciful God. Unless they need killing."

Jack's hand trembled, but he dosed himself with his liquor, and Bill did the same. My glass had been filled with liquor this time, which I let be.

"Gentlemen," Bill said, "and Jack, I am about to play cards."

With that Bill moved away from us, over to the table. The chair available had its back to the entranceway, and Bill said to the man across the table, a fellow by the name of Charlie Rich, "Sir, would you change chairs with me? I have an aversion to sitting with my back to the door."

"So do I," said the man. It surprised me a little, as most folks were quick to give Bill his way. I remembered that table of men that night in the Gem, how they had given us their table so we could have a private talk. I didn't know if Bill's reputation was slipping or if Charlie Rich was just one of his constant card buddies, but it made me kind of proud of that fellow for standing up like that against the fastest and best shot there was.

Bill was taken aback, but he didn't want to show it. Pride. That damn savage thing, which can be as much a burden as a quality, took over. "Very well," Bill said. "But I sure would prefer that spot."

"As do I," Rich said. There wasn't nothing mean in his tone, and he smiled when he said it. I think he knew he had Bill over a barrel, in that if Bill protested he would seem to be a whiner, and if he insisted he would appear to be a bully.

I glanced at Jack. He was taking a certain delight in this performance.

Bill nodded, took the seat with his back to the door. I turned to the bar, ordered another sarsaparilla for myself and nothing for Jack. As the bartender was pouring it, I seen an image in my glass. It was just a blurry reflection, but it was the man across the table, Charlie Rich, the one who had refused Bill his seat, and I can't say for sure, but it seemed to me that blurry image nodded to Jack.

As I turned, Jack stepped forward, pulled a hidden .45 pistol from under his coat, said, "Damn you and your cheap charity. Take that, you son of a bitch," and fired a shot that struck Bill in the back of the head. Blood sprayed from Bill, and I seen and heard the fellow to Bill's right yell out in pain; the bullet had gone through Bill and hit him in the wrist.

Bill tipped forward with his face on the table, his open eyes turned toward me. That wild spark he had in them was already gone. His arm hung loose, and his hand dropped the cards it held. In that quick moment, them lying there on the floor, an incomplete hand, I seen they was aces and eights. The last card had yet to be drawn from the deck. Bill's body slumped, and his weight dragged his face across the table, and he tumbled to the floor.

I came unfrozen, glanced at Jack. He lifted his pistol to shoot at me, but it hit on an empty cylinder or a dead load. He yelled out, "I have killed the son of a bitch," and bolted.

I threw my sarsaparilla glass at Jack as he ran and missed, shattering the glass against the wall by the door. Then it was a footrace.

I come out of Mann's hauling as fast as I could go, and that damn short-legged McCall that couldn't keep up with Wild Bill was damn sure moving briskly along the boardwalks and planks that was draped across the muddy streets. Racing after him, I thought of pulling one of my pistols and plugging him, but I couldn't bring myself to shoot him from behind, though that was exactly what he had done to Bill. I also thought it bad form to take a shot at him and accidentally shoot a child off a stick horse or some such.

I stomped over a long plank across a wide puddle, and damned if I didn't slip and bury my leg knee-deep in mud, about two pounds of it seeping into my boot. By the time I got my leg yanked up and was back in the race, my boot was heavy with mud. Jack had done hit the other side of the street and was running with that pistol still in his hand. He was yelling, "I killed Wild Bill. I killed him."

I was gaining on him as he reached the open door of a butcher shop. He acted as if he might dart inside, perhaps to run through and out the back, but a leg poked out from a doorway and stuck itself right in front of Jack, who did a tumble over it and landed in such a way, on top of his head, his hat come down near over his eyes. Then that leg kicked out again, and this time it caught Jack in the teeth. I seen it was Colorado Charlie Utter that had done the leg work. He gave Jack another kick, this one causing the little bastard to spit out a tooth. Jack was crawling, trying to get to the pistol he'd dropped, but another man come along, scooped it up, put it in his coat pocket, and walked off with it.

It was then that a bunch of men jumped on Jack, some of them coming out of the butcher shop. Jack was pulled up and hit a few times, then carried away in such a hustle that his feet wasn't even touching ground.

Charlie was pulling his pistol, and had not a handful of men grabbed him he'd have shot Jack sure as rain is wet. Some of those men looked at me, knowing I was Bill's friend, but there wasn't any need. The heat had gone out of me. I was breathing heavy, and I leaned on the wall.

Jack was gone then, and Charlie stumbled over to me with tears in his eyes. "Say he's a lying bastard, Nat."

"I can't," I said. "I seen it done with my own eyes," and I went about laying out the details as I knew them. Before I was even finished telling my story, Charlie had sunk to the boardwalk, his back against a storefront. I sat down beside him and pulled off my boot and dumped the mud out of it right there on the boardwalk. I was daring a man to come to me with an angry attitude about it, and it was a good thing none did.

Bill may have been a preening peacock, a little mean-spirited, and willing to screw a dead cow if he was drunk, but he had been my friend and had treated me decent all the time I had known him.

I decided right then and there to put the shooting match out of my mind, gather up everything I had, including Win and Madame, give my good-byes to Cullen and Wow, all them other China girls, and head out for the great beyond; anything to get away from that hellhole they called Deadwood.

# 20

I was sick to my stomach, and me and Charlie spent a few moments together cussing McCall's name with oaths that would have made a preacher and a schoolteacher want to put a gun to their heads, then Charlie went to find out what was going on. I went wandering along the streets for quite a time, not really going anywhere, stopping now and again to lean on a building wall, and then I would lurch back into the street and walk some more. Finally I climbed up the hill to the shack where Win and Madame was.

Win and Madame was outside, as they was doing laundry and had their big wash pot boiling on a fire of broken lumber and sticks. Win seen my face and came running over to me. When she did my feet went out from under me, and I sat down on the ground. I don't know how to explain it, cause me and Bill wasn't the best of friends, but we had a bond in blood and gun smoke, and that's a kind of bond can't be explained; it fits tighter than a hub on a wheel.

"It's Bill," I said. "He's done been killed by a coward."

Win squatted down by me, and Madame came over, sat on the ground beside me, and threw an arm over my shoulders; it really felt good. I hadn't had that kind of motherly attention since my ma died. Madame pulled me in close, and Win held me, too. I started crying. I wasn't caterwauling or nothing, but I was crying, and this went on for some time. I figure, looking back on it, I wasn't just crying for Bill but for my pa and ma and Mr. Loving. They all just wadded up together like bread dough in my mind. I felt as if everything that had ever been worth anything had just been sold cheap at auction. I couldn't hold back the tears.

Between sobs and wiping my eyes with the back of my hand, I told them all that had happened and how it was that I wanted to head out no later than tomorrow, tonight if possible, and the shooting match be damned.

I hadn't no more than finished telling this when I looked down and seen Charlie Utter in a fresh set of clothes. For a moment, way he was dressed, his long hair and all, I thought he was Wild Bill come back to life. I wiped my eyes quick and watched him slog up the hill.

He come up and took off his hat and nodded politely to the women, said, "Would you ladies mind too much if I had a private word with Nat here?"

They agreed as they would be good with that and went back to their laundry. But when I looked at them, I seen both was watching me close, just to make sure I didn't come to pieces and need recollecting.

Charlie's face was red, especially around the nose, and his eyes was bleary. "Walk with me, Nat?" he said.

"You have duded up," I said as I followed him down the hill toward Main Street.

"I have. I went over and saw the body at the saloon, and me and some of the boys carried it over to the barber's for cleaning, and from there we have plans to bring it out to a tent I've put up. I'll watch over him, and tomorrow there'll be the burial. Me and some others have chipped in for a coffin and some funeral doings."

"I can chip in as well," I said.

"That is appreciated," he said. "But let me tell you the chip you need to give."

"All right."

We was down the hill now, wandering along Main Street. Word had gotten out about Bill, and the air around us was buzzing with it. There was people practically swarming down the street, yakking about what had happened as they went, talking almost all at once, rushing out of alleys and stores, fluttering down from the high-perch streets thick as flies in a bowl of molasses.

"Look at those goddamn vultures," Charlie said. "If I didn't have him hid out in the barbershop, they'd be in Mann's Number Ten pulling his hair out and yanking the threads from his clothes, trying to dip handkerchiefs in his blood for souvenirs. They'd steal the boots and drawers off him if they could."

Charlie paused to gaze at them with his face twisted up, and then he relaxed it and looked at me. "That shooting match. Bill told me you were a part of that, correct?"

"The desire for it has flown," I said. "Why do you ask?"

"Cause we wanted to give Bill's widow something lest he look like he died poor, which in fact he did."

"I see," I said.

"We have him a funeral now, and a coffin, and he'll be buried tomorrow before he ripens and swells, but it would seem right for him to have had a bit of a financial gathering for Agnes, who, by the way, I had no truck with and no interest in. I don't know how much dearness Bill had for her, either, other than telling me about how flexible she was. But she is still his wife, and we would prefer Bill not die under circumstances that might have him considered a pauper."

"He seemed well stocked when we met at the saloon," I said.

"He liked to make a show," Charlie said. "The gambling mostly emptied his pockets. He had a few dollars in his pants, a few on the card table, but those have gone to the funeral, along with what the rest of us tossed in. Well, you see how it looks."

I didn't care how it looked, but I did care about Bill.

"So how does this tie in with the shooting match?" I asked.

"We would like you to try and win that," he said.

"Didn't plan on trying to lose it," I said. "But now I'm not planning at all."

"If you win the prize, we thought you could donate that to be sent to Agnes, like Bill had been saving it up, and we will all make side bets in a way that you'll make some real money for yourself as well. You will get your share from the bets; Bill's widow will get her share from the prize money."

"Who is the 'we' you mentioned?"

He named some men; some of them I knew, some I didn't.

"You may be misplacing your faith," I said.

"Bill had faith in you, and that's good enough for me," he said.

"Some days are better than others," I said. "I don't know the kind of day I'll have if I shoot."

Upon Bill's death, my confidence had taken a departure. Before that, I was stuffed full of it.

"I can take that chance, and my friends can, too," he said.

"Very well," I said.

Moments before I had planned to walk away with nothing, forget the whole thing, head out of Deadwood. Now I was going to be shooting not only for myself but also for a friend, too, even if he was white and dead. I told Charlie, "Bill made it so I could compete, but there are some who might take exception to the hue of my skin now that he's not here to provide support."

"No, they won't," Charlie said. "I can guarantee that. Any row comes about, I will be there, and so will some others. It would be unwise for you to be excluded."

"Very well, then," I said.

"One more thing. Bill told me about the one he said you called Ruggert, about him and his henchmen. My guess is he may have been behind Bill's death. He may have wanted him out of the way, as he would have stood up with you, and in a straightforward fight he would have been a load. Damn. I can't believe Bill sat with his back to the door. Anyway, that Ruggert was involved is only a guess, but there is more than a strong rumor that he has paid for your competition."

I gave him a blank look.

"Bronco Bob," Charlie said.

"Who is Bronco Bob?"

"He's a famous trick shooter. Famous to everyone but you, apparently, and he's not just one of them that uses devices to make things seem like they're more than they are. Doesn't load his revolvers with buckshot, for instance. He's a hell of a shooter in the real world. Travels about, makes his day-to-day on it. Bill would have got around to telling you about it eventually. He heard about it from McCall, his assassin, but he didn't know what stock to put in it. Wasn't sure if Broken Nose was playing him or not. But I seen Bronco Bob's wagon roll into town right before Bill got killed, saw him pulling up at the livery. He's over at the hotel. So it's quite a coincidence, is it not?"

"Why would McCall warn Bill about it?"

"That is a confusion, to be sure," Charlie said. "One moment I think Jack wanted to be Bill, another he wanted to be his best pard, and another he wanted to trip him up, which in the end we have to say he did. I think Ruggert may have paid him. And there's them other fellas. The one Bill said was called Gobbler and the little one."

"Golem," I said. "Not Gobbler."

"Golem?" Charlie said. "What in hell is that?"

"Bill didn't tell you?"

"If he had, would I be asking you as much?"

"Reckon not." So I told him what Bill had told me, though there was little material there to make much of a story from.

"Them Jews have some queer ideas about things, sounds to me," Charlie said, "but if I know what a golem is or don't, I know who that big son of a bitch is that goes by the name. And I know that little son of a dog turd with him."

"They call him Weasel," I said.

"Weasel it is, then. Bottom line, me and Bill's friends will be there to check your back, make sure a bullet don't nest in it. The shooting match, how that comes out, that's up to you. If the cards don't land in your favor, I know you will have done your best. I trust Bill's judgment that much. But that's all there is in a nutshell. That is the favor I'm asking you. Money for Bill's widow."

"I've done agreed."

"I wanted you to know the perils of it, though. I have built up good how you are protected, and how we will have your back, but I should add as a measure of honesty, nothing is certain."

"I know that from experience," I said. "But with you at the lead, it is certain enough."

I stuck out my hand.

We shook. "You come and see Bill laid down tomorrow," he said.

He crossed the street, and I started back to Win.

Before I made it there, I seen Cullen coming toward me at a goodly clip, passing the crowd that was hustling to Mann's saloon.

He caught up to me. "I heard, Nat. I know he was a friend. I'm sorry."

"Ain't no going backwards now. The killer has been nabbed."

"This is a bad time to ask, you and me being friends and all, but are you still planning to shoot tomorrow? I put considerable money on you."

"I will be shooting," I said.

"Good," he said. "It's how I figure to make my dowry for Wow."

"You need one?"

"No, but we need money, so I thought I'd call it that."

"Come with me," I said.

He walked with me back to where Win and Madame were. Actually, they had all met, but I took the time now to properly introduce him. When the visit had reached its natural course, I kissed Win on the cheek and went away with Cullen.

I said, "Ain't you working today?"

"Wild Bill getting killed has kind of made it a holiday," he said. "Not that I'm suggesting it's a good thing, though I can use the time off."

Arriving at my place, I took Cullen inside, and we sat down on the floor. "I'm going to give you some papers to hold for me, at least for a

short time," I said. Then I explained about Mr. Loving and the arrangements he had made.

Wild Bill's funeral was a big ballyhoo.

At Charlie's camp, under a tepee-style tent, they set up a black-cloth-
lined coffin on wooden blocks with the guest of honor in it. Charlie laid a
Winchester rifle beside him, said it was his favorite shooting piece. This
was a lie. Bill always carried revolvers and was right proud of them, far
more than any long shooter. I think Charlie felt he needed to lay Bill out
in style, with some kind of weapon beside him, but didn't want them
fine and famous shooting irons of Bill's to go to waste in the ground. It
kind of bothered me about the Winchester, to speak frankly, as it seemed
false to Bill's memory.

Folks paraded inside the tent and around the coffin. Everyone, no
matter sex or color, was let in. There was even a few dogs wandering
about, and Charlie had to grab a cat off the edge of the coffin and throw
it under the back of the tent, as it was sniffing at the corpse.

After a lot of flapdoodle was said, some of it accurate, the body was
toted to a hillside, where Bill was put down. Some more flapdoodle was
said by a couple of fellows, one of them a weepy Chinaman none of us
understood. He apparently knew Bill, and it was whispered that he sup-
plied our man with opium. I don't know if there was truth to it or not.
Charlie come up when the Chinaman got finished, or was made to finish, and said some heartfelt words. Then a board he had carved on was
put up at the head of the grave. Charlie had whittled into it Bill's age and
about him being murdered by the assassin Jack McCall. One man suggested that "assassin" be changed to "dick sucker," but Charlie was against
it. It would have required an entirely new board.

The grave was covered with dirt, and that was all there was for the
great Wild Bill Hickok.

This is off the trail a little, at least as far as the layout in time, but I
thought I'd put it here cause I learned about it later. Jack McCall was let

off by a miners' court, even though he snuck up behind Bill and shot him in the head and there was witnesses to what was clearly cold-blooded murder. I was one of them witnesses, but I was not called to testify. I didn't even know there was testifying to be done. It all happened quick and was done with.

In his defense Jack said that his brother had been killed by Bill back in Abilene, Kansas, but he had nothing on that but his word. That's why I think he had been paid by Ruggert and knew how safe he was because some of the jury, such that it was, had probably been paid, too. Jack got off, and you can bet he got gone. Had Charlie not been so broken up about the funeral and needing to be there to protect me at the shooting match, I have no doubt he would have snuck off after him, left his bones out there in the wilds for grass to grow over.

Getting off didn't do Jack no good, though. Later on, in Wyoming, he bragged about the deed. The Wyoming folks, bless them, didn't consider the Deadwood trial a real trial, as it wasn't an incorporated town then. They nabbed him and tried him and found him guilty and hanged him. I hope with thirty pieces of silver in his pocket.

I went to my room and sat alone. I cleaned my weapons again, as if they needed it, laid out all my ammunition. I thought about things Mr. Loving had taught me. I tried to do as he said I should do anytime I became overwhelmed, and that was to think about nothing at all. Course, the more I tried that the more I thought about every damn thing you can imagine. Finally I settled on thinking about being up in the hayloft in Mr. Loving's barn, looking out the opening at the countryside in the springtime, when the trees grew thick along the creek bank and there was wildflowers and the limbs of the trees got filled with bright-colored birds.

It was with that thinking that I found my peace.

# 21

I planned to shoot my Colts and the Winchester, but I carried the LeMat for backup, not wanting at any point to be with an empty gun. The Colts would be better for target shooting and more accurate, and for long shooting you couldn't beat that Winchester.

When I come out of my little room for the last time, there on the dirt street was Charlie and some others, about ten men if I remember my count. There was Tater Joe Wingchip, as he was known, and Smooth Ride Smith, known by that name because he was always falling off horses, and Frank Penn, and some others I knew just a little, mostly by name or by sight.

"We come to walk with you, so as you won't get lonely," Charlie said.

"I am a mite lonesome," I said, "and would enjoy the company. Shall we stroll, gentlemen?"

They gathered up around me and marched with me through the streets. There was people watching as we came, and I'm not sure what they made of a wad of white men with a darky in the center of them. Maybe they thought I was being led to a hanging.

Finally we arrived where the match was. There was a banner stretched across the street, right close to where it broadened and fanned toward a great hill of dark dirt. The banner read simple enough: DEADWOOD

SHOOTING MATCH. The shooting range was plenty wide and plenty deep. There was ropes stretched across it on poles at either end. I wasn't sure what that was about, as nothing had been explained beforehand, outside of there was going to be targets, and some of the shooting would take place on horseback.

There was also on the ground at the far end some stacks of bricks, and on those was big jugs with corks in them. I knew what that was all about. I counted ten across. They was bigger jugs with bigger corks than Bill and I had shot, but they was also set back a mite more in distance. There was a youthful man there, string-lean to the point of being mostly bones, wearing a checkered coat and bowler hat. He was introduced to me as Checkers Chauncey, which led me to believe that coat stayed on his back a lot. He was the one that ran the match, though he was not a judge, this being the job of six well-dressed men, three on one side, three on the other, all of them seated on stiff wooden chairs with cushions on the seats.

While I was signing in, some other men came up, and pretty soon there was ten of us signed. Then there was a murmur in the crowd. I looked back and seen people parting to let a little fellow come through. He had on a tall white hat with a wide brim. He was broad-shouldered but small everywhere else, except he had big hands and long fingers. I noticed that even as he was coming from a distance. His face was long and friendly-looking. He had dark hair and a mustache and a beard to match. He was wearing a milky leather jacket with fringe, dark stovepipe pants, and high boots that matched the jacket. He wore a vest with all manner of colorful curlicues on it. Around his waist was two black leather holsters of the sort Mr. Loving had made. The pistols he was freighting on his hips was pearl-handled Remingtons.

A ragged, redheaded boy, probably fifteen or sixteen, was running alongside him and had long leather bags slung over each shoulder on straps; the bottoms of the bags was banging against his heels as he ran.

The man signed his papers for the match, studied on me with fine, clear eyes, and with that boy following with the bags come over and stuck out his hand. Charlie and the others stood close to me. I noticed they had their hands on their pistols in case things went in the wrong direction.

On instinct, I handed my rifle to Charlie, took the man's hand, and shook it.

"I take by the tint of your hide you are Nat Love," he said.

I agreed I was the same.

"I am Bronco Bob, and this here is Tim."

"Jim," the boy said.

"I will call you Tim," Bronco Bob said, then turned back to me. "I have been hired by Mr. Ruggert to shoot against you, meaning he has covered a number of bets in my favor. I have heard a few say you are quite the shot, though none of them can claim to have actually seen you shoot. I think their judgments are based on the say of the lately departed Wild Bill Hickok, God bless his gambling, whoring soul. I knew him well at one time, back in Abilene. I was just Bob Brennen then."

"There are nine other men shooting here tonight," I said. "They may prove to be of an ability better than either of us."

"If the rumors are correct concerning you—and those about me are quite true, I assure you—it will be up to you and me. Maybe one other, Prairie Dog Dave Jiggers. I shot against him once, a year back, in Fort Smith. He is no slouch."

"Fortune has a way of shifting in near any direction," I said.

"It does, at that. But them that prepare have better fortune than those who don't. Gun shooting is a science, but it is also an art, and those of us who are artists do better in the long run than those that are merely scientists. They know how it works and which way to point it, but we feel how it works and feel which way to point it."

"That so?" I said.

"Creativity is far more important than skill alone, though you got to have one for the other to matter. That big loop rifle is quite nice. Made for you?"

"In a manner of speaking," I said.

"Let me add that though I have been hired to shoot against you, it's nothing personal. It's my profession. I would have been here anyway. I have a piece of the side bets provided in my name by Mr. Ruggert if I win. And I intend to. But that is where our contest ends."

"Very well," I said.

"And if I should lie about such, may these men crowding around me blow my head off."

"We will," Tater said. "And then shit in your mouth, if you got a mouth left."

Bronco Bob looked at Tater, said, "That could be most unpleasant for me if you fail to do them in the order suggested."

He tipped his big ole hat, and he and the boy went stepping away from us.

"What do you think, Nat?" Charlie asked, handing me back my rifle.

"I think he speaks truly," I said. "There was no need for him to speak to me at all."

"To throw you off guard," Tater said, and the other men nodded and grumbled about for a few seconds.

"I take him at his word," I said.

"Good enough," Charlie said, "but if you're wrong, and he kills you, know we will take care of him and bury you some place nice, but with a service less fine than Bill's. Another funeral like that and we'll have to take up honest work to pay for it."

"I suppose that's some sort of comfort," I said.

By this time that Chauncey fellow was calling for all the shooters to come to the scratch line. Charlie and the others wished me well, and I went over to where the other shooters had gathered.

"Now, this here is going to be as fair as if God himself was here to take score and say how things was done," Chauncey said. "I want that figured on right now, provided any of you think you're going to get away with buckshot in a pistol or some such fool shenanigans. Me and the judges is wise to all that. I'm the referee, and I will call any stepping over the line right away. For that matter, I'll call anything I think of as unfair. The judges will make conclusions on who has shot what if there should be any confusion or disagreement. Their word is final. We ask you to leave, you leave, or we'll all give you a whipping. Everybody understand that?"

We all agreed we did.

"Now, what I'm going to do is put some slips of paper we got here, stick them in my hat, and you're going to draw numbers as to when you shoot. Understood?"

Again we all agreed.

Chauncey took the slips of paper, which he had produced from his coat, took off his hat, and dropped the slips inside it. He held the hat about chin high and one at a time we all reached in and drew from it. I got the number 4. Prairie Dog drew 2. Bronco Bob drew 8. Number 1 was a big blustery fellow with leather holsters and his guns stuck down in them in such a way that if he had to pull them it would be like reaching into a sack to find them. I figured him to be out of business right quick. He didn't know how to carry guns, then most likely he didn't know how to shoot them. The others drew until all ten of us had numbers.

I scanned around, searching for Win and Madame, finally located them to the back of the match on a rise, sitting on the ground on a blanket. They had a good view of things. While I was looking at them, I seen Cullen come up with Wow, them other China girls walking in behind them. They had blankets, too. They rolled them out on the ground near Win and Madame, and I could see Wow and the China girls was introducing themselves to Win, as they hadn't all met her. It did my heart good to see them up there.

I glanced around some more, seen Ruggert had a seat in a chair in the front row of the blocked-off street. I hadn't noticed him at first, there being a crowd of men standing in front of him, but now they had all gone to find their spots, and the view was clear. I seen Weasel and Golem coming along through a split in the chairs that had been set out, and they was followed by seven or eight other men. It was easy to see they was all together, and all of them had the same sour face of men who had been paid to do something distasteful. I had an idea what that might be.

Charlie eased up beside me, said, "We see them. You concentrate on your shooting, and we'll concentrate on them."

"Thanks," I said.

We was all called to the scratch line, and according to number took our places in front of our targets—the corked bottles, about forty feet away. That's a damn good shot for a pistol.

"Way we do is we go by numbers, and if there is any man in line don't know numbers, let him speak now," Chauncey said.

A man standing to my left, who looked old enough to have lived when Methuselah was a child, said, "I don't know writing, and I can't add too good, but I know numbers. I know my number."

"Then you didn't need to say nothing, now, did you?" Chauncey said.

"Guess I didn't," the man said and looked forlorn, having brought up his lack of certain skills to no good purpose.

"It ain't nothing," I said. "I can't add so good, neither."

He worked his mouth into a grin. "Lots of people can't," he said.

"There you have it," I said.

"Now," Chauncey said. "Everyone knows their target, which if you are in line proper is the one in front of you. We will begin with the first round. Everyone has to make the first round or they are out. No one survives the first round, we have another round for all you lousy shots. No one makes the second round, then we retire for the afternoon in mortification. Understood?"

There was some nervous laughs along the line, but we all agreed we understood.

"You got to hit the cork, which may bust the bottle," Chauncey said. "But if the bottle busts and the cork ain't hit, it don't count. Any quarrel, we look at the cork. Number one, get ready."

I took cotton balls from my pockets and stuffed them in my ears and took a deep breath. I was ready as I was going to get.

* * *

Number 1 couldn't have hit his own chin with his fist. He was out, and by the second round it was down to those who was going to be there for a while. I was among them, of course. So was Prairie Dog and Bronco Bob and a little fellow I had never seen before, number 10. He could shoot really well and was always looking back at the crowd between shots, showing them the tobacco he was chewing when he grinned.

We set to shooting ten targets apiece, still corks, but not in bottles this time. They was tied to strings dangling from those stretched-across ropes. You had to hit six to stay in for the next round. Second round you had to do better. My Colts shot smooth, and I hit nine out of ten my first run, the far one on the right being a little off-angle for me, and I think maybe the wind kicked up a bit.

The shooter who didn't know his ciphers had made it through round one, but that second round of cork shooting put him out of the game.

Prairie Dog hit eight.

The little guy with the chewing tobacco hit ten, and so did Bronco Bob, who was as cool a shooter as I have ever seen. Both of them had outshot me by one cork, and I found that matter surprising, but then again they didn't have the angle I had, and the wind hadn't been working as hard when they took their turns. It was the only thing I could figure.

"That's all right," I heard Charlie yell. "You did fine. As for them others, even a blind pig can find a corncob now and again."

I looked toward the hill where Win was. She and the others all gave me high signs and smiles, except Cullen, who looked like a man who might have started to think he had bet too much on the wrong shooter.

Now it was time for the long guns. Dimes was set up at a distance slightly farther than the corks. They was set with their edges toward us, between grooves in wooden blocks weighted down with rocks. We only got one shot and one dime. That would be the nut-cutting shot and would lead to who was in and who was out. If only one man was standing, the match was over. If not, then it moved to more rapid firing and horseback shooting.

The tobacco chewer, whom I thought of as Tobacco Mouth, was first. He leveled his Springfield and popped off his shot without so much as breathing, and damn if he didn't send that dime spinning. It was Prairie Dog's turn then, and he was more deliberate about it. He was shooting a Winchester, same as me, though it was of a more recent model. He fired and hit his dime, turned, and grinned at me. I noticed he trembled slightly, and he was probably a little surprised he had made his shot.

I was next, and, like Prairie Dog, I took my time. Mr. Loving told me that the idea was to make your target seem big as the moon in your gun sights. I aimed down that barrel, but that dime's edge was mighty thin to me, nowhere near big as the moon. I carefully pulled off my shot.

I sent the dime spinning. I was still in.

Bronco Bob took a fresh rifle from one of the bags the boy was toting for him, a Henry—what some called a Yellow Boy due to its coloring. Bob hadn't no more than pulled that rifle from the bag than he wheeled. With the stock of the rifle on his hip, a position that couldn't never be worth much, or so I thought, he fired and hit that dime as sure as my name isn't really Nat Love.

"Damn," I heard Prairie Dog say. It had come out of him without him knowing it was going to. Just beyond him, I saw the tobacco wad fall out of Tobacco Mouth's piehole.

I felt weak in the knees.

"We move on," said Chauncey, "though from the look of things, anybody whose name ain't Bronco Bob is pretty much ass-poked."

We was at the stage of the match where it would come fast and furious. This was the throwing of glass balls and bottles for us to shoot.

We started with bottles.

They had a big colored man throwing, maybe twice my size, and he could really wing those bottles. They went high up and away from the sun. That was the idea, to keep the sun out of our eyes. We was to fire at them in turn. None of us had any problem with the bottles. I think we shot about fifty of them, and by that point my Winchester had heated up so much I could hardly hold it. Prairie Dog's Winchester was warm, too, and I saw him trade it off to a man in the crowd who was holding two rifles for him. Tobacco Mouth's Springfield, being a one-shot, one-load affair, wasn't heating up the same, but we had to take more time for him to load and shoot. He would shoot, load again, shoot, load again, shoot. He'd shoot till he missed, then when the rest of us had a turn we fired more quickly, therefore the heat-up.

Charlie watched me shift my rifle back and forth in my hands, came over and handed me a fresh Winchester. I was happy for this but worried as well. It wasn't my rifle, and I hadn't had occasion to sight it in or learn its personality, as Mr. Loving used to say.

It was time to shoot at the glass balls.

Glass balls was done same as bottles. You got your turn, and the tosser throwed them till you missed.

Bronco Bob, having edged us all out by a couple of points, got first shot. The colored man threw the glass balls for him, with Bronco Bob yelling "Throw" between shots, and damn if he didn't hit all ten that was thrown for him.

Tobacco Mouth was up next, and let me tell you it was quite the boat to China waiting on him to reload his single-shot weapon, and he was nervous about it. He fumbled around like his fingers was sausages. I think that shot Bronco Bob made from the hip earlier had flummoxed him a smidgen.

The crowd had started talking during the reloading, and Checkers Chauncey yelled at them. "Shut the hell up and let the man concentrate."

The first six shots went well, but by the seventh Tobacco Mouth started to miss and missed all the shots thrown thereafter. It was like he had gone blind. When it was over, he was given the ax, so to speak. As he walked off the field everyone yelled and clapped for him, and then he was swallowed up by the crowd and I didn't see him again.

I went next, and, like Bronco Bob, I hit all ten, shooting them out of the air as fast as I could yell for them. Prairie Dog passed muster too.

A break was taken, and Win brought water down the hill and gave me some. Ruggert had not moved from his chair, and the way he looked at me it was as if he was trying to set me on fire with his eyes. I seen some of his men in the crowd, too, though how many there actually was I had no idea. They could have been scattered all throughout. As Win walked back up the hill, I tried to not think about them. If I was to win this thing, I had to tuck them kind of worries away.

Charlie brought my Winchester back to me, took the other, and then we was shooting again. This time there was twenty balls to be thrown, and since we all had repeaters, the match moved more quickly.

Up went those balls. The three of us took our turns. We all hit ten out of ten, and then the next ten. Twenty balls thrown for each of us. Twenty balls hit. We looked at one another and grinned.

Bronco Bob traded out for a new rifle. It was a sort I had never seen before, but it had the general look of a Winchester. It was thinner and longer, the stock being cut down to a smaller size. I could tell it was light by the way the boy handed it to him.

"Thank you, Tim," Bronco Bob said.

"Jim," said the boy.

"As I said, you will be called Tim."

We all returned to the scratch line. The cotton in my ears was sweaty, and when I plucked it out to put fresh in, I seen the cotton was dark with gun smoke. Putting in fresh, I cradled my rifle in my arms, letting my arms dangle as low as possible. I was starting to get a pinch in my shoulder, a stitched feeling in the middle of my back, and my neck hurt, to boot.

"All right, now," Chauncey said. "The balls is going to be thrown from a farther-out position, twenty-five of them. There can be no pause between shots, and no need of it, as you have repeaters. Is that understood?"

We all understood.

Bronco Bob went first, and this time he missed on his first shot. It was like seeing Zeus miss with a thunderbolt. After that he hit all the balls tossed. Like Bronco Bob, I only missed one. Prairie Dog hit the first three, missed the fourth, hit the fifth, and then he wasn't worth killing after that. I could tell it was his arms that had worn out, not his aim. He was having trouble keeping the rifle lifted.

That was it for him. He come over and shook our hands and told us what fine competitors we was and how on another day he felt he could have outshot us, and then he moved into the crowd amid much yelling and hooting and clapping.

It was me and Bronco Bob.

We was given a half-hour break, and during that time I asked Cullen to go saddle up Satan and bring him around. The last round was the horse ride, shooting at targets on sticks on either side of the street. This meant the path was cleared to the sides, and the targets was set solidly.

Cullen collected Satan and saddled him, without saddlebags or any unnecessary trappings, and he was led up to me. The crowd made with a sighing sound he was so shiny and black, and he was trotting and tossing his head as if he knew he was on show. And he probably did.

Then came that redheaded boy leading Bronco Bob's horse, a big white stallion that might not have been a great long runner but was bound to be good for the short run and probably had the stamina of a mule.

Me and Bronco Bob shook hands and wished each other luck, which was lies through our teeth. He gave his rifle to the boy, and I gave mine to Cullen. I checked my pistols and their loads. For the time being, Bronco Bob held pat, left his in the holsters. When we was satisfied, we mounted up. The crowd split, and chairs was moved farther apart so we could ride two abreast. As we rode up to the starting line, I passed Ruggert and looked down on him. He glared up at me, then spat on the ground, then stared at me again. The glare in his eyes was the same as that day I saw his wife's ass, and now here I was, a colored man riding on a big horse well above his white head; it was almost more than he could stand. For a moment I thought he might pull a gun from under his coat and go at me. I know I wanted to shoot him. Instead I tipped my hat to him as I rode by.

# 22

Me and Bronco Bob took our places side by side.

Chauncey had come along the street to be in front of us. He said, "Bronco, you will shoot to your right, and you colored fellow will shoot to your left."

"Nat," said Bronco Bob to Chauncey. "His name is Nat."

This from the man who couldn't remember the name of the boy he'd hired to tote his weapons.

"What?" said Chauncey.

"His name isn't Colored Fellow, it's Nat. And he is on top bill with me. We are the only ones left, and we have both earned our position, and he deserves the respect of his name. His name is Nat. I'd like to hear you say it."

Chauncey nodded, not wishing to bother a man with a loaded revolver in his hand.

"Nat," Chauncey said, "you will shoot to your left. And then when you come back riding this way, the arm will reverse. There are six targets on each side. Is that understood?"

"Yes," we both said, pretty much at the same time. Bronco Bob said, "I have to trade out." His boy was running toward him with a small leather case, and when he come alongside Bronco Bob's horse he opened up the case, and Bronco leaned out and took two fresh Smith & Wesson revolvers from it, traded his five-shot Remingtons for them.

When he was positioned, Chauncey said, "Riding back, try not to stray your shots and kill nobody. I seen it happen in Abilene once, and that lady wasn't doing nothing but minding her own business on her porch."

Chauncey stepped to the side, pulled a red scarf from his coat pocket, said, "Soon as I drop this here rag, you ride, no sauntering. This here is a run. And remember, don't shoot until you come to your targets."

This seemed common sense to me, but I guess you can never be too sure. Chauncey lifted his hand with the scarf in it. A tiny wind breezed up, and I took note of which way it was blowing the scarf. It wasn't in favor for my shots, but I was hoping it wasn't going to blow any harder than it was and that I could judge it wisely. With my left hand I pulled one of my pistols.

The red scarf dropped.

It was like Satan knew the score. He leaped, all four feet coming off the ground at one time. We had a good plunge on that big white horse and was immediately at a gallop.

The targets was coming up on my left, and if you have never fired pistols from the back of a running horse trying to hit a square about the size of a woman's pocket handkerchief, then you have done very little that counts as real shooting.

As I have said, my left hand never gained the currency of my right, but it wasn't bad, and I had shot from a running horse before, having been trained by Mr. Loving who had been a rebel on horseback and was as good a rider and shooter as a Comanche. I had those reins in my teeth, my right hand folded over my chest, and with my left I lifted the shooter and shot low; it would rise with the discharge, and I had to keep in mind the changing height of the horse as it ran, not to mention the shifting of the wind, which was wiggling my ears like a dog listening for footsteps.

The shot was good. I hit another square, and then another, kept firing.

When I come to the end of the ride and took the reins in my hand again, wheeled Satan about, I had hit all six targets.

And so had Bronco Bob, who came riding in about a horse length behind us, the reins in one hand, the pistol in the other.

"Them leads in your teeth is a good trick," Bronco Bob said.

"I learned it from a master."

"That horse runs at the touch of the knees, don't he?"

"When he ain't got a mind to do what he wants, he does."

Measurements was taken to see who was closer to center on the targets, and we both come out so near the same they called it a draw. I looked over at Bronco Bob, and he touched the brim of his hat in salute, and I did the same.

I put my left-hand revolver in its place and pulled the other with my right. I took a deep breath, waited for the signal. Checkers Chauncey had walked down to meet us with the scarf in his hand. He took a position in the middle of us, and then lifted his hand. That scarf seemed to dangle there forever, but the thing I noticed was there was no wind. We would both be at our best situation.

The scarf dropped, and Satan leaped forward before I could spur him, damn near surprising me right off his back. But I managed to keep my place, though I had to shoot too quick. I hit the target, but it was only at the edge. I had to get my mind right for the next target, which was coming up between breaths. I shot five more shots, hit all the targets, and once again me and Satan arrived ahead of Bronco Bob and his mount.

I sat there on the back of Satan, pulling the cotton out of my wind-whipped ears, waiting to hear the word on the measuring of who had the closest shots, and the answer arrived quick.

Bronco Bob had missed two shots.

I was the winner of the Deadwood shooting contest.

Bronco Bob strolled over, grinning, and seemed genuinely friendly. He shook my hand and patted my back, said he'd lost a few matches in his time, but when he did he wasn't always up to his mark, having a cold or some soreness or such, but this time he had been beat fair and square.

"Thank you, Bronco," I said. "But I need you to know I come into this match with a little indigestion."

Bronco let out a big howl of laughter and commenced to slapping me on the back some more. "You are one hell of a shooter, you are a regular Deadeye Dick. No . . . Deadwood Dick is better. Yes, sir. When I give up this life for the writing life, which has always been my great love and concern, I will write of this day."

"In that version will I still win?" I said, and I was smiling big now.

"You will, sir. I am one thing for certain, and that is fair."

"You are also a damn good shot and a worthy opponent," I said. "I thought I was whipped there more than once."

"So did I," he said, and went to laughing and patting me on the back. Then came Charlie and his bunch, and finally down from the hill came Win and Madame and Cullen and Wow, and all them Chinese gals whose names I never could get right, having the same problem as Cullen.

I checked around for Ruggert and his men. I saw Ruggert slowly rise from his chair and walk into the crowd along with his compadres.

When all the whooping and hollering had died down, I was given first place and the money I had been promised. I gave that straightaway to Charlie, who then brought me a wad of loot he and the others had collected on bets.

I stuffed it in my pocket without counting it, and we all walked to Win and Madame's place on the hill. We relived the match over and over, and then when we was all tired of it, I took a break to wash the gun smoke off my face. Madame brought out some of her medicine and had a swig, then passed the bottle around. By the time it got back to her it was empty.

"Deadwood Dick," Tater said, "ain't that what that Bronco Bob called you?"

"Yes," I said.

"For me, from now on and forever, that's who you will be," he said.

"Mr. Deadwood Dick is best," I said.

There were some more laughs, but by now we was all starting to wind down. I realized by this time that I was exhausted. All the strain and worry of the match and concern over Ruggert's men made me feel like I had done a day's work with a pickax.

Charlie said, "We done our part. You have your money. We have ours for Bill's widow, and you ain't been shot."

"Yet," I said.

"Since you plan to leave our fair town, we can ride along with you until you are out of sight," Charlie said.

I looked at the sky. It was not far off dark. It was hard to believe the match had gone on that long.

"No," I said. "I think a crowd leaving town would only call attention to us. We'll wait until the night is just about down on us, and we'll depart."

"We are packed and ready, Nat," Madame said. "Though I bought a couple of cows."

"What?" I said. "Why would you do that?"

"Milk," Madame said.

"Ask a stupid question," I said.

"Exactly," she said.

"Then I suppose we'll take your cows with us. Where are they?"

"Behind the shack."

"It is nice to have fresh milk," Tater said.

"That's what I thought," Madame said.

I looked at Win. She was laughing.

"You're sure you don't want us to follow you three and your cows out?" Charlie said.

"I'm sure," I said.

I shook hands with Charlie and Tater and so on, and then they all went down the hill. I checked around for Ruggert, any of them men I thought to be his, especially Golem and Weasel. I was delighted not to see them.

The stars and moon hung bright in the sky, and our path through the hills was a good one. We had the wagon packed tight with goods, and

Win and Madame was on the driver's seat, Madame driving. The cows was tied to the back on lead ropes and were trotting along behind the double-mule-drawn wagon as smooth as if they had been training for just such a trip. I rode alongside the wagon on Satan with six hundred dollars and two bits in my saddlebags from the shooting match. Once I was away from everyone but Win and Madame, I had counted it out to myself. Twice. I couldn't believe I had all that money. I was as rich as I had ever been, and though they say money don't make you happy, it damn sure don't hurt your feelings none.

Cullen rode with us until we was well out of town, then we stopped the procession and climbed down from our horses. Win and Madame came off of the wagon to bid him adieu, hugging him and telling him bye, then me and him shook hands. That wasn't enough. That turned into a hard, and I like to think manful, hug. When we pulled apart we both had tears in our eyes.

"I will write you soon as I can," I said. "And at some point I will have you mail me the papers I gave you to hold. We are gone south by tomorrow."

Without another word, Cullen climbed on his horse and rode away. I climbed on Satan and watched him. He was waving his hat above his head as he galloped off.

It was my intention to travel about half the night, get some shut-eye, and start when we was comfortable the next day, knowing we wouldn't always have a full moon to light us. But this night I wanted away from Deadwood, due to my worry about Ruggert and his men.

Now that we was out in the wilds, I began to have concerns about Indians. I worried enough about it that I stopped our procession twice to adjust pots and pans in the wagon that was clattering, so as to bring about silence. Bill once told me an Indian, even a deaf one, could hear a June bug fart under a bucket a half mile away.

I guess we traveled about half the night, and it was still a moonlit sky, when we stopped to rest. The air was cool, with a light wind, and it was comfortable. Win and Madame got ready to bed down in the wagon.

I hitched up the stock and fed them and staked them out. I put my bedroll out on the ground by my saddle, which I was going to use for a pillow, laid my rifle nearby, and wished me and Win could sleep together. But that might lead to Madame shooting me with her pistol.

I cleaned and reloaded my pistols and the rifle, which is a thing I do at the end of most days. The moonlight made it pretty easy to do, though I can do that job in the dark if need be. I listened to Win and Madame settling down inside the wagon. I was pretty excited, as I was about to start a new life with a fine woman.

I felt I needed to stay awake and on guard, and decided stretching out for a few minutes was all I required, then I would get up and keep watch until morning. I am ashamed to say that no sooner had I laid my head on the saddle than I was sound asleep.

I don't know how much sneaking they had to do to get up on us, but I figure they could have ridden up on the backs of buffalo and been ringing cowbells and I wouldn't have noticed. I awoke to a boot in my ribs.

When I opened my eyes, I was looking up into Ruggert's ruined face. He was bent over me. "Did you sleep well, nigger?"

Actually I had, but the outcome of the sleep was nothing to brag about.

Weasel appeared above me, holding my rifle. He glared down and snickered, said, "I done got all your guns." He said this because I had put a hand to where one of my pistols ought to be, but it wasn't there.

"It wasn't no problem," Ruggert said. "Them rocks on the ground wasn't no more asleep than you was."

By this time I was sitting up, looking around. I seen Win and Madame was being pulled out of the wagon by Golem. Win wasn't saying anything, but Madame was calling those men everything in the book. And when I say men, I mean quite a few of them. Twelve. I had seen most of them before, back in Deadwood at the shooting match, and they was a rugged bunch from a distance. Up close they was scarred and haggard-looking; all of them appeared on the edge of being too old to live comfortable on the frontier except one, a sixteen-year-old boy with a bit of fuzz on his chin. His eyes was darting about like fish in a bowl. He had on what looked like a new gun belt with deep holsters, the butts of his revolvers just showing. The belt was a little big for him, and he kept tugging it up.

They all had their heads turned toward Madame and her cussing, at least they did until Golem pulled Win along the ground from the shadow of the wagon and full into the moonlight. My blood chilled.

Ruggert looked at me, his eyes drooping, like maybe he was tired.

"Want to tip your hat now, you black son of a bitch?"

I said nothing.

"Chasing you, I have gone through much. A scalping, my face burned by savages with hot knives, my toes cut off by one of them, and thorns shoved in my dick, right at the tip, and deep down. Long thorns, you hear? I was cut on near all over, and all the while they're doing it to me, you know who I was thinking of?"

"Jesus?" I said.

"Not at all. I thought of you, Willie — or is it Nat or Deadwood Dick, which is what they was calling you around town? I thought of your black face leering at my wife's rear end. That's what I thought of. And when you done that, you was disrespecting me, a white man. You was being bold, Willie, like you was good as me. It wasn't about her ass, boy, it was about me and how I was being treated — that you, a nigger, would come through our yard without your head bent and your eyes on the ground, looking around like you was a white man with all its privileges."

Golem came over and squatted down in front of me, kind of studied on my face. There wasn't any expression to him. He pushed his hat up, and I seen there was a deep and ragged scar across his shaved head. I hadn't seen it before because he always had his hat on tight, but now I could and could tell it was a horseshoe shape; he had been kicked by a horse. That explained some things, not that it gave me any comfort. Besides that wound in the middle of his forehead was that odd mark made with what I now decided was ashes.

"He thinks God has made him of mud," Ruggert said. Then Ruggert reached out and patted Golem's shoulder. "And surely he has. Good old thick, river-bottom mud."

Ruggert let his hand drop from Golem's shoulder, said, "Proper way for a nigger to die is by the rope and fire, but there's nothing but rocks and a trail here. That's not nigger-hanging landscape. I like a good high tree with a good firm limb. It's best if you don't tie a hangman's knot, just a slipknot. Last longer that way. You see, Willie, we got the rope but no limb."

"Why don't you boys wait here," I said, "and me and the ladies will go find you one. I'll send someone back to tell you where it is, and we can meet there."

Ruggert punched me in the face. It was a good shot and knocked me back against my saddle and blood from my busted nose ran into my mouth. I rolled my head to the side and spat it out.

"Take care of the ladies," Ruggert said to Golem.

"As if they are given to me by God," Golem said, each word no more level or unlevel than the other. If you could figure on how a dead man might speak—if he could—that would be how Golem sounded.

"God can't be here right now," Ruggert said to Golem, "so they are given to you by me, the next best thing. But I am vengeful, Golem. Vengeful, and I wish for you to be the same, my strong right hand. You got a pocketful of nice coins I gave you. That shows how I take care of you, don't it?"

Golem barely nodded, pulled his hat back down, and moved toward the women. My heart missed a beat.

"Then there's fire," Ruggert said, as if he had only taken a breath in the conversation, "and I have considered on it profoundly, but then decided any nigger that dies is bound for hell, so you will have that. I think some-thing else might be more appropriate, and I'm deciding what that is. I am giving you," he paused, "much thought. You have come to think of yourself as highfalutin, but you are to me nothing more than that nigger who some time ago so insulted me by looking at my wife's behind with lustful intent."

I started to say that her face cured that but decided my best approach at this stage was not to anger him further, though, truth to tell, I figured it didn't matter one whit. He was all het up to do me in, make me suffer, and had been after me for so long he would have to have satisfaction, and he wanted to draw it out.

"It was an accident," I said. "I was walking by, and I just happened to look. There was nothing lustful about it."

"A white man," Ruggert said, "even a poor one, must maintain his position, and if those I knew in town thought I let a nigger slide by on such a thing, then what would they think of me?"

By now I knew there was no smoothing it over, so I went for it. "They don't even remember you or me, and what makes you think they ever had a high opinion of you?"

"She left me, Willie. I believe it was because I couldn't honor her womanhood by making you pay. For that I blame you. She still has to be taught her lesson, she and the man she run off with, but Willie, I had to see you first. I had to take care of you before the other. Did you know your mother and father were once owned by my grandfather? They were. Did you know my grandfather liked dark meat, and that your mother was his special pick? You wasn't even born when he owned her, but he did, and he owned your pa, too, and he knew what Grandfather was doing with her out in the milk shed."

"I don't believe you," I said, and I didn't. I figured he was just yanking my chain.

"Don't make it less so, Willie. But when you seen my wife's butt, it was in the same position my old grandfather seen your mama's, except he hiked up her dress. And you know what? She didn't have no say in the matter. That's when white men were as they should be, and the idea of a free nigger — well, that just wasn't something that could be imagined, or should be. I was just a boy when Grandfather told me to come out to the milk shed with him and your mama and to come stand on a bucket and have me some."

"You lying son of a bitch."

He shook his head. "No. It's true. I didn't do it, Willie. I was young and scared, and I didn't do it. Now I wish I had. But if I didn't have your mama, now I got you. In a different way, of course, but you are owned as she was owned as your papa was owned. You are owned right this moment by me. You are the root of my problems. You have undone my life with the insult you showed my wife. I won't be outdone by a nigger, Willie."

I looked him in the eyes, and the words finally came back. I said, "You got to have someone to blame, because your life is just as low-account as any slave's ever was. You think you deserve better. You don't. Spending your life chasing after some fellow caught a glimpse of your wife's ass is no way for anyone to live. You are outdone by your own dumb self."

That's when he hit me again, this time with a backhand, a really solid blow that knocked me back and made me dizzy. I didn't try to sit up after that last hit. Just lay back with my head on the saddle, blood running out of the corner of my mouth. I glanced out of the corner of my eye and seen that Golem had Win and Madame on their knees on the ground, one big hand on each of their heads, like they was resting posts. He was looking up at the moon.

Weasel came over, said, "You figuring what you can do with him, ain't you?"

"Of course I am, you idiot," Ruggert said.

Weasel reacted to being called an idiot as if it was nothing more than his middle name.

"I know I'm just paid help," Weasel said. "But why don't you do what the Indians do—some of them, anyway?"

"What would that be, Mergatroit?"

Mergatroit! That was a disappointment. To me he would always be Weasel.

"Kill one of them cows and skin it, wrap him in it, tie him up tight as a papoose. Wet it down, and when the sun comes up that blood inside the skin and that wet on the outside will start that skin drying, just like how you soak rawhide to get it tight. It'll tighten and tighten and blow his guts out. My daddy did it to a fellow once wouldn't pay him money he owed. I helped him wrap the skin."

"It killed him?" Ruggert said.

"And real slow. He got so he couldn't scream anymore it was so tight."

Ruggert turned his head to one side, as if measuring that suggestion like a woman thinking of cutting cloth for a dress. "Slow, huh?"

"Oh, hell, yes," Weasel said. "When we cut him open, his insides busted out of him and all over us."

Ruggert nodded. "Kill a cow."

They didn't waste a bullet. Golem grabbed the poor cow by the horns, twisted its head, and Weasel stepped in and cut the critter's throat. Golem brought it down to the ground with blood splattering on him and coloring the grass. They was on that beast before it was dead, started the skinning with it still trying to bellow, which it couldn't do with its throat cut; it could only gurgle. They ripped its hide off quick and easy, the cow still breathing, and then finally someone, one of those men, shot it in the head, which was a mercy.

Win and Madame was still on their knees, and Win had started to scream at them, knowing full well that they was about to do something to me. Madame, who had paused in her cussing, went back to it, least until she was hit in the head with a rifle stock and knocked back on the grass. Ruggert started tearing my clothes off, yanking my shirt to pieces and tossing it aside, unfastening the belt and buttons on my pants while Weasel yanked off my boots, which he measured against his feet, then flung in the grass. Then Ruggert tugged off my pants. For no reason at all they left my socks on.

"I'm going to take your horse and ride it," Weasel said, "and I ain't going to feed it, just ride it, and then when it falls over, I'm going to cut its heart out and eat it."

"Damn wasteful of a good horse," one of the men in the crowd said, for now they had all gathered around me to watch what was being done.

"Yeah," Weasel said. "You're right. I'll feed it and keep it and sell it later."

"He ain't nothing but muscle," said the young boy, looking down on me.

"Good," Ruggert said. "That means he'll last a long time."

They bound me with wet rope, which they had made that way by all them taking turns pissing on it, then they wrapped me firm in that bloody, stinking skin with only my head poking out and dragged me away from the wagon so there wouldn't be any shade. They propped my head up with a rock so it was facing where the sun would come up. Next they unstrapped one of our water barrels off the side of the wagon, brought it over, and poured it on the skin and on my face, which at that moment was kind of refreshing but would soon be anything but.

Ruggert bent down and stared into my eyes. "To make the time pass, let me tell you what I'm going to do. I made a lot of money placer mining, had me a good run, only good one I ever had in my whole life, and now I've spent near every dime to hire these men, and after this moment, I am done with the coins. I am going to give the wagon and those women to the men, if anyone should want the old woman. And there will be at least one. There are those here who would do her and the cow that is still standing and maybe the dead one. Do it at high noon on a city street and be proud of it."

"You best hope I die," I said. "I've had chances to kill you and didn't. That was a piss-poor mistake. I won't repeat it again."

"It was a mistake, Willie, but you ain't going to have another chance. God is on my side. He protected me."

"He wasn't so good on watching out for you when it come to those Apache."

What there was of Ruggert's face twisted up.

"I don't know why he made that choice, but I believe in the end the Indians will be conquered and butchered like the animals they are. And

God is not on the side of your sort, either. On some sweet day the South will rise again, and the North will be overtaken and driven down to the ground to mingle with the dust, and things will be as they were before."

I felt the burden of my foolishness, my napping while my enemy crept up on me, and it was as if that great sky I had gloried in that night on the trail sometime back had fallen and was lying smack dab on me.

The men cooked up the cow, using some dried buffalo chips they collected as well as the tailgate of the wagon, which they broke apart for firewood. They drank whiskey, ate some of that poor beast, mainly the sweetbreads and a haunch, and left the rest of it in the grass for the ants. Then they pulled Win and Madame, who was still knocked out, over to the side of the wagon. I will not describe what happened next, but will only say that Golem went first, and there was so much screaming I began to cry, which was an absolute delight for Ruggert.

It was near morning when the men loaded Win and Madame, naked and bloody from abuse but, thankfully, still alive, into the wagon and threw their clothes in after them. If Win had been dead, maybe I would have just gone on and died myself without there needing to be any sun to squeeze the life out of me inside that skin, but the fact they was alive gave me some hope.

Weasel saddled up Satan, who let him, much to my dislike, and then mounted with my rifle in the rifle sheath and my pistols stuck in his belt and coat pockets. He also had my money in the saddlebags, though he didn't know it yet.

Two of the men took over the wagon, having hitched the mules back up and having tied their horses and the lone cow to the back of it. As they rumbled over the grass, heading toward the deeps of the Black Hills, I turned my head as much as I could and watched them and all those men on horseback go. Weasel, sitting on Satan comfortably, turned and looked back at me and grinned. At least he was far enough away I couldn't see those damn ugly teeth.

He and those men rode on, leaving only Ruggert and me.

So there we was. Stars was beginning to dim. The moon had slid to one side of the sky and faded. A crack of flame grew on the horizon. Ruggert was squatting next to me, facing away from the rising sun. Now and then he would reach out and pat my cowhide-covered chest.

"Seems to me," Ruggert said, "this is going to be a hot day. You know, I think those women of yours might last until sundown. When the men get hungry and probably eat that cow, get full up, they'll want their pleasures again. After that, they'll want to split up, not having my money anymore to hold them together. At that point, I figure they'll put the waste to that pretty little gal and that old lady. Though I was them, I'd keep that gal alive and in fair condition, take her down to Mexico and sell her. Down there they are always buying. Then again, they'd have to feed her, watch her, and so on, so maybe it's best they just have their fun and end it for her. What do you think, Willie? That sound right to you? I am a little saddened that I didn't take me a piece off the nigger gal, but the truth is, Willie, I can't get it up. Not after what those Apaches done, and I blame you for that, Willie. You insulted me, and then you took my manhood."

"I did nothing to you," I said.

"I had a place in the world, and you upset it."

I didn't understand him at all, and so I said nothing. There was nothing left to say.

Ruggert looked at me and smiled. He shifted to one knee, picked up the rifle that lay on the ground beside him, and stood up. I saw he was looking off in the distance at something.

"I have to leave you near as satisfied as I can be. What the hide don't do, others will."

Then he was up and moving swiftly toward his horse. He rode away in a westerly direction. Slow at first, then a little faster, looking back over his shoulder at something behind me and beyond my sight.

Knowing that Ruggert had finally been in a place of enjoyment after all this time, I wondered what could scare him like that, but no matter what it was, I was glad for it. I didn't want him to have the satisfaction of seeing me die.

It took some time before what had put the fear in Ruggert came up to scare me. It was horses, and on them horses was six Sioux warriors that I could see. They had come up behind me as silent as the rising of the sun. They was armed with bows and rifles that was fixed up with brass tacks driven into the stocks for decoration. A couple of them rifles was old muzzleloaders, and had I been them I'd have been afraid they'd blow up in my face.

I didn't know how many more was behind me. They didn't chase after Ruggert. Wasn't no need in it. They had me. I was a bird in hand, not one in the bush.

Well, them near-naked savages sat there on their ponies eyeing me for some time, then there was movement behind me, and a fist grabbed my hair and picked up my head as far as it would go, that cowhide being tight around my neck. He was wearing a worn beaver top hat he'd probably bought at a trading post at one time, and the only other thing he had on was a frown, a loincloth, and a scabbard with a big knife in it. He gave out with a little yip, pulled the knife, and put it to my forehead. I was going to be scalped alive. But as the blade pricked my skin, blood trickled down my face, and it caused the scalper to pause. He stuck the knife in the ground and rubbed that warm blood on my forehead furious-like. He jerked his head around to look at the others so fast his top hat flew off. It took me a moment, but I realized they had never seen a colored man before and thought I was painted up. When the blood slipped out and didn't run the paint, they was startled.

They gandered on me all together, and pretty soon all them that was on horses in front of me climbed off, and then them behind me did the same. There was eight altogether, and they gathered around me and studied me like I was a cipher problem. They bent down and took turns rubbing my forehead, which was painful, as they damn near chafed it raw.

I didn't say a word. I didn't know what to say. And whatever I would have said, I figured they wouldn't have understood it. They, on the other hand, was chattering about, and one brought over a skin of water and poured it on my face and went to rubbing with his breechcloth. After a bit they decided my hide was indeed black and there to stay. The Indian who had started to scalp me picked up his knife, and I figured, well, here it comes. I hoped if he did it he went on and killed me, because I was growing mighty uncomfortable in that warming skin.

He put the knife away and gave a chuckle. The other Indians started to laugh. They got so tickled and guffawed so long I almost laughed with them.

I don't know why they didn't scalp me, as I had a really full head of long hair back then, and it would have been a prize. But instead, that same Indian, one with the scalping knife, got a smaller leather bag out of a large one on his hip, opened it, and dipped his fingers in. They came out white-tipped. I figure it was some kind of clay, but whatever it was he bent down and went to work on my face with it. As he rubbed it on me, all the others laughed, and one even giggled like a little girl. I was a little embarrassed for him.

After a time my painter got done with his intentions, stood up, turned his head first to one side then the other, and practically hooted he was so happy with his work. They all started laughing about it, and then the laughter died out easy as it had started. They got on their ponies, and each of them rode around me, leaning off their horses and touching me with their bows or rifles. Then, hollering it up, they rode off.

Why they left me like that I don't know. I guess they decided I was a curiosity, one that deserved whatever fate had been given to me. After that little lapse in boredom for me and the Indians, they abandoned me.

The sun rose up high and turned hot as hell's oven. That hide began to clench me something terrible. Steam come off the hide and rose up in slow wads of white, and the stink of it was so thick in my nose it was like plugs of rotting meat had been shoved in there. I was starting to have trouble breathing as that skin tightened. I wouldn't have been no more uncomfortable if a blacksmith had come in and laid an anvil on my chest and then sat on it, and I was messing myself in that damn cow skin. I could feel it squirting down my legs. It wasn't just painful, it was humiliating.

A slight shower came up, and though it wet the hide again, which wasn't a good thing in the long run, in the short run it actually caused it to loosen a smidgen. The shower went on for hours. I could feel the paint on my face cracking and crusting up, but it was a rough sort of paint and wouldn't wash away easily.

When the sun was back out, I began to stew again. But the day was near an end, and I had been given some breathing room. The hide, though still tightening, had loosened just enough to allow me a long night and another miserable day tomorrow that would end as it might have ended if not for that rainstorm.

That's when I heard horses behind me. I figured the Indians was back and had thought it over and decided to come and scalp me after all. But I paused that thought. I could hear these horses, where I didn't hear them Sioux until they was right up on me. That was because these here horses was shod and coming from a distance.

I waited, listening.

It was two horses. They rode up in front of me.

The riders got off their mounts.

I began to weep silently.

It was Cullen and Bronco Bob.

# 23

There is no way I can express the gratitude I felt as Cullen cut me free of that skin with a hunting knife, folded it back, and clipped them ropes that held me.

Bronco Bob had squatted down to watch Cullen work, and when the cowhide was folded back, he stood up and stepped back a pace, which, due to the stink, was understandable.

"You got white stuff on your face," Cullen said.

"Some Indians thought I needed painting." My words was as dry as the dust in a summer street, hardly understandable.

"It's clay and ashes mixed with animal fat," Bronco Bob said. "They've made of you a white man. I suppose it is from their point of view an insult."

I tried to stand up but couldn't. Cullen got his canteen and gave me a good swig, said, "Just a little right now."

"Thank goodness you come," I said. "But why are you here?"

"Bronco Bob here was in the Gem, and it was mentioned by a fellow there that some men planned to take care of that Deadwood Dick fellow."

"He seemed quite happy about it," Bronco Bob said. "I overheard him speaking to a young gentleman, and when the speaker went outside, I went, too. I spoke with him. We had a very enlightening conversation."

"Bob means he beat the hell out of him," Cullen said.

"It was a mild beating, though it made a wound or two over his eyes. While lying on his back in the dirt, he spoke to me at my urging, which means I kicked him a lot with the toe of my right boot. Said he had been paid to be one of the bunch to follow you out, but had gotten drunk instead. He had his money already, an error on the part of his employer, so he decided to spend it and not follow you. That was your good fortune, for I heard word from him, and me and Cullen followed you. Or rather we took the obvious route you would take with a wagon."

"How come you're here, Cullen?" I asked.

"My doing," Bronco Bob said. "I had seen this gentleman with you. When I saw him in the street, I told what I had overheard, and what I had been able to get out of the loudmouth. Though too late to keep you from suffering. We came when we knew the situation."

"All that matters is you came," I said.

I was on my feet now, but still having trouble.

"They got Win and Madame."

"I feared as much," Cullen said. I knew what he was thinking. Men who would do what they had done to me might do the same or worse to women. I didn't mention that they already had.

The barrel they had poured the water from lay on its side in the grass. I hadn't seen it until now, as it was behind me. The lip of it was slightly raised on a rise of ground. I waddled over naked to the barrel and tipped it up. There was some water in it.

To make it short, Cullen and Bronco Bob helped me gather up the pieces of my shirt, and I used them and the water to clean myself, wiping the paint off my face best I could, cleaning the shit from my body. Then I put on my pants and boots and socks.

I pointed. "That's the direction they took," I said, "and if you don't want any part of it, loan me a gun and a horse, and I'll take care of it. You two have done more than anyone could ask."

"Hell, I'm already out here," Cullen said.

"I'll come along," Bronco Bob said. "Though I have had a few adven tures, I admit readily that I have never fired a shot at a human being. Not that I want to do that now, but I might write better about such things if I experienced them."

"Close enough," I said.

I rode on the back of Cullen's horse, him complaining about my stink all the way. Wiping myself down had only gotten rid of the main of it. We rode through the night. The moon was still rich, so the seeing was good. My head ached, and I felt weak. Part of it was lack of having eaten.

We rode for a couple of hours, following the moonlit wagon tracks. Then I seen Satan standing in the grass, head dipped, chomping. He raised his noggin as we came, and damn if he didn't start trotting over. He still had his saddle on, and the rifle was in the pouch. I slid off Cullen's horse, held out my hand, and made clicking sounds until he come up. I petted his nose.

"He's bucked Weasel," I said. "The devil let him climb on pretty as you please, and then he bucked him."

"That would be his way," Cullen said as I mounted Satan. "He has always had a sense of humor."

We three rode on. Wasn't too long before we come to a white mound in the moonlight, and as we got closer, I seen it was a body. It was a woman.

I rode over quickly, and from the saddle looked down on the dead and badly mistreated body of Madame. There was hardly a place on her that didn't appear to have been cut, stabbed, or clawed.

Slipping off Satan, I went and bent down and looked her over. Her eyes was open and full of the moon. I tried to close them, but they was contrary.

"We have to bury her," Bronco Bob said.

"Ain't no time for that," I said. I pulled my bedroll off the back of Satan, unrolled it, and threw it over her corpse. "Win is still with them, and she might be alive."

It bothered me to no end to leave that poor lady there with nothing but a blanket over her ravaged body. I didn't like the idea that varmints and bugs would be about her, but she was beyond help. Win, maybe, could be saved.

I guess we had gone another couple hours when we seen a man staggering along in the moonlight ahead of us. I could tell from the way he moved it was Weasel.

I halted Satan, shifted in the saddle, pulled the rifle, and shot Weasel in the back of his lower right leg. He let out a scream and collapsed. I rode up on him. He had rolled on his back and pulled one of my Colt pistols. When he seen there was three of us, he started in to begging. "Now, boys, don't do nothing hasty. I was just hired. Nothing more."

"Put that gun down," I said.

He laid the pistol in the grass. I dropped off Satan, picked my Colt up, then took the other Colt and my LeMat from him as well as my knife. I handed each of the weapons to Cullen except for the Winchester, which I kept. Cullen brought his horse next to mine and dropped the pistols in one of my saddlebags. The money I had wasn't in there.

I gave Weasel a hard look, said, "You was the one suggested the cowhide, as I recall."

"It was just a suggestion," he said.

"Uh-huh," I said. "And Ruggert took it."

"Listen here, Deadwood," he said, trying to sweeten things with that name. "I found that money that was in there, and that big Jew took it away from me. It was him that stole it. I ain't got nothing against you. I'm leaking a river here. I need someone to bind my wound."

"That there is a sad complaint," I said, squatting down to keep an eye on him. "Where have they gone?"

Weasel hesitated only a moment, realizing his chances was slim in any direction, and decided he might could get in on my good side. He pointed. "There's a split in the hills there. There's a natural camp just inside them, around the first real run of rocks. They are going to bivouac there."

I looked. The split he was talking about was some distance away, nestled in white rock between higher rocks darkened with trees.

"The young woman? Is she still alive?"

"Was when I seen her last, though them boys was rude about her."

"And you, of course, wasn't?"

"I ain't saying one way or another."

"You just have. How come you're out here all alone?"

"Me and the big man, one they call Golem, went off together cause we was to meet up with Ruggert in Kansas, where we was to get the last bit of our pay. That black devil of a horse threw me and run off. Golem, he went on without me, and me calling to him. He said he didn't like me."

"Imagine that, a weasel despised by yet another and larger weasel," Cullen said.

"You bind me up," he said, "I can ride you to their camp."

"If you split with Golem, how do I know you know where they are?"

"I been to that campsite," he said. "I'm the one told them about it."

"All right, then," I said. "Give me the coat you're wearing."

"It gets chilly at night," he said.

"Not if you're wearing a bloody cowhide it don't. But right now I'm a little on the cool side. Give me the coat."

He pulled it off and tossed it to me, sat there holding his leg.

"You'll take me with you?" he said.

"No."

I stood up, leaned the rifle against my leg, and put on Weasel's coat. It fit all right as long as I didn't try to button it. I got on my horse. Weasel looked up at me with spite in his face.

"All right," Weasel said. "I can tie my own leg off with something. I can take care of myself without help from any of you."

"You ain't going to need no help," I said.

Weasel knew then. He said, "Now, Deadwood Dick, you don't want to do that."

"That's where you're mistaken, Mergatroit."

I lifted the Winchester and shot him through the forehead. He fell back from his sitting position and lay in the grass on his back.

"Damn, if that wasn't severe, sir," Bronco Bob said.

"Yes," I said. "Yes, it was."

The Black Hills have stretches of prairie as well as rumbles of rocks spot-ted with grass. Then there was the hills. The trees that grew on the hills was thick, and in the moonlight they looked like one great wave of dark-ness creeping down from the sky.

We rode until we came to the split Weasel pointed out. It was a long, wide break in the rocks.

As we rode up on that split, Cullen said, "Hold up."

We did, and he pointed to his right and high. I could see floating above a short rise of rocks and trees a gray puff of smoke. It looked like fairy dust in the moonlight.

"I smell meat cooking," Bronco Bob said.

"I think we have found our men," I said.

We climbed off our horses, led them into a clutch of trees, and tied them up there. I said, "Y'all wait here."

Carrying my rifle, I started climbing through the trees, a large num-ber of them dwarf pines, along a trail spotted with rocks and scrub brush. It was tough going, but when I got near the top, I stopped and squatted among the trees. I seen a lone sentry up there and recognized him as one of the men who had attacked us. He was standing so he could look down, and I suppose he was in that position so that if anyone rode into the split he could see them. He wasn't looking back, as the idea that someone might know they was inside the split and would come up through the trees hadn't occurred to him. If they could guard the split, they felt they could keep attackers out. What they had actually done was boxed themselves in.

He was looking down, probably wishing he was there eating whatever was cooking. There were little red sparks from that cook fire, and they fluttered up and dotted the dark like fireflies, then faded. I could smell the meat really good now. My stomach turned over a couple of times in want of it.

I squatted there for some time, watching.

Finally the man turned and went into the tree line, leaned the rifle he was toting against a pine, and unfastened his pants. With his pants hanging around his knees, he took what looked like a dime novel out of his pocket and squatted, let his back rest against the tree to support him while he took care of nature's business, that book there for ass wiping.

He was quite loud about his straining, and was finally making good on his intentions when I gently laid my Winchester on the ground and crept up behind him. Pulling my knife, I inched around the side of the tree and drove the blade into his throat. I struck him so hard the knife went through his neck and into the tree, pinning him there. He turned limp, and blood gushed like a spring. I jerked the knife free. He sat down in the pile he had been making, dropping the magazine on my boot.

Putting my knife away, after wiping it on his shirt, I got my rifle, eased over to where he had been standing guard, and looked down. It wasn't a long drop, maybe thirty feet, and with the fire and the moonlight I could see all of them real good.

They was all gathered down there around that big fire, and Madame's other cow was on a spit that had both ends racked in forked limbs they had cut and set up as supports. I seen Win right off, and though it was a relief to see she was alive, my heart sank for her. She was completely naked, leaning against some rocks with her arms crossed over her breasts. She was trembling from the cold, being some distance from the fire. I felt a kind of quiet madness seep over me, and it was all I could do to control it.

One of the men was wearing Win's yellow dress and one of Madame's sun hats. He was prancing around the fire, playing the fool, and I could hear the men laughing. It went all over me like a splash of icy water. They was the biggest fools alive to do what they had done and not finish me off, and then to box themselves into that great hole in the rocks.

I counted the men. Seven. I thought about that. I had killed Weasel, and Golem had ridden off on his own, and then there had been Ruggert, who did the same. I had killed the man on watch. That was four out of the picture, and I remembered there had been twelve. That meant there was probably one either in the wagon, which was not far from the fire, or off in the bushes. Or maybe he had gone off on his own earlier. Then it come to me if one had gone off on his own it was the younger one among them, for he was missing. I counted the horses. Plus the animals they had taken from us, there was eight, not counting ours. Nope. He was still around.

It was then that I seen him come out of the wagon, sleepily putting on his hat. The men started in on him about something, but I had lost interest in them.

I glanced once more at Win, took in a deep breath, and moved down the hill and through the trees, trying to get down as fast as I could without making a sound.

When I come to Cullen, Bronco Bob, and the horses, I said, "They're down there. So is Win, and she's alive."

"Thank God," Cullen said.

"She's in a tough way, though," I said.

"What do we do?" Bronco Bob said.

"We're going to kill them all."

"I second that," Cullen said.

"I don't know," Bronco Bob said.

"You are not obliged," I said. "You have done me a great favor as it stands."

"So you say your woman is there?" Bronco Bob said.

"I do. And one less man, on account of me cutting his throat."

"Shit, I'm out of my element," Bronco Bob said. "I'm just a good shot, not a killer."

"I guess I joined another club some time back," I said.

"I ain't never lifted a weapon against nobody. I don't even like to hunt."

"They ain't no different from targets," I said. "Except they shoot back and bleed all over the place, and there's that whole business about dying. Them or maybe you."

"Bronco, it's up to you, but we are going down there," Cullen said.

Me and Cullen got in the saddle, and Bronco Bob, after a brief moment of hesitation, did as well. He pulled his Henry from its sheath. I had just put my Winchester away. I said, "It will be close work mostly, and a rifle might not be the thing. You choose your own weapon, though. Me, I'm starting with pistols."

"Very well," Bronco Bob said. He replaced the Henry and pushed back his coat to reveal his Remington pistols.

"I got a two-shoot shotgun and a pistol," Cullen said. "That will do me."

I pulled two of my pistols from the saddlebag—the Colt and the LeMat—and stuck them in Weasel's coat pockets. "Way we got to do it is to come on the sneak until we get to that big rock, then we got to ride around it like we was running from a stampede, yelling and shooting. I'll go to the far right immediately and take them head-on. You two ride straight ahead, veering a little to the right. You'll see the wagon. Come on around it, and make sure you don't shoot my head off as you come. There's a big campfire, and when last I seen them they was all gathered around it. Watch for Win; she's against the rocks on the far side, or was. A man is wearing her yellow dress and Madame's bonnet."

"Luck to us, then," Cullen said.

"Luck ain't got a goddamn thing to do with it," I said.


We went slow, trying not to make noise, but as we neared our spot the horses' hooves sounded loud on the rocks, so I took out at a run, and Satan plunged forward like he had a flaming brand tied to his tail.

I put the reins in my teeth, freeing my hands to draw my pistols from Weasel's coat pockets. I dug my heels deep into Satan, and we made the turn at the rocks well ahead of Cullen and Bronco Bob. All of a sudden I was looking at the fire, men moving in front of it. I lifted my pistols and fired. One of those men went down, and the one in the yellow dress yelped and dropped to the ground, pulling his own piece out from under the dress and firing, missing me so bad he might as well have been trying to shoot a squirrel out of the trees on the hill.

I galloped past the fire and swung under Satan's belly, hanging only by a heel. The others had drawn their pistols and was firing. They couldn't hit me or Satan. We galloped right past them. It was like me and him was touched with some kind of strong Indian medicine that made bullets swerve, though I knew the truth of it was they was just lousy shots.

I swung back into the saddle, swiveled so I was backward on the horse, and shot at them, hit one right off and saw him go down as if a hole had opened up under him. Then I heard other shots. Cullen and Bronco Bob. I twisted back to the front of the saddle, wheeled Satan, and started back. I seen Win by the rock wall, then got my mind back on my business. Bronco Bob, yelling at the top of his lungs, the reins in his teeth, same as me, rode into the fray. He threw out his right hand, which was clutching one revolver, and laid the other across his legs so it pointed in the same direction, and shot that way. Two of them men went down like they was wet blankets that had slipped off the clothesline. One rolled into the fire, knocking over the cow on the spit. The flames grabbed at his hat and ate it, and then the fire swarmed around his body like ruffians.

Cullen was right behind Bronco Bob. He cut toward the fire, riding and firing his pistol fast as he could and not hitting a goddamn thing. The young one took off running, away from the fire, and was soaked up by the dark.

More gunfire. Cullen's horse was hit and went down, and Cullen was thrown from its back. He went rolling, bullets being fired at him all the while. By the time I rode around on that side, Cullen had scuttled up behind his dead horse and pulled the shotgun free, which was a good thing, because one of the gents was running at him and firing.

Before I could help Cullen out, his double barrel roared, both barrels, and I seen pieces cut off that fellow fly along in the light of the fire, and he was dropped to the ground. It was then I seen Bronco Bob, who had made a wide turn, tumbled off his horse, and hit the ground. There was two of them left—the kid who had run off and the one in Win's dress that I had wounded. He was on his knees, one hand clutching his groin. The yellow dress was stained with blood. He threw his gun on the ground, saying, "I have had enough."

I rode around to him, clicked the baffle on the LeMat, and shot him in the face with the shotgun load. I just felt mean, and that's all there was to it.

The ones Bob had shot was mostly dead. I dismounted, went over and kicked their pistols away from their hands, tucked mine in my belt, then checked on Win.

She fell into my arms. I pulled off the jacket I had taken from Weasel. Win put it on and buttoned it up. I grabbed a horse blanket stretched on the ground for a bedroll, and she wrapped it around her for a skirt.

"Win," I said. "Are you all right?"

It was the kind of question you ask, but soon as I said it, I felt like an idiot.

"In a fashion, Nat," she said. "In a fashion. Oh, God, everything is so close. The sky is falling, and the ground's coming up."

"You been through a lot. You got to sit down here, against the rocks."

She did, then said, "Your friend is wounded."

Bronco Bob was on the ground, but before I could reach him he was already getting up. "I am not hit," he said.

"The hell you ain't," I said and touched his arm gently where it was turning wet.

"Oh, hell. Yes, I am. Ah, shit. I won't live to write about it."

He sat down in a way that made you think his legs had been sawed off under him. I used the bullet hole in his shirt to get my fingers in and rip it open for a look. The fire crackled and gave me light. "You got a hole through the meat at the top of your shoulder, more of a groove, really. It ain't so bad."

Bronco Bob said, "Shit. That is good news. Good," and then he fainted straightaway.

Cullen came over, said, "You get the one left. I will take care of Bronco."

He went to tearing Bronco Bob's shirt some more, using a piece to plug into the wound and another strip to bind it.

It will sound harsh, but these many years later I am dedicated to the truth, mostly, so I will tell you this honestly. Though bad off, one or two of them men we discovered was still alive. If we had loaded them in the wagon and hauled them back to Deadwood, which was a two- to three-day ride, they might have lived. Thing was, we didn't want them to. I caught up Satan, tied him to the wagon, got my rifle, and walking by them wounded men I admit to you I shot them the way you would a dying horse.

After that I went after the kid.

I trotted in the direction I had seen him take, and wasn't long before I could hear him breathing ahead of me, trying to climb into the rocks, dribbling pebbles and dust down on me. I climbed up after him. When I got to the top, the sun was bleeding through the trees, and I seen blood drops on the rocks, glimmering like rubies. One of us had hit him. I kept on the trail and climbed up to where it was flat, near where I had cut the lookout's throat. I seen him then. He was running. His gun belt sagged loose, fell around his legs, and tripped him up; down he went.

I was on him then. When he tried to roll over and draw his guns I had a bead on him with my rifle. He looked frantic. His hat was pushed up on his head, and his blond hair hung out long like a woman's; his face was as soft as one's, too.

"I didn't mean nothing," he said. "I was made to do it."

I squatted down and held the rifle on him. He took his hands off his pistols, turned them palms-open.

"I didn't want to," he said. His voice was squeaky, like his balls hadn't yet dropped. "But they said I had to. I ain't nothing but a kid. I got a girl back home. Me and her are going to get married soon as I get a job."

I could see the fear on his face, hear it in his voice. I couldn't help but think of that time I was being chased by Ruggert through the swamps back home, how I had felt about it, the way my heart beat and my head buzzed.

"I didn't mean to have it happen," he said. "I was just caught up in it. If you and she had been white, I wouldn't have had nothing to do with it."

That's when I shot him, and I tell you, to this day he's the only one I feel a little guilty about. It's not a guilt that shows up much, but it's there, and about once a year, for a few minutes when I'm shaving, I feel it.

# 24

I will make short work of our trip back to Deadwood, for that was the only wise place to go under the circumstances. We didn't bury a one of those men but left them to the things that wiggle and the things that fly.

We gathered their weapons and tossed them in the wagon, took their horses, which we tied to the back of the wagon, except for one animal Cullen took in place of his, and started back swiftly as we could, considering Win had taken considerable mistreatment and the wagon's rumblings was hard on her aching body. I will not spend time on what was done to her. I think that is obvious, but she was not only mistreated in as vile a way as a woman can be, she was also sick and bloody and headwise confused. But that is enough. I'll draw the curtain on that.

Before we got back we seen some Sioux, perhaps some of them that had painted my face white. There wasn't too many, and as an Indian is a smart opportunist, they probably decided since we was on horseback and well armed, the scuffle might not be worth the prize, so they let us go without bother.

We passed Weasel's body, flocked with vultures, and when we did the birds rose up and flew away. Win asked if we would pause. I helped her

out of the wagon, as she had grown mighty stiff. We did that so she could
spit on his corpse. She was able to work up quite a wad and frighten a
flock of innocent vultures.

Later, when we come to Madame's body, Win found the strength to
get out of the wagon again and look, to tell us that after the hooligans had
done all they wanted, Golem twisted Madame's neck like a chicken and
threw her out of the back of the wagon, which is when he and Weasel
went off together before having their divide. It was at that point, looking
down on Madame, that some of Win's mind took flight, and she didn't
say another word during our journey.

As for Madame, we had tools in the wagon, a shovel and hoe among
them, some of our new supplies for a possible farm somewhere. It all
seemed silly now, all those tools and supplies and nothing to do with
them; it was like they was there to mock us.

We buried her out there on the plains, and Bronco Bob, who was also
an ordained preacher of sorts, said some words over her. We gathered
up a few stones and made a mound and went on.

Rolling into Deadwood, we was a despondent bunch, you can bet on
that, and now me and Win had no home. When Madame and Win left
their house there was no shortage of squatters waiting to move into it,
and my little room was no longer mine, either. We ended up staying with
Wow and Cullen in their small place, and Bronco Bob, having money and
being white, went to the hotel, coming each day of the following week
to check on mine and Win's condition.

One day after a visit, I walked with him outside, said, "What do you
think, Bronco?"

"Time could heal her."

"What do you really think?"

"I can't say for sure. Who can? But since you asked, I'm of the thought
her spirit has gone out through a hole in the wind, and it's not coming
back. I say that knowing full well it's only a guess. I had a cousin that had
a very bad experience. She went through that hole, and somewhere her
spirit is still rambling. One thing for sure, though: it never came home."

"I must be hopeful," I said.

"Of course," he said.

When I was able to slow down, what had happened to me took hold, and I was laid up for three days, hardly able to move. It was recommended by the China girls that I drink lots of water, and they brewed some foul-smelling stuff to drink as well; it tasted like someone had peed in some dirty water with a dog turd at the bottom. I resisted, but Ching-a-ling, as she was calling herself that week, insisted I drink it. I did, and I am here to say I think it did much for me, renewing my physical energy to such an extent I was out of bed by the end of the week. Or maybe I just wanted to get well so I didn't have to drink any more of it, and that may have been its most important curing property.

It was slower for Win, there being more than just bruises and humiliation but an assault upon the spirit, as Bronco Bob called it. Sometimes I'd take her for a buggy ride up to our hill, but it was like riding around with a bag of flour, bless her heart. I had hoped for some renewed vigor by stirring old memories, but no correction of spirit was forthcoming.

Sometimes I would wake up in the middle of the night and she would be in a corner, her back to the wall, her knees drawn up, and I would have to coax her back to bed, which was a pallet on the floor. I would try and hold her, but she wasn't having any of that. I'm sure it made her think of other things.

Though it was a tight squeeze there with Wow and Cullen, and I felt I was stretching their hospitality, I made no rush to head out again, though I had firmly made up my mind to track down Ruggert and the big Jew and kill them both. I was tempted to do it slowly and in some horrible fashion, and had dreams of tying them down and putting hot coals to the bottoms of their feet and forcing a gun barrel up their ass and firing until the trigger didn't work no more. Actually, that was just some of the things I considered.

To be honest, my spirit, though not broken, had been twisted considerably. It was a day-to-day measure to regain my piss and vinegar and to

think about starting out after them. I remembered that Weasel said he
and Golem were to join Ruggert in the Kansas Territory, but that was a
long ways off, and they could be any place there, if they went there at
all. I decided if they was going to Kansas, Dodge was likely.

I couldn't presume what Ruggert would have left to do with his life
now. He had chased me for some time, and if he reckoned I was done
in, and if he had stored some money secretly for himself, he might go
from Kansas back to East Texas and take up residence again. I had no idea
what the crazy Jew might do. A man who thinks he's made of mud is not
someone with average plans. It was all guesswork. But I was determined
to find them. I should have killed that bastard Ruggert when I first realized who he was. Mercy has its limits.


Due to Bronco Bob being a talker, there was questions about things and
all that had befallen us. Bronco Bob, having been the one who shot his
mouth off in the first place, handled it well, explaining how I was set
upon by those fellows, and he and Cullen come along just in time, and
then we had to seek Win out and rescue her. He told in detail about how
those boys died on account of their own actions and went into great detail about Cullen and his shotgun, having the fellow Cullen shot flying
through the air from the blast, which any one of us knew was a lie, knowing full well them shotgun blasts didn't push, they tore right through
you. That was a detail the crowd was willing to let pass. The highlight
of his story, and I am certain he told it many times, was my horseback
ride with the reins in my teeth, shooting like a madman and hitting what
I shot at. My pursuit of the younger one up on the hill became a little
windy, and it turned into a glorious shoot-out, and of course it had been
no such thing. I had told Bronco Bob exactly what happened up there,
but I reckon he figured it sounded too much like murder, which I suppose it was. I never corrected him on his version of events. The part
about his own self, and how he was wounded and how bad it was, swelled
in the telling, too. Bronco Bob even favored his arm a little to make sure
it was known he was well in the fight. He had a way of letting his arm

dangle and twisting his mouth in just the right way so you might think
the bullet had cut fresh; it gave his story a feeling of truth, and mostly it
was true, though the wound had been nothing and was pretty much done
with by the time we returned to Deadwood. I have never known a man
that wanted to be a hero more than Bronco Bob, and in my eyes he had
been one and didn't even know it. He claimed I had been set upon for my
prize money, and as they had taken it and I hadn't gotten any of it back,
the bodies not carrying a coin of it, that was a good enough story. He
left Ruggert's claim that I had stared at his wife's butt and made advances
on her out of the telling, not wishing to give any of the ex-Confederates
in our midst any ideas that I might in fact be uppity. Bronco Bob said he
was writing a book about it. *Deadwood Dick and the Dark Riders of the Black
Hills, and What Befell Them.* He did, too, some years later, but I'll come
back to that.

Some of the fellows went out there to Split in the Rocks, as it was
called, and seen what was left of the bodies, and come back saying
Bronco Bob had told it true, even as to where the bodies was. They
found bones they figured belonged to Weasel, which they left (ain't nobody in town had liked him anyway), and come across the marker for
Madame. The killings actually gave me a bigger name than I had right after the shooting match, and people took to treating me nicer. This irked
me more than being treated like a black animal, because it wasn't based
on my character, just on my ability to kill folks.

The days turned into weeks, and I hadn't worked a lick and didn't
know how much more I could ask Wow and Cullen to put up with us.
I was thinking on this one day when Cullen came up to me, said, "You
might think you are a hindrance to us, but you aren't. You stay long as
you want."

"I appreciate that," I said. "I believe I will be leaving very soon, but I'd
be obliged if Win could stay for a while, at least until I take care of some
business."

"I know what the business is," he said.

"I'm sure you do."

"She may stay as long as she likes," he said. "As long as you would like for her to."

Well, it wasn't but a few days later that Cullen figured he had enough to buy him a spot of land with a cabin on it at the edge of the town. The cabin was built of whole logs and split logs, and there was dried-mud patching. It didn't have no shingles, just an open roof, because the man who owned the property died from eating too many sweet potatoes—that's what his wife told me—and never got the roof on it. She said she was selling on account of she was going back to Alabama. "I didn't like my husband much, really," she said. "And it's kind of a relief."

It made me wonder if something other than butter had been on those sweet potatoes.

It was a pretty big place. Me and Cullen roofed it ourselves, though I must admit my side of the roof was a little uneven.

Thinking Ruggert was in Kansas Territory was a high wish, but I felt I had to go there and see. I talked to Win about it, and she listened. Usually, that was all she did, as her willingness to talk, or even play her flute, which I had recovered from the wagon, wasn't there. I laid out what I intended like she knew what I meant.

When I finished, she turned her head, for she had been eyeballing a corner in our room like it might be a path to glory, and said, "You kill him, Nat. You kill him good."

I couldn't have been more startled to discover green manure could be turned to gold.

"I will," I said.

Then she went through that hole in the wind again, became silent as stone.

A few days before I was to leave, Cullen volunteered to go with me.

"Ain't no man I'd rather have with me, Cullen. But you got a woman here, and I need you to look after Win best you can, and I will at some point need you to mail me those papers you're keeping."

"Wow can do that," he said. I could tell he was serious about going, but I could also feel he didn't really want to. He had Wow, and he had a life in Deadwood.

I told him no, I couldn't do that.

He let out a sigh of relief, and I didn't blame him.

I rode over to Charlie Utter's camp, told him I was leaving Deadwood. Charlie shook my hand firmly, and his eyes got wet. He told me they sent that money to Bill's widow, Agnes, added they hadn't gotten nothing back from her on the matter, not even a goddamn two-word thank-you note.

"I'd have been happier with 'Fuck you' than silence," he said.

He also afforded how the mail was slow sometimes, and maybe that was the problem, but he didn't sound sincere about it. He said he was saddened by all that happened to me and Win, and that did sound sincere. He forced some money on me. I didn't want to take it, but I did. It was well needed and much appreciated.

"I'll pay you back, Charlie," I said.

"No, you won't. Because I won't take it. It's yours. Good luck to you, Deadwood Dick. At least you will miss a Black Hills winter. It is a frozen hell of snow and sleet and a wind so sharp it'll blow up your ass and freeze the turds inside you."

I thanked him for that parting information, and last on my list of good-byes was Bronco Bob. When I told him, he said, "Nat, I am going with you. You are a source of stories and a man of action, and I plan to write them all down and become rich for it, and you will, of course, receive a cut of the monies."

"That would be grand, Bob, but mine may be a rough trail, and I don't think white audiences much care to read about a colored man and his adventures."

"We will see," he said. "As for the journey, I can handle that, at least as far as Kansas. There I may choose another path. I've already sold my wagon and some of my guns, so I have traveling money. I'm willing to share it if the need arises. My days making my living as a shooter are quit.

I have run out that string and have lost interest. I would delight in your company, as I have plans to leave anyway."

This is how Bronco Bob became my traveling companion.

The night before the day I was leaving, in bed, I made a small effort to hold Win close, and she let me. It made me feel good to see she was getting better, if only in small doses, but it made me feel, too, that maybe I shouldn't leave, that I should stay and help in her recovery. But I was too set in my plans to change them; at that point it would have been like turning a petrified tree back into common wood. Wasn't going to happen.

Next morning I saddled up my horse, and Bronco Bob come and joined me, and Win even came out in the yard. I kissed her gently on the mouth, without any real response, hugged Wow and Cullen good-bye, and climbed on Satan. I said to Cullen, "Keep Win warm. Charlie Utter says the wind blows hard and sharp and cold come dead of winter."

"She will be as warm as we are," said Cullen, "and I like it warm."

"Good enough," I said.

As me and Bronco Bob rode away, I turned and looked back, seen Win turn quickly into the house. It hurt my heart to see her so eager to return to her spot in our room. But we hadn't ridden far when I heard a sharp note cut the air, and then it was followed by a number of sweeter notes.

I turned on my horse for a look. Win had come out of the house with her flute and was playing us off on our mission. With a smile on my face, I raised my hand to her, and we rode on out of Deadwood to that high, sweet sound.

# 25

Having gone only a short distance, we realized we was being followed. This follower wasn't so sneaky, as he was riding a mule and coming right behind us, purposely keeping some distance. I turned in the saddle, looked back, and recognized him. It was the boy Bronco Bob had hired to tote his guns and stuff at the match.

I said as much, and Bronco Bob said, "Tim?"

"Jim," I said.

We slowed down, and Jim stopped coming, halting on his mule, just looking at us. Then Bronco Bob waved him in, and he put his heels to the mule and came riding up to us. We sat there on our animals and talked.

I tell you, that boy was worse-looking than the mule. He had gone down considerably since I had seen him last, the day of the shooting match some months back. His red hair was long and caked with mud, and his face was spotted with it, too. His knees and elbows, which was bony as an old cow carcass, was sticking through his clothes, and the soles on his oversize boots flapped like nags' tongues when he came riding up. He was scummy around the eyes, and his teeth was a little green at the gums, like they was little trees with moss growing against them.

"What in hell are you doing out here, Tim?" Bronco Bob asked.

"I ain't got no family. I been living under a porch. I hadn't done nothing until you seen something in me and hired me, Mr. Bronco. It meant a lot to me."

"Hell, boy, you just happened to be handy. It might well have been anybody."

"Oh," Jim said.

"He just don't want you to get the big head," I said, sensing right off that any confidence the boy had gained from having been the aide to Bronco Bob had just run down his leg. It was like someone had told a worm they was too high off the ground.

Bronco Bob seen how I was heading, and after having had that rare dull moment, said, "Yeah, I don't want you getting all blowed up in your thinking, your head such a size you can't walk through a doorway."

"Yes, sir," Jim said.

"Listen here," I said. "You ain't doing yourself any good out here with us. We got a long ride ahead of us."

"I ain't got nowhere to go," said Jim. "Dogs like under that porch where I was sleeping, too, and when it rains I got to find a place higher. Just staying halfway dry and warm is some real work."

"You'll get wet out here, too," I said. "And where'd you get that mule?"

"I borrowed it," Jim said.

"I bet you did," I said.

"It's as poorly as me," Jim said. "I was packing out goods for some miners, but they took to butt-fucking me and the mule, so I stole it when I seen you fellows leaving and come after you."

"What was that you said about the miners?" Bronco Bob said.

Jim said it again.

"We should go back and kill them right away," Bronco Bob said. This from a man who until a few days ago had never shot at a living human being.

"They moved on and left the mule to fend for itself cause it's skinny, but that's because they ain't fed it good," Jim said. "I get older, learn how to use a gun like you boys, I come across them butt-fuckers I'll kill them myself."

"What say you, Nat?"

I didn't like it, adding a responsibility, as I hadn't managed so well my last time out with my charges, but I said, "All right. But we got to decide on something right now. Are you Jim, or are you Tim?"

"I got called Jim by somebody sometime back, and I've kept the name. I don't recall what I was named when I was little, as my folks run off and left me with a boot-shine kit and a cold potato in a sack. They just moved off and took their tent and supplies with them. I stayed with a Chinaman for a while, but I couldn't understand him, so I left."

"How long ago was that?" I asked.

"I don't rightly reckon," he said. "But I think I'm about sixteen, and that's been seven, eight years ago I left. I ain't got that boot-shine kit no more." He added that as if we was about to ask him for a boot polish.

"My God, you were practically a baby," Bronco Bob said.

"I ain't never been a baby," said Jim.

"All right, then. We still don't know which you prefer," I said. "Jim or Tim."

"I come to most anything," he said.

"Naw, that ain't going to work," I said. "Decide on your name."

The boy looked at Bronco Bob, said, "I like Red, actually."

"Then Red it is," I said. "And remember, you got to tote your own weight if you're going to be with us."

"I been doing that and can keep on doing it."

And that's how Red, formerly Tim and formerly Jim, became our companion.

That first night we stopped to camp, we did so down in a ravine. We had a cold supper of beans, as we was worried about Indians. It was a clear and dry night, so the ravine was fine. It was lined with rocks, and there wasn't no water in it right then. It was dry and a good windbreak. Bronco Bob dug around in his bedroll, where he had wound up his possibles, and pulled that white fringed jacket he had worn at the shooting match out of it, tossed it to Red.

"Put that on, and take care of it," Bronco Bob said. "It's yours, but you got to take care of it. This one will fit you better than me. I'm gaining in girth, and I prefer my big cotton one. It'll warm you well enough."

Red held the jacket like he had just been given baby Jesus's fresh swaddling wrap. "Thank you, Mr. Bronco." It was obvious he wanted to say something else, but his tongue had grown too thick and was blocking his throat.

"I catch you leaving it laying about," Bronco Bob said, "I will take it away from you and give you a kick. You understand?"

"Yes, sir," Red said.

"You got a few manners," I said. "Where'd you learn that?"

"An old woman took me in for a year, and then she died. I didn't tell no one right away, cause I figured I'd have to leave her house, and the weather was bad. I stayed there awhile longer, then she took to stinking too bad. I was going to bury her in the night, but she died in her big cloth chair and I waited too long and she melted into it. Her and that chair was one and the same. I was too little then to drag it. I just left. Someone finally found her, cause of the stink, and dogs had broken in and eaten part of her. I heard all about it on the street. She was buried sitting in that chair, or what was left of her, as most of her by then was in the cushions. She loved that chair, though. She was the one taught me manners good. I liked her a lot. I hated she died. She could sure cook good cornbread. I didn't know until I come to live with her that you was supposed to wipe your asshole, even if it was with a rag or paper or leaves. I didn't know it mattered, as hadn't nobody told me until she did."

"We get the idea," Bronco Bob said. "Here is another thing. From here on out, you'll take a pinch of salt, and when we have it, soda, and you will fray a small stick and dip it in the salt and clean your teeth with it. You almost got enough growth on your teeth there to cut and winnow. A young man like you may want some ass in the future, and I am not speaking of the lady mule you're riding. If you prefer fairer ones to those less fair, nice teeth are important. From what I can see, those chompers are fair enough, just grimy, but they'll go bad if you don't get to work on them."

Bronco Bob opened his bag, took out a small willow stick that was bunched up with others in a tied bundle, and handed it to him. It was a trick we all used to keep our teeth clean—that and a finger dipped in salt rubbed on the gums as well. Bronco Bob followed this up with a pinch of salt he put in the boy's palm.

"Now, son, you spit in your hand, on the salt, fray that stick with your teeth, then use the frayed end and the salt to clean yourself. You start on it tonight so we don't have to look at that grass growing on them in the morning. When we get somewhere where we can buy it, we'll get some baking soda or tooth powder. You do that maintenance every day, and they'll clean up. I got a mirror you can see into during the day, and you can do a more serious job of it. That will be your job until we arrive where we are going."

It was a long ride, and we did see some Indians, but they looked more ragged than Red. They was few in numbers and kept their distance. We passed buffalo hunters and skinners who was hunting the herds, and they stunk so bad we could smell them coming for half a mile at least. A few lessons from that old lady who had taught Red to wipe his ass might have been of some benefit to them.

We didn't spend any friendly time with them, as me and Bronco Bob was not taken by their lot, and neither was we proud of their profession. We came across carcasses of them buffalo they had shot and skinned, the meat left rotting on the prairie. For a fellow like me that had grown up looking for something to eat pretty much day up and day down, it was a terrible and senseless waste.

Anyway, we passed them and others, folks in wagons heading out to Deadwood for the mining, though the finds there was already playing out. We did camp with them a time or two, though there was those, mostly Southerners, who didn't like the idea of being so near a colored on the prairie, thinking I might in the night murder them all and rape the women. Mostly folks was friendly, though. We asked if they had seen a burned-up man or a big fellow with a mark of some such on his forehead.

No one said they had at first, but when we was near across Nebraska, a man and woman with two young children told us they had in fact seen the burned-up man, and he had bummed a meal from them. They felt sorry for him and fed him supper, and come morning he decamped early, taking with him their frying pan, a bag of sugar, and some bacon. We hastened to add he wasn't no friend of ours, and we was after him for other reasons, but didn't dig into the details.

"It just goes to show, a fellow burned up like that might not need no more pity than a fellow that ain't burned up," the woman said. "He was just as bad as if he was everyday-looking."

When we was back on the ride, Bronco Bob repeated the woman's lines to me, the ones about a burned-up fellow not being necessarily any better than one that wasn't. "There is a philosophy in there somewhere," he said.

We rode on across Nebraska and come to the state of Kansas. We was certain of when we come to it, as Bronco Bob had traveled all that area when he was living off shooting matches. There wasn't much out there in Kansas (not that there had been much in Nebraska), and I have to say I didn't take to it at all. It was just too wide with nothing on it but tall grass. Bronco Bob said it was so tall cause there wasn't enough buffalo coming through anymore, least not in the numbers they once was. Considering all those rotting carcasses we'd seen, this was understandable.

Along the way we started teaching Red how to better handle himself in polite society. We made sure he understood that farting at a meal was not a sign of respect for the vitals but was foul. We explained women especially disliked this, and when it was built up in you too tight, you had to find a place by yourself and let it go. I had learned this from Colonel Hatch back at the fort during my soldiering days.

We taught him that clean hands was best for eating, when you could wash them, and if you had a chance to eat with a knife or spoon you ought to. We discouraged eating with a knife, unless that's all you had or there was no women around, which was our case right then.

Bronco Bob showed the boy a few boxing moves, and it was fun to see Bob dancing around, quick on his feet, his fist held up, throwing punches. He taught the boy how to do it, and they had a few matches, thumping each other in the chest, avoiding the head. I even took to doing it, too. I learned more about fisticuffs than I knew there was to learn. I thought before it was just about who was the strongest and how fast you swung your arms, but Bronco Bob taught me different. I couldn't lay a hand on him, even though I was bigger and taller. Had he not been hitting me in the chest and ribs and pulling his punches, I would surely have taken a beating, especially if he decided to include punches to the head.

Red took to boxing and really seemed to enjoy it, though he always moved as if his ankles was tied together. He had good hands but not good feet. He couldn't dance about and move like Bronco Bob, who said people use the weight of the arms too much, don't apply the twisting of the hips, which he felt was the secret of success as a pugilist, as he referred to himself.

We also taught Red about gun shooting, and we was the right ones to do it. Still, Red had a knack right from the start, more so even than with boxing. He could hit targets right away, and he seemed to be one of those like me — if I do say so myself, and I do — who instinctively has an ability to point the gun and shoot and figure on its rise and sighting mostly by touch alone.

Red wasn't no gun hand, but he was well on the way to being one if he wanted to put in the work. I even gave him my old Navy Colt and some shells. I figured with the Colt, LeMat, and Winchester Mr. Loving gave me, I was armed enough for most anything and could spare the pistol. Bronco Bob gave him a derringer, which is a good weapon if you can hold your man down and put it to his forehead, shoot him with it, and then go to beating on him with the butt of it to make sure he feels something.

By the time we got to Dodge City, Kansas, Red could shoot and box well enough, and his teeth was cleaned up and he had learned how to comb his hair and put a part down the middle. That red hair looked mighty odd to me, and the part in the middle made it look like someone had dragged a rake through some blooded grass. But over the weeks he had actually put on a few pounds, as had the mule, and had started to look manly.

Dodge City stank like cow shit and unbathed men on the day we showed up, and it was my figure it stank that way on the days we didn't show up. There was cloud cover cloaking the town. It was as if we was having a sack pulled over our heads the air was so thick. It was cold, too, a dry kind of cold that was given a knife's edge by a prairie wind blowing at our backs.

There was tents on the outskirts and large signs posted up that said we had to turn in our weapons. That was different from Deadwood, as turning in guns was only that way at the Gem, an idea I put into action, and as soon as that idea come about the murders in the place dropped considerable if didn't disappear. There was always someone who sneaked a pistol in or was willing to gnaw someone's throat out or beat them to death with a chair leg, but on the whole it was a little less rowdy. Thing was, after I quit being the bouncer, I can't say if the rule was enforced anymore.

We rode by a big cannon in front of an army fort, and I tell you I got a little nervous passing by the fort for fear I might be identified as a deserter. But as this was a white bunch of soldiers, that was near impossible, unless one of the ranking white soldiers from my old regiment had been transferred and might recognize me. I knew it was unlikely, but it made me jittery just the same. I still carried more than a little guilt for having left my job with them.

We passed by the cattle yard, and there was cowboys hustling longhorn cows down the street and into catch pens. A goodly number of the cowboys was colored, and I seen a lot of Mexicans in their crowd as well, though some was so covered in dust I couldn't quite figure what color they was, only that they were cowboys and knew how to move cattle.

There was a general store, the Long Branch Saloon, a dry-goods store, and all manner of business buildings along both sides of the street. It was a much more organized and better arranged line of buildings than Deadwood, none of it built in such a way as to be treacherous. The street was wide and hard enough there wasn't any mud puddles, only a few holes here and there, most likely made by herds of cattle being driven through. There was lots of cow pies in the street and flies to go with them.

Bronco Bob said, "When I first come through Dodge it wasn't nothing more than a line of tents and a handful of cows. Look at it now."

"It still smells like shit," I said.

We arrived at the livery, unsaddled our horses, turned them into a corral, took off our guns, and gave them to the liveryman, a short little guy wearing a wool cap—which had been home to some moths at one time—and loose red gallusses that could be seen when he moved and his blue-jean coat swung wide. He appeared to have some Mexican or Indian blood in him, way his skin was colored and how his eyes was dark, but I figured his bald head was all Irish. He gave us what he called claim checks; it was a piece of paper with our names written on it and a brief description of our weapons. It matched the papers that was tied to our guns.

Bronco Bob said he and Red was going to the saloon where he intended to buy Red his first beer and maybe a whiskey. Then they might go whoring. Knowing Red's upbringing was in good hands, I chose to find a place to sleep.

Thing that was different in towns out there on the plains was that a colored could occupy any hotel if the owner was willing to room him. There wasn't no law against it, as there was in the South. I can't tell you it was all even out there for people my skin color. I can only say it was more so.

I got a room in a hotel run by a fat white man. I was given a key. I felt strange about it and very good. In that moment I had been accepted as an equal, if for no other reason than I had the price of a room. I thought that was fair enough.

It was midday, and I was as tired as if it was midnight. I paid out for a tub and some hot water and retired to my room until the bathwater was brought to fill the tub, which was already there under one of the windows. I pushed up the windows to let some air in, being used to the outside those long weeks, and the smell of cow mess sailed in on the breeze like birds. I finally pushed the window closed except for a crack and sat down in one of the two chairs that was there. It was thick with cushion and comfortable.

The bathwater come in trips delivered in steaming buckets, carried a bucket at a time by a very nice-looking colored girl who gave me a friendly eye.

Had I wanted, I surely could have had a sweet night with her, but I didn't act on it. I wouldn't do that to Win. I pretended her beautiful face and dark brown skin was of no allure to me, and when the water filled the tub and she left, I stripped down and soaked, washing my long, wild hair. Drying off, I fell into bed without a stitch on, and even with the light shining in through parted curtains I fell into a deep sleep in the nicest and softest bed I had ever spent a night in.

I didn't wake until the rest of the day had passed, the night had journeyed, and late morning arrived and crept on well past first bird's song.

I dressed, went downstairs, and had breakfast, which was two pickled eggs, toast, and coffee. I asked the fat man at the desk where a colored man like myself could get his hair cut.

It was a tent at the back of Main Street, and when I stepped inside I saw at least four colored men ahead of me. The barber was a big, dumpy, coffee-colored man with a bald head. Bald barbers make me nervous.

Some chairs was provided, so I sat and read a dime novel that was laid there for the purpose. It was the biggest batch of balderdash I have ever read, as it had to do with Wild Bill Hickok, and the personality of the character in that story wasn't anything like Bill, but it was pretty entertaining once I made up my mind it wasn't no true-life story.

When my turn came, I had to lay the book aside right when Bill was about to have a shoot-out with a dozen men. I never did learn how that come out, but I had a pretty good idea. I sat in the chair and had my long hair cut short and shaved at the neck and powdered. It might have been nice had the barber run the razor over the strop a little more before he went about his work. There were times when it dragged over the back of my neck like a plow over solid rock.

I threw in another coin to have myself shaved. It was done quick and rough, and I was only cut twice. The barber gave me a mirror to look in. Without all that long, thick hair, my ears really stood out. I had almost forgotten about them.

I paid up, strolled over to the dry-goods store, and bought me a fresh shirt.

I went back to the hotel and put on my new shirt, which was bright red, and waited around for what I didn't know. What I needed to do was start asking around about Ruggert and Golem, but I was a little uncertain where to start until the obvious hit me. I walked over to the livery and asked the liveryman, who was currycombing Satan as I got there.

He turned and seen me, said, "If I remember correct, this here is your horse."

"It is," I said.

"He is one fine animal—a little too lean, I figure, but well taken care of."

"He is a little lean," I said. "We been traveling."

"Few days' grain, and he'll fatten up," he said.

"Sir," I said. "Might I ask your name?"

"Cecil Jenkins," he said, like it was a title akin to captain or governor.

"There are two men I'm trying to find, and I was wondering if you might have seen them." I then went on to describe them.

"Should I tell if I have? You sound like you don't like them much."

"Do I?"

"You do."

"You haven't seen them, no problem. If you have, it's up to you if you want to tell me about them or not."

He hesitated for only a moment. "I have seen them. They quarreled right here in this livery."

"Quarreled?"

"They did. Big one decided he didn't want to go with the scarred fellow, and I think it had to do with money."

"So he don't think he's a mud monster so much he can't worry about money," I said.

"What's that?" Cecil said.

I waved it off, saying it wasn't important.

"I don't suppose you have any idea where either one of them is now, where they went?"

"The big man's horse is still here," the liveryman said, "and he is paid up through the week, so my guess is he's in town. As for the other, he said he was going out with some cattle drovers, got a job as a cook."

"Do you know where the drovers was going?"

"To get some cows, I reckon."

"He told you all this?" I asked.

"Nope. He told the big man. I'm an eavesdropper of the first order. I was also paying attention to them because I didn't like the condition of their horses. I can't abide a man that mistreats horse flesh. That's why I'm telling you about them. I usually keep a tight lip, but anyone that mistreats a horse—rough-rides it, doesn't feed it, or doesn't curry it good—they get a special place on my shit list."

"Do you know where the drovers are going to get those cows?"

"Texas. That's where they always go. Pretty sure the scarred one said he was going on his own when they reached Texas, or maybe he said before he reached Texas. I was listening in, but I wasn't writing it down."

"If I tell you the hotel where I'm staying and promise you a full dollar for letting me know if the big man comes for his horse, will you do it?"

"I will," he said.

I thanked Cecil for the information and how well he was treating my horse, then decided my next step was to find Golem. Golem was an odd duck and hard to figure, but my first thought was he might be at the saloon. I started over to the Long Branch, as it stayed open pretty much around the clock due to all the cowboys that passed through town at all hours. If Golem was there, even without a gun, he would be a handful, but I needed to know if he was still in town and where he was. If he saw me, things could go south quick, so I was thinking how I might just peek in the saloon then slide out and figure from there. I hoped I could hold my anger back enough to be sensible.

I was crossing the street, considering on all this, when who should I see coming out of it but Bronco Bob. He was heading my way. He hadn't put on fresh clothes. His hair was matted where it hung down from under his hat, and his beard was so tangled an owl could have nested inside it.

He seen me, and I noticed he was taking some time to look me over before deciding I was in fact Nat Love with a haircut and a shave. When he was satisfied it was me, he come to me with his hands waving. "Nat. What a set of ears. And with that shirt, you look like a robin redbreast."

"Thanks for noticing the ears," I said. "I never do."

"Nothing by it, Nat. They are manly. I want to tell you something. I'm worried about Kid Red."

"Who?"

"Red. We got to drinking, and he got to drinking more, and he played cards and had a knack for it, and by the time I cut him off from my money he had gambling money of his own. He got really drunk, and the boys in the Long Branch started calling him Kid Red on account of his hair, and by early this morning he was so drunk you could have laid cucumbers on him and they would have pickled. He borrowed some fellow's horse and a rope, roped that cannon at the fort, and dragged it along the street. They found him at the far end of town, having fallen off the horse, asleep by the cannon. I think he had taken his boots and pants off, but he had managed to keep his shirt and hat. The law come and got him, and he's in jail."

"Goddamn it, Bronco, he shouldn't never been allowed a drink. He's just now learning how to eat food. That's why I don't drink, all that kind of foolishness."

"You may have a point there, Nat."

We went over to the jail. The town marshal was a fellow named Deger. He was built near in the shape of a box and had a mustache like a resting caterpillar. He said the kid was in the back and had thrown up all over the cell. A man he was sharing it with took to beating him so bad they had to pull the kid out and put him in a cell by himself, which was not a thing they liked to do, their jail being stuffed pretty tight with troublemakers and drunks.

"It was pretty funny, though," said Marshal Deger. "He pulled that cannon through the streets, and when we brought him in, he said he did it so he could take it back to Deadwood and fight the Indians."

"He's never been drunk before," I said.

"That's true, Marshal," Bronco Bob said. "I gave him his first taste of liquor."

"He looks mighty young," said the marshal.

"He's nineteen," Bronco Bob said, lying with an authority so strong I damn near believed him.

"Well," Deger said, "he damn sure put a wet one on."

The short version was Bronco Bob paid a bit of money, and the sheriff went back and got Red, or Kid Red, as he had been called by the saloon boys. He had his pants on, and we pulled his boots on him, and we hauled him out of there. Pretty much toting him by the arms, we took him to the hotel where I was staying. Bronco Bob got himself a room, having spent the previous night in saloons, mostly the Long Branch, and in a bordello, where he had met what he referred to as a temporary fiancée.

"She was a honey," said Bronco Bob. "I told her I would take her away and make her my wife, and it seemed like a hell of a good idea at the time. But when I woke up this morning and realized what I said, on sober reflection I decided against it. I snuck out while she was asleep. That's when I realized I had lost Red somewhere. I found out about him when I went over to the Long Branch."

I had some coffee sent up, a whole pot, and we went to work having Red drink it. It took another pot to get Red so he could at least uncross his eyes. He had taken a pretty good beating in his cell. He had a knot on his forehead, both eyes was blacked, and his lip was cut open. The jacket Bronco Bob had given him was stained up, and his shirt was torn. When we pulled off his boots, we found the derringer in one of them. He had either forgotten to check it or had chosen not to. I was surprised it hadn't been discovered when he was arrested, him having pulled his boots off and all.

"Good thing he forgot about that," I said. "Or someone might have gotten shot."

"I would agree with that," Bronco Bob said.

The coffee may have uncrossed his eyes, but it didn't do much else, so we finally stretched him out on my bed and took ourselves downstairs to have a meal. I was eyed a little uncomfortably, but people in Dodge didn't want to insult someone who might be part of a team of drovers and free with money and had friends with pistols, so I was let in without incident. We was put at a table in the back, so as to keep my colored face from shining too bright near the front door. Still, for me, it was a real change being able to eat with everyone else. I enjoyed it.

Bronco Bob, being better-heeled for money than I was, ordered us both steaks and taters and bread. He ordered himself a warm beer and me a warm sarsaparilla, there not being any ice on hand.

"I take credit for foolish choices," Bronco Bob said. "I thought a boy that hadn't never done anything and had lived from hand to mouth might deserve a good night on the town. It got out of hand."

"I'll say."

We ate a few bites, and I said, "Golem is in town, and Ruggert is headed toward Texas."

Bronco Bob paused a fried potato on its way to his mouth, said, "Where'd you learn that?"

I told him.

"Do you know where Golem is exactly?" he asked.

"Not yet," I said. "I was going to start the search when I come across you."

"Without a gun, you will have hell to pay," Bronco Bob said.

"Already thought about that," I said.

Bronco nodded. "If you need me while you're here, Nat, if you come across him, I am your man. But after that, I'm sticking with Dodge. I think I can manage some card games and may even go back to shooting matches a bit. I'm sick of riding and being out in the wilds. I think I'll encourage the boy to stay with me as well. I might try and get some newspaper work here until I can write books about you and me and our adventures. Some of them will be true."

"I understand," I said.

We bought some biscuits with meat in them, wrapped them in a red-and-white-checked cloth they gave us, and carried those back to the hotel. On the way up to our room, we ordered and paid for another pot of coffee. In the room we found Red sitting up on the side of the bed, holding his head like Atlas holding up the world.

"I feel bad," he said.

"You and Bronco Bob had quite a toot," I said.

"If that means we drank a lot, that's what happened," Red said. "I think I even got some pussy. Though I'm a little shaky on the memory."

We gave him the biscuits, and he went to wolfing them down and drinking more coffee. About the time he got to the second biscuit, he paused in midbite, said, "Hey, wait a minute."

I was pouring a cup of coffee. "What?" I said.

"That Jew fellow. He was in the jail with me. He was the one hit me."

I put the cup down. "You mean Golem? He was back there in the jail?"

"I forgot about it until just now. My head ain't right. My brain is all twisted. But he was back there. Had that ash mark on his forehead. I know it was him. I seen him around Deadwood before. I think what happened is I knew it was him, said something to him about how he was a big coward and a backjumper. I got sick on him, and he beat me up. I'm not really sure in what order all that happened, but it happened."

I put on my hat. "Guess I'll go over and see him," I said.

"No," Bronco Bob said. "You can't go in the jail and try and kill a man with your bare hands, Nat. That is frowned on by law officers, and in the long run, considering his size to yours, foolish."

It was all I could do not to rush out the door, but of course he was right, and I wasn't stupid, no matter how bad I wanted to kill Golem. If I was going to go back to Win with all my parts, I had to play it wise.

"Tell you what," Bronco Bob said. "I will go over and check and see what Golem's status is, make sure the kid here didn't dream it."

"I didn't," Red said.

"When I know what the situation is, I will come back, and we can lay plans. Maybe I can go his bail and get him back on the street, and then you can kill him."

"Fair enough," I said.

Bronco Bob went out, and Red said, "I forgot I had that derringer in my boot. I should have shot him."

"Against a man like that it would be like trying to knock a mountain over with a well-thrown rock," I said. "It's best you didn't shoot him with that. He might have killed you."

I quit talking and sat down in the stuffed chair, but now it didn't seem so comfortable. I looked at my hands resting on my knees. They was shaking. Not from fear. I was too mad to be fearful. They was shaking with anger.

It seemed like I sat there for hours, but it couldn't have been more than a few minutes. Bronco Bob come in and said, "He was there, but he's been released. He sobered up and paid his own fine. I had to shoot shit with the marshal and pretend Golem was an old pal and I was look-ing to buy him a beer and some such story line, but he didn't know where he went. Just that he paid up and left. My thoughts are he has gone out to take a nip of the hair of the dog that bit him, to get over that hangover."

"Maybe that's what I need," Red said.

"No," I said. "You don't." I turned to Bronco Bob, said, "Listen here. How about one last favor, and then you are out of it. Go over to the Long Branch and peek in and see if he's there, check the other saloons if he ain't. I would be noticed a lot quicker by him than you, as you have grown in the hair and beard department, and you aren't wearing your show clothes."

"That's a for sure good thought," Bronco Bob said, and went out.

Well, that time an hour or so did actually pass before he came back in and said, "I looked in all the saloons and didn't see him. He may have found a place to sleep last night off."

"All right," I said. "From here on out this is my problem."

"I told you I was game to stay with you as long as you were in town," Bronco Bob said.

"I'm in for whatever comes," Red said.

"I know, and I appreciate it, but I'd prefer neither of you got involved. That hasn't worked out for them that's been friendly toward me in the past. Red, you stretch out on my bed and rest some more. You wouldn't be of any use like that anyway. And Bob, you look like hell yourself. Sleep some, and then get you a bath, or in the other order if you like. Me, I'm going to take a walk around town."

"I don't feel good letting you do that, Nat," Bronco Bob said.

"You look out on your feet," I said. "You wouldn't be of much help."

"That might be true, but let me sleep a few hours, and we'll go out together."

"All right," I said. "You two stretch out and rest, and we'll talk it over then."

"Now you're using your head," Bronco Bob said.

Bronco went to his room, and Red stretched back out on the bed, and in spite of all that coffee he was out right off. I closed my eyes thinking to relax a moment, but I went out like a candle in a high wind.

When I awoke it was to noise in the street, and it was dark.

I looked at the bed, and I could see Red's shape. He was still asleep and snoring loudly. I got up, went to the window, and looked out at the street, which was lit up with flickering streetlamps and the lights from the saloons. The street was full of folks, a lot of them obviously drunk.

I slipped the derringer from Red's boot, and with it tucked in my coat pocket, went downstairs and asked if the liveryman had left me a message, but he hadn't.

I went along the streets looking for Golem, even glancing in the saloons Bronco Bob had looked in just in case he had shown up. I didn't see him. I walked all over Dodge and back again but didn't see my man. I went to all the saloons again, managing to be called nigger only twice, once affectionately. I even had some warm sarsaparilla at the Long Branch, but still didn't see the son of a bitch.

Finally I slipped out of the saloon for a last stroll around town and had the same results. I was about to give it up when I decided I might amble down to the stockyards, take a look there. Closer I got to them, the stronger that cow shit smell became. There was a few cowboys in the area, but it was mostly just pens of cattle, the drovers having left their herds there and glad to be shed of them.

No Golem.

As I was crossing the street back to my hotel, I come across the liveryman, who was coming toward it. I called out his name, and after determining that I was who he thought I was, he threw up his hand in greeting and came over to me. He said, "I ain't seen your man. He hasn't come for his horse. But I thought I might tell you something of interest, if you can tell me why you want to find him so bad."

"My plan is to kill him deader than a goddamn post, and I have my reasons. I'll put them in a nutshell for you if you'll stand for it," I said.

"I will," he said.

I told him what had happened, leaving out a bit of it here and there but giving him the story in a fairly honest manner.

"My God, man. No wonder you want to find him. But you ain't even got a pistol."

"There's the law," I said.

"If you're going to break the law and kill him, you ought to have something to do it with. Come by the livery and let me slip you a pistol. Just one."

"All right," I said. "But wasn't our agreement that I tell you what happened to make me want to find him, and then you'd tell me something?"

"It was, but let's go to the livery to talk about it."

There was a part of me that was concerned. He was, after all, mostly a white man, and he could have an arrangement with Golem to lead me into a trap, and all I had was the popgun. I reached in my pocket and gripped it, but not with confidence. It was like the fellow that grabs at a straw when he's drowning.

The walk to that livery seemed the longest in my life, and when we got there he unlocked the door, which had been padlocked, and let us in. There was soft lantern light glowing inside, and it gave the place a pleasant look. There was some smell of horses and their leavings, but mostly it was a comfortable aroma, and it was warm inside. Golem didn't jump out of the shadows and hit me with a rock or shoot me with a gun.

Fact was, Cecil guided me to a desk where he kept his business ledgers and took a bottle out of the drawer and got out two glasses. I didn't say anything about not being a drinker of alcohol, not under the circumstances.

"I suggest just a swallow," he said. "Enough to warm you but not enough to give you liquid courage, which could get you killed."

I sat in a chair in front of his desk, and he sat in one behind it. I pulled my hand off the derringer, picked up the drink, and put it to my lips but didn't drink it. I can't even stand the smell of it. I put the glass back on the desk.

"He is about Mabel Jean's business," he said, leaning forward to take hold of his drink.

"Mabel Jean?" I said.

He downed the whiskey, poured himself another from the glass.

"She is a guide to peculiar interests, is how she describes herself, or maybe that ain't exactly what she says. Something like that. She comes over here once a month, on Tuesdays, that's today, and hauls my ashes for a free buggy anytime she needs it. It's kind of a lease agreement."

"She's a madam?"

"Yeah," said Cecil. "And a little more. Not all them she services want to get the standard piece of ass. I say she caters to peculiarities, more so than the China Doll brothel. It's pretty much straight in and out there."

I sat silent, waiting for him to get to the point.

"Thing this man of yours likes is different. He likes beating the whores, and Mabel Jean arranges it."

"The whores know this? That he's going to beat on them?"

"They expect a certain amount of abuse and a certain amount of extra dollars for it. He wants to hit them with whips, but Mabel Jean only allows cloth strips bound into a wooden handle. That way the whores get a sting, not a wound, and a man who likes that kind of thing gets his feelings settled. The man you call Golem, I'm sure it's him, as he was described to me today by Mabel Jean during our moments of lease payment. She rarely mentions her customers, hers being a private business. But she's scared of him. I think she thought I might do something, which I won't. I'm not crazy. Not after what she told me. She said she was glad to come see me to get out of her place. Said your man used the handle of that cloth whip on her girls, and not just to hit them with it. He won't leave. He's tanked up on liquor and hasn't paid for a drink or a fuck. And the two bouncers she's got, both colored like yourself, they both got broken up by him. Went home in a hurry, one on a stretcher. When me and her finished our business, I locked up and was on my way to the hotel to find you or leave a note. I was hoping you might want to kill him. I figured that was your plan. It could work out all around."

"He's at the whorehouse now?" I said, half rising from my chair.

"He may well be," Cecil said.

"Where is this place?"

I was shaking like a leaf in a storm as Cecil gave me directions, and a bloody haze was swimming before my eyes.

Cecil finished his drink, looked at mine, then at me.

I nodded.

He took my glass and downed it. He got up, got my guns.

He said, "I said one pistol, but I figure I'll get in as much trouble for one as all of them. The rifle, too, right?"

I started digging in my coat for the claim checks, but he said, "Naw, I know what's yours. Two of them is real interesting. That pistol with the shotgun load, that looped rifle."

He tore the tags off and gave them to me. He said, "Marshal asks if you gave me your guns I'm going to lie, and if it comes down to me getting in trouble with the marshal, I'm going to call you a nigger and say anything I need to say to keep my ass out of the jail. We understood?"

"We are," I said. "You keep the rifle here. It don't work out for me, I don't come back for it by tomorrow evening, then you can have it."

I took a breath and put the pistols in my coat pockets, made sure they would pull free quickly. "You telling me about this to help me get my man or to get in good with the madam?"

"One thing helps another," Cecil said.

I walked out of the livery and started up the street. It was a goodly walk. It was a building down below the stockyards and holding pens. I slid around back, seen there was lights at the back windows and some sliding out from under the door. There was a lantern with red glass in it hung over a long nail above the doorway.

Getting my grit up, I opened the door and slid in. It was a hallway, and on the walls there was cloth hangings of all colors and designs, and there was a painting of a naked woman riding a horse in a wide gold frame. She was lying sideways on it, and she had long blond hair and looked sleepy, like maybe she'd forgotten her nightgown and had gone riding not fully awake. To the left was a flight of stairs with the wall on one side and a railing on the other.

An older, meaty white woman with hair as rough-looking as a horse's mane came sliding into the hallway from a wide opening that led into a room where I could see a fancy red couch, a blue chair, more paintings, and a broken-down piano. I took a guess right away that was the place where the bouncers got bounced. The woman was wearing a pink dress, and the right side of it was torn. A titty that looked like it belonged to an old milk goat was dangling out.

The woman said, "You got to be the one Cecil's sending." She tried to poke that wild titty back behind that ripped dress, but the rip didn't leave it any place to go. It stayed free and in action.

I almost laughed. Cecil had set me up to do this job, just as I thought. The woman, of course, had to be none other than Mabel Jean.

"Unless you're overrun with colored men with pistols in their pockets," I said, "I'm the one he sent."

"He's up there," she said gesturing up the stairs. "He's got girls with him, and I don't want them hurt. Some of them are still working off their room and board."

I could hear him then, and I recognized that voice as surely as I would have recognized that of my mother. He was yelling about how they should arrange their asses, and he was saying, "Sing, you jezebel, sing."

I could hear the girls start in singing "Buffalo gals, won't you come out tonight." Not a one of them whores could have carried a note in a bucket with the lid tapped on tight.

"You look smaller than my niggers, and they got broken up," she said.

"This here pistol improves my stature," I said, drawing my LeMat from my coat pocket.

"That's what they thought," she said.

"Them bouncers was armed?"

She nodded. "I think that big bastard got shot once, but nothing he took note of."

"You don't say?"

"I do say."

I took that into consideration, put a foot on the stairs.

"Be sure and kill him," she said. "I think he's the unforgiving sort."

"I'm not going up there with the intention of giving him a flesh wound," I said, and continued up the stairs.

I was about at the top when I heard a smacking sound, like someone had slapped their hands together. Then one of the girls let out with a yip, and on behind that came a bloodcurdling Indian-style yell that I knew had come from Golem. It was so loud and surprising I almost filled my pants.

There was three doors along that upstairs hall, but he and them women was so loud up there I didn't have any trouble knowing which door they was behind. There was also smoke drifting out of a wide crack at the top of the doorway, and I could smell that it was tobacco smoke, strong enough to be that of a cigar or a pipe.

I practically ran to that door, and, lifting my leg, I drove my boot into it.

# 26

The door cracked loudly, swung back, and slammed against the wall.

It was a little room filled with smoke and the smoke was wrapped around a bed and some of it rose up and grew thick and covered the ceiling like a cloud. On the bed were two nude white women, both of them striped with blood and crying, and there was a colored gal bent over the end of the bed rail, her head lying against the sheets, her face turned from me, and Golem, fully dressed, had a whip in his hand—a whip made of cloth and a wooden handle. He was holding the cloth and snapping that wooden handle upside that colored gal's head. She looked to be unconscious, as she was just dangling there, not trying to move away from the blows. Blood had dripped down from her and was on the bed and on the floor.

Golem turned his head and showed a mouth full of a big black cigar. It was the source of the smoke that filled the room. I raised my pistol. His forehead had that mark of ash on it, and that was to be my spot to shoot.

"Deadwood Dick," he said, around that fat cigar.

"Big bastard," I said, and I was about to squeeze off a round but was denied the pleasure.

Golem wasn't so out of his head thinking he was some Jewish monster who couldn't be hurt that he didn't have the sense to whip that poor woman's body around in such a way it come in front of me and spoiled my aim. After he pushed her forward and she went tumbling to the floor in front of me, he wheeled and ran toward the open window behind him, grabbed at a rifle leaning against the wall, and jumped. That big bull of a man went through that open window with that rifle as easy as if he was hot molasses sliding along a greased pan.

Running to the window, I looked down. It was quite a fall, but if he was hurt, it wasn't enough to keep him from getting up and running off, heading toward the stockyard. I got a glimpse of his rifle lying on the ground.

Instead of jumping out the window, I decided on the stairs. I wheeled and stepped over the girl on the floor—for that's really what she was, a girl—and was in the hallway, down those stairs, and out the back so fast I don't really remember the trip. Next thing I knew I was outside and running along the back of the building until I come to where Golem had landed. His cigar was on the ground, smashed up, and I could see why he left the Winchester. It was busted from the fall.

"He's got a pistol in his boot," I heard a voice call out. I looked up and seen it was one of the white girls. Little beads of blood caught the light as they fell from her mouth and nose and dripped down not more than half a foot in front of me.

"Obliged," I said, and moved on after my intended target.

I came alongside the stockyard pens, which was packed with longhorns. There was cow manure that had oozed from out of the lot and under the pen slats, and there was enough light I could see Golem had run through it, for there was his big boot marks. I eased along careful-like then, staying close to the pens, trying to not take to mind what I was stepping in, for it was near ankle-deep.

The cows was stirring restlessly, and I seen that the tracks I was following had ended. There was cow manure on one of the slats of the pen where he had climbed up and had taken off through their gathering. I climbed up carefully and looked out over the cows. I seen Golem moving through them, trying to stay low and slide under their necks. One moment I'd get a good view, then a cow would take his place, then Golem's head would bob up, and then he'd stoop and be gone again.

It was a crazy thing to do, but I put my pistol in my coat pocket, worked my way to the top slat of the fence, and stepped off of it. I landed a foot on a cow's head, leaped to another's back, and then another. It was easy enough to do, as they was so tight in that holding pen.

Then there was a shot. A cow that hadn't done anything but walk a thousand miles to be a steak dinner took the round in the head and went down. I was by this time having less luck with my cow jumping, as they had really started to stir. I fell in between some cattle and splashed in cow mess, which didn't smell like a bed of petunias.

That shot and my fall got the other cows frightened, and they began to shove and push and thud about even more, and then one fell over the dead one. I was just able to avoid its horns as I worked to my feet, but this had started other cattle stumbling, and pretty soon there was a big, kicking pile of them.

There was another sharp snap from Golem's pistol, and if it hit anything I'm not in memory of it. The cows went loco. Horns flashed, hooves thumped, beef rushed by either side of me. I grabbed a running cow around the neck and swung my feet up over its haunches, dangled under its neck as it ran. It knocked other cows aside, tripping over one, stumbling a bit, but not so much either of us hit the ground. It got its hooves under it, and away we went again, striking a row of slats full-on, me at the forefront of the cow's battering ram. This split the slats and broke the pen and sent the cow into the open. I was flung off my ride as it made a wild turn, tripped, and went rolling along the ground. Cows came rushing through that split in the fence, hooves flying by me, stirring the dirt into clouds of dust and manure.

Another shot was fired, and a cow bought the farm—threw its head forward and stuck its horns in the dirt so hard it flipped, like an acrobat trying out a failed headstand. Cows was bumping against me. A shot rang out, and Golem managed to pop him another cow. He wasn't shooting anywhere near me, but he was hell on cattle.

I'd been damn lucky and had only been shoved about. I was well beyond the gap in the fence and had rolled up against a building wall. As fortune would have it, those cows turned toward the lights and the sounds of the cowboys in the streets. The cowboys was firing guns off and yelling, which meant more than one of them had been unwilling to turn in their pistols and would most likely be spending a night in jail.

The cattle was hastening through that alley like they was being shot out of a cannon, perhaps confused on where the shots were coming from, knowing only that they should flee in some direction, and any direction would do.

I hauled myself into a doorway as the longhorns charged by me. When their numbers thinned, I went running along the wall, away from the direction they was taking. I seen Golem a good ways ahead, between the holding pens and that building I was up against. I ran after him. He turned as if to shoot, but I fired first. I know it hit him, because I could tell by the way his body jerked and the fact that I don't miss much if I'm in range. The shot didn't put him down, though. He darted into an alley, and I went after him.

There wasn't much light down that alley, but there was plenty of stinking trash barrels and plenty of shadows to go with them. I pulled the Colt from the other pocket and, armed with two revolvers, started down that alleyway feeling as if I was naked. There was all them barrels, of course, but it was still about twenty feet before I could reach one to hide behind, and a bullet might pass through one, meaning they wasn't necessarily all that good a protection, though they was working for Golem in that I didn't know exactly where he was hiding. But I reasoned he hadn't had time to reach the other end and make his way into the street. Won't lie to you: hesitation came over me for an instant. Then I remembered Win and how we had been on that hill in the dark, the sweet sound of her flute when she was happy, that so-fine kiss, and then there was that stinking, bloody cowhide wrapped around me, holding me tight like a fist squeezing a grape. Golem pulling Madame and my Win from the wagon, those men in a lusty crowd around them, Madame's mutilated body, Win naked in the firelight, that blank look she had as she turned her head toward the wall. It put steel in me, brother. Cold blue steel.

So I inched onward, my hide prickling, and then, well, I don't know what overcome him. Either he was bored with the whole thing, mad, or thought he had the advantage, because I hadn't gone more than a few feet when a large shadow swelled up from behind one of the barrels. It was without question Golem. His pistol barked red fire, and mine barked back. He tried to shoot another time, but either his gun was empty or his hammer hit on a bad load. I fired with both pistols—two shots from the LeMat, one from the Colt. It made Golem dance about a little, and then he threw his pistol aside, snatched a barrel above his head, trash flying out of its mouth, and charged down the alley at me.

I couldn't have missed him. It was like shooting at a buffalo tied to a tree. I fired two more shots, one from each pistol. Then that barrel come flying. I tried to dodge, but it hit me, and all the trash flew out. The Colt went skittering from my left hand. I fell on my back, tried to get up, my boot heels scratching in the dirt.

I flicked the baffle on the LeMat as Golem leaned over and grabbed my shirtfront, lifted me up like I was a pocket handkerchief. I stuck my pistol straight in his face and squeezed the trigger. The shotgun load roared like a lion.

There was a scream, high-pitched for a man of his size, and the next thing I know I'm on my back, and Golem is lying on the ground holding his face with both hands. I got up and eased over careful-like to look down on him. The light wasn't good, but since he wasn't wearing a shirt, I could see he was all shot up and bleeding right smart. He was still holding his face as if to keep it together, moaning and rolling his head from side to side. I couldn't believe he was alive. I couldn't believe he was sitting up. I squatted down beside him.

I said, "My name is Nat Love, as you may well know. I am also called Deadwood Dick, and you have wronged me and the woman I love."

I know how that sounds, but that's how I spoke to him, if not exactly those words, making it as dramatic as I could. It was stuff I had read out of that dime novel about Bill during that trip to the barber's. "I have avenged that wrong, or will have done so shortly, as you're shot up something awful and won't be pulling daylight." I think I even called him a scoundrel or a rascal. I hope I did.

A tooth dripped out from under his hands and fell between his legs.

Now that it was done, I didn't feel all that satisfied. I won't say that disappointment set in. I was glad I had done it, but seeing him suffer like that wasn't giving me a bit of pleasure. I slipped the LeMat in my coat pocket, pulled the derringer out of it, stuck it into Golem's ear, and cocked back the hammer.

He didn't try to move away. In fact he quit rocking his head. Blood squeezed through his fingers and dripped. He pushed his head toward the derringer; let the barrel rest there like a steel earwig.

I heard him say in a voice that sounded as if he was trying to talk under water, "I'm God's avenger. I'm not supposed to die."

"I think you're mistaken," I said.

"I'm made of mud," he said.

"Well, your mud's got runny," I said.

He lowered his hands. A chunk of his face, including one eye, was gone. The other side of his face was riddled with buckshot. "This doesn't make any sense. I can't be hurt."

I squeezed the trigger on that little gun, and the next moment he made a liar of himself. His hands fell loose from his ruined face, and his legs snapped apart, like he had mounted an invisible horse. He fell back so hard his head sounded like a bag of flour hitting the ground.

I saw then that a watch chain was dangling from his pocket and his turnip watch had fallen out of it. It was a lidded sort, and it had popped open, like maybe he had been trying to look at the photo inside of it in the dark before I come into the alley.

I tugged the watch loose of the chain. I don't know why I did it, but I did. Maybe it was some kind of trophy.

I put the watch in my pocket, tucked the derringer away, gathered up my own guns, and hurried out of the alley.

When I got to the street it was full of cows. More had broke free of the pen. With all those cowboys firing pistols and hooting, the cattle had gone wild and were pounding down the street in a mad stampede. I got close to the buildings and kept walking. I seen a few of the critters had gone into the saloons as if to order beers. They was causing quite a ruckus. Women had gone to screaming and men was yelling.

I felt a little guilty.

I made my way to the livery, dodging horns and thousands of pounds of beef. I knocked on the wide door, and after a moment Cecil opened it a crack and let me inside. "Don't let those cows in here," he said, as if me and the cattle were plotting together to charge in and steal his cash box.

Inside the livery, I wandered over to some loose hay and sat down in it, my back to some slats that made up an empty horse pen.

Cecil stood over me, said, "You done it?"

"He ain't with the world no more," I said. "He's gone back to mud."

"What?"

"It ain't worth the story, Cecil."

"Any whores survive?"

"All of them, I think, but they was in a poor way, having been beaten by him. One of the girls was bad off. You might get a doctor over there."

"You done a good thing," he said. "You have done those whores right."

"I did it for me," I said.

"Maybe so, but it worked out for a lot of people. How do you feel?"

"I don't feel all that good, to tell the truth."

"All right, then. Stay settled there. I'll get you a drink."

"Just water," I said.

"I got coffee."

"That'll do."

He brought the coffee to me. It had a lot of sugar in it. I drank it, and it made me sick. I turned my head and threw up in the hay.

"Must be all the excitement," he said.

"Something like that," I said, leaning back against the pen, feeling like everything inside me was draining out.

Cecil went then to check on the whores and to get a doctor. He was gone for some time, and during that time I didn't move except to fix myself another cup of coffee and sip on it. I kept it black. I think it was all that sugar that had made me sick, what with my stomach feeling as if it was turned over. I took Golem's turnip watch from my pocket. It was silver, scarred and nicked up from having been carried in his pocket with coins and the like. I thumbed the lid open and looked at what was inside. It was a photograph of Golem with his hair shorter and slicked back and parted down the middle. His face looked firm and gentle, like life was good. There was a woman and a little girl in the photograph. The woman was nice-looking, with black hair in a bun. The child looked like the mother. I remembered what Bill had said about how Golem had lost his mind and killed them with an ax. Whatever had come over him, them deaths he caused had turned him into something new and wrong, and worse, sometimes I figured he knew it. I was surprised to find I felt a little sorry for him right then. I closed up the watch and tossed it into the hay. I didn't like how it made me feel.

When Cecil came back, he said, "That colored whore will be laid up awhile, and she may have a hitch in her get-along."

"How bad a trouble am I in?" I asked.

"You killed a man, but as far as I know ain't nobody found the body. Mabel and the girls only tell it like he was there and jumped out of the window because he was drunk. That's all they're telling. They ain't even saying you was there. I think you're in the clear, but his body is damn sure going to show up, so my thinking is, far as Dodge goes, I wouldn't linger. Nothing to tie you to him yet, but a whore might talk in time to someone, so I'll say it again. I wouldn't linger."

I got to my feet, using the pen to lift me up. I hadn't realized how much those cows had banged me around. I was terribly sore and weak. I gave my pistols back to Cecil.

He had his own water pump in there, and I worked the handle and cleaned up as best I could. Then Cecil came out with some clothes and told me to change into them. They wasn't much—a ragged shirt and some worn pants and patched socks—but I took them gladly. I stripped, washed myself good, dressed, then washed my manure-stained, brand-new red shirt, scrubbed my pants with a bar of lye soap Cecil had, and laid them over the top slat of one of the pens.

"You can pick your clothes up here tomorrow," he said. "Keep them ones you got on, you want to. Man left all his belongings here a year ago and never came back. I sold his horse and saddle and other goods already. I figure he got dead somewhere."

I nodded and went back out onto the street.

A hell of a roundup was going on. Cowboys was in the streets, trying to herd them cows. They was hooting and hollering and driving the cattle back up the street. I damn near got horned a couple of times but made my way to the hotel.

When I got inside, looking out the windows was a bunch of folks that was housed there, among them Bronco Bob and Red. They was at the window by the door. As I come in, Bronco Bob raised his eyebrows. I got my key at the desk, leaving everyone to the show at the window. I hadn't no more than started up the stairs than Bronco Bob and Red was beside me.

"How come I have this feeling you didn't just go out to change into those old clothes?"

"Because I didn't," I said.

We went upstairs into my room. I felt like everything around me was closing in. The walls seemed tight, and the gaslights seemed dim. I said, "I'm leaving tomorrow, boys. I have a direction on Ruggert."

"I could go with you," Bronco Bob said.

"Don't change your plans now," I said. "You said you was through when you got to Dodge. Stick to it. You've been good friends. That is enough."

"I have really felt good riding with you," Red said, and hung his head, like it was uncomfortable to meet my eyes.

"I borrowed this derringer," I said, holding it out to him.

"I come to know it was missing when I put on my boots," Red said as he took it. "I didn't figure it was anyone else other than you that took it."

"I have underrated this little gun," I said. "It needs reloading."

Next morning I wrote a letter to Win, though I wasn't even sure she would read it, and a letter to Cullen. I wrote them out and at breakfast downstairs gave Bronco Bob some money for posting them, asked if he'd mail them the next time he went past the post office.

I shook hands with him and Red, trucked over to the livery, and when a crowd of cowboys left out of there after doing business, I got my clothes, which was now dry, and put them on. I rolled up the ones Cecil had given me in my bedroll, saddled my horse, collected my guns, and went to pay up.

"You can keep your money," Cecil said. "You done them women a favor last night."

"I would have done it anyway," I said.

"It don't matter. You done it. Keep your money. Tell you another thing. They found that big moose in the alley, but not before they ran some of the cows through there and penned them up. After they done that they found him trampled over. I heard about it from a customer who walked over there when he seen a crowd gather. I went over there, too. Big man was where you said you killed him. There was barrels and trash knocked all over hell by them cows, and when I looked at his body, I couldn't have told you if he was a man or a mud hole he was so mashed up. Ain't no one going to even know he was shot. For all they know he got caught in the stampede, maybe sleeping one off in the alley when they brought them cows back through last night. You'll be good."

"Thanks," I said.

"You're shy of money, there's a colored preacher and his children want to go to Arkansas, and they'd like to have a gun hand. I don't know how you're set for plans. Pays meals and company and a few dollars. They got a cow with them, so that means fresh milk."

I didn't really want company, but meals and money and fresh milk might be nice. I was getting down to the dregs.

"Where would I talk to them?" I asked.

"They were here this morning. Told them I knew a man leaving today might be interested in riding along, a man that had some gun skills but wasn't no gunman by trade. I threw that in to make you sound better as a person."

"Thanks. And I'm not a gunman by trade."

"They're on the far side of town, a half mile out of it. They're living out of a mule-drawn wagon. Seem nice enough folks. What might be a thought is to ride out there and talk to them, take their measure, if your plans are loose enough."

"I'll think on it," I said.

I put my rifle in the saddle sheath, led Satan out to the street, and swung onto his back. He trotted along comfortably, having enjoyed his rest at the barn. We passed the hotel. I looked up at the window where my room was. I didn't see anybody there.

I rode south with it in mind not to stop and talk to anyone. But the farther I got out of town, the more I began to think about having my meals given to me and some money to boot. I didn't have anything but a few dollars, a canteen full of water, and enough jerky to last for a day or two—three if I let my belly growl a little. I'd have to depend on game appearing and my marksmanship to feed myself.

It was the idea of company I didn't like. My heart wasn't in it. Truth was, as of that morning I had been looking forward to being alone for a while. The thought of that had been like a tasty fruit, the tomato being a member of the nightshade family notwithstanding.

But it was a long ways to Texas, and the more I figured on it, the more I thought it might not be bad to take it by way of Arkansas.

# 27

I seen the wagon and the mules, a cow roped to the back of it. There was a big colored man sitting on the wagon with the reins in his hand, a pipe tucked up in his mouth, and clouds of smoke floating up from it.

Truth was, though I was wearing a coat of high, cold lonesome, I knew within a day or two I'd start to miss someone to jabber with. I like to be alone from time to time, and that's what I had been considering, but basically I am the friendly sort. My pa was a talker, as long as the day's work was done. Told stories, let me know all the things about my mother I didn't know about (this after she died), and they was all good things. He told me about himself, how it was to be a slave in the old days, and how happy he was I had only been one for a short time. He told stories about jaybirds and dogs and wild hogs and stories he said came from way cross the ocean, where there was a country full of colored people, which I later learned from Mr. Loving was some place on a continent called Africa. Pa had a way of telling stories that made you want to sit up on your hind legs, throw up your front paws, and beg for more. Mr. Loving was like that, and even Wild Bill could be that way.

As I was looking at the man, he turned his head toward me and lifted his hand. I guess he figured I had to be who Cecil told him about, as I was the only colored riding along the road out of town. A slip of a girl dropped out of the back of the wagon and come walking around to get a look at me. She was dark of skin and lean, but with good hips. She wore a faded calico dress that might have once been green and blue, and had on a white bonnet. She was wearing men's lace-up boots, but they wasn't laced and the strings hung down and dragged the ground. Right behind her came a little boy who I reckon was maybe ten or eleven years old. He had on overalls and a blue shirt and was barefoot. He was black as a crow's wing. He strutted about like he had just whipped a grizzly bear in a fair fight.

When I was up to the wagon, I seen the large man was really compact. You might think him fat at first glance, but he wasn't. He was as skin-tight as a wild animal, but he had a hard plumpness about him, as if the sack of skin he wore wasn't quite enough to hold all his muscles. His head was large and rolled about on his neck like a boulder, and his face glistened he was so black. His eyes was just as black. He had a wide and friendly face with a smile full of white teeth. I couldn't help but be drawn to him. He climbed down off the wagon to greet me. It was like he come unwadded and grew to a height well over my own. He was bigger than Golem had been. His arms was about the size of my legs, and his legs was about the size of me.

I swung off Satan, stuck out my hand to meet the big man's. I learned from Wild Bill to always have the other hand ready to draw, and if you couldn't shoot left-handed, it was best not to shake. But it wasn't a way I wanted to live. In spite of all that had happened to me, I was by nature a trusting soul, or at least I wanted to be. My pa was like that. It seemed like a better way to live, and frankly I still hold by it. It has cost me some over time, but on the whole it has given me greater joy than not. That said, I didn't throw alertness to the wind.

"Luther Pine," he said. "Glad to meet you."

"Likewise," I said.

The girl came over then, loosening the bonnet strap, pushing the hanging brim of it back so that I could see her face. She was lovely, and I noted she wasn't as young as I first thought. She was just small, and her dress was loose. The boy was all grins, and I could see right off that face was the same as Luther's.

"This here is Ruthie, and this little troublemaker is Samson."

Both of them said hi.

I greeted them both back, tried not to let my eyes linger too long on Ruthie, for there was something about her that held my attention. All right, let me be honest. She was a good-looking young woman, and I have the same animal in me that all men do. I was only looking, but I figured when you come across something pretty, you ought to take it in, same as watching a blue jay or a clear night sky. They're a joy for the eyes.

"We can feed you, and I got twenty dollars if you complete the trip," he said.

"I'm going to Texas," I said. "I can get you to Arkansas, though, and then it's up to you."

"You been there before?"

"No, but I reckon I know the way well enough."

Luther plumbed the depths of that idea like a well digger shoveling for water. I guess he struck it, cause he said, "I got the money for you when we get to Arkansas. Food along the way. You are responsible for your own sleeping arrangements, care of your horse. I have some grain for my mules, but there's enough for your critter, too."

"All right, " I said, and we shook hands again.

"Are those your guns?" Samson asked me. He had been scooting over closer and closer to me so that his head was about even with where the butts of my revolvers was standing out of my coat pockets.

"Well, little sir," I said. "They are indeed my guns, or I wouldn't be wearing them."

"Samson," Luther said. "You will hold your talk for now. We need to go on."

Samson scuttled to the back of the wagon and climbed in without another word.

"He is a scamp," Luther said, "and I fear when a little older he will be about the devil's business. I should know. I was there once myself."

That's when I remembered he was a preacher. "I think he'll make a fine young man."

"Actually, so do I," Luther said.

"We're glad to have you along," Ruthie said.

So away we went. Me and Satan leading, mostly, but now and then dropping back behind the wagon to make sure it was settling good and the cow was all right; and when I was honest with myself, I knew I did it because Ruthie sat at the back and looked out. I looked at her so much a kind of guilt settled over me. What with Win up there in Deadwood waiting for the snow to fly, her mind drifting, it didn't seem right for me to even look at another woman, even if it was just to raise my spirits.

In short time guilt settled on me heavy as stone, and I made a point of riding up front more, and when I took to the back of the wagon as a change of pace, I made myself concentrate on how well the big barrels (three to a side) was fastened on. The barrels had ribbons tied around them along with the ropes that held them. They was in different colors. Yellow, blue, red, and green, and they was tied off in firm bow knots.

First day out the sky turned the color of a pearl-handled revolver. Then it started raining. It rained hard right off, so I pulled on my slicker and we kept going. After a while it was too much on me, even with that rain slicker. Rain blew up under my hat and down the neck of the slicker and wetted my knees where they stuck out from under it. I rode back to the wagon and said how miserable I was. Way the wagon was set, Luther could sit back under the covering a bit, if not completely, and though he, too, had pulled on a rain slicker, he couldn't avoid getting wet in the same way I was. He tugged the mules up and set the wagon brake, suggested I tie Satan off and climb up with him.

I did that. We settled in the wagon, putting our feet inside and turning on the driver's boards so the rain was to our backs. We was mostly dry that way. It was the wind that hurt you, especially if you was soaked as I was. Under my slicker, my coat was damp, and so was my guns. I had brought my saddlebags inside with me. I had my gun-cleaning equipment there, along with extra ammunition and some rags. I unloaded the weapons and dried them and cleaned them and reloaded them.

"You seem quite concerned with your weapons," Luther said.

"Indians or rowdies show up, you'll be glad of that," I said.

I looked up and seen Samson eyeing my every move. He was fascinated with these weapons. Ruthie had lit a lantern at the back of the wagon and was reading a book by its light. So far, me and her hadn't had much to say to one another.

"Do you live by the gun, Nat?" Luther asked me.

"I try not to," I said.

"I would hate to see a young man such as yourself let them be his guide through life," he said.

"You didn't hire me because you suspected I was a good conversationalist, now, did you?"

He laughed. "That is the truth. I have your guns in my hands through you. I'm not innocent of their use."

"Innocent or guilty has nothing to do with it," I said. "I'd just soon lay them down and never pick them up again, but that ain't the life I got. Least not yet."

"What sort of life do you want?" Luther asked.

I started in then about the farm I wanted. Said I had a few things I had to do first, but that was my plan. Settle down on a farm. I didn't mention Win. I didn't want to have to go into where she was and what condition she was in or how she had been put in her bad way.

"You should add prayer to your ambitions, son," he said.

"I've had about as much luck with that as I have had with hoping," I said.

He nodded, smiled pleasantly, the lantern light laying on one side of his face like a big swath of yellow paint. "Very well."

I glanced up then, seen Ruthie had turned her head away from her reading and had set her eyes on me. I said, "What are you reading?"

"*Ivanhoe,*" she said.

"I read that myself," I said, it being one of the books me and Mr. Loving had read together.

"The women in it seem fairly dumb and always have to be rescued. There's times when I wish they would just get their heads chopped off."

"But other than that you enjoy it?"

"I suppose I do," she said. "Robin Hood is in it. I rather like Robin Hood."

"Ruthie is one peculiar girl," Luther said. "She wants to be a schoolteacher."

"That sounds like a good idea for a smart woman," I said.

"I agree," said Luther, "and I second it. She's just peculiar is all. She talks to ducks."

"Birds in general," Ruthie said. "They are good listeners."

"She says they talk to her," Luther said. "What can you do with a daughter who talks to ducks?"

I laughed. Then I saw Ruthie's face. Hell, she and Luther was dead serious. That gal talked to ducks.

Luther changed horses, so to speak, said, "I'm a preacher, but I don't take the Good Book just as it is." He took a fat, floppy Bible from an open box, held it in my direction. "This is no more than a guide. I don't believe that the words of the Bible are divine or to be taken exactly as is. There are as many bad things in the Bible as there are good, and the bad things are often held up as good because some Bible hero did it, and that doesn't set right with me. The Old Testament I pass over completely. As for the New Testament, I follow Thomas Jefferson's lead. I have underlined only the things that are said to have been spoken by Jesus. The rest is of no importance, really. The Beatitudes. How Jesus said we should treat people, do unto others as you would have them do unto you— those are the things I teach."

I told him about Mr. Loving, how he believed God just sort of started the clock then stepped off the stage.

Luther nodded. "Perhaps, but I think he helps in our lives. Maybe not the way we want and when we want. I know it's hard for some to accept, but I think there is a plan to things. I think he has laid it out, but not in stone. We can vary that plan. We can do better, or we can do worse. There is an afterlife, son, and not all of us will go there, but I don't believe God sends anyone to hell. I don't think of him as that mean. I think the bad die and cease to exist; their souls fade. But the good, they live on in paradise."

"With harps and such?" I said.

"I seriously doubt that. I don't think it's a corporal place, but one where we are all part of something that is impossible for man to define. Some part of our great universe."

"That actually don't sound much like a preacher," I said.

"I'm not with the Methodists anymore."

I liked Luther pretty much right off for his manner. And for him not being a Methodist.

"You teach me how to shoot?" Samson asked.

"No, he will not," Luther said before I could answer. "You will learn to read and write and make something of yourself." After this exchange, Luther turned to me. "No offense meant, sir."

"None taken."

Next morning Ruthie milked the cow into a bucket and poured the milk into one of the barrels, except for that which was used to drink or for cooking. The way they had it worked out is that as the day went on and the wagon rolled, it sloshed that milk in that barrel until it was the same as having been churned. In the evening the churned milk was salted into butter, then stored in tins. There was usually more butter than could be eaten, but it was also used for easing the pain of cuts and such, and it was even used to take the place of grease for the wagon wheels. Most important, it was poured on flapjacks and mixed with molasses. The flapjacks was made from flour from one of the barrels, which when mixed right with milk and butter can be stretched out for a long time.

We traveled like this for quite a few days with no trouble in sight. The meals was good, if pretty much the same, and the company was good, too, and it made me glad I had come along with them.

One night after we stopped and the cow was milked again, the milk being drunk with a dinner of boiled pinto beans and cornbread, the cornmeal coming from yet another barrel, I said to Luther as we sat around the fire, our bellies full, "I seen three of the barrels used. What's in them other three?"

Turning to look back at the wagon, Luther said, "Of the three on the other side, one is full of salted meats, which we haven't broken into yet, and if we can start scaring up some game, we may not have to for a while. As for the other two, well, one has our old dog Scratch salted down in it, and the other contains Geraldine, my wife and the children's mother."

I thought for a moment he was tugging my leg, but when I looked at him, glanced at Ruthie and Samson, I could see he was dead serious.

"You have your wife and family dog salted down in barrels?"

"I just said that."

"I know, but I felt it needed repeating."

"Pickled, to be exact. Brine water, and a bit of this and that to keep them solid and without odor. I had to bend Geraldine's knees under her chin to make her fit, but she is a small woman, so it's not that bad."

"Why would you do that?"

"Bend her at the knees?" Luther asked.

"No. Pickle her." I said this and watched my back in case Ruthie or Samson might come up on me, whack me in the head with the intent of pickling me for a later trail lunch.

"It's not as grim and mysterious as it seems," said Luther. "Scratch is a beloved pet, and he come down sick and had to be shot. When my wife died a day later, we decided we had had enough. I had already made the break with the Methodists as a preacher, and the house we lived in belonged to a little church not far from Dodge, and they were forcing us out, so we decided to head to Arkansas. I have kin there, though I've never been to Fort Smith. They're on my wife's side, actually. I know them from letters. Geraldine was from Arkansas and always wanted to go back, so back she's going. The idea of leaving Geraldine and Scratch behind for the wind to blow over without any kin nearby was too much. I dug Scratch up, and though he had already been visited by the worms, I pickled him and then Geraldine, set them aside for a few days until we had to leave. When we did, we took them with us. And there they are."

I didn't have anything to say to that. I just sat there while Ruthie came over and plopped more food on my plate, poured me more milk.

"I guess that's understandable," I said.

"Sure it is," he said. "We couldn't bear to leave them behind. The thought of it made me sick. I considered it, mind you. It would have been the easy way, but we had a family meeting, which is where I tell them what we're going to do, and I did it."

"How's that settle with you, Ruthie?" I asked.

"I want my mother buried in soil where I live," Ruthie said. "And if she can't be where I am, I just want her to be some place nicer in the winter."

"I hear Arkansas can get pretty brisk in the winter," I said.

"It's got to be better and prettier than Kansas," she said. "If it's pretty, I can stand the weather."

"Scratch was a good dog," Samson said. "Mama liked him, too."

"Sounds like to me you got it worked out," I said. Then I ate and drank the milk and then had coffee. That night I slept a little greater distance from the wagon, and I didn't sleep solid or comfortable.

More days passed, and I mellowed on the pickling news. I come to think of Luther and his family as odd, but not crazy or dangerous. I guess if you was a generous thinker, you could look at them making big pickles out of their family member and a dog as a gesture of love and kindness. That said, I made sure not to dip from the wrong barrel when I was helping with the flour or dipping out milk or butter. I didn't want to come up with Geraldine's eye or one of Scratch's ears in a flour scoop. I also wondered about Ruthie and her talking to ducks. I wondered what the ducks had to say. Since none was on hand at the moment, this was a question that had to go unanswered.

We came to the Indian Nations. There was plenty of Indians there, many of them said to be tame, but I felt it wise not to chance their friendly dispositions if we should come upon some. My plan was to cock my weapons and keep a sharp eye out in case they was overtaken with a sudden loss of hospitality. I knew for a fact Comanches wandering through there would soon skin us as look at us.

We met a few travelers now and then—whites, mostly. Some of them had been bushwhacked and robbed. We met a colored couple on their way to Kansas. They said they had two children when they started, but they'd come down sick and died. Had it not been for a friendly Cherokee that was wandering about on foot, they would have died, too. He gave them some food and pointed them the right way to go, and then he was gone.

They ate supper with us one night, and the next morning, loaded down with milk, butter, and such that Luther felt he could spare, they headed north, toward what I figured would soon be weather cold as a witch's tit. Before they left I asked them if they had come across a burned-face man, partly scalped, and they said they hadn't. I figured if they had, they'd have remembered it.

We came to the base of the Ozarks. The land had gradually moved from prairie to a rise in the earth and finally into tree-flecked mountains. When we got up in the mountains a ways, we stopped one night and decided on a two-day wait. The mules was tuckered out from pulling the wagon, and the cow was starting to have trouble keeping up. The milk had started to dry up, maybe from her not being milked as properly as she should have. We thought with rest and a good feeding for a couple of days, the animals would regain their strength. Only Satan seemed fine and even bored from waiting around.

On our first night there, after Ruthie and Samson had disappeared inside the wagon, me and Luther sat around the campfire. We enjoyed doing that. I had come to look forward to it every night when we camped. First there would be dinner, and for some of the stories Luther told, Ruthie and Samson would be about. Then they would grow tired and turn in. Me and Luther would tell stories about this and that, and if the fire was bright enough, sometimes we'd read books from the wagon, now and again reading aloud to one another. On this night we wasn't reading nothing, just had blankets wrapped over our shoulders to fight against the cold. There was a night bird calling, kind of pretty, and way out where the mountains was standing tall, a cry like a dying woman came down from them and seemed to roll at our feet like a ball.

"Cougar," Luther said. "They ain't much for bothering someone, but it happens now and then. When I was growing up, we used to lose chickens, hogs, and dogs to them from time to time."

"East Texas has bobcats, a few cougars," I said. "I've seen bobcats, but not cougars."

"They are elusive critters," Luther said. "And out like this, it's best not to come up on one. They mostly won't bother a person, but they don't have a code against it if they're hungry enough or we get in their way."

Luther picked up a stick and stirred it around in the fire.

"What brought you to being a preacher, Luther?"

"Sin," he said. "My own as well as that of others."

"What could you have done?" I said. "You're about as affable a fellow as I've ever met. You steal some apples?"

"It was more than that," he said.

I waited to see if he was going to volunteer a reason. It was a long wait. I heard the distant cry of that cat again. It brought a chill to my bones that was worse than that brought to me by the wind.

Luther pulled the stick from the fire and dropped it on the ground. He looked at me, said: "It's not a simple answer. I was a young man, twenty-five, and I wanted a pistol I saw in a store."

"A pistol?" I asked.

"It's kind of a long story," Luther said.

"Not like I got a meeting to attend to," I said.

"I guess you are pretty much trapped here. I lived in Missouri then. A small town, though actually it wasn't much of town. That store wasn't much of a store, either, a clapboard building with one room and some shelves with things on them, and there was a big potbellied stove. White men liked to go there and sit around the stove and swap stories, drink some, chew tobacco, and spit at a can. I was fresh from being a slave, but we weren't treated a lot better afterward. You know about that, I'm sure. I seen that pistol on the shelf when I was running an errand for my former master, as my pa still worked for him, except now he got some wages of a sort; they weren't much more than what we had when we were owned. I think I was feeling my freedom, Nat. I was feeling bold. I was supposed to be free, so why wasn't I? I wanted that pistol. I knew there wasn't any way I could have it, and I was supposed to have the same rights as everyone else.

"Old Man Turner had a rule, and there was even a sign. It said: I DON'T SELL FIREARMS OR AMMUNITION TO NIGGERS. The resentment built up in me. I had been secretly educated by my pa, who was educated himself, at least to some degree. He had been stolen from the North and brought to the South as a slave when he was young. He had been a free man and could read and write and cipher, but he had to act like he couldn't do any of those things. That wasn't tolerated in a slave. After he was stolen, he tried to slip away a few times, but all that got him were terrible beatings. One time Master used pliers to pull out his back teeth as punishment. Pa finally gave up and accepted things. I had been there twenty-five years and accepting it myself. My mother had long died. There were brothers and sisters, but they had been sold off. I was kept because I was strong and Master needed someone sturdy to work the way he worked us. It never occurred to me that I was accepting things same as Pa. It only come to me that he was accepting it. I can't explain that. Maybe because he was my pa I thought he was supposed to do something, and whatever he did was supposed to include me. I realize now that he was whipped down, body and soul. That pistol became more than a pistol. I wanted to defy that sign and have that gun. It was like a statement, I suppose. I am free and should be treated like I am.

"Well, one night I snuck out and crept over to the store, pried the back door with a claw hammer, and went inside. There was a safe there.

It wasn't any bigger than a shoe box and was about as secure. I was able to pry it open with the claw hammer and steal thirty-eight dollars that was in there, though I left a copper in it out of spite. I stole that pistol, too. I looked around for some shells but couldn't figure out which ones went to it. I didn't know a thing about guns then. I stuffed a bunch of shell boxes in my pocket and lit out. I decided I was going to make my way north through the Ozarks. I thought things might be better up north. The weather was good. I was strong as a bull. And I was spiting not only Old Man Turner, I was spiting my pa, who at that moment in time I saw as a coward.

"I hid out in the woods and tried to make my way north, but I hadn't been anywhere much and couldn't figure out which way to go. I tried to use the sun as my guide, and that way I could find north, but what I hadn't thought about was that you couldn't always take a straight route. The mountains, the trees, the creeks, the available paths didn't always suit a straight direction.

"What happened is they sent my pa after me, along with a white man, and they had dogs with them. After a few days they run up on me. That white man wanted to let them dogs on me, but Pa kept begging him not to, saying he could talk me in.

"Well, he wouldn't have had to talk too hard. I had stolen the wrong ammunition, hadn't eaten anything but a few wild foods, and was so hungry and weak I wouldn't have cared what they done to me.

"This white fellow, I think his name was Ennis or some such, had been hired to bring me in. Old Man Turner had figured out pretty neatly it was me, as I was the only one missing. He was the one sent them out to get me. I bet it cost him more to catch me than it cost to bring back the money.

"Pa came into the brush where I was at, the dogs having pretty well surrounded me. He asked me to toss out my pistol, and I did, saying it wasn't loaded. He picked it up and gave it to Ennis, and I come out. Ennis said, 'Now, this nigger is going to take a whipping, and you'll take one too, being his pa.'

"Pa offered to take a whipping for both of us, and that hurt me to hear it. All of a sudden I didn't exactly know how I felt about him. I didn't want him to take a whipping for me, and I didn't want to take no whipping, either. Ennis said we would both take a whipping and told Pa to strip off my shirt and tie me to an elm so my back was facing away from the tree. I had had many a whippings, but I had come to the point then when I wasn't going to take no more of them voluntarily. But I didn't let on that I had turned rebellious again in less than five minutes. Pa started leading me toward the elm. He didn't like it, but I think he didn't see any other way out, and he had many times coated my whip lashes with lard and butter and a bit of coal oil. I have the scars to prove that.

"Ennis came over to stand by Pa so as to watch and see he tied me right. I knew then I wasn't going to take a whipping come hell or high water. I snatched a pistol from Ennis's belt, and I shot him. Right in the face. Pa tried to take the gun away from me, maybe thinking Ennis was alive and we might find our way out of this yet. Or maybe he wasn't thinking. But I tell you what I did. I shot Pa."

"Hell," I said.

"Didn't kill him. I shot him in the leg, and he went down. I figured the only thing I could do was take Ennis's horse and get on out of there. The dogs didn't know what to do when Ennis was shot, and they sort of drifted off on their own, not having anyone giving them commands. Now they was free, too. All the time I'm getting ready to ride out of there, Pa was begging me not to do it, and then I couldn't go through with it. Least not without Pa. I got him on the horse, and we rode down a trail and into some valley land. There we come across a colored man running an errand for his former master. Not much had changed for him, either, except in word. I asked him about a doctor. Course, no white doctor was going to help us, and there wasn't any colored doctors. But he said there was an old woman who was pretty much left to her own devices in a cabin on the edge of a planter's property. She was once a slave there. She was said to do good things with wounds and sickness.

"We hid out in the woods, and that night I got Pa over to her place.

The old woman said the bullet was too deep to come out, but that he'd heal over, and if he didn't die of infection, which she called the rot, he'd live to pull a cotton sack another day. It was my plan to leave him there, thinking that bullet would work for him, not against him, and that he could say I shot him and Ennis when they tried to take me back.

"That old woman gave him something to drink, and Pa passed out. She said it was for the pain and he'd get over it in a few hours. That was naive of me. I rode out of there into the trees, and at that point it was like I couldn't go no more. I just fell off that horse, down between some sycamores, and lay there. The horse ran off. I was so weak I couldn't move anymore. I had been going without rest, and now I was drained by fear and confusion. I was up pretty high in the hills, but I had a good view of that old woman's shack. I seen that old woman come out of her shack and head toward the little settlement down below. I tried to get up and move on, but my legs had quit on me. I decided if someone, or dogs came, they could have me. I didn't have no more fight left. I just laid down there in the cold and slept.

"I don't know how long I was out, but when I woke up my will had been somewhat restored, and so had my strength. Down below here come that woman, and she was walking fast for someone old as she was, and right behind her on horseback, and some on foot, was a bunch of men with lanterns. They come to her house, and I knew then she had gone and told on us. Pa was knocked out from her so-called medicine. They went in and brought him out, and the only thing I'm thankful for, Nat, is he was still mighty drugged and couldn't walk. He was literally dragged. They put a rope around his neck and found a tree limb and pulled him up. His neck wasn't broken, like in a clean hanging, but he was strangled. Again, I hope that medicine kept him away from too much pain. He kicked a little, but it wasn't any time at all before he was still. That old woman wasn't anything but a Judas.

"I eased back on my hands and knees, got to my feet, and started running. I still had that pistol I had taken from Ennis, and I told myself if they come up on me, and I saw there was no chance for me, I would use it on myself before I would be strung up. But the odd thing was, no one ever came after me. Maybe they thought I was long gone and not stupid enough to be sleeping on a hill just up from that old woman's house. As for her, I entertained going back to kill her, but it came to me that she didn't know any better. She had been a slave all her life, and to let Pa live, and possibly have it found out, could cause her harm. For an old slave woman she had it pretty comfortable by then, too old to work and around long enough she was beloved in the same way you like an old dog that has been about for years. For what she done to Pa she probably got a ham and an extra scoop of flour from her former master.

"I lit out. I just kept going. I started heading north. I stole chickens, killed and ate them to survive."

"Better dead chickens to eat than alive," I said.

"That's the truth. I stole eggs, stole food from houses when no one was about. I even robbed a couple of white men on the road with my six-gun and whipped one of them about the ears just because I could. I was on the road one night, going into Illinois. I had stolen an old sway-back horse and was getting bolder as I went. I come upon a colored fellow lying beside the road. He was dead. It appeared his neck was broken. I guess he had fallen off his horse or been thrown by it. The horse was nowhere to be found. That's what I was thinking then, about the horse. Not thinking there's a poor man lying dead at my feet, but that he had a horse, most likely. I searched through his pockets, found a flask of whiskey in his coat and two bits in change. I never did find his horse. I wanted to. I figured it had to be better than that old swayback. I left there with that flask, drinking, not thinking one whit about that poor man.

"I went on, and the night turned cloudy. I swear, a bolt of lightning, blue-white and sizzling with fire, came down out of the heavens and hit that swayback smack in the head and gave me the burning trembles. When I woke up that horse was lying on top of me, and I could smell its hide sizzling from the lightning strike. It was then that the clouds parted and I saw the stars. Nat, it was then I saw the face of God. He wasn't angry. He wasn't mad. He wasn't seeking vengeance. He was there to let me know I had a chance to turn things around. What do you think about that?"

"That God liked you all right but didn't have the same feeling for horses."

I couldn't help saying that, and feared soon as I said it Luther would take offense. But he laughed. "That's a good point, Nat. I've thought on it. And you know what?"

"What?"

"I don't have an answer. But what I had from that point on was faith that I was placed here by God for something better than robbing the dead. I worked for a long time to get out from under that horse. That lightning bolt had knocked us to the side of the road, and the ground was soft there. I wasn't crushed on account of that, as the ground gave with me and made enough of an indentation I was able to slip out from under that dead swayback. I was numb for a while, being stunned from the legs down. I grew a lot of hair after that. My legs and balls got hairy, and so did my chest. It was overnight. That lightning stoked me up inside with the spirit of the Lord."

"Along with hairy balls," I said.

"That, too. I walked out, Nat, walked into Illinois, and first colored church I come to I went in during services and dropped to my knees and prayed. I prayed not for ownership of things but for my eternal soul. I prayed to be a better man. A little later I got a job there at the church, cleaning the place, and pretty soon I was doing a bit of preaching, time to time, you know, when the preacher would let me. He didn't let me for long, because I started getting a following, a big following. He came and told me I was too good at it. I was taking his job altogether. I didn't want to do that to him, and he didn't want it done to him. I moved on through the country, stopping at colored churches and preaching when they'd let me be a guest at their pulpit.

"It was heady stuff for me. I went from being a Church of Christ for a while to being a Seventh-day Adventist. All I remember about the

Church of Christ is they argued over musical instruments. Some were for it, some weren't. Adventist I don't remember anything at all. I met some Catholics and prayed with them some. I was a Baptist for a while, but frankly, I found them too stupid. I know that's a harsh thing for a preacher to say, but they believed the Bible word for word, and common sense didn't stir them in the least. If the preacher told them a handful of shit was honey, they'd eat it. They lacked the desire to question. The Methodists I was with a little longer, but they thought they were special because they could go to dances and didn't see the devil in their soup, meaning they were down on the Baptists, who could service a goat and shoot a man while doing it, and think if you had been baptized, you were forgiven. Catholics had too many beads and such makings. There were some other branches, but they hurt my feelings about the same. That's why I started my own church and took to my own way of preaching."

"What's this church called?" I said.

"It hasn't any name. It's just me, and I preach what I think Jesus meant, with the understanding I could be wrong, though not so wrong as the others."

I smiled at that.

"So you see, Nat, I was once a very bad sinner. I shot a man—"

"He deserved it," I said.

"Just the same. I shot him and I disrespected my pa for no good reason but pride. I stole. I lied. I actually did service a goat once. I was on the road and I came across it at a farm where I stole some chickens, and one thing led to another. Anyway, that's not for the children to know."

"Of course not," I said. "Do you and the goat write?"

"No. But we parted friends. Later on, when I had religion and my head screwed on tight, I met Geraldine, who was from Fort Smith. We married and were very happy. I continue to be happy because I am thankful I had her and our time together. God took her, for whatever reason, but I feel blessed each day that she was mine. That I have these wonderful children, Ruthie speaking to ducks notwithstanding."

That night I slept under the wagon, and three or four times the cry of that cougar brought me awake. Last time it did the sound was close, so I didn't really sleep anymore, just lay there under the wagon, cradling my rifle, eyes open, alert to shapes, thinking about Luther and his religion and his need to be a better man. Me, I was out to shoot a bastard.

# 28

When we finally came into Fort Smith I saw it was a fairly lively town. There was a lot of bustling about, people on the streets and boardwalks, wandering out of stores and such. We come to the livery, but the man there told Luther there was a colored livery on the edge of town and that he ought to take his animals there.

"I'd take your stock," he said, "but there's lots of white folks in town for a hanging, and they come first."

We didn't really have no other choice but to rattle onward. At the edge of town there was a big tree where there was some horses tied, and next to it was a ramshackle shed that had three sides closed in. The open end showed us a row of horse and mule asses. There was a bit of open room at the far end. Enough to house five or six animals if they all agreed to be friends. The owner of the shed was a big redbone with one good eye. The other eye had the lid pulled down and sewed shut due to some ancient injury. He said we could go cheap if we wanted to just put them under the tree.

Luther paid up for the shed for his mules, my horse, and the cow. He was allowed to pull the wagon under another tree down from the tied horses and turn it into a camp spot. Me and Luther both saw this as short-term housing and animal boarding. It wasn't a whole lot better than just having the animals stand out in the rain. Anyway, we pulled the wagon there, then took the animals back to be housed in that shed.

I was supposed to be done with Luther and his family and get my twenty dollars, but I told Luther to forget it. He gave me five dollars anyhow, told me I had a place there in or under the wagon. I thanked him, said I would see him again, but for now I was on my own. Truth was, I didn't want to stay around Ruthie. She was starting to stir my blood, and I felt guilty about it.

"You ain't got to go," Samson said.

"You don't have to go," Ruthie corrected Samson. She wasn't speaking to me. She didn't seem to care one way or another.

"Guess I do," I said. "Maybe I'll come back and have Ruthie teach me how to talk to chickens."

"Ducks," she said.

"Ducks, then," I said.

"I doubt they'll speak to you," she said. "I don't know they'd like your attitude."

"How do you feel about my attitude?"

"I could probably learn to tolerate it. How do you feel about me talking to ducks?"

"I could probably learn to tolerate it."

"Actually, I do speak to chickens and other birds, and they speak to me, but I've always found ducks to be the most informative."

"That's information I can hold to my heart," I said.

"You do that, Nat Love."

I must admit she made me feel pretty good and at the same time pretty bad for feeling that way, what with poor Win back there in Deadwood, her head like a cleaned-out room, and me out here flirting with a pretty girl that talked to ducks.

Me and Samson shook hands, and he did it like a grown man. Then I shook Ruthie's soft little hand, took what money Luther gave me, and walked into town. I needed to figure on what to do next. I hadn't so much as heard a word about Ruggert, and I feared I had seen the last of him. Golem was out of the way, but the worst of them seemed to be lost on the wind. I figured the best thing I could do was find myself a place to stay and a steady job, at least until I could figure on things. I had left Win alone to kill them, to avenge her, yet being away from her made me feel confused. I thought back on her, and all I could remember was how she looked at me as if I was a stranger.

I come upon some colored boys playing in the street and asked them about a place where I could stay. They gave me directions to a colored boardinghouse, and to get there I had to go back part of the way I had already come. I got a room, and it cost me three dollars for a week. I figured a week would maybe give me time to find a job. I reckoned, too, that I could deal with Luther for a bit of supplies to get me through until I cornered a job.

My little room didn't have a real bed in it, just a cot, and when I laid down on it I had to bend my feet a little so they didn't hang off. The room was slanted because the undersupports wasn't even, and there was cracks in the walls and the wind whistled through like a butcher knife. It was worse than the room I had in Deadwood. I bought some newspapers and looked for job ads, but there wasn't any, so I used the papers to clog the worst of the cracks in the wall. A couple of blankets came with the room, and there was a small stove with a smoky stovepipe that went up and turned and poked out of the wall.

I was told not to burn the heater too long, else the pipe would catch on fire and burn the place down. They hadn't even done a good job of putting it in the wall, didn't surround it with mud or some such that could take the heat and not flame up. I figured I might manage to fix that myself.

It took me three days, but finally I got a job sweeping out the general store. I worked three days a week, about four hours a day, and got paid a dollar a day. The white fellow who did it on the other days made two dollars a day. My employer was a Mr. Jason, a porky fellow with muttonchop sideburns and a patch of hair that was thick on the sides and at the back. It looked as if there had been a brush fire on top. When he first offered me the job, he stood before me holding a broom. He explained to me how it worked, in case I might think it was a horse.

He told me when I went to work that I had to understand he paid white men more, but he felt the War between the States was over and I deserved a chance to work—at half price, as he didn't believe colored were animals the way some did, but that didn't mean he felt they were on par with a white man, one of God's true creations. I guess I was an untrue creation, along with the worm or the traveling salesman. He then told me something about how to hire me he had to cut something at home that he was used to having and really cared for, cause it would mean money was spent on me that couldn't be spent on items of his desire or some such. I don't remember exactly. It made about as much sense as believing the moon was made of green cheese.

I did this job for a week, then I got a kind of promotion and was put on six days a week, not just sweeping but unloading supplies and such. I didn't get any more a day, just more days. Mr. Jason made it clear that he was quite the positive sort of fellow giving me such a position, and I heard his lecture again on how he felt he was the fairest man in Arkansas when it come to niggers. I secretly harbored the view that one night I'd have liked to burn his store down, but since he didn't live in it, I didn't see the reasoning.

I managed during this time to write some letters. I wrote one to Cullen, even sent one to Dodge City in hopes Bronco Bob was still there. I wrote that lawyer in East Texas, even though I didn't have my papers Mr. Loving had given me. I wrote him and told him I had them, and I sent it to his name in care of general delivery.

In the letter to Cullen, I gave very detailed accounts of my travels, though I left Ruthie out of it except for mentioning her name as Luther's daughter. I put in things for Win, tried to touch on a number of events she might find amusing, even though I didn't know for a fact any of it would mean a thing to her. I asked about her playing the flute and mentioned our fine place on the hill, in a very modest way; told her I was tight on the trail of Ruggert and had only stopped in Fort Smith for supplies, which was a mild lie. I was neither on Ruggert's trail nor merely stopping for supplies. I was at a standstill. But that's how I told it, and then closed out with all my love to all of them. I thought I ought to write Win her own letter but decided against it. If she was still confused, it was better I kept things general, let her hear it from Cullen. Maybe that way some of it would sink in.

In Bronco Bob's letter I was even more entertaining, and I threw in a couple or three lies to liven up the whole thing where I thought it might be sagging. I mailed the letters with hopes of them all finding their intended, then waited for a reply.

One day as I was sweeping out the store, I came out on the front porch and seen a big colored man riding on a sorrel horse. He sat straight in the saddle, had a bushy mustache, and wore a ten-gallon hat and a shiny badge. He looked firm as an oak tree. He had a rope leading from his saddle horn to another horse behind him, and on the horse was a white man big as the man leading him. He was hatless, riding with his head down, his hands tied together in front of him to the saddle horn. He looked as if he had been chewed on by a cougar.

There was another colored fella working there with me by the name of Washington, and he walked up beside me to see the man ride by. He was somewhat younger than me, a boy, really.

I said, "He's got on a marshal badge."

"Marshals wear them," Washington said.

"They got colored marshals?"

"Judge Parker does. That there's the toughest and best marshal there is, black or white, red or brown. That's Bass Reeves. You don't want him after your ass, cause he'll sure as hell find you. Want to fight, he'll fight, and he'll bring you back lying across that horse if need be. That fella there, looks like he wanted to fight. Lucky he's alive."

"A colored marshal. I'll be damned," I said.

"Most of us are," Washington said, "and you going to be damned and without a job you stay out here on the porch too long."

I went back to work, but by pure chance my stepping out on that porch and seeing Bass Reeves was to change my life more than a little bit. But that was to come.

As time went on I began to save some money back. I visited with Luther, Samson, and Ruthie on a regular basis. Ruthie still said she talked to ducks, or would if she could find one. She said in the meantime she listened to the mockingbirds and took in what they had to say. It wasn't about much, she explained, but they was upset about how many trees was being cut. I can't say for sure that was accurate, having never spoken with a mockingbird myself, but I decided to take her word for it.

I missed Win, but all things considered it wasn't a bad life, and I admit to the fact that I was beginning to notice that, like a flower at spring (though it was still winter), Ruthie was starting to blossom. Her skin was smooth and her eyes were wide and bright, seemed as if they were pools that you could fall into. I told myself what I saw in her was some of the traits Win had, but to be honest the two of them couldn't have been any further apart. It's hard to match up anyone with another if one of them talks to birds.

My habit of working and visiting with Luther and his family was spun to the four winds when I went to the post office one Tuesday. I did this daily after the first week of writing those letters. On that day, after waiting a month or more, a letter and a package showed up. The letter was from Cullen, and the package was from Bronco Bob. Both, of course, had come to me general delivery, Fort Smith, Arkansas.

It was noon, and I was on my lunch break. I had a bottle of sarsaparilla and a couple of fresh-cut slices of bread and a slab of cheese. I put the cheese between the bread and sat down under a tree out back of the store. I rested the bottle on the ground, the sandwich on my knee, and held the letters in my hands. The letter from Cullen was the most tempting, as I felt it might hold news of Win. I decided as it was the most important, I'd read it last.

I laid it on the ground beside me and opened the package from Bronco Bob.

Inside was a letter and a dime novel. The novel was titled: *The True Life Adventures of Deadwood Dick*.

*Dear Friend Nat,*

*It was a pleasure to receive a letter from you and to hear of your time on the trail and your friendship with Luther and Ruthie and Samson.*

*As I promised you, I have written up your adventures and have managed to place three novels based on them. I am happy to say they are selling well, though by the same token I am not getting rich, and so far I have no money from them for you. I should also add they wouldn't let my hero be colored, so he has become white. Still, he is based on your adventures, the ones you told me about on the trail when we were with the redheaded boy who is now better known as Kid Red. I will come back to him.*

*Anyway, if there is any money to be made beyond my expenses on the dime novels, I will see that you get some of it. I will write a new story that will tell of your leading a wagon train through the Ozarks and how you fought a cougar and Indians to get to Fort Smith. In fact I have already started the story. This one, you will see, covers mostly the time we fought those desperadoes that stole your girl and the old woman and wrapped you in a cowhide. I gave the Indians you told me about a bigger part, and just so it would be sure to be exciting, I added more men to the final gunfight. I also gave myself and Cullen bigger roles than we actually had in the gunfight, but not so much that there isn't some truth to it, though I thought the part about the trained circus lion taught to attack at the use of a foul word (that I left unnamed) was a good addition. I felt the lion was a symbol for the kind of mean things you and me and Cullen fought against, even if there wasn't any lion present. In other words, it's a windy, and I'm trying to justify it to you. I became carried away when I was writing it and couldn't contain myself. That is why they call it art, and that's why it has a cougar and a lion in it.*

*I added in a wild dog who only answered to your commands as well, and the dog died bravely while battling the lion, managing to drive itself and the lion off a cliff in the process. I hope that will be okay. I figured if some-*

one figured out the story was actually about you, then you wouldn't have to explain where the dog was. He has been taken care of.

As for Kid Red. Well, Nat, he has gone bad and become a gunman. He got so good with the pistols, having had good training from me and you, he began to enter shooting contests, as I used to do and as I now and again still do when the money dries up. He acquired quite a name around Dodge. But he also took to carrying his pistols in town, hidden under his coat, and he took to drinking something furious. I regret the day I took him to a saloon to toss back one. That is on me.

Thing is, while drunk, he got in an argument with a man in a saloon and shot and killed him. He also shot a saloon girl who screamed when he shot the man. I guess the scream made him jerk around or something, because he wheeled about and shot her right through the head. He hightailed it, and word around Dodge is that he joined up with a gang of thieves noted for robbing travelers on the trail, and as of late they have taken to a couple of banks and are currently, like Jesse James, robbing trains; it is said he and these men are led by—and I want you to hold on to yourself here—a man scarred by knife and burns. He has four men in his gang at all times and sometimes more. The kid has gone bad, Nat, and that is all there is to it.

I know the man you are after may well be the leader of this gang, as he fits the description, and I hesitated for some time if I should tell you about him. I know how your heart cries out for vengeance, but I don't want to be the one to lead you into something you might not get out of. As your friend and biographer, I thought it right of me to inform you of this change of events and to inform you I have heard and read in the newspapers that he and his gang have moved into the Indian Nations, where they figure to go about their robbing sprees with greater ease. I know you are near there.

I am living in Dodge and have taken up with a young lady who I might marry if I don't wear her tail out first. I thought I should try it for a while and see how I feel a year from now. We are, I guess, engaged. She has spent nearly all the money I have gotten from the books. I have two more payments that will be sent to me, and they send me several copies, so if you

*want these further adventures of Deadwood Dick, all you have to do is let
me know, and I will mail them to you wherever your address might be.*

*If you are back in Dodge, look me up.*

> *Forever, as always, your dear friend,*
> *Bronco Bob, Esquire*

*P.S. I really am sorry there was no money, but the girl, her name is
Beatrice, is expensive and worth it, and surely I will make enough to give
you your share in time if we both live long lives.*

Now, that was a turn of events, all right.

I hated what I had heard about the kid, but the idea that I might have
some kind of lead on Ruggert, vague as it might be, was inspiring. I was
thinking on how I might go about hound-dogging that lead when I remembered the letter from Cullen.

I hesitated opening it. I ate my sandwich and drank my sarsaparilla. I
looked at the sun, determined I probably had about fifteen minutes before I was supposed to go back to work.

Finally I took a deep breath and tore the letter open.

*Dear Nat,*

*I am glad to have heard from you, and I read your letter with great in-
terest. I should say up front that Wow is doing well, and so are the other
China girls. I think the one whose name always seems different was indeed
messing with me. I think she finally told me her real name, but you know
what? I can't remember it. It's harder to remember than the names she made
up, so I just call her Peg Leg Pete. She doesn't seem to mind. She and the
other girls come by to see us from time to time, and they have all spent time
with Win.*

*I read aloud to Win what you wrote to her, but she didn't seem to un-
derstand it or who it was from. I'm sorry. But that's how it was. She asks
for water now and again. She never asks for food, though we try to make*

sure she's fed. This is not always successful. She doesn't have much of an appetite, and I must confess she has grown quite thin and pale.

We have had a couple of doctors come to see her, but their verdict is that she has ceased to thrive, which is what they say when they think she has just quit, doesn't care anymore. I hate to lay it out like that, but here it is, Nat.

Wow and the China girls have been through much of what Win has been through and maybe some worse. I don't say this to say Win is weak but to say some manage to get past it, and some do not. There is no way of knowing what all experiences were in Win's background that led to her current state. I was told that by Wow, by the way.

I must be very blunt with you, Nat. The weather here is terrible, and I wouldn't want you to saddle up and come this way for fear you might not make it. But you must brace yourself to the idea that Win may not see the spring flowers bloom, and if she does she may soon be underneath them. I want you to understand the depth of her despair. She is lost inside her head, and I fear there may be no way back out.

As for your vengeance ride, I would not continue it. I am glad, as of your letter, that you caught up with Golem, and I am glad you and me and Bronco Bob put the burn on those others, but Ruggert, if he has gone on to leave you alone, might be best left alone.

Lastly, I can't predict the weather, but it might be best to come as far as Dodge and be ready for when the weather changes. I would hope you will be here to see her at least one more time.

Perhaps she will rally. After you left she seemed better for a time and even played her flute. Then she laid it aside, and not a peep since. It seems to me she is having a harder and harder time identifying me, Wow, or any of the girls. She never leaves the house, as the weather is too bad, and she is too ill to leave now. She mentioned the hill once. That's all she said. "The hill." And then she said, "Nat." And neither your name nor mention of the hill has come again. It's like the last of what she knew of life had gone out with those words.

Forgive me for writing such a sad and direct letter, but when you can, keeping in mind you do no one any good if the weather captures you and

*kills you, please come back. Forget Ruggert. I can't say Win needs you,*
*as I can't say she knows what she needs anymore. Still, I feel you would*
*like to be here for the end, which is undoubtedly coming. Be assured if*
*you cannot make it back, we will take care of her until there is nothing*
*left to do.*

> *With sadness in my heart, but with great memories of you still,*
> *Cullen*

Now, I've said that I have had some low moments, but not even when I
was wrapped in that cowhide and Win and Madame had been taken from
me, have I felt lower than I felt in that moment. I could hardly stand up
when it came time to go back to work; stunned and confused, I did go,
and I put in the rest of the day, though I hardly remember it.

When the day was over I went to the only place I knew to go,
Luther and his family. I went there, and they was glad to see me.
Luther had some rocks laid in a circle outside his wagon, and it was
there they cooked when the weather was dry. As I came up, he stood
from where he was squatting near the fire, stirring it up with a stick.
Leaning against the wagon was a coffin he was building out of white
pine. He had been shaving it down and sanding it, as there was sawdust on the ground by it.

"Nat," he said. "How are you?"

"I ain't so good," I said.

About then Ruthie walked up, as she had been busy about her toilet in
the woods, or so I guess. Samson stuck his head out of the wagon. "Hi,
Nat."

I greeted him and Ruthie. They had dragged some logs around the fire
spot, and I sat on one of those without being asked. Luther said, "You
need to say a thing or two, Nat?"

"I don't know," I said.

"Tell you what," he said. "Don't think on it too hard. Have a cup of
coffee and see how you feel then. You haven't anything to say, don't say

it. If you do, well, I'll listen. If you prefer the children go off, and you just want to talk to me, that can be arranged."

"I'm a grown woman," Ruthie said.

"Maybe just enough in years to call yourself that," Luther said. "But you're still a child as far as I'm concerned."

I looked at Ruthie. Even in my deep bewilderment I had to say she looked womanly to me. She had really come into her own after we had arrived in Fort Smith.

Luther had a pot of coffee on the fire, and he got a rag and lifted it out, poured me a cup. I sipped it. If it was hot, cold, fresh, or old, I couldn't have told you. It was like my taste quit working.

"Well, then," Luther said. "Let me tell you our plans. Our relatives, the ones here. They aren't here now. Least not alive. The influenza killed them well before we arrived."

That pulled me out of my own pit. I said, "I'm sorry, Luther."

"Well, it's not like we knew them that well, but we have brought my dear wife home and our faithful dog, and they are both going to be buried."

"Together?" I asked.

"Separate holes," Luther said.

"Of course," I said. "I see a coffin is almost ready."

"Wife gets the coffin, dog stays in the barrel. Her relatives have a graveyard, and since there ain't no one to protest against it, she'll end up there, I reckon."

"What about the dog?" I asked.

"I think he should be buried there, too. It's out a stretch. I rode a mule out there after I was told where it was and was told all her people were dead. Frankly, it's kind of a relief. I wasn't sure I wanted anything to do with them. Relatives can be a pain in the neck."

"That's a rough thing for a preacher to say," I said.

"Isn't it?" he said.

"Would you like a top-off on that coffee?" Ruthie asked me.

"I suppose I would, Ruthie, thank you." I of course didn't even remember drinking it I was in such a state.

She got the rag, took hold of the pot, and poured me a cup. That cup wasn't no more than full when I started telling them about the letter I had gotten from Cullen, leaving out what I didn't want them to know. I had the dime novel with me. I had dropped it on the log beside me. Samson picked it up and was thumbing through the pages. I didn't mention that it was supposed to be about me. I think Samson might have been reading all the while I was talking. That's one good thing about being young. You don't always feel obligated to pay attention to sad stories.

I spilled it all out—about how I needed to start back to Deadwood and how I was planning on supplying myself and starting out in spite of the winter. When I finished telling it all, Ruthie said, "You are a damn fool, Nat."

"Ruthie!" Luther said.

"Well, he is," she said. "He went off and left her to kill a man—"

"How do you know that?" I said. "Luther?"

"I didn't tell her," he said.

"We both know it," Samson said. "We listened when you was telling Pa."

All right, Samson was paying some attention after all.

"You got big ears," Luther said, "the both of you. Too big."

"Not as big as Nat's," Samson said.

"That's true," I said.

"Well," Ruthie said, "we heard it, and that's all there is to it. Nat left her to kill a man." She looked at me. "Now you want to go back, and you shouldn't have left in the first place."

"It's not your business to say," Luther said.

"No," I said. "She's right. I shouldn't have left."

"And you shouldn't go back now," Ruthie said. "The winter is bad up there, that's what the letter said, and if you go, you have as good a chance of dying as she has. You won't have accomplished a damn thing."

"Watch your language, young lady," Luther said.

"I'm not a lady," Ruthie said.

"I'm noticing that," Luther said. "But you act like one just the same.

Nat, I apologize for Ruthie. She's been taught better manners than that."

"She was taught to be honest and thoughtful, is my guess," I said. "I think that's what she's doing. I didn't have any right to go off and leave her, not with her being that way."

I stood up to leave.

"Won't you have supper with us?" Luther said. "We needn't talk any more about this if you don't want to."

"It's not that. I need to start out tomorrow, after I get some supplies. I've got enough money put back for that. Enough to get me to Dodge. I got a friend there who can help me out. I need to go and think things out."

"Nat," Ruthie said. "I apologize. I didn't mean to get you all guilty and stirred."

"Don't blame yourself," I said. "You just wiped the looking glass for me. Now I can see through it."

Luther put his hand on my shoulder. "Come tomorrow morning for the funeral. I would be pleased if you could be there."

I nodded.

I walked back to my place. I had forgotten the dime novel. Guess I'd been in that shack about a half hour, looking at the wall, when there was a knock. Opening the door I found Ruthie staring at me. She was holding the dime novel. She held it out to me. I took it, and when I did, she said, "Nat, I didn't mean what I said. Hell, maybe I did."

"Come in, Ruthie," I said. "Leave the door open. A young woman ought not to be in a man's quarters."

"Dog-diddle propriety," she said.

"Maybe you ought to watch your language more," I said. "Luther might be right about that, way you're talking and all."

"Listen here. I'm going to talk straight. You said I was being honest before, but I wasn't."

"How's that?"

"I don't want you to go back. I don't want you to worry about her anymore. I know you got to, that's what you should do to be a man worth a plug nickel, but the simple fact is I'm in love with you, Nat. There you have it."

"That can't be."

"It can be, and it is."

"I mean, that won't work."

"Doesn't change the facts. When I saw you the first time, I thought, now, there is a man of substance."

"That's ridiculous," I said.

"That's how I felt. I told myself I would be proven wrong when I got to know you, but I wasn't."

"You're a child," I said.

"I'm eighteen years old. My mother was married when she was sixteen. Thing is, I'm jealous, Nat. Jealous you can love your woman like that, and here I am wanting the same sort of thing. Be honest with me. You look at me pretty often, don't you, Nat?"

"You're very attractive," I said. "Beautiful, I think. But that's just me looking, not me thinking."

"Mama once told me if a man is looking, he's thinking," Ruthie said.

I didn't say anything, as there is a certain truth to that. It's the birds and the bees, I reckon.

"Okay, I guess I thought some things I shouldn't have, way a man will."

"It's more than that, Nat."

"How do you know what lives inside my head?"

"Because you don't look at me the way a wolf looks at a staked goat. That's how some men look at me. You look at me the way Pa used to look at Ma, way he used to smile at her, even if she was fussing at him. That smile would make her madder, but he was always taken with her. Think he would have salted her down and put her in a barrel to bring all the way here if he didn't feel something special?"

"Hell, Ruthie, he salted down the dog, too."

"Well, he loved the dog, but I'm not saying it was the same. He didn't look at the dog the same way. I don't think you can make a case it was on the same level. Come on now, Nat. Tell me you don't see something in me you like."

"I see plenty in you I like. You're not only pretty, you have a strong heart and a good mind, and you seem to me to be a planner. Like you want something out of life."

"I do indeed," she said.

"I like the way you walk."

"Do you?"

"Yeah, I do."

I sat in a chair and tossed the dime novel on the floor. Ruthie closed the door. She said, "Tell me when you look at me all you see is someone who is a good planner."

"I said about your head and heart."

"Tell me you don't feel just the slightest something for me. Tell me you don't think I would make a good wife."

"Of course you would," I said. "Just not my wife."

"I want you," she said. "In my bed, such as it is—a pallet under a tree—and in my life forever."

"You shouldn't talk like that. Your pa will shoot us both. Listen, Ruthie, it's not that easy."

"Tell me you don't love me."

I looked at her and opened my mouth, but it didn't come out. I put my head down and shook it. "I have obligations."

"You loved Win—that's her name, right?"

"Right. And it's 'I love Win,' not 'loved.'"

"You loved the Win you knew. She had a breakdown. She wasn't strong enough."

"Don't say that," I said. "Don't ever say that."

"But she wasn't."

"Who would be?" I said.

"I didn't mean to make you mad," she said.

"But you have. Don't ever say that about her. You can't say things like that if you haven't been through it, and heaven forbid you should. It's not always about strength. It's more complicated than that."

Ruthie sat down on my bed, put her hands on her knees, said, "I shouldn't have said that."

"You're right about that," I said.

"I know that. I'm jealous of Win, and I don't even know her. I just wanted to say something mean. God says judge not lest you be judged, and now I wouldn't be surprised if he brought a mess of troubles on me for saying it."

"Forgive yourself. I have."

"Nat, you never said how you feel about me." She turned her head and laid those beautiful eyes on me. Outside the wind was starting to whistle and the sun was starting to set, and I was thinking what Luther was thinking about now. He had to have guessed she would come here.

"I don't love you, Ruthie," I said. "I love another."

"You love who she was," she said. "You don't want to be a coward. Want to stand by her, but you lost her. You been away too long, and she's not herself. You know that's true."

There were tears in her eyes.

I had a hard time doing it, but I knew it was the right thing to say. "Ruthie. I like you. But I don't love you. I love Win."

"All right," she said, and she could hardly get the words out. She got up, went to the door, and opened it. "All right," she said again, and stood there in the doorway, the last of the sunlight resting on her as she turned to look back at me. "You got to do the right thing, Nat. But you know how I feel."

"You're young," I said. "It'll pass."

"I don't think so," she said, and went away.

I sat there in my chair looking out the open door, watching the night fall down. I sat there and thought. I remembered what Mama had said, about how I had to go out and have a future, and that I was destined for greatness. Right then I didn't feel so great, and my future wasn't that shiny. I had let her and Pa down, and I had let my own

self down. If you could buy bad choices, it was like I had asked for a
bag of them.

I sat there and felt ill. I cried a little. I feared I might have lied to
Ruthie. Win was becoming a ghost, and I was starting to feel like a rotten son of a bitch.

# 29

Early next morning I bought some supplies and gave Mr. Jason my best wishes and said so long. He took this more kindly than I meant it. I paid Satan out of the livery, led him over to Luther's wagon.

Luther, Samson, and Ruthie was dressed in their finest, and they had laid out the coffin with the wife and the barrel with the dog on a sled. They had the mules hitched up to it with some equipment I figured they had borrowed or rented from someone, perhaps the owner of the sled.

Ruthie nodded at me. Samson made a few of his usual attempts at jokes. He was not a funny child, but he thought he was. I hoped he'd grow out of it.

Out at the graveyard, Luther had already dug the grave, maybe with help from Ruthie and Samson. There was a couple of shovels sticking up in a mound of dirt. He had two long pieces of rope with him. Me and him took one end of a piece of rope, while Samson and Ruthie took the ends of the other. We hooked the ropes under the coffin and lowered it into the grave.

When that was done, Luther said, "I found she wasn't as pliable as expected, but I got her mostly straightened out. She and me both smelled like pickles before it was over."

Luther went into a rambling sermon that should have been boring, as it wasn't all that interesting if you took it word by word, but he had a way of talking, a tone of voice, that could make reading a grocery list sound fascinating. I almost got religion myself.

When he was done, I helped cover her up, then we dug a fresh hole for the dog. Down it went, and we shoveled dirt in the hole. That done, he said a few words for the dog, wrapped up with "Amen," then said, "I plan on getting my wife a headstone next. Blacksmith said he needed some help. I told him I was a good hand and showed him how I could heat up and hammer a horseshoe. He seemed impressed. Said he could only use me three days a week, and sometimes when there is a lot of activity in town. He does shoeing for the marshal service."

"Judge Parker," I said.

"One they call the hanging judge."

"That would be him."

We talked a little more, then I told them good-bye, shook hands with Luther and Samson. I shook hands with Ruthie, too, but she didn't look right at me, and her hand was like holding a dead fish.

I got on Satan and started riding. It didn't take me long to leave Fort Smith and wind my way into the mountains.


By the time I reached Dodge, the weather was really bad. Cecil took in Satan for nothing, feeling like he owed me one. I let him think it. Maybe I felt it was true. I got a job shoveling horse shit at the livery.

Next thing I did was I looked up Bronco Bob.

Bronco Bob was happy to have me stay with him. He had acquired a mean-spirited, redheaded, heartbreaking strumpet who lived with him, but not the one he wrote me about. That great love had passed. During the nights he wrote while she whored and brought in money. What he wrote he sold to the dime novel company. I was the inspiration for many of his books, though he had taken to writing about a fellow called Broke Hand Bob, who was a one-handed fellow who could throw a knife real well with his good hand. He was made of thin air, Bronco Bob not having any real adventures to steal from for that character. Course, way Bronco Bob wrote it, my adventures and his wasn't all that different.

Well, I began to get the feeling I was wearing my welcome out, though Bronco Bob was nice as he could be. But the strumpet gave me looks, and there was the fact that her and her customers humping all night, and her and Bronco Bob humping all day, not only kept me from sleep but kept my hand in my pants. I had been caught going at it twice already. Once by the strumpet and once by Bronco Bob. It was embarrassing, but I owned up to it. Bronco Bob said his strumpet had friends, and one night I broke down and took pleasure from one. I felt horrible the next day, having violated Win's trust. I was no better than Hickok, who I had judged not so long ago. And then again, it was possible Win had no idea who I was anymore.

A week or so later I talked Cecil into letting me sleep in the livery. I moved out with Bronco Bob telling me it wasn't necessary, but I could see on his face a look of grateful good-bye. We played it out, though. Him asking me to stay and me saying how I appreciated it but needed more room. I even threw in I wasn't fond of having someone walk in while I was priming my pump. I was easily embarrassed when I was younger.

I moved to the livery.

It wasn't a bad life, really, if you didn't mind waking up and going to bed to the smell of horse manure. I did my job, Cecil paid me some, and at night I stayed in the loft in the hay with a couple of thick and very used horse blankets. I always had the faint smell about me of a mount that had been rode hard and put up wet. I didn't go out much, as there wasn't much to do. And as Dodge became more civilized, they became more aware of the color line. I didn't drink beer or whiskey, so there was no real pleasure for me at the saloons, and at the cafés where they still let colored in I was too short on money for the grub. I ate cheap, and I ate in the loft.

When spring cracked the country with brighter light and warmer air, the grass turned green and the flowers jumped up. I packed my little bit of belongings and said good-bye to Cecil. By this time he was almost weepy to see me go. He knew he'd have to take over the shovel.

"You're as good a hand as I ever had," he said, taking one of my hands in both of his.

"Glad for it," I said.

"My best goes with you." When he let go of my hand, it was almost with reluctance.

"Thanks, Cecil. You been all right by me."

"Here's fifty dollars to go with you, too," he said, pulling the bills from his coat pocket, shoving them into my palm. "I think it'll do you better than my best wishes. Your helping out the gals at the brothel, that's got me free tail for life, so I kind of owe you."

I thanked him again, got Satan, and rode to Bronco Bob's place. Satan, having been ridden little during the winter, was a bit sassy, but I knew after we got on the trail he'd work off his fat and be all right. Me and him had come to an understanding.

Bronco Bob's abode, as he preferred to call it, was off Main Street. I rode down the very same alley where I had killed Golem. I had been down it many times since I had been back in Dodge. Being there always made me feel a little odd, as if Golem might leap out in all his bloody glory and try and grab me. I tied Satan to a hitching post, climbed some stairs, and knocked on the door. I could hear Bronco Bob and his lady making the springs squeak.

I thought it best to leave a note, but I didn't have pencil or paper on me. I was about to go down and get some out of my saddlebag when I heard Bronco Bob yell out, "Wait just a goddamn minute. I'm almost finished here. I'm at the peak and about to descend the mountain."

The springs squeaked a little more, then there was a sound like someone happily sinking down into a feather bed after a week without sleep. About five minutes later, the door opened, and there was Bronco Bob in his filthy long johns.

"I didn't know it was you, Deadwood. I thought it was a bill collector. I owe everyone for something. Be it meat or milk or whiskey. On top of that I need a new lambskin for my pecker. I'm about to break through the one I got. They don't come cheap."

"I have one made of rubber," I said, "but I've never had the desire to lend it."

"Or me to wear it."

"Still, didn't mean to interrupt you while you was mining for gold."

"For what it's worth, I found my nugget."

"I'm leaving, Bob."

"I knew you would before long. Guess I've been a little less of a friend than you might have expected."

"You been all right," I said. "You've got your life, and I got mine, such as it is."

"I think my life is what led Kid Red into the arms of ruin. I should never have got him drinking. He was just a kid. That liquor made an outlaw of him."

"That was a mistake, Bob. But we've all made a few. He's young and may still straighten out. Should he come back through, give him my best, and then turn him in to the law. Could be the best thing that happens to him. Jail for theft before it's jail and the gallows for murder."

"Might be too late for that already," he said. "There are rumors."

"Let's hope that's all they are. Good-bye, Bronco Bob. I hope our trails cross again."

"I'm sure they will. And where should I send the money for the dime novels?"

"Same place you been sending it."

"Yeah. I know. I'm just talking. I mean well."

"It's all right, my friend. Adios."

Within minutes I was out of Dodge and on the trail to Deadwood.


I come to the Dakotas, and spring or no spring, it was cold there. There was snow in the trees and over the rocks, and breathing the air was like breathing razors, but the trail was clear and no Indians tried to scalp me.

I didn't even see one, though I bet they saw me. They was supposed to have been tamed by this time, but I wasn't going to count on a newspaper article that said it to be true. I kept my weapons loaded, my eyes sharp. I slept poorly. That wasn't all about watching for savages. I was thinking about Win, and damn me, I was thinking about Ruthie, too. When her face would come to me, I'd try and push it from my head, but it would float right back up. I hate to say it, and I'm ashamed, but at that point I could hardly remember Win's face—just her explosion of dark hair, that flute playing she did, and that sweet kiss up on the hill. The one that could never be matched.

Deadwood was less of a ragged town than it had been, though I should add that just a few years after I saw it for the last time (and this was the last time) a fire blazed through and burned the whole town to the ground. Some folks said it was the best thing that ever happened. Them that said it mostly lived somewhere else. But some of the Deadwood folks thought the same and was glad to see it rebuilt. That was, they say, the first beginnings of it as a real town, not just a wild outpost for gambling and killing and all manner of wild activity.

Banks and churches just about ruin everything.

There was new buildings and new streets, but it wasn't so different that I had trouble finding where Cullen and Wow lived with Win. When I rode up in their yard Wow was outside hanging wash on the line. When she saw me ride up and dismount, she came running up and threw her arms around me and kissed my cheek. Once, I thought she had a face that could blow out a candle, but seeing her now, I thought she was quite beautiful. Her spirit made her glow. I gave her a kiss on the cheek, and she shed some tears and hugged me more.

"It's good to see you," she said.

"And you."

"You got that same black horse."

"I do. And he's as mean as ever."

"Cullen is asleep. He's working nights cleaning out stores, doing your old job, too, emptying spittoons. He's hired someone to do some of the work for him. He's trying to start a business like that, where he farms out hands for jobs and everyone gets paid. Mostly him."

"Sounds like you're prospering."

"In a fashion."

"Win?"

I already knew the answer from Cullen's letter, but I was hoping against hope that in the last few months she had improved.

Wow shook her head. "Not well. You should brace yourself. Her mind is gone, and her body is nearly gone as well. I think she may well have some kind of disease. Maybe she always had it, and when she . . . Well, when what happened to her happened, she wasn't strong enough anymore. She hardly eats, and if you try and force her a little, well, she chokes. We give her broth a lot. She can do broth."

I said, "She's in the house, I assume?"

"Yes. I'll wake Cullen. He'll want to see you. Win may be asleep; she may be awake. She hasn't any set hours. She catnaps."

"No need to wake him—or her, if she's asleep."

"There certainly is," she said, and went ahead of me into the house.

I tied Satan to a post out front, waited for Wow to come back. When she did she had Cullen with her. He had thrown on some clothes, and his shirt was buttoned wrong. He looked thinner than I remembered—not bad, just wolf-lean.

"Nat," he said. "You son of a bitch."

He grabbed me and hugged me so hard I thought he'd break my ribs. It was good to see him. When he let go, he said, "You'll want to see Win."

"Yes," I said.

"Quit standing out here in the cold, then," he said. "Where's your manners, Wow?"

Cullen led me into the house, and Wow, with tears in her eyes, stayed outside to finish with her wash. Cullen led me to a doorway at the back of the house.

"You've built on," I said.

"We own more land now. It's my plan to be a property mogul, rent shitty houses, and hire out men and the like, not have to work so hard."

"Sounds like a good plan."

"She's here," Cullen said, and opened a door.

I took off my hat and gave it to Cullen and went inside.

I would forever remember that kiss on the hill, and I will forever remember the skeleton in the bed, for that was what Win had become, and had I not recognized her hair, wild and loose on her pillow like a nest of snakes, I wouldn't have known it was her at all, her face being a dim memory as it was.

Light from a window shining through thin curtains framed the bed, and what should have looked warm looked cold, like butter on ice. A blanket was over her, pulled up to her armpits. There was a bowl on the table beside her, and there was food in it; rice and some kind of stew. There was a spoon in it. It appeared untouched. There was a pitcher of water and a glass beside it.

"My heavens," I said. I didn't mean to say it, it just came out. I thought I had prepared myself, but seeing her was like discovering the world was a lie and we all lived in a little tin cup.

I sat on the edge of the bed and took her hand from under the blanket. It was light as a false promise and paper-thin. Her skin that had been so lovely dark was now ashen as a week-old campfire. Her eyes were huge in her skull, and they held nothing; they were dark and bottomless. They didn't even search to find me or move at all; they lay flat in her skull like stones.

"Win," I said.

I began talking to her. I told her everything I could remember about how we met, the kiss that had meant so much, her flute playing, the times we had on the hill beneath the great tree, the crawling shadows of oncoming dark, the stars at night, the color of moonlight, but nothing moved her. I told her how she had changed me inside. How all the bad things I had in me, all the anger, had washed right out, and that I couldn't lose her. That she had to get better, cause if she didn't they might wash right back in. I told her every dream and hope I ever had. I told her about my pa and about my mama, even told her my mama thought I was cut out for something great, and Mama had meant Win, cause I couldn't think of nothing greater.

I said, "I love you, Win."

I like to think I felt her hand squeeze mine a little, but to be honest I can't be certain. I was there for three days, and then on the fourth day, Win was no longer with us. It was as if that bed was a pool of deep water and she was sinking deeper into it every day, and then one day she reached bottom. But I was there when she left completely, and I was happy for that.

She was buried on that hill we loved. Me and Cullen, Wow, and the China girls did it. Buried her up there in a fine coffin that Cullen helped me pay for, one lined with shiny white silk. I laid her flute in there with her, the way Charlie had laid Wild Bill's good rifle with him. We buried her deep and covered her grave with rocks to keep the wolves and bears out. Cullen bought a headstone, and me and him set it in place at the head of her grave. Her name was on it; her birthday was a guess. From my remembrances, conversations with her, I knew she had been born in the summer. I called it June. I guessed the day. I guessed her age, and we put the date she died behind that.

Underneath was carved something I had asked for: WIN, WHOSE KISS MOVED ME FROM EARTH TO SKY.

Cullen and Wow and the China girls all hugged me and went away. I stayed up there with Satan. I stayed up there all day. I talked to the grave. I cursed the world. I yelled at the mountains. I screamed at the sky. I grew so weak my shadow seemed heavy. For a while there I wanted to die.

In time it got dark and the stars came out, and there was a shiny sliver of moon. I sat there and looked at it, sitting with my back against the tree, my head turned slightly toward the grave.

I swear to you a snow-white owl came down from the dark sky and rested on the headstone, its moon shadow falling across the grave like a blanket. It turned its head the way owls do, which doesn't seem to involve the turning of a neck, and looked at me and made a hooting noise and flew away.

Reckon if I was an Indian I would say it came for her spirit, carried it off into the sky. And like those Greeks and such Mr. Loving told me about that was always getting put among the stars, I fancied that's where she was. It seemed right to me she would be among them heroes and beauties, shining down forever like the star she was.

The wind through the trees sounded like notes from her flute.

# 30

I left out of Deadwood without saying good-bye to anyone on a cold spring morning with the sky chock-full of dark clouds covering the sun. The shadows from those clouds rolled over the ground and covered me. At some point those clouds went away, but for me the darkness didn't. I rode on across Nebraska and into Kansas, the days going by with the speed of a bullet.

On the day I was close to Dodge the prairie flowers was starting to bloom and the grass was high and bright, green and yellow, rolling like the waves of the sea. If there had been buffalo out there the world would have seemed as of old, except for the heaviness of my heart.

When I rode into Dodge I stopped off at the livery, and Cecil said I could stay overnight, which is all I did. I didn't look up Bronco Bob, but I wrote him a letter. I told him I was passing through, that Win had died, and that I was on my way to Fort Smith. I said he could write me there. I had some plans, but I didn't mention them to Bronco Bob, as I was uncertain how those plans would go. I mailed the letter and traveled on.

On the edge of the Indian Nations I saw some Comanche, and they saw me. There was four of them, and they came riding toward me with their hands held high, palms open, working their horses with their knees. They was a skinny bunch and looked beat down by life. They couldn't have looked no rougher if they had been boiled in oil and pressed out with a hot iron.

I stayed cautious. They wanted tobacco and whiskey, and I didn't have either. I finally gave them some cornmeal, and they dropped off their horses and opened the bag and went to eating it as it was, just by the handful. They was starving, and it made me ill to see these once mighty warriors on their hands and knees scooping out cornmeal. White man's whiskey had something to do with it; it had been the hot oil they were boiled in, the hot irons that pressed them out.

This lay on my heart like a rock, so I gave them about half my jerky, which meant I'd be on half rations until I reached Fort Smith. They gave me a blessing, I think, but for all I know they may have been saying, "Thanks. Kill you later, black asshole."

I went on my way but kept an eye in the back of my head for a couple of days in case they was following, thinking maybe they might want what was left of my possibles. They wasn't following, though. Up into the mountains I went. The trees was emerald green, plants was blooming and busting with color, flowers was pinned to the earth like jeweled brooches. It was like riding along in a fairyland. I had the sad feeling that soon it would all be gone, cut down and sawed into boards, the animals shot out and the mountains filled with nothing more than leaning shacks in graying shambles. It was a cheerless way to think, but I couldn't get it out of my head. My experiences had gone on to sour everything I saw.

In Fort Smith I went to see if I could rent my old room, but it was already occupied by a family of four, and since I had felt tight there by my lonesome, I pitied them. I went to the livery there, tried to make a deal like I had in Dodge, but the liveryman was nothing doing. I didn't consider trying to get my old job back, as charming as Mr. Jason had been.

I sauntered to the post office and looked on a pinup board there to see if there was places to stay announced. I saw a few that housed coloreds. Also saw something that made my heart jump up in my throat. It was a wanted poster pinned next to the information about places to stay. It was from the Pinkerton's, so it was serious. There wasn't no drawings of anybody, but it said they was looking for train robbers, and they was suspected to be in the area. They was offering a reward of five hundred dollars for a robber called Burned Man, who they figured was in his forties, and the same for Kid Red, who they thought to be anywhere between sixteen and twenty. They had murdered a couple of men in the course of a robbery, and a stray bullet had killed a boy. There was a smaller reward for two other criminals—Indian Charlie Doolittle and Pinocchio Joe, named such, it said, for his long pointed nose, which hooked on the end. I pulled the poster down, folded it, and put it in my pocket. I made note of the address for rooms that housed coloreds and went away.

After several turndowns, I found an old colored lady with a hitch in her get-along who had a back porch I could stay on. It was closed in, but at night it was cold as a well digger's ass. There was no stove, just a small table by the bed. But the days was warming, and besides, I had me a plan. I spent my first day relaxing on that back porch, and for a bit more money the old lady would give me something to eat about noon. That first day she brought me out some dried cornbread that was hard enough to throw and kill a squirrel. I dipped it in some milk that was on the edge of turning and got through the day, which considering the old lady liked to sing gospel songs to herself while she rocked and knitted, and had a voice she could have used to teach a frog how to croak, wasn't nearly all that uplifting an experience. By nightfall I was starting to look for a place I could hang myself. Thank goodness she finally quit singing, having grown hoarse, and my neck and a rafter was spared.

Next morning I left my guns there on the porch under my blanket and strolled over to where Judge Isaac Parker held his court. I was early enough and lucky enough to catch him when he wasn't on the bench or about law work. I was told to take off my hat by the man outside the door, a white fellow who looked more than serviceable if it was necessary to wrestle a grizzly to the floor and later tame it for janitorial work.

I was let into Judge Parker's office. The great man was at his desk drinking out of a large cup. He was sharply dressed in a black suit and had a long, graying beard that come to a point like a spike. His hair was thick and neatly combed and maybe touched up with shoe polish. He wore eyeglasses. He could have been thirty-five or fifty-five. It's hard to tell with bearded white people. He set the cup down and laid his other hand on a big black book. He said, "So you come here to tell the truth?"

"About what?"

"About anything."

"Yes, sir. Reckon so."

"Reckon? Or you do plan to tell the truth? Got my hand on a Bible here."

"I plan to tell the truth. But shouldn't my hand be on the Bible?"

"That's true. We may come to that. How's the weather out?"

"Nippy, but the sun is starting to burn off the cold. It'll be short-sleeve weather by noon, or at least you won't need a coat."

"You have on a coat."

"Yes, I do. But it isn't yet short-sleeve weather, and it is far from noon."

"You're young. Get older, nothing is that far away timewise, including your own demise. In the blink of an eye it'll be noon. I like noon. It's dinnertime."

"Dinner is all right if you got a good one to eat."

"So you aren't eating good dinners?"

"No, sir. Can't say that I am. I've only had one meal since I've come to town, but I got it set in my mind that where I am dinner ain't going to improve much. Supper don't come with my stay, either, and breakfast is the morning air."

"No coffee?"

"No, sir."

"What are you having?"

I was more than a little confused by his interest in the dealings of my stomach, but as I had come there with the intent of looking for a job, I figured I should go along to get along.

"Cornbread, if you can call it that. Cornbread and milk on the edge of disaster. It's like eating a brick and washing it down with phlegm."

The judge let out a laugh.

"What do you want with me, son?"

"A job, sir."

"Cleaning up the office? Working in the courthouse? What you got in mind?"

"I'm looking to be a deputy marshal."

"Are you, now?"

"Yes, sir, I am. I figure as a deputy I could at least eat a better dinner, though since I don't know the pay, I don't know what kind of breakfast or supper I would be having."

This made him laugh again.

"What attributes do you have as a marshal?"

"I have been in the army, first off," I said. "Buffalo soldier with the Ninth. Fought Indians."

I didn't mention I had run off from the army.

"What else you got?"

"I have been a bouncer in Deadwood, and last year I won a title there as best shot. They called me Deadwood Dick on account of it."

"Like the books?"

Three or four books about me was out and about by this time.

"Yes, sir. Them books is based on me. I think you could say it's a loose sort of thing."

"Isn't Deadwood Dick a white fellow?"

"Only in the books. They're based on me, and the fellow writes them is named Bronco Bob, though that's not the name he works under. He came in second in the shooting contest."

"You know what? I have heard of that contest. Story of it has gotten around."

"It has?"

"Yep. Story that a colored man won and that he outshot everyone there. Here's another thing. I know Bronco Bob."

"That's a surprise."

"He had a situation once where he appeared before me in court. He was traveling through doing his shooting matches. It had to do with a woman and a fight. He lost the woman, won the fight. The other guy lost the woman, too."

It was my turn to laugh. "That sounds like him."

"It not only sounds like him, it was him. I liked him. Very personable. Gave him the letter of the law, though. Time in jail. A sizable fine. It wasn't his wife he was with, you see, but a whore. Had it been his wife the time would have been cut in half, and so would the fine. I have read a number of the Deadwood Dick books of late, but until this moment had no idea he was the writer or that you were the source."

"Well, I might be the source, but them books about me is about as close to real life as the moon is to Denver."

"Fair enough. That is honest. I figured as much. So you can shoot and you can bounce drunks and rowdies, and you got books written about you, and I take it you can ride pretty good."

"More than pretty good. Like I was the horse itself, and I got my own mount. I wouldn't be expecting one from the local government."

"Good. You wouldn't get one. Speak any Indian dialects?"

"No, sir. I don't."

"Well, that can be a holdback, but not altogether. A bump in the road. Can you track?"

"I'm okay at it," I said. "There are better, but I'm all right."

"If it's a big tracking job, we got Choctaw Tom on retainer. He's as much Negro as he is Choctaw, but the Choctaw name stuck cause he lived with them so long, his mother being Choctaw. He can track anything that walks or rides and maybe anything that flies. So he's available now and then. Something you can't handle trackingwise, we could hire him. The Bible. Do you read it?"

Right then I knew I was on loose ground. But seeing as how the judge had his hand on one, I ventured it meant something to him.

"Now and again. I'm not as educated in it as I should be, but then I'm not educated in a lot of things."

Judge Parker pursed his lips, pondering my comment. "Well, now. I suppose that is reasonable enough. You should know I am a Methodist, and in my court, God is a Methodist, so you might want to read up on the Good Book a little. I'd stay away from the Baptists if you come across them. Heathens. I'm not all that fond of other false versions of Christianity, either. They are all going to hell, the way I see it. Except the Methodists. And some of *them* are going. Let me tell you a little something. I hire you, I expect you to bring men to justice. Kill if you got to, but not for the convenience of it. I'd rather a man be brought in and punished as the law decides."

I decided it would be best if he and Luther didn't meet to discuss theology.

"Yes, sir," I said.

"You would need to study up a bit on what is expected and acquire some idea of the law, though mostly your job would be to go out and catch folks. And, as I said, not shoot them. Unless it was called for, of course, and it often is. There's men—white, red, and black—that will not want to come back with you for obvious reasons. They may take it in their heads to kill you. That warrants you shooting them, killing them if you have to. They may not shoot at you, but just won't come. You may have to shoot them and bring in their dead bodies. Best if you got a spare horse to lead for that, cause a dead body sure raises a stink. Summer's coming soon. Spring blinks, summer waits, and waits and waits, and then winter comes and it won't go away. Kill a man in winter, the odor problem is lessened. You may also have to shoot them on the run. I suggest from a distance with a long gun. Being the shot you are, I can reasonably assume you have a long gun and a pistol?"

"You can reasonably assume that," I said.

"Good. Well, I guess we can swear you in right now. Come put your hand on the Bible."

"Sir, I got one thing I'd insist on."

"You do, do you?" he said.

"Yes, sir." I took the poster out of my pocket, unfolded it, and walked over and placed it on his desk. "I want to start with them."

"Why?"

"I know them."

"This a personal grudge?"

"To some degree, but not to such a degree I wouldn't be wise or cautious. I know two of these men on sight. I might be able to talk the kid into putting down his guns and coming in."

"He killed a man. You know how that's going to work out, don't you, son?"

"I do. If it goes bad, I'll go bad with it."

"It does sometimes, and as I said, if you shoot a man in the line of duty—"

"It's all right."

"That's the size of it."

"The other, I figure he'll come in dead and stinking."

The judge leaned back in his chair and pulled at his beard a little.

"Know them on sight, do you?"

"What I said. Now, I'm not saying I won't do whatever I'm called to do before I get to them, but I'm saying I'd like the chance to deliver their warrant, such as it is. Someone else comes across them, they can have them, but I don't want anyone else sent for them."

"I don't see any problem in that. That way they aren't being kept from being caught. It's just you are the prime hunter. But I may not send you after them right away. I've had my eye on that gang for a time, and right now the leads have gone dry as a South Texas ditch. Put your hand on this."

He pushed the big book forward on his desk, and I put my hand on it. He said some words and had me repeat them, ended our talk with, "Show up here tomorrow morning, say, seven sharp."

"I'll be here."

"Wait a minute." Judge Parker dug in his coat pocket, came up with a silver dollar. "Have you a good meal. Advance on your salary, though. I'll mark it down. Pay sometimes comes a little slow, but I can give you another dollar or two you need it."

"I'll be all right," I said. "And since this comes out of my pay, I'll take it."

I was nearly to the door when the judge said, "By the way, I expect my men to be forthright and God-fearing and honest. I'm taking your word you are just that."

"Yes, sir," I said.

"And if you have to shoot a man in the back or sneak up on him and shoot him anywhere, that's all right if it's in line with the arrest and, of course, if your target is resisting. Remember, the byword is justice."

We were back to that again.

"Of course," I said, and left out of there.

I didn't look up Ruthie or her family but heard through the grapevine that Luther had started his own church, called Luther's Church, and somehow it got around it was Lutheran, but it wasn't. You can see how such confusion could set in.

Far as the job went I delivered a few light warrants, and the worst I had encountered was when I arrested a drunk man for theft and his ten-year-old son showed me he had acquired quite a vocabulary, none of it words to be used politely.

Up to then it was simple work, and I was paid all right, and I got a little extra payment for them that I captured and brought in. One day I was in town and coming out of the store where I used to sweep up, and there was Ruthie, a big brown-paper-wrapped package under her arm. She was wearing a bright blue dress, and her hair was in pigtails. She had on a pair of black shoes that looked new. She looked more beautiful than when I had last seen her.

I was coming up the steps, going in, planning to buy some goods, so I couldn't hardly dodge her. I took off my hat. "Ruthie. It's good to see you."

"Why, you liar. You been in town for a month at least, and you haven't so much as come by and said hi or 'Kiss my ass' to any of us."

"It wasn't that I didn't want to or didn't mean to."

"Want to or mean to doesn't get it done. You've forgot us since you left . . ." And then her face collapsed. "Oh, dear, Nat. I forgot about Win. Forgive me. I keep being selfish, and you've already told me how you feel."

She nearly dropped her package as the memory came over her. I reached out and took it, said, "Let me walk you home."

"Okay. I . . . I'm so sorry, Nat. Is she all right?"

"No. She has passed on."

"I'm so sorry. I mean, you might think I'm not after what I said, but I am sorry. Truly."

"You shouldn't be apologizing to me. I should have come by."

"It's the other direction, Nat. We aren't living in the wagon anymore."

We turned and started in that direction.

"I heard Luther got a church."

"He did, and it comes with a little house. It's not much of a house, but it's better than that wagon. We got a corral there, and we've bought some chickens for eggs, and I have started a spring garden. There's bugs in it, but the corn and potatoes do all right . . . Dang it, Nat. I really am sorry about Win."

"You said that."

"I know, but I said some bad things to you when you were here last time. I know it hurt."

"Hurt because it was true," I said.

"About you and me?"

"I assume you have outgrown your fancy by now?"

"I wouldn't say that. But after Win dying I don't think you could have an interest in me other than a ricochet. I don't want anything like that."

"I understand."

We walked along without speaking for a while. It was a pretty good walk.

I said, "You still speak to ducks and such?"

"When they want to talk. Frankly, I haven't seen a duck in a long time."

"I suppose it's a limited enterprise, the plans of a duck."

"I get a sense of things from them and other birds as well. They told me you'd come back."

"They did, did they? Was you ever dropped on your head as a child?"

"That's no way to get on my good side."

"Think that's what I'm trying to do?"

"Not when you talk like that," she said. "There's the church. We got twenty colored families come all the time, couple of Creek Indian families, and even a white couple. No one likes the white couple in town, so they come to us."

"That's generous of them," I said. "Slumming like that with the colored folks."

"The Lord doesn't care about color," she said. "Not even white skin."

"He might be the only one."

We walked a little more, and then Ruthie stopped.

"That's the house."

It wasn't far from where the church was and looked to be about twice the size of the room I had lived in before in Fort Smith. There was a little fenced garden and some poor-looking crops inside the fence. I saw a chicken coop and some chickens running about in the yard, which was grown over with weeds.

"You might want to come in and say hello to Pa and Samson."

"Not today. I really wanted to see you all, but I didn't know if I was ready. Thing is, Ruthie, I loved Win, and in some ways I always will. But you were right. I was in love with Win as I had known her, not as she had become. That alone made me ashamed of myself."

"That's human nature," Ruthie said. "You didn't change her."

"Knowing me led to what happened to her," I said.

"You can't go through life worrying about that kind of thing," she said. "You couldn't get out of bed in the morning if you did. God wants us to move on. He wants us to thrive."

"What about the ricochet?"

"Give it some space, Nat. Come see us in a week or so. Come and have dinner. We'll see how things develop. I have others courting me, you know."

All of a sudden she was in a good humor and sure of herself again. Sometimes Ruthie was hard to figure.

"I don't doubt that," I said. "And I'll tell you something. That soil you got there, reason your garden has bugs and the crops aren't growing is the soil is too rocky and acidic. Some ashes from your stove would help with that. Mix it with some cow manure and keep that chicken mess out of it, as it's too hot unless it's cured. I can tell you ain't composting it none."

"You know about gardens?"

"I do. I had a good teacher. I'll tell you about the nightshade family next time."

"Nightshade family?"

"It's a bit of a story, but I'll share it later."

I gave her the package. She came close to me as she took it.

"I have to go in now," she said.

"Sure."

"You will come by soon?"

"Couple of weeks. I think what you said about not having a ricochet is right. We wouldn't want that."

"No, we wouldn't."

I could smell her skin. It smelled like lilac soap. Her breath was like mint leaves.

I turned around and walked away, and I must tell you I wanted badly to turn back and look at her, maybe go back and plead with her to let me take her in my arms. But frankly, I was worried about that ricochet.

I was put with Bass Reeves for a while so as to get some deputy marshal training. That big colored man was so full of wind that every time he talked he near knocked my hat off. But he could do most everything he bragged about doing. I was with him once when a white marshal who was in pursuit of a fellow sent word back to Fort Smith that he had him pinned down near a place called Gibson Station and assistance would be appreciated.

Bass was dressed up for a church social that day, and besides his usual black hat, had on an orange-and-black-checked suit and a striped bow tie. I was sitting with him out front of the courthouse, him about to leave for that social, when this fellow the white marshal had sent came riding up. He was the one told Bass they had a man pinned down in the brush but he was putting up a good fight and was bound to shoot one of them if they went in. Worse, the fellow seemed to have plenty of ammunition.

This had to do with a stolen pig. The thief in the brush had wounded some men and shot at this other marshal so much the marshal had developed a tic to one of his eyelids. When we rode up we tied our horses to a tree and scooted low along an embankment till we come up on the marshal, whose name was Ledbetter. He was there with three other white men and Choctaw Tom, who had helped track him. Choctaw Tom was a really lean man with wild twisted hair and a hat that nestled on top of it. It always looked as if it might blow off at the slightest wind, but it never did. I think he had it pinned there somehow. It had a few feathers in it, one of them broken and dangling.

All the men, including Choctaw, was shoved up tight behind that bank, out of bullet range.

The white marshal, Ledbetter, his eyelid hopping like a frog, said, "I'm glad to see you, Bass."

"I bet," Bass said.

One of the men said, "He shot off part of my finger. I don't think that's what he was aiming for, but he shot it off. Will it grow back?"

"Of course not," Bass said. "You've lost that. Let me look . . . Ah, hell, that's just the tip. You don't need it for nothing. You can dig a booger with the other hand."

Bass was like that. He talked the same to anyone, white or black or red.

"He has got me buffaloed," the marshal said. "I need you to shoot him, Bass. You can do that. I've seen you do it. I've seen you make some fine shots. None of us here have even come close."

"Choctaw didn't come close to hitting him?" Bass asked.

"He didn't try," said Marshal Ledbetter.

"I'm not shooting a man that stole a pig," Choctaw said. "I stole a pig once."

"How long ago?" Bass said.

"I was a kid," Choctaw said.

"Well, then," Bass said. "I guess we can let that go." Bass nodded at me. "This boy here is more than a fair shot, or so I hear. He will back me up."

"Good enough," Ledbetter said.

"Ha! You mean you'd rather see a nigger get dropped than a white man," Bass said.

"Now, Bass," Ledbetter said.

"Shut up and give me a rifle," Bass said.

Ledbetter was carrying one, and he gave it to Bass. I had my Winchester.

Choctaw Tom was rolling a cigarette. "I'm no marshal," he said, spitting tobacco off his tongue, "just hired help, but I'd keep my head down."

Bass said, "You can give him a round of fire, Nat, and when he comes out I'll pop him."

"All this over a pig?" I said.

"It was a nice pig," Marshal Ledbetter said.

"Was?" I asked.

Marshal Ledbetter nodded. "He stole it from Mr. Evans. Evans wants it back, and this fellow, Chooky Bullwater, part Creek, I think, don't want to give it back on account of he thought Evans owed him for something or another, some old debt Evans doesn't seem to know anything about. Chooky yelled out to us it was something to do with his father. I don't know. I think that incident with his father had to do with a pig, too, but it could just be an excuse. We told him to turn over the pig, which he'd trussed and throwed on the ground after we shot his horse out from

under him. We said if he gave up the pig, we'd see it went lighter with
him than if he tried to keep it. He shot the pig. He said that would show
he was serious."

"It showed the pig he was serious," I said.

Bass and me snuck along under the edge of the embankment, keeping
our heads down. It sloped up, and we sloped up with it. We come to a
spot where there was a couple of large trees and you could see between
them, and unless the fellow with the dead pig was a crack shot, it would
be hard to pick off a man, as there wasn't but a hand's width apart between those trees. Bass stuck his face through the gap in the trees, yelled
out, "I'm Bass Reeves, deputy US marshal. I'm calling you to come out
and to bring that dead pig with you. I reckon it's still fresh enough for
cooking."

"You can come get me," Chooky called back. "I will be glad for some
company. As for the pig, you can kiss my ass, and you can kiss its dead
ass."

Bass called out to him. "You've decided, then?"

"I have," Chooky said.

Bass said to me, "You fire into those bushes and keep him busy. If you
hit him, all the better, but if he rises up to run, I'll shoot him."

"Wing him, Bass," I said.

"I don't think so. When he runs, I'm going to shoot him in the back of
the neck. That cuts the spinal cord. He'll be as done as the pig. I think I can
talk the owner of the pig into giving us some of the meat if you want it."

"You keep it. And shoot him in the leg. Ain't we supposed to always
try and bring them in alive?"

"Sure we are. And I'll bring him in, though he might be turning stiff
when I do. I can see Judge Parker gave you the talk, but he didn't mean
it. He don't give a damn long as we get them."

I could see how things was, and did as I was told, Bass being the senior
man. I flicked the baffle on the loop-cock Winchester so it would be
rapid-fire, rose up quick, and started blasting shots into the brush where
Chooky was hidden. I shot high, clipping the tops of the brush, trying to

make sure I didn't hit him, hoping he'd give it up and come out. Then, like Bass said, Chooky rose up and ran, dragging that pig with him.

True to his word Bass stood up and from between that cut in the trees he fired, hit the man, and brought him down. When we went out for a look, sure enough he had hit him in the back of the neck, severing his spine. He was a real ugly customer, with a long nose and a round head with lots of black hair that had fallen loose when his hat was knocked off.

"I had to do it," Bass said.

"Why?"

"He'd have got away."

"He's a pig thief," I said. "Not a desperado."

"One is as good a black mark as the other in my book."

"You keep odd books, Bass."

Bass was bent down, looking the pig over.

"Have it your way. Look there, he had to shoot the pig twice. He's got one in the snout, and one between the eyes, which is the one did him, I think. Hell, you have to shoot a pig twice close-up, you need to practice your shooting."

I didn't get down and make sure Bass was right about the pig. The others was coming up now, along with Marshal Ledbetter. "Good shooting, Bass."

"I know," Bass said.

Without saying anything, I left them there, walked past Choctaw Tom, who had not gone over to see the dead man. He said, "So Bass shot another one, huh?"

"He did," I said.

I got on Satan and rode back to Fort Smith. I rode on out to where Luther's Church was and tied Satan to the hitching rail. The door to the church was open. I went inside. It was small, six pews to a side. I went to the one up front and sat down. There was a lectern up there, and behind it on the wall was a carving of Jesus on the cross. I sat there and studied on it. I heard someone else come in, turned, and looked. It was Luther. He was wearing overalls and a dirty hat.

"I thought that was Satan tied out front," Luther said, walking toward me.

"Coming from you," I said, "that's funny when you think about it."

"You get religion, Nat?"

"I came here to see if I felt anything, but I didn't. It is a little stuffy in here, though, and at first I thought that might be God, as I figure he's got to be a big fellow. But no, it's just stuffy."

"How come you're really here, Nat?"

By this time Luther had took the seat beside me on the pew.

"I'm a deputy marshal," I said.

"I've heard."

"I just seen another marshal kill a man for stealing a pig. The man had been shooting at folks, but he took a run for it, and the other marshal shot him in the neck and killed him."

"You're saying it wasn't necessary?"

"I'm saying I'm a marshal, too, and I got to wonder if being like that just comes with time. Wondering if you get so you can kill without it mattering."

Luther sat silent for a time. "You've killed. You've told me about it."

"I think they had it coming more than a fellow stole a pig. Fellow did shoot and kill the pig, and maybe that counts for something. It was an innocent pig, and it was meat wasted, though it's possible Bass will eat it."

"You have to make your own decisions. You have to make sure you're right with God. I can't speak for the pig."

"What if you don't believe in God?"

"I won't try to convince you. We've had that talk. But I will say this. If you can't get right with God, then you better get right with yourself."

"That's what I thought you'd say," I said.

"Does it help?"

"As much as anything could."

"People are an odd bunch," Luther said.

"Sometimes I feel odder than the rest."

"Should I pray for that man's soul for you, Nat?"

"I guess it couldn't hurt, even if I think your words are bouncing off the wall."

"You're saying it's the thought that counts."

"I don't think anything counts much, to tell the truth."

"I'll say a prayer for him anyway. What's his name?

"Chooky Bullwater. I wonder if he stole the pig cause he was hungry. They said it was an old feud, but maybe he just wanted something to eat. I been that low before."

"So have I, as I've told you. I had a Saul-on-the-road-to-Damascus moment. Maybe this is yours."

"I don't know what it is."

"You didn't shoot Chooky or the pig, Nat."

"True enough."

"Ruthie told me you were in town. She told me about Win. I didn't know her, but I remember how you talked about her. I'm sorry."

"I should have come to see you sooner. I don't know why I didn't."

Luther put his hand on my shoulder. "Ruthie has feelings for you, you know that?"

"I do."

"I know there's been some bad things in your life, and Win was important to you, but if you have feelings for Ruthie, I think you ought to let her know. And if you don't, then you ought to let her be."

"I guess I'm sorting out how I feel about things."

"Don't sort too long," he said. "There's other fellows that have an interest in her. I fear the Baptist fellow the most."

"What about a nonbeliever?"

"You got room to come around. He don't. He's solid Baptist."

"Judge Parker says God is a Methodist."

"Better that than a Baptist or those fools that play with snakes."

"Somewhere along the line I figure you got bit by a Baptist instead of a snake," I said.

"I do hold a certain prejudice, but that is neither here nor there. It's good to see you again, Nat. You know, Samson greatly admires you . . . Let me ask. Does this event today mean you've given up on the man hurt Win?"

"I'm still a deputy marshal, and he is in my sights as an officer of the law."

"And that's all there is to it? A man doing his duty?"

I didn't answer that. I dodged around it. "You know what? Say a few words for that innocent pig. He wasn't killed to be dinner. He was murdered."

I got up, patted Luther on the shoulder as I passed, and left out of there.

# 31

A few days later, one sunny morning, I was at the courthouse. I had testified in court about a fellow I had arrested for stealing a couple goats. It had been an easy arrest. I found him asleep on the trail and the goats he stole wandering about. He wasn't much of a rustler. Another hour of him asleep and the goats would have walked home.

I finished up my testimony and was coming down the courthouse steps with a warrant in my pocket for a fellow who had robbed another fellow of a horse, when who should I see riding along on his big sorrel but Bass Reeves. Riding along with him was Choctaw Tom.

There was a white marshal with them, Heck Thomas, and he was driving the prison wagon that was rattling along behind them. In the back of it six men was peeking out of the bars at me. Three of them was colored, two was maybe Indian or Mexican, and the other was white. I recognized him. Kid Red, the boy me and Bronco Bob had taught to shoot. He was as skinny and ragged as I had first seen him when he was carrying Bronco Bob's shooting gear. He was hatless, and his red hair had grown long and stringy. He was chained to the others by wrist and ankles and the main chain was locked down to a ring in the middle of the wagon.

"Hold up, Bass," I said.

Bass raised his hand, and Heck pulled the wagon to a stop.

"I know one of your prisoners," I said.

"You knowing him won't help him none. These are the worst among a bad lot," he said.

"They steal full-grown hogs instead of pigs?"

"That's funny shit, Nat. You are something of a softie, I fear, and it will get you killed. My prediction is every one of these dog turds will hang, including the one you know."

"I'd like to speak to one of the turds for a moment, the one I know."

"All right," Bass said. "Heck, Choctaw, let's get a cup of coffee. These fellows ain't going nowhere."

Heck climbed off the wagon, and Bass and Choctaw dropped down from their horses.

"Bass, let me have the redhead off the trot line," I said.

"That ain't a good idea, Nat."

"Leave his leg manacles on. Just take him off the main chain, let him out so me and him can talk."

"You're sure?"

"I am."

"Which one is he?"

I pointed out Red.

Bass pushed up his hat and gave me that dark, burning look he used on men who didn't agree with him. I have to admit, that was some look. I tried not to let my knees buckle.

"I get a feeling that someday you and me are going to tussle, Nat."

"Not unless I steal a pig."

Bass grunted. He went around and unlocked the back of the wagon and unchained Red from the main chain and brought him out. He pushed him to me. Red's leg chains tangled him up, and he fell. I got him under the arm and pulled him up.

Bass locked the back of the wagon.

"You got as long as it takes us to have a cup of coffee in the court-house."

"Have two cups," I said.

Bass did that grunting thing again, went up the steps of the courthouse and inside with the other two. I led Red over to the courthouse porch, and we sat on the edge of it.

"How you been, Nat?"

"Just happy as a duck in water. What the hell, Red? What are you doing? I got a letter from Bronco Bob. He said you'd gone wrong and thrown in with Ruggert. You know what he did to me?"

Red hung his head. "I feel deeply sorrowful about it, Nat. I do. It's the whiskey. I got on it, and then I got to liking the guns and the thrill, and next thing I know I'm with Ruggert, and . . . I wish I could explain it better."

"Me, too. What have they got you for?"

"The big man had a writ, and he served it, and it had a lot of things written on it."

"Did you do them all?"

"Yeah. And some more wasn't on it."

"How bad was what was on it?"

"Murder, six times, train robbery, stagecoach robbery. Burglary. Public lewdness. I showed my pecker to some ladies. I was drunk on that one, Nat. I mean real drunk. On all them charges I was drunk, Nat. I ain't like that now. I'm a changed man."

"Save it. You've crossed the river, and there's no boat back. You might be lucky with time in prison, but I figure it's the rope. That's a lot of mischief, Red."

"I know."

"It's bad enough you done all that, but Ruggert? You teamed with him? What did I ever do to you, boy?"

"Nothing, Nat. You always treated me straight and upright. I ain't got no excuse for it. You won't believe this, but when I first got crossed with him I had been rustling some cattle, and he was the man we sold 'em to. Me and these others, and I thought, I know him from Deadwood, and that's the man done them bad things to Nat, wrapped him in a cow skin and raped his woman and killed the other one. I knew all that from you and Bronco Bob telling me. Shit, Nat. Really, I meant to kill him. And then he had us all stay the night. He was staying in a shack, and it turned out he'd killed them that owned it, and they was propped up out back. It was cold weather, so it wasn't as nasty as you'd think. He put them stolen cows in their corral. Ruggert, he had a buyer, and he paid us for them. He also had some men with him, four of them, so I was waiting on my chance—"

"This sounds like bigger bullshit than Bronco Bob writes."

"Hey, I read some of those books, and they're good. I'm in a couple of them, though he's not real nice to me."

"Goddamn it, Red. Give me your shitty explanation. Give me something to believe."

"I know how it sounds, Nat. But it's all true. I was going to kill him, but he had whiskey."

"You sold me out for whiskey?"

"Sort of."

"Jesus, Red."

"I didn't mean for it to happen how it did. It was sort of like a little creek—that would be me—flowing into a larger river, and that larger river would be Ruggert. Next thing I know I'm drinking, and he's talking. I never mentioned you, but he did. He has it bad for you. Told me how you violated his wife and so on and so on, and how he had killed you by wrapping you in a cowhide. Word hadn't gotten to him yet. I told him I knew you some and that you was alive. I didn't make out we was friends."

"Thanks for that," I said.

"He was beside himself. Got so mad I thought he was going to mess his pants. He jumped up and hobbled around—that's how he walks, with a hobble."

"I know. Go on."

"He said you was the reason every bad thing had happened to him, including his being burned and scalped and his balls carved on. It was a long, sad story, Nat. And I was moved. Not that I thought you was responsible, but he'd had some deprivations. I learned that word from one of Bronco Bob's dime novels."

"Congratulations on your vocabulary."

"Next thing I knew me and him was planning a robbery. I didn't have nothing against you, and I didn't think you was responsible for nothing, but he was really sad."

"Well, boo-hoo."

"So before I know it I'm in with him, and we're robbing trains and getting into scrapes and he's praising my gun handling and all that, and I'm liking it. I did mention to you in the past how I hadn't gotten a lot of attention."

"You did," I said.

"Now I was getting some. It went to my head."

"That's it? That's why you were with him?"

"I suppose that's all there is to it. And then we did this last job, which was robbing a stage up near Kansas, and things went bad. I got in a shoot-out, killed the driver and the shotgun rider, and damn if a stray bullet didn't pick off a kid. We had brought everyone out to stand in front of the stagecoach, and there was this boy dressed in a suit and a bowler hat, holding a little dog, and that's when the shotgun man, who we had disarmed and told to stay up on the seat, pulled a derringer and shot at me. He missed, but I didn't. Then I shot the driver for good measure, and Ruggert yelled, "Watch them prisoners," and I don't know how it happened, but I just turned and shot. Bullet went right through the dog and hit that kid. He just sort of sat down out from under his bowler hat. That dog and him didn't so much as whimper. I knew then I was through. We split up. Ruggert took the money. Days later I got lost somewhere in the Indian Nations. My horse broke a leg. I shot it and then got lost worse than I was before, if you can imagine that, come out finally on a clay road and knew where I was. Didn't help me none. Here come that big colored man and with him that other fellow driving the wagon and the mixed blood, and there was five men in there. Deputy marshal, one you call Bass, has a memory like a steel trap. He figured me for someone on the run, which I guess isn't that hard, but he remembered a description of me and Ruggert. I wasn't anywhere near where we robbed that stagecoach, but he had already gotten word. Goddamn telegraph."

"I don't like him," I said, "but he is a hell of a marshal."

"He said, 'You fit a description, boy.' I tried to hold out on him, but after that kid and that dog, I'd had enough. I shot my mouth off. I told him everything I had ever done, and that included stealing a comb when I was a kid in Deadwood."

"You're still a kid."

"I don't feel like one."

"I'm sorry for you, Red, but there's nothing I can do for you."

"You want Ruggert, don't you?"

"You know the answer to that."

"I can give you a lead on him, but I'd like something in return."

"I can't let you go."

"Hell, I know that. But maybe you can talk to this judge, Parker."

"He's a hard one," I said.

"You could talk to him about how I helped you marshals out. Ruggert, he's the brains behind all this, and he wants to kill you. He knew you were here he'd come for you. I bet he would. But I bet it would be better and easier you just went to him."

"You know where he is?"

"I know his running path. He don't know I've been nabbed. He's expecting me to show up again. You can use that. Besides, I ain't going back if I could. I think he might be planning to kill me. There was a fellow in our gang disappeared and no one knew where he went. I figured it was Ruggert got rid of him. Got him alone and killed him on account of it was more money for Ruggert. He always seemed to have more than the rest of us. He was the leader, but he was supposed to split whatever we hauled in even-steven. I don't know he ever did. Maybe that fellow called him on it."

"I don't care about any of that. Who else is with him?"

"Pinocchio Joe Bullwater is one. And then there's this other fellow, Indian Charlie Doolittle."

I had never heard Pinocchio Joe's last name. It was not listed on the warrant, but it certainly rang a bell now.

"Pinocchio Joe have a brother named Chooky?" I asked.

"He did. He didn't ride with us, but he put us up in his cabin some. I was planning on going there when I got caught out on the road."

"That's interesting," I said.

"You got to watch Pinocchio Joe. He'll cut down on you in a minute. Doolittle not so much. He's kind of like a chicken. He's just as happy pecking corn out of cow shit as he would be eating fresh corn. But he's a sneaky bastard. Look here, Nat. Will you talk to Parker?"

"I will, but I won't guarantee a thing."

"But you will talk to him? Put in a good word for me?"

"You tell me where Ruggert stays, and if you lead me on a wild-goose chase I will put in a different kind of word with Parker. Hear me?"

"I do," he said. "I do. You put in a good word, that's more than I deserve. Goddamn it, Nat. I am so hungry. I haven't eaten in days. Bass gave me some water, but when I asked for a bite, he gave me his best wishes."

"I'll get you fed. You can count on that. This information you got, you can't tell nobody but me. Say anything to anyone else, our deal is off."

"That's how it'll be. Thanks, Nat. You were always good to me. I want to make things square with you and me. No matter how it turns out, me in prison or bouncing on the end of a rope, I want to make things square."

He told me where he thought they were hiding. I placed him back in the cage and secured the lock through the chains that fastened him to the wagon.

I went over and seen Judge Parker right away. I told him what I knew from Kid Red, and I put in a good word for him on account of him giving me some information that might lead to me coming up on Ruggert and killing him. I also told him there might be something to me checking out Chooky's cabin.

"Kid Red has quite a list of serious crimes, Nat," the judge said.

The judge was sitting at his desk, but now he stood up, walked around, and looked about his room like he was searching for cobwebs in the corner.

"I know," I said. "I'm only asking to put it into consideration. He isn't really any more than a boy, and he's had it tough."

Judge Parker stopped walking, put his hands behind his back, and looked at me.

"Nat, would you say you've had it tough?"

"I don't know, sir."

"Surely things have not all been slick sledding for you as a Negro."

"I suppose not."

"Have you committed any crimes?"

"Not that I'd own up to."

"All right, then, let's take another tack. Lot of men brought in here have had hard lives and can tell you stories so sad it would make you and your horse weep. But they still had a decision to make, and they chose to go wrong. I know some of the men who work for me haven't always been on the up-and-up. Maybe that's your case, son. But what I will tell you is this. I find out they aren't square, find out they aren't doing their duty, then they have to answer to the same laws as those they arrest. Understand me?"

"Yes, sir."

"I don't want to know your past. Way I look at it, I don't have a warrant, I don't have a thing to say to you for anything. But this boy, he murdered a boy and a dog. The dog doesn't rest as heavy as the child, but it has some weight with me. I like dogs. You look at the list of his crimes—hold up."

He went to his desk and ratted around in some papers, came up with one.

"This is the latest information I have on the Ruggert gang. And it's quite a list. Your boy, as you call him, has murdered and robbed—"

"I said as much."

"Hold your water. Listen. They have raped in the Nations. Indian women. Negroes and white folk as well. Your boy is said to have raped a young girl. That's what it says here."

"That doesn't sound like him," I said.

"It's not what he'd tell you. Look at it this way, Nat. A boy like that with bad raising has made choices you wouldn't make. You may have some knots in your life's rope, but I bet you haven't raped any young girls. Now he whines. He could have gone either way, and he chose one way and you chose another. He's a criminal, and you are a US deputy marshal. You kept your word to him, and now you're done with it. I will tell you true as the direction we call north I'm going to hang that boy. That's how it is. Now, if you have something that will let you get this Ruggert and whoever is involved with him in his criminal enterprises, go forth and do it. Good day, Nat."

"Good day, sir."

I left the courthouse stunned, walked over to where the wagon had been. Bass had moved it under a big oak tree so that it was in the shade. It would be emptied soon enough, and into the jail those six would go. I stopped and leaned against the bars.

I was close to Red. I said, "There's a new warrant, says you raped a girl. You didn't mention that."

"Why should I, Nat? I was just getting me some. It was an Indian."

"And if it was a colored girl how would you feel?"

"I don't know. I think of you as different."

"I'm colored."

"Yeah, but you're different."

"And if she was white?"

"Of course not."

"So you did rape her?"

"I took some advantage of her, but I wasn't the only one, and I wasn't the first of us."

"So the number and position somehow make it different?"

"It was just some girl you don't know, Nat."

"Listen to me. Listen good. I told Judge Parker you helped me out. Right now I don't know you did. You may have lied to me."

"I didn't."

"Good. Because I'll get Ruggert, and you know what?"

"What?"

"You're going to hang like drapes."

"You said——"

"I said I'd talk to the judge. I did. That was before I knew you raped a girl. You did it, and you don't seem bothered by it in the least."

"It gets to me a little. I was drunk when I did it. Wasn't entirely myself."

"Shit, Red. You've become one of them. Only reason you are talking to me, befriending me, is you thought I could help you out. You put everything on being drunk. It's you that's drinking, Red. It's not being forced down your throat."

"You've killed before."

"Not for money. Not for sport. And I never did the things you did. That boy and his dog. That wasn't no accident, was it?"

"Nat."

"It wasn't an accident, was it?"

"I never had a dog. I never had a fancy suit like that punk had, or a bowler hat. He looked right proud of himself in that garb, holding that damn dog. I never had nothing."

"So they should have nothing?"

"You're turning on me, Nat."

"You turned on yourself, Red. All I can hope for you is the drop through the trap is clean, snaps your neck, and you don't strangle."

"You're like all of them. You're just like Ruggert said."

"Like all of who?"

"Like all the goddamn people like you."

"How do you mean?"

"He said no matter how good a nigger is, in time the nigger will come out in him. You just let it come out in you. You sold me to the rope."

"You sold yourself, boy. And I ain't getting you a damn thing to eat. Suck your thumb."

I turned then and started walking away. I felt like a fool. Tears was running down my cheeks.

"Nigger," he kept calling out, over and over until I was gone.

# 32

I bought myself lunch, something I could eat out under a tree, and later
when I seen that the wagon had been emptied of its prisoners, I walked
to where Ruthie stayed with her family. I found her out in the yard with
a hoe. She was trimming around some tomato vines that she had staked.
They wasn't real healthy-looking tomatoes. I stood at the gate of the
fence they had built around the garden, which I guess was about half an
acre, and watched her hoe for a while. It wasn't that I enjoyed seeing a
woman work, though I damn sure like one that is willing to, but I found
myself trying to figure if she was the sort that would have gathered rats in
a bag and beat them to death or drowned them. I couldn't see that. And
I couldn't see Win talking to ducks. There was a lot of confusion in my
head, but some of it sorted out that very day. I opened the gate and went
through the path between the crops. Ruthie lifted her head when she saw
me coming, leaned on the hoe. I could see Luther out back cranking a
bucket of water up from the well. He looked like a tree wearing a hat. It
was a nice well and a nice house. Samson was out in the distance tossing
corn to some free-ranging chickens.

They both looked up and saw me. I lifted a hand in a wave. I went
right up to Ruthie.

"I'm going on a hunt for a dangerous man. I think you know who I mean, as you've heard me talk about him. I'm done with him, and you ain't been claimed by any of them other suitors, I would love to be your main man, as long as you don't think it's a ricochet and you know I'm serious about marriage."

"That's a lot of words," Ruthie said.

"It is."

"What if I said we should start slow?"

"I would start slow. About those other suitors . . ."

"I don't care a hoot for any of them," she said.

"That's good."

"It's good for you. And just so you're clear on matters, Nat. No one claims me. I decide if I want to be with them. That's how it works."

"Fair enough. I want to give you something to think on while I'm gone so maybe it will help you decide if it's a ricochet."

"All right, then. What have you got?"

I pushed up my hat and took hold of her shoulders and pushed my lips to hers. She didn't fight. We kissed. It was a long and good kiss. It wasn't the same as that kiss with Win on our hill in the high Dakotas. It tasted a little damp with sweat, but mostly it tasted sweet and right.

I heard Samson make a hooting sound. When I looked up Luther was still out by the well, but he was smiling at me. Samson's hooting had scattered the chickens. He wore a big grin. I tipped my hat to them all.

Ruthie was a little teary when she said, "Don't get killed. For God's sake, don't get killed."

"Wouldn't think of it," I said. "And more for my sake than God's."

I turned and went along the path and out of the gate.

I started that very afternoon. I went and found Choctaw Tom over at the courthouse. He was sitting out front whittling on some wood. I said, "I'd like to have you come with me."

"I'm taking it this ain't no invitation to a dance."

"It kind of is. The music might be gunfire."

"I don't like getting shot at."

"Hell, who in their right mind does?"

"I like it less than most."

"Well, I'm asking, and you can say what you want."

"You ain't crazy like Bass, so that's in your favor."

He tossed the piece of wood on the ground and folded up his pocket-knife.

"Judge going to pay for this?" he asked.

"It's marshal business, so yes."

I told him who I was going after and asked if he knew Chooky, who he saw killed.

"I knew him. He was harmless as that pig. His brother, though, he's not on the harmless side. He's a snake and then some."

"He's running with other snakes."

"I know."

"Could you find them?"

"I can find anybody if I have a start."

"That's what I hear. I also hear that Pinocchio Joe is running with a man I want, Ruggert, and another man named Indian Charlie Doolittle."

"That little shit. He ain't much."

"But he has a gun."

"He probably does. My guess is there might even be more of them than those three."

"That's possible," I said. "I'd like you to go with me. I said you'd get paid. I told you who it is, and now all I need is your agreement."

"How about one bottle of whiskey when the job's finished?"

"Fair enough. When it's finished, not before. I don't ride with drunks. But I'll bring the bottle with me. I'll decide when the job's done."

"Well, then, I'll go get my horse and saddle."

"One goes with the other," I said.

"That it does."

"More important, bring a rifle."

"I got a Yellow Boy. Thing is, though, I'm a tracker, not a marshal, so I'm not going to promise I'll get down in the thick of it. I'll get you there, but three men or more, that's a lot of men. We could get Bass and some others."

"We could, but we won't. I think it'll be easier to find them with a light crew. It's more than you want to handle when we find them, you can step out."

"All right, then."

"Meet here in an hour, ready to go."

He went to get his goods, and I went to get mine.

I put some possibles together and made sure of my ammunition and was on the hunt. We left out of Fort Smith with the sky freckled like an Appaloosa, a sure sign of bad weather and a sure sign to turn back and wait for better weather.

But we went ahead. Bad weather would cause them to hole up somewhere, not to expect someone out in it and after them. I thought about Kid Red's information, and I told Choctaw Tom where he said they might be.

"Hell, Nat, that could be anywhere. That's a place so wide and long it's like saying there's a tick out there with a top hat and he lives there somewhere and you can find him if he yells at you and waves his hat and has a voice like a buffalo. That's no help at all. That's just as general as saying, 'There's stars in the sky. Watch for the one on the left.' "

"Is that where the tick with the top hat will be?"

"Most likely."

"He seems to have moved from the ground to the sky."

"They are tricky bastards."

"Here's how we'll start. Pinocchio Joe being Chooky's brother, it might be best to start with Chooky's cabin."

"Did you know Pinocchio was wanted?"

"Yep."

"You didn't tell Bass the connection?"

"Nope."

"Why not?"

"I don't like him. Killing a man over a pig seems on the harsh side to me. Besides, I just discovered the connection from Kid Red."

"I see. Ever ate a pickled egg?"

"What?"

"A pickled egg. I'm going to have me one. I got two."

"No. That's all right. Keep it for yourself."

Choctaw pulled a bag from his saddlebag. It had a box inside it, and as he rode along, he opened the box and took out one of the eggs. It smelled awful. He ate it, and then he ate the other.

"I knew I'd eat them right away," he said. "I was going to save them for a time when I was really hungry, but I love the goddamn things."

"I don't need an explanation," I said.

"I eat all the time, Nat. I'm always hungry. I got enough supplies here for a whole wad of sawmill workers. I could feed ten or twelve. I eat all the time and don't gain a goddamn pound. I stay skinny as a rail. I could use a bit of meat on me. Other day the wind blew, and I found myself in a tree."

"Sure you did," I said.

"Would I lie to you?"

"I think you might," I said.

"Not about the eating. That's true. I think I got some kind of worm."

We came to where Bass had shot Chooky, and then we rode on farther up the hill and then onto a flat slab of land and into some trees. On the other side of the trees was a cabin that Choctaw said belonged to Chooky.

We stopped and sat on our horses and looked at the cabin. There was no smoke, and there was no horses to be seen out front or in the open-ended shed to the right of the house. I rode around back of the house, going wide, and didn't see no horses there, neither, though there was a corral there. Without getting down off my horse I could see that the horse turds there wasn't fresh, but they wasn't old, neither. A few days or so, I guessed. We met around front and tied our horses off. Choctaw carried his Yellow Boy, I pulled my Colt, and we went up to the door, which was already partly open. I nudged it with my boot. It was dark in there, and it smelled like sweaty men.

Choctaw lit a match and moved past me and went inside. It was a small cabin, one room, and we was quick to see wasn't nobody there but us.

"They must have holed up here with Chooky," Choctaw said. "There's been several men here. I reckon he stole the pig to feed them. He wasn't no bad fellow, but he'd have helped his brother hide out. He just up and lied about why he stole that pig. Stood by his brother to the end."

"And Bass didn't come here after the pig thief was killed," I said. "That would have been a smart follow-through, don't you think?"

"It would have, but I think Bass was thinking about free pork chops more than detective work," Choctaw said. "He's got his mind right, though. Ain't no one better than him. I just don't like his attitude."

We strolled out back to the corral.

"There were several horses here, and not too long back," Choctaw said.

"Way I figured."

"There was some cows, too."

Choctaw got off his horse and climbed over the corral and started feeling around in piles of shit. Soon as he mentioned it, I could see there was cow pies and horse piles in the corral. It ain't that hard to tell them apart; same with chicken shit and hog shit. They all got their look and smell and feel. Choctaw went out to the well and cranked up a bucket of water and rinsed his hands off, came back, and got on his horse.

"There was three cows rustled from Old Man Turner over on the other side of the bluff there. He had them put up, but someone came in the night and took them. My guess is these fellas was the ones that had them, cause there was three cows in that corral, and on the far side there was horses."

"You can tell how many cows from a pile of shit?"

"Hoofprints and such. Every hoof looks different, you make the effort to study them. My figuring is they stole them to sell, or maybe for food.

They drove them off when they rode away."

"Can you follow them?"

"Trail isn't too warm, but I can follow it if it doesn't start raining, and maybe even then. Long as they got those cows with them they can't move too fast. Then again, they got quite a few days on us. I can't guarantee your man—what's his name?"

"Ruggert."

"I can't guarantee he's with them, but Pinocchio Joe is. I know his horse's print. It's not the horseshoe, it's the way the horse wears it."

"You can wear it different ways?"

"You ain't much of a tracker, are you?

"Why I got you."

"A horse has his own way of walking with a shoe—how it steps, way it puts its print down. Trust me. It's him. And I figure one of the other prints to be Doolittle. They never get far apart, and the print is light. Doolittle rides light. He don't weigh enough to hold down a newspaper in a light wind. And there's another. That might be your Ruggert fellow."

I nodded, glanced at the sky. It was starting to darken. "Looks like rain will be soon."

"Yep. Let's get on the trail. See how much ground we can cover before it comes down."

We wound up into the mountains and the sky got dark and the rain started to come down hard. We pulled on our slickers, and that helped, but pretty soon it was damn near dead dark, and the sound of the rain on my hat was making me loco. There was an old cabin high up in the mountains Choctaw knew of, and he said it wasn't much off the trail and we should go there to ride out the storm. We rode there, being cautious to note if our outlaws might have had the same idea a few days back and was still there, but they wasn't.

We brought our horses into the cabin, which wasn't really much more than a shack. It was dark in there, but we had some waxed paper twists and we lit one. There was an old kerosene lamp, but there wasn't any kerosene in it. We stuck a few lit twists here and there and tried to figure where we could put our bedrolls. First thing we did was block the door from being pushed back by wedging a slicked piece of wood underneath it. It would take some determination from outside to move it, and by then we should be on the job in case defending ourselves was necessary.

There was a fireplace, and the flue drew smoke well enough, and there was a bit of wood, so we made a fire. That gave us more light. Choctaw got out his cooking goods, warmed us up some beans. It was a lot of beans, actually. I ate a plateful, and Choctaw ate three plates full. He wasn't kidding about always being hungry.

"What do you think they got in mind?" I asked Choctaw.

"Not getting caught. Bunch like that, they done played out their cards, but they don't know it. They ain't got nothing left now but to keep doing what they're doing, and then in time they'll step in a pile somehow, and they'll get caught."

"Think we'll be the ones to catch them?"

"Hell, yeah."

"What makes you so certain?"

Choctaw smiled at me, wiped his bean-juice-coated mouth with the back of his sleeve. "You got me. Course, once we catch up with them they could kill us both."

The rain came down like bullets, and the cabin was shabby and leaked. We hobbled the horses, but the rain and the lightning made them restless, and between the rain and them stirring and me worrying about our prey coming upon us by accident, I had a sleepless night. Here is what I had wanted for so long, and now that I was getting close I wasn't sure how I felt about it. I wasn't sure I'd live through it, and if I did I wasn't sure how I'd feel about myself. My mother said I was destined for greatness. I doubted when she said that she thought I'd be up in the wet mountains with plans to kill a man, even if he deserved it. I remembered what Ruggert had said about her, and that made me a little sick. I didn't like what was running through my mind, the ideas he had put there.

When morning light slipped through the wet cracks of the cabin, I was already up and tending to the fire. There was hardly enough wood to make a blaze now, but it was enough to warm more beans. I had my plateful and Choctaw had his three, this time the beans coming from my possibles. At this rate we'd have to eat the horses by noon and each other by noon the next day.

The day was fresh, and the rain was drying fast as the sun was growing hot. By ten the freshness would go out of the air and it would turn sticky, like someone had poured hot honey over the woods and mountains. It was that time of year when the weather could change from one thing to another as quickly as a child can change its mind.

Choctaw, to my surprise, could still find sign of where our bunch had traveled. He said it was because they had those cows with them when they passed through. The cows had torn the earth up a lot. I looked. I couldn't tell the difference from what the rain had done and what the cows and horses had done a few days back. As I said, I'm not a great tracker, though I can follow fresh sign all right, but Choctaw could follow a ghost in moccasins.

By late afternoon we come upon a white man walking. He didn't walk like someone used to it. He was a heavy, bowlegged outfit of a man without a hat, and he was holding a hand to the side of his head. When he seen us he threw up a hand. "Hold on there, men. I been robbed."

We got down off our horses and helped the man to sit on a fallen tree by the side of the trail.

"Who robbed you?"

"Three men," he said. "One of them I knowed, so that's why I think I'm alive. They gave him me to kill, and he took me off in the woods and said I'd wake up with a headache, and before I could ask him what he meant I woke up with a headache. I see two of each of you, by the way, but I doubt you is two sets of twins. And you got all them horses."

"You're going to need some bed rest," I said.

"I ain't far from my house if I can take the right trail."

"There's only one," Choctaw said.

"Not the way I'm seeing," he said.

"What's your name?" I said.

"People call me Bump. Now that I got this lick on my head, that fits right nice. You got a chaw?"

Neither me nor Choctaw had a chaw.

"Smoke?"

Choctaw rolled Bump a cigarette, licked it closed, put it in Bump's mouth, and lit a match to it.

Bump took a few puffs.

"Bump, who was it you knew?" Choctaw asked.

"Doolittle, that little shit. He used to work for me. He's all right, I reckon, but he has a tendency to stray here and there, and now I'm mad at him, hitting me in the head like that."

"He was supposed to shoot you," I said.

"Yeah, well, that's true, but I tell you, my head stays like this I won't even be able to sort my socks. There'll be too many."

"What did they steal from you and when?" I asked him.

"I been walking all day . . . Well, I laid out some on the ground in some trees for a while. Yesterday near evening was when Doolittle hit me. They already had some cows with them when they come up on me, three, I think, and then they took my cows. Eight of them. And my horse. I was driving the cows on some green range. I don't own it. No one does that I know of. I run them there now and then to give them a kind of spring tonic. Hell, they're not prime cows or nothing. Just some old sagalongs. Some I was gonna butcher and smoke the meat; a couple are milk cows. I've had them awhile. I like my milk. They'll need milking, too, and I told them that. You gonna steal them, I says, then you gotta milk 'em, otherwise they're in pain, and in time they can quit giving milk. I don't think they was listening. But I tell you, they don't milk them, they'll be bawling by sundown."

"Any idea where they was going?"

He shook his head.

"I have an idea," Choctaw said. "There's a fellow named Chet Williamson on the other side of the bluff, two, three days' ride at their pace with the cows. He buys stolen anything that can be made into meat. He's a butcher. He's good at buying what ain't his and butchering what ain't his. We all know he does it, but ain't no one ever caught him red-handed. He buys cows low and butchers them right away and makes his money off the meat by selling high. He don't ask much in the way of questions. Them rustlers need some quick money, is my guess, and they're gathering cows and horses, which Williamson also buys, kills, and smokes and says is beef. He wants what you got, you're quick in and quick out. By the time money has changed hands and he's got the stock, Williamson's sons go straight to the butchering. They're all butchers, though I heard one of them likes to make brooms or some such horseshit."

"Oh, hell," said Bump. "They butcher them. Ah, shit. I hate that to happen to my milk cows. They're like family. They're the only family I got, actually."

"Maybe we can get to them before they sell the cows," I said. "Tell me about them."

Doolittle we all knew about by now, and then he described one that Choctaw said was definitely Pinocchio Joe. Then Bump said, "And the other one looked like he had been caught on fire and it had been put out by a stampede. Not only was he ugly, he was also mean, and he was in charge. I thought him and the long-nosed one was at each other's throats a little, on account of I think Long Nose thought he should be running things. Doolittle, he don't care who runs things. He's good to figure out what day it is and which hole to shit out of. He wasn't much of a worker when he worked for me. I thought I might as well be honest about that."

"That's a note we'll make," I said. "All right, we'll get you to your place then go after these assholes."

"Hell with that. Go on and do your job. My place ain't far, soon as I figure out which of the trails I see is really there."

"We can set you on it," Choctaw said.

"Just get my cows back," he said. "Especially my milk cows."

"We'll do what we can," I said.

We set Bump on the trail, and with his hand to his head, he went wandering along. Back on our horses Choctaw picked up their trail again, and we followed.

As we rode along, Choctaw said, "The cows are slowing them down quite a bit, and now that they've added some they'll go slower still. We'll catch up with them by nightfall is my figure. Not then, early the next morning."

"Good," I said.

"I want to remind you," he said. "I only signed on to track."

"When we find them, you can go back if you like."

"Just so that's understood that I can if I want to. I ain't going to, just wanted it understood I'm my own man."

"You're sticking, then?"

"I think so, yeah."

"When will I know so?" I said. "Something like that I ought to have a better idea of, considering the circumstances."

"Yeah, I'm sticking."

"I ought not look a gift horse in the mouth, but why?"

"You ain't bossy like some of the others. Bass—damn, now, there's a boss. I think him having been a slave taught him how to be a boss, too. He learned from his master. You know, story is he run off from being a slave, got clean free, and never went back. He was a good friend to his master is the story I heard, and they got in an argument over a card game, and Bass hit him and then run off and stayed run off."

"Good for him," I said.

"Yeah. But I think he did it not just because he was a slave but because he wanted to be boss. He likes being boss a little too much. Had his way, he'd have slaves."

"But you're fine with me?"

"You got an easy manner, Nat."

It was all birdsong and roses right then, but we had yet to find them, and sometimes if you hunt bear, the bear wins. A thing I had solid in my mind as we rode along higher into the Ozark Mountains.

# 33

What I told you about how weather in that part of the country can change in the blink of an eye was coming true. The skies had darkened again, and not only was rain threatening to wet our heads, it was also threatening to darken our trail and wash it away. Choctaw had been able to follow it so far, but even he said another rain and he might not be able to stay on it, least not without some serious hunting here and there to pick up on it again. He said that wasn't a worry, though, as he was certain where they were driving them cows and he didn't need to track them anymore.

It made sense, but then again you can make all kinds of guesses that can get your ass in a tight crack. I was hoping we wasn't making one, and I was hoping it wasn't going to rain before we come up on them, as that would make our business more difficult. That hope got wet not long after.

It began to drizzle, and then real rain came down. It was a cold rain, driven by wind that near slashed you out of the saddle.

As it was dark with cloud cover and rain, we wasn't trying to follow sign anymore. We pulled on our slickers, and Choctaw headed us where he thought they might be going. By nightfall the rain was still going full blast, and it was very dark, and we come upon a huddle of trees, hardwoods that had broad limbs and full leaves, and we decided that was the place to camp. As we was preparing to do that, we seen a red glow about three hundred yards away. Sitting on our horses just inside the trees, we could see that it was a huge fire built into the front of a cave that was hollowed out of a rise of rock; the kind of caves that litter parts of the Ozarks. What we couldn't figure was just how far it went back, but we could hear cows mooing in there, and a couple of the critters seemed distressed.

"That's them that are in need of milking," Choctaw said.

"Yeah," I said.

"Well, I don't reckon you plan on just riding in on them."

"I don't. This is as good a place out of the rain as we got. I say we get our horses fed and do some planning."

We dismounted, leaving the saddles on in case we needed to ride quick, and led our horses into the thickness of the trees and put feed bags on their snouts and tied them to tree trunks. We stood there watching them eat, glancing now and then at that big warm fire and that large-mouth cave. Here we was, representing the law, and we was cold and wet, and there they was, representing assholes everywhere, and they was warm and dry. That alone made me want to shoot them.

It was then that we seen a figure coming across the clearing between the cave and the trees. I think he had been coming all along, but because of the rain and the shadows we hadn't made him out. He was wearing a hat pulled down tight and a rain slicker.

"It's a little fellow," Choctaw said.

"Doolittle?"

"My figure."

We moved through the trees, in line to where we thought he'd enter, and waited.

Our man edged into the trees and walked right between us, as we was hid up behind some elms. As he got past us, Choctaw stepped out and whacked him a good one in the back of the head with the Yellow Boy barrel, knocking him down.

"Aw, hell, that hurt, shit, damn it," said the man on the ground.

"Shut up or I'll give you another one," Choctaw said.

"That hurt," the man said.

"I reckon so," I said. "You Doolittle?"

"Who wants to know?" the man said.

"A fellow that's going to smack you again with this rifle," Choctaw said.

"Yeah, I'm Doolittle. What have I done to you?"

"Breathe air," I said. "I'm Nat Love, deputy marshal, and you are under arrest for theft and a bunch of stuff that would wear me out to list."

"You ain't got nothing on me," Doolittle said.

"Let me think," I said. "Yeah. Yeah, I do. I got papers on you and your friends."

"They ain't all that friendly," he said.

"I also got word from Bump that you hit him in the head a lot harder than you just got hit."

"Goddamn it, I knew I should have gone on and shot him. I liked him, though. That's what my problem has been all my life, just like my mama told me. She said my good heart would lead to my downfall."

"That's one way of looking at it," I said. "Here's what we're going to do. We're going to tie you up and gag you."

"Oh, hell, not a gag. I been gagged before. That's just miserable."

"Shut up," Choctaw said.

"We will gag you and tie you up, or we can just go ahead and shoot you. If we shoot you, that will let your companions know we're here, but on the downside for you, you will be dead."

"I don't like that side of it at all. Go ahead and gag me."

We tied his hands behind his back with some leather strips, bound his feet, sat him up against a tree, tied a rope to the bind that held his hands, and wrapped that around the tree.

Choctaw said, "You are in luck, Doolittle, as I got some dirty socks that will fit right into your mouth. But let me tell you a thing or two. I seen a man gagged once that fought the gag so much he swallowed it, and that didn't do him any good, I can assure you. You got to be still and wait for us to return or you might choke."

"And what if you get killed?"

"That wouldn't be good for you at all. We get killed, and your buddies get killed, too — or don't know you're here or don't care — you're going to be in quite a pickle, now, ain't you?"

"I reckon I will be. But it don't seem right I got to root for you fellows."

"It is a confusion," I said. "Why was you out here anyway?"

"Looking for a place to shit. At least I don't have that problem no more. It's all stove up inside of me now."

"You can't shit in the cave?" Choctaw said.

"I suggested it, but my pards was against it."

"I can see that," I said.

"So you came out in the rain to shit in the woods?" Choctaw said.

"I'm modest. They're going to miss me, you know?"

"Maybe not soon enough," I said.

Choctaw got one of his socks and some rags out of his saddlebag. You could smell that sock even with the rain and the wind blowing. It wasn't pleasant.

"You really going to use that sock?" Doolittle said.

"I am."

"Ain't you got no clean ones?"

"I do."

"So you're just being mean?"

"I am. I used it to wipe a little cow doo off my boots when I changed socks yesterday, so there might be something in them you can chew on."

Choctaw pushed the socks up close to Doolittle's face.

"Oh, that's smells terrible. I've changed my mind. Go on and shoot me."

"Don't tempt us," I said.

Choctaw shoved the sock in Doolittle's mouth and tied it in there with a couple bands of what was now wet rags. When he was done, he stood up from where he had been squatting and patted Doolittle on the head.

"Be good, little boy," he said.

There wasn't no choice but to go to them, as pretty soon they might wonder what happened to Doolittle. Way we decided to come at it was I'd go to the right, far around, and try and come along the line of rocks that led to the cave and surprise them at the mouth of it. Choctaw would cross the clearing off to the left side of the fire. We figured if they saw him at all before he was right on them, they'd think it was Doolittle coming back, though the problem there was Choctaw was considerable taller. I pointed this out to him, and he said, "I'll hunker down."

"Hunker good," I said. "Give me about a five-minute lead before you start hunkering, though."

I took my deputy marshal badge out of my pocket and lifted up my slicker and pinned it on my shirt and set out along the trees with my rifle in hand until I was far right of the cave. Then I took to a trot across the clearing, out of their line of sight, or so I hoped. I glanced back and saw Choctaw had started his way toward them. With all that rain and wind blowing, I didn't think they figured it was anyone other than Doolittle until he was right up on them. I was close enough I could really hear them cattle in the cave now, and I could hear voices, but not what was being said. I felt pretty confident we had put the sneak on them, but as I reached the rock wall, I looked back and seen a surprising sight.

It looked like a giant rabbit wearing a hat. Doolittle had somehow freed himself from the tree. Rope was rotten or the knot wasn't good, I didn't know, but there he come, his hands still tied behind his back and his feet bound. He was hopping up and down, right past Choctaw, who decided to go to one knee there in the clearing. I could make them both out from where I was, and since there was two of them, if the men inside the cave looked up, they'd see them both and know they couldn't both be Doolittle.

Now, I got to give it to Doolittle; he could hop fast. He went right on past Choctaw and just kept on his mission. We could have shot him, but that wouldn't have helped us none, as our shots would have announced us. I decided it was best I moved on toward the cave, and just before I started in that direction I seen Choctaw stand up from where he squatted and start out after Doolittle the Rabbit, most likely to brain him again with his rifle.

I hadn't no more than pressed against the rock wall and started moving when shots rang out, and Doolittle the Rabbit caught one and stumbled but kept to his bound feet and went back to hopping. The gag had shifted, and he had managed to spit the sock out, cause he started calling out, "It's me—don't shoot."

Instead of stopping fire, this seemed to draw it. Bullets ripped from the cave, and down went Doolittle, right on his face. Then them inside the cave took note of Choctaw, who had tried to widen his position, and I heard a shot and seen him toss his head back and yelp and fall to his knees, and then to his face.

I didn't know the disposition of either him or the rabbit and had no choice but to continue on my path to the mouth of the cave. When I wasn't no more than twenty feet from it, I seen a man step out of it, just past the fire that was raging inside the cave. The fire was hissing as the wind was blowing rain into the cave and into the fire; it was like someone was constantly spitting into it.

I knew the fellow standing there was Pinocchio Joe, because I hadn't never seen a nose like that on anything outside of a possum. It stuck out and then hung down like a door latch at the tip.

"I got them both," Pinocchio Joe said. "But I'm starting to think one of them was that little shit Doolittle."

"Which one?" said a voice from the cave, which I recognized as belonging to Ruggert.

"The one hopping, I figure."

"What the hell was he hopping for?"

"He might have thought it was funny."

"He ain't laughing now, is he? Didn't you know it was him?"

"I thought the other one was him, but then I seen he was taller. I'd already shot Doolittle by then, so how tall one was to the other don't really matter."

"Who the hell is the other one?"

"I don't know no more than you do."

"Well, least make sure Doolittle's dead," Ruggert said. "You shot him, you finish him. We'll call it an accident if we got to call it anything. It makes dividing the money easier. And see who that other fucker was. See if you know him."

"Why don't you go out and take a look?"

"Cause I'm the goddamn boss."

"Boss of what? Ain't nobody left but me and you."

"Don't get no ideas, Joe. I ain't going to hop up and down till you shoot me. I might prove a bit more trouble."

Pinocchio Joe stood there as if thinking to respond. I was leaning tight against the shadowed wall, and if Pinocchio Joe didn't turn and look right at me, he wasn't going to see me. I held my breath.

Pinocchio Joe tracked across the clearing to where Choctaw and Doolittle lay. I took a quick study of my situation, and as I was putting together what I should do, for some reason or another, Pinocchio Joe turned and looked back just as I was moving out of the shadows of the rock wall with my rifle.

"Son of a bitch," he said when he saw me.

Ruggert yelled out of the cave, "What did you call me?"

It was then I brought my rifle up and started cocking it fast as I could. I had the lever pushed so that each time I cocked it, it hit the trigger. I must have missed him three times, but I figure I got him on four. He went down in the grass and started cussing.

"You got me in the nuts, you coward. You shot my goddamn nuts."

"I was aiming for your goddamn pecker," I said. "You in the cave. You better stay put."

"Willie?" came Ruggert's voice. "Is that you?"

"It is," I said, "and your hide is tanned."

"You ain't got me yet," he said.

"I'm laying out here shot in the balls and you're having a talk with this bastard," Pinocchio Joe said. He had started to roll around on the ground a little.

"It's that nigger I told you about," Ruggert said.

"I don't care," Pinocchio Joe said. "I got a bullet in my sack."

All the time Pinocchio Joe was rattling on, I had been moving with my back against the rocks, toward the mouth of the cave. Pinocchio Joe might have thought I wouldn't notice he was trying to get up on his knees with his rifle. But I noticed. I was just waiting for him to set up high enough I could pick him off.

When he rose up suddenly and the rifle lifted, I popped off a shot. He shot, too. His shot went wild, but mine hit him. He fell back in the grass and yelled out, "Now I'm shot in the goddamn neck. I'm dying in the rain. Oh, Jesus. I got blood in my mouth." Then I heard Pinocchio gurgle, and then he was silent and still. I watched toward the mouth of the cave to see if Ruggert was coming out on me, which he didn't, and then I darted my eyes out to where Pinocchio Joe lay, hoping he wasn't playing possum. He didn't move, but I decided to put another shot into him to make sure. I shot him twice, actually. He didn't so much as flinch either time. I was counting him dead from that moment on.

"Ruggert, I'm coming in after you."

"Then come ahead. I'll put on the coffee, you black bastard."

I heard the cattle and horses stirring inside the cave. Those shots had gotten them worked up.

I leaned my rifle against the wall and pulled the LeMat and put the lever on the shotgun load, then I put it back and loosened the Colt in its holster. I picked up the rifle again. I considered for a moment.

"Well, you coming in, or do I need to give you a piggyback ride?" Ruggert said.

I took a deep breath and moved swiftly along the wall to the mouth of the cave and the bright burning fire. I poked the rifle inside and started cocking and pumping shots. The cows bellowed and the horses snorted and then they all went wild. I could hear them stomping around in there, and then one of the horses leaped through the fire, knocking big logs about. I heard more stomping inside, and then Ruggert yelled out in pain. I dropped the rifle, pulled both pistols, and stepped inside.

There was a wall of cows, and they near knocked me down, running in a circle as they was. The cave was small, but I could see between the dancing shadows of cow bodies and flickering firelight that there was a kind of drop-off at the rear. I could hear Ruggert screaming down there, so I knew he had been knocked into it by those frightened critters. They was wide-eyed and getting crazy, and within an instant they all started toward me and the fire. I stepped back outside the cave as they came rushing out, sending logs and fire a'winding, sparks floating up into the wet night sky. The logs that was knocked outside the cave steamed white smoke in the rain.

I watched the animals rush off across the clearing, tramping on Pinocchio Joe's body so solidly I could hear his bones crack from where I stood. I waited a moment, then stepped inside. It was darker at the back of the cave, as the fire had been knocked about, so with my LeMat in one hand I picked up a burning stick with the other and used it to guide me back into the shadows.

Ruggert was moaning down in that dark drop-off.

At the drop-off I stuck the blazing stick over the edge and peeked down.

"Had a little fall, did you?"

A shot flared up and punched a hole through the brim of my hat.

"I ain't dead yet, nigger. I'm stomped on and broken, but I ain't dead. I been burned and cut, shot and beat, and still I ain't dead. But what I don't understand is why in hell ain't you dead."

"Ornery as you, I reckon," I said.

"I'll second that, goddamn it. Ah, shit. I hurt."

"Ruggert," I said. "I could just sit up here and wait you out, or you can give yourself up."

"And have you kill me?"

"I wait you out, you'll be dead, and I'll haul your dead ass into Fort Smith just the same. I could kill you easy. Get some rocks and push them over on you. Fire down there with my pistols until I hit something with meat on it. I could drop this here firebrand down and shoot you in the light of it. Or you can give yourself up."

"You'd let me give up?"

"I been talking to the preacher. He thinks I'll do better about myself if I don't kill for vengeance."

"Does he, now?"

"I can't say I've got Jesus, but I think he makes some sense there. You know I killed Golem?"

"You did? That big, contrary son of a bitch? Well, damned if you ain't the resourceful nigger."

"I got an ass full of resource."

"You could be lying to me, Willie."

"I assure you Golem's dead."

"About bringing me in alive."

"I could be."

"You ruined my life."

"I didn't do nothing to you. Who the hell cares about such a thing as someone seeing your wife's clothed ass?"

"I do."

"And what's it got you? A burned-up face, some cut-up balls, and now you been stomped on by a cow. On top of that, you're a wanted man. And you'll love why I'm taking you in."

"The reward, I figure."

"That's true, but I'm also a deputy marshal, and it's my job."

"Now, I'll be damned to hell if you're a marshal."

"Have it your way."

"I got another solution. I could shoot myself."

"Go on ahead. It's nothing to me. You do it, I'm off the griddle. You give me trouble and I do it, I'm doing my job. And I could change my mind and feel less forgiving in the next five minutes. Hell, Ruggert. You get to choose. But you don't choose soon, then I will kill you in the name of the law, and for Win, Madame, my pa, and a hog that never done nothing to you. And I'll kill you for my mama just on general principles."

"I forgot about the hog," he said. "Damn it, boy. Drop a rope over. Pull me out. I'll go in with you."

"Your voice has got real sweet, but I don't trust you. Let me tell you how we're going to do it. I'm going to go check on my man. Then I'm going to come back, and you are going to throw your guns up here—"

"I just got one. I dropped my rifle. You tend to do that when a fucking cow steps on you."

"I see it here on the ledge. You throw what guns you got up here, and then we'll see about getting you out. How bad are you hurt?"

"Leg's twisted under me, coiled up like a rope. It hurts."

"It'll get worse. Throw the gun up."

"I don't trust you for shit."

"You might want to throw it up anyway. I walk away with this fire it's going to get awful dark down there."

I grabbed the burning brand and started out the front of the cave. Ruggert yelled after me. "Don't leave me down here, Willie."

I ignored him and went out of the cave to look at Choctaw. He was sitting up when I got there, holding the side of his head. The rain made my burning brand waver.

I kneeled down next to him.

"I got creased in the head," he said. "There's blood all over me."

"Move your hand."

He did, and I turned the brand in that direction. His ear had been cut in two. The bottom half dangled.

"How's it look?"

"Your ear's hanging by a strand. I can cut it loose for you."

"Don't do that."

He put his hand back over his ear. "Help me up."

"Not just yet. You sit."

"Guess I can't get no wetter."

I sauntered over to Doolittle. I waved the burning brand over him. He had collected quite a few bullets. His hat was pushed back on his head, and he had a look of surprise on his face. Part of the cloth gag hung down around his neck.

I checked on Pinocchio Joe. Also dead.

I went back and helped Choctaw up. I said, "Go in the cave. Stay away from that drop-off at the back. Ruggert's down there. He's still alive, and he's got a gun. I'm going to get our horses. Can you make it?"

"I can make it." I gave him the torch, and I trotted after the horses.

By the time I got back with the horses, Choctaw had built the fire up again. Logs that had been gathered up in the cave had been thrown on the fire. Cows and one of the horses was wandering around outside the cave like they wanted back in. We didn't let them. The rain had stopped, and there was grass for them to eat. I unsaddled our horses, rubbed them down, hobbled them, fed them some of the grain we had left by putting it in the feed bags again.

Choctaw had tied a white rag over his wounded head and blood was seeping through it. He had started heating up some beans. He never quit thinking about food, even with an ear shot off.

"You cut off that strand of meat?"

"No. I'm going to ask you a favor."

"First let me check on our friend in the hole."

I got a fresh brand out of the fire and went to the back of the cave. I said, "How you doing down there, asshole?"

"Well, there's too many women down here and a lot of free drink, and that's getting old . . . How the hell do you think I'm doing?"

"Toss your pistol up."

"I can't toss it. I can't get my legs under me, and it's too high to just throw it up with my arm, without no leverage."

"Have it your way, then."

"I smell beans. Ain't you going to feed me?"

"Nope."

I eased back to Choctaw. Ruggert had started bellowing by then, partly in pain but mostly in anger.

"He don't shut up I'm going to shoot him, Nat, and I don't never like to get involved in this business. Hell, how did I get shot? I didn't mean to get into all this."

"Not very smart is my guess. Let my look at your ear."

"Listen here, Nat. I want you to sew it back on."

"What?"

"You heard me. Sew it back on. I got some heavy thread and a needle. I want you to sew it on. You got some whiskey for me, don't you? You said when the job was finished."

"I don't know it's finished."

"Ain't it close enough?"

I got my saddlebags and got a small bottle of whiskey out of one of them. I had wrapped the bottle in a lot of rags to keep it from getting broken easy. I brought it to Choctaw. He had moved closer to the fire and had pulled a needle and thick black thread out of a bag he had tied to his belt under his slicker.

"This is going to hurt," I said.

"Give me a snort."

He uncorked the whiskey and took a swig. "Oh, that tastes good. You know what you should tell me before you stick that needle in me?"

"What?"

"What the Irishman tells his wife on their wedding night. Brace yourself."

I threaded the needle, then poured whiskey over it and stuck the needle over the fire until my finger and thumb started heating up. I dripped whiskey over my fingers and the needle again, leaned in close to Choctaw, and removed the rag from his head.

"No guarantees, Choctaw."

"Sew it on tight. I was a kid, I had a dog got its ear tore off by a bobcat. My daddy sewed that ear back on, and it grew back."

"You ain't a dog," I said.

"Go on ahead and do it, Nat."

"Brace yourself, honey. Here I come."

Choctaw found a stick, put it in his mouth, and leaned his head against the cave wall. I sewed, all the while listening to Ruggert screaming in pain down there in that hole. Choctaw didn't make a sound.

That stitching made me ill, the way the needle would slide through that near cut-off ear and the flesh on the side of Choctaw's head, but I tell you I did a right nice job. It took me a long time to do it, though, as I had to make many a stitch to get that sucker back on. It looked a little tighter to his head than his other ear, and that worried me some, but I figured it was better to leave it as it was than to cut it loose and stitch it some more. I was running out of room to poke the needle. I poured whiskey over the whole operation, gave Choctaw some to drink, then wrapped a fresh bandage around his head.

Not for one moment during this entire operation had Ruggert quit caterwauling down there in that hole. It made me sick to hear it, what with a bloody ear to sew back on, and him howling like a dog, I could hardly eat my beans once they was warm. But I did. Choctaw ate his usual three plates full.

Next time I asked Ruggert to toss up his gun, he tried to, and it took him three tries to get it to the edge, where I could catch it. Choctaw felt spry enough to have me tie my rope to him and lower him down. I had a couple of firebrands on the side of the hole, and they gave some light down there. It was a pretty good drop. Twenty feet or more, I reckon.

"Well," Choctaw called up. "The good news for you is his leg is broken. The bad news for him is his leg is broken."

"Oh, shut up and pull me out of here," Ruggert said.

"He wants out," Choctaw said.

"You bastards," Ruggert said. "Pull me out of this hole."

Choctaw tied the rope around him and then helped him as I pulled him up, Ruggert screamed in pain all the way to the top. I dragged him against the wall and looked him over for weapons, but he didn't have any on him. His leg was like a limp dishrag. I had removed my slicker, and Ruggert looked at the badge on my shirt.

When Ruggert got his breath back, he said, "You really are a marshal."

"I am," I said.

I untied the rope from him, used it to pull Choctaw up.

It was bright in the cave with that big fire, and Choctaw used the light to look Ruggert's leg over. "Well, if you was one that could do the reel on the dance floor, you ain't going to do it again. You might can skip a little."

"Up to Judge Parker's trapdoor," I said.

Choctaw and I tried to take turns sleeping, but Ruggert was in such pain he moaned and carried on all night. First light Choctaw got his hatchet and went out and cut some limbs to bind up Ruggert's leg. Ruggert passed out when Choctaw set it straight and tied it up.

In the meantime I went out and caught up two of the stolen horses and was able to herd up Bump's two milk cows. They was anxious to let me milk them, they was in such pain, and I squatted down and did so, squirting the milk out on the ground. They had lots of it, and when I finished their tits was slack. They followed me like dogs to the mouth of the cave.

The fire had gone out, and the morning was warming up when we put the bodies of Pinocchio Joe and Doolittle side by side across one of the horses I had caught. We got Ruggert mounted on another.

We got our horses out of the tree line, and with the milk cows following us, we started out. We made Bump's place by nightfall, returned the milk cows, and barely managed to keep him from killing Ruggert with a hoe. What worked to Ruggert's advantage was Bump was still seeing double. Anyway, we left the cows, which Bump hugged a little too warmly for my taste, and went on a piece and pitched camp. We had thought about staying at Bump's place but was afraid his vision would clear in the night and he'd chop Ruggert's head off like a snake, or we would find him and his cows in positions that could embarrass all of us.

Our camp was uncomfortable, as the ground was still wet, but it was what we had—a place under a tree laying on damp bedrolls. Ruggert moaned and cried and started complaining nonstop of how he couldn't sleep, as he was in too much pain. After a bit Choctaw got his rifle and went over and hit Ruggert a solid blow in the head, said, "That will help him sleep."

It did, too.

As we roughed that night through, I thought on what Ruggert had told me about his grandfather owning Mama, and you can bet I thought about asking him about that, if he was lying to me, but then I thought there wasn't no use. If I asked he'd say it was so if it wasn't, and in the end it didn't matter. But the idea of Ruggert or his kin having their way with my family in any kind of fashion set on my stomach like spoiled milk. But damn if I was going to give him the satisfaction. And what did it matter? Mama had done all she could, considering the circumstances. What she had been forced to do, or forced to be, was no consideration, really. I looked over at Ruggert lying there, having taken a lick to the head, and to be damn honest, in a small way I felt sorry for him. In that very moment I let go of any kind of anger I might have had about his kin owning her. It didn't mean a thing now. I had the bastard.

Next morning we started out again, and when Ruggert started moaning too much, Choctaw suggested his pain cure, which would be a short nap with a bad headache on awakening. This caused Ruggert to keep it down considerable until we reached Fort Smith, though that blow to the head caused him to throw up most of the trip there.

# 34

We dropped Ruggert off at the jail, and a doctor was brought over to look at his leg. We said there was cows and horses that had to be rounded up but me and Choctaw wasn't the men for it, so there was some herders put together right away, and Choctaw gave them the general location.

I came out of the courthouse feeling as if I was a new man. I can't explain it exactly, but I think I felt good for not killing Ruggert—not something I would have considered just a short time ago. As it began to get evening, I rode over to Luther's house, and when they let me in it was to the sound of laughter and the smell of good cooking, which was shared with me.

I told them all that had happened, including the sewing of Choctaw's ear, and about how when the doctor came to look at Ruggert he looked at Choctaw's ear, complimented my sewing, said it had about a fifty-fifty chance of reattaching itself, which was about fifty percent more of a chance than I expected. Ruthie joked that if the marshaling didn't work out, I could take on seamstress work.

We finished up supper, then me and Ruthie took a walk out to the gate, and when I figured Luther or Samson wasn't looking out the window, I gave Ruthie a kiss, then I gave her some promises. Some of it I had already said, but I felt it deserved repeating. I wanted her for my bride. I wanted a new life. I wanted a calm life and wanted to rethink on being a marshal. I told her I couldn't give it up right away, but I wanted a farm, as I knew how to do that as well as I knew how to shoot a pistol.

"I say we marry in the fall," Ruthie said.

"I say that's fine."

"I say we have children, but not right away. And we get a dog."

"I say all right to that, too."

"I'd like to live near my dad and brother."

"We can build a house right behind this one if you want."

"Not that close. But if they're in Fort Smith, I'd like to be here as well."

"I like here fine," I said.

We went on like that for a while, and then I got more sweet, and the way I talked kind of embarrasses me, so I won't recite what I said here. But it was loving and a little mushy, I can tell you that much, and it had to do with things that wasn't about farming.

I rode back to the stable, got my horse boarded, then walked over to where I was staying and went to bed. But I didn't sleep much.


Judge Parker ran a quick court. Ruggert and Kid Red was condemned to hang from their necks until they was dead, dead, dead, and this was set up to happen quickly. On the day before the hanging, I got word from Choctaw, whose ear had begun to heal and attach itself, that the kid wanted to see me over at the jail. I thought about not going, but then decided me and him had been friends once, so I'd oblige.

When I got there he was sitting on the bunk inside his cell, and when he looked up and seen me he smiled. "I wasn't sure you'd come, Nat."

I could see Ruggert across the way behind his own set of bars. His head was wrapped from where Choctaw had hit him, and his leg was bound up with slats and fresh bandages, and he looked as if he had just eaten a sour persimmon. At least he wasn't howling and moaning.

I looked back at Kid Red. "I wasn't sure I was coming, either."

Kid Red got up and came over and grasped the bars with both hands.

"I spoke bad to you, Nat."

"Yeah," I said.

"I didn't mean it."

"All right."

"Can you find it in your heart to forgive me?"

"For what you said to me, yeah. For what you done, no."

"I don't blame you for that. I can't forgive myself. I thought it was all right when I was doing all of it, but now I know it wasn't right."

"Little late," I said.

"But at least I know the difference."

"You knew the difference then," I said.

"A preacher come in here and told me I would be forgiven if I admitted my sins. Stood right where you are with a Bible and told me that. You think that's true?"

"No. But if it's any comfort, I think when you're dead you don't go to hell. You don't go nowhere. It's over."

"I didn't want to hear that."

"You asked."

"But you could be wrong, couldn't you?"

"I'm wrong about lots of things. I was wrong about you."

"Shit, Nat. I didn't want to go out like this. I wanted to be important."

"Doubt anyone wants to grow up to hang. But you will, son. You will."

"You don't have to rub it in. I know I talked bad to you, but I was mad and scared."

"You're going to hang not for what you said to me but for all you done."

"You done some bad things," he said.

"My killings was justified by self-defense and rescue. You killed because you could. And you raped."

When I said that, I immediately thought of Win and that empty look in her eyes.

"At least you forgive me for what I said to you. You said you did, right?"

"I did. And Kid, I hope the rope breaks your neck quick."

"You'll tell them to tie it right, won't you?"

"Executioner knows what he's doing."

"They say he wears a hood."

"So will you. That's how it's done."

"I hear when you hang . . . I hear you mess yourself."

"Most do."

"I was thinking if I don't eat, I won't have that problem."

"I'd eat," I said. "You'll shit yourself anyway."

"Jesus, Nat. I don't want to go out like a coward."

"Then don't."

"Easy to say from your side."

"True enough," I said.

"Will you promise to be there?"

"You want me to see you hang?"

"I want to look out and see you. You're the only person I know."

"You know me," Ruggert called out.

"Well, and him. But I don't like him."

"You liked me fine before," Ruggert said.

"I like Nat better."

Ruggert stirred on his bunk, like he was going to try and get up, but didn't. He just said, "Nigger lover."

"He can really hold a grudge," Kid Red said.

"Tell me about it," I said.

"So you'll be there?"

"Sure," I said.

I reached through the bars and shook the kid's hand.

"I wish I had rode with you instead of Ruggert."

"Me, too," I said.

I looked at Ruggert, but he didn't say another word.

That very day I got word I had a good-sized amount of money coming from the arrest of Ruggert and for the bodies of those other two desperadoes. Even split with Choctaw it was a large amount. A letter arrived from Mr. Loving's lawyer. It said if I was who I said I was and could prove it, I should come to Abilene, Kansas, and collect my money, which was sizable. That's why my letter had taken so long to find him and why he took so long to get back to me. He wasn't in East Texas anymore. He was in Kansas.

I was excited to hear it. I wrote him I couldn't come right away but would come soon. I went and told Ruthie about the reward money and the money promised in the letter. Her face lit up.

"Do you feel bad some of the money come from dead men and another man that's going to hang?" she said.

"I feel fine. How about you?"

She shrugged.

"We can buy that farm," she said.

"And I'm going to get some ducks, too. I want to see you talk to them."

Next day I went to the hanging, which was the last they had where a crowd could attend. After that they built a fence and hanged them behind that, deciding maybe everyone bringing peanuts and food and such, picnicking on the grounds, set a bad example for justice.

But on this day there was a good crowd, and they was loud and laughing and having a hoot of a time, and there was a fellow telling jokes in the center of the crowd. They gathered around him and laughed. He could do some acrobatic things, too, like walk on his hands, stand on his head, and flip and such. That kept folks entertained until it was time for the main event.

They was hanging not only Ruggert and Kid Red, they was hanging a colored man named Franklin who had got drunk and killed a white woman cause he said he thought she was a deer.

There was a big platform built up for the gallows, and the hanging took place in the early afternoon, about two hours after the crowd gathered. I got my place up front so Kid Red could clearly see me. I started to buy some peanuts from a walking vendor, but thought that might set a bad example for a marshal, and it certainly wouldn't do Kid Red any good in his last moments watching me enjoy a snack. I had missed lunch, though, and those peanuts was on my mind.

There was two guards per prisoner, and they brought the three out. Franklin stood on the far left of the gallows from the way I was facing. Then came Kid Red to the center, looking small in oversize boots, and on the right side, facing me, was Ruggert, limping on his boarded-up leg, his head still wrapped. None of them wore hats, and they all looked like they was dead already; the bones in their shoulders and chests seemed to have gone thin and slack. Ruggert and the kid seen me right away. The kid sort of perked up when he did, but his knees was shaky.

"I don't want him standing there," Ruggert said to the executioner, a plump man with a black hood over his face.

"Well, he's a marshal, and he can stand where he wants," said the executioner, being quite clear in spite of the mask over his face.

"Damn you," he said to the executioner.

"Well, sir, you'll be damned first," the executioner said.

Ropes was already draped in place, and nooses was tied. These was put over the three men's necks, and the knots was pulled tight to the sides of their heads. That way the neck broke better. The three men was told to stand on the trapdoors, and they done it. I guess by that point they didn't see no reason not to.

Each man was allowed to say his piece.

Franklin said, "I sure thought that woman was a deer. Usually I can tell a woman and a deer apart, but that day I was good and drunk, and I could have swore it was a buck with a big rack. My mama told me not to drink, but I did. And look where it's got me. That is all."

The executioner pulled a bag over his head and readjusted the rope.

Kid Red said, "I ain't never had much of a chance, but when I did, I didn't take it. I'm sorry for all I done, but I know God is in his heaven, and he's forgiven me, and he's waiting on me with a harp."

"I don't want to hear you play it," a man in the crowd yelled out.

Kid Red ignored him, tried to stand in his spot without lowering his head. "I go to see Jesus now," he said.

"Have him send me a present," said the man in the audience. I looked around to find who had spoken, but didn't locate him.

I looked back at the kid. He was still holding his head up. I was proud of him. The executioner put the bag over his face.

Ruggert was next. He spoke in as loud a voice as he could muster.

"My whole life I've tried to live the kind of life a white man ought to live, and all that has come to me and brought me here was caused by a nigger who looked boldly at my wife's bottom while she innocently hung clothes on the line. And there that nigger stands with a marshal badge pinned to his chest, good as a white man. I say to you, take that darky down and free me from this gallows. I'm not to blame for my ways. He is."

"Ah, shut up," said the man who had spoken before about the harp. I recognized his voice and spotted him this time. He wore overalls that was as worn as his face. "We don't care none about you or your nigger or your wife's ass. Take your goddamn medicine, you burned-up old fart."

That seemed to sap Ruggert. I think the boards on his bad leg and the rope around his neck was all that was holding him up. I don't know what he expected, but maybe he thought the white folks in the crowd was going to rise up and pull him down from there and put me in his place and forgive all his killing and robbing. He was one of those that could never see himself wrong, and I figured he hadn't until that moment truly realized that this was all she wrote and he was a fool.

After a pause, Ruggert said, "All right, then."

They put the bag over his head.

I was thinking how my life had changed because of that man, the bitter and the sweet, when the traps was dropped and the men fell through with a sound like someone snapping a leather belt between their hands. The kid kicked once, throwing off one of his boots and hitting a man in the head in the front row. The colored man and Ruggert moved not at all. I could smell shit in the air.

\*   \*   \*

I'm tired now. I will say again there was many dime novels written about me by Bronco Bob, but this here is the straight record. There's more. But I'm too tired to write it out. I spent some time with Buffalo Bill's Wild West show, even went to Europe and seen the queen of England. Oh, and I married Ruthie. She went to Europe, too. I had a family. Fortunately, none of the kids got my ears. By the way, Ruthie really did talk to ducks and chickens, but in dedication to honesty as I see it, I never heard a one of them talk back, nor feel anything Ruthie told me they said was all that beneficial.

I had many adventures before I became a porter on this long, black train, where I sit and write in my spare time and read the old dime novels I can find that was written about me. Perhaps those other adventures of mine are for another time. Perhaps in a fashion I did turn out great, way Mama thought I would. I had me some times, that's for sure.

But this here is what happened to me up to where I've told it. It's how I became Deadwood Dick, and most of it is as true as I know how to make it, keeping in mind nobody likes the dull parts.

## AUTHOR'S NOTE

Parts of this novel were loosely borrowed from my short stories "Soldierin'" and "Hides and Horns." I have also slightly condensed certain historical events to suit my storytelling purposes, though I have on the whole tried to present these, as well as the contribution of black cowboys, soldiers, and lawmen in the West, accurately while adhering to the mythology-building tradition of all great western storytellers of the time, including the real Nat Love, who inspired so much of this story, at least in spirit.

## ABOUT THE AUTHOR

Joe R. Lansdale is the author of more than three dozen novels, including *The Thicket, Edge of Dark Water, The Bottoms,* and *A Fine Dark Line.* He has received the British Fantasy Award, the American Mystery Award, the Edgar Award, the Grinzane Cavour Prize, and nine Bram Stoker Awards. He lives with his family in Nacogdoches, Texas.